TILL THE BUTCHERS CUT HIM DOWN

MARCIA MULLER

TILL THE BUTCHERS CUT HIM DOWN

A SHARON McCONE MYSTERY

THE MYSTERIOUS PRESS

Published by Warner Books

A Time Warner Company

Mysterious Press books are published by
Warner Books, Inc., 1271 Avenue of the
Americas, New York, NY 10020.

W A Time Warner Company

The Mysterious Press name and logo are registered
trademarks of Warner Books, Inc.

Printed in the United States of America

ISBN 0-89296-455-3

For Kit, Arthur, and Tiffany Knight
Thank you'ns

Thanks also to
Marcie Galick, for organizing me
Jerry Kennealy, for bringing McCone into the computer age
Suzanne Rampton, for yet another piece of her life
Patricia Wallace, for fine-tuning on Nevada
Collin Wilcox, again, for his aviation expertise

Oh! didn't he ramble ramble?
He rambled all around
In and out of the town,
Oh didn't he ramble ramble.
He rambled till the butchers cut him down.

From *Oh, Didn't He Ramble*
by Will Handy

TILL THE BUTCHERS CUT HIM DOWN

Touchstone

July 4

    I made the best decision of my life on a high meadow in California's White Mountains, where I'd gone to watch for the wild mustangs.

At least watching for mustangs was what I planned to do when I declined to ride into Big Pine with Hy to pick up some supplies. But now that I was nestled in a drift of dry wheat-colored grass at the base of a dead-looking bristlecone pine, I realized that once again my sight had turned inward. Decision time, I thought. Middle-of-your-life crossroads, important stuff. Make the right choice and it's golden; make the wrong one—

I didn't want to think about that.

Lately too much thinking had been my chronic ailment. Sixteen days of relaxing about as far from civilization as I could get should have cured me, but instead I'd picked and prodded at my current problem—charging it from one side, sneaking up on it from another. All to no good purpose; the problem

1

remained a stubborn, inert lump in the exact center of my psyche.

I burrowed down into the grass, sniffing its bitter fragrance. It rustled around me and tickled my face. Above me the pine's branches creaked in a light breeze; I glanced up and saw bursts of green at their very tips. Not dead, just faking it.

Lulled by the whisper of the tall grass, I leaned against the pine's rough trunk. Closed my eyes. And began obsessing some more.

Decide, I told myself. You're going home in a few days. For God's sake, just make your decision.

When I opened my eyes some moments later, I was looking a wild mustang straight in the face. He stood not five feet away, pale mane blowing in the breeze, head down, long roan neck stretched to its limits as he studied me. His soft brown eyes met mine, and he blinked. Clearly I was the most curious animal he'd ever come across in his meadow.

For a few seconds he continued to stare, nostrils quivering. Then he snorted, as if to tell me that he found humans not nearly as impressive as we find ourselves. With a shake of his head he wheeled about and ran, kicking up his hooves, tail and mane streaming proudly—a shining, free creature.

And then the solution to my problem came so clearly that I jumped up, wheeled about, and ran too. Ran through high grass, kicking up my heels; leaped over fallen branches, laughing. Ran till I was breathless and fell on my back, panting. Lay there and laughed some more—really giving the mustang something to tell his herd about.

* * *

When Hy got back to our borrowed cabin some two hours later, I was sitting on the raised hearth, my hands wrapped around a glass of wine, a big grin on my face. My lover set the box of groceries on the rough pine table and studied me, stroking his droopy mustache. He'd pretty much stayed off the

2

subject of my decision these past sixteen days—as I'd stayed off the subject of some plans he was making—but now his curiosity got the better of him.

"You decided," he said.

I nodded.

"You're going to cut loose and go out on your own."

I nodded again.

"Good choice."

His words swelled the happy bubble in my chest. I grinned more widely, deciding not to tell him just yet about the part of my scheme that made it perfect.

Hy took a bag of ice from the grocery box and began dumping it into the cooler. "You must've known I'd like the idea."

"Well, yes. But it's good to actually hear you say so. Your opinion's kind of . . . an acid test for me."

"I call it a touchstone. Black siliceous rock. Metallurgists use it to test the purity of gold or silver." He hesitated, arranging beers on top of the ice, then added, "You're my touchstone, too."

There was an uncharacteristic shyness in his tone that made my eyes sting. I blinked and busied myself with lighting the fire I'd earlier laid on the hearth. When I finished, I turned and asked, "So, Ripinsky, this decision of mine—is it silver or is it gold?"

Hy raised a beer bottle in a toast. "It's gold, McCone. Pure gold."

Part One

San Francisco

August

One

"Are you sure this'll clear the bank?" Ted Smalley, All Souls's office manager, held the check that I'd just handed him up to his desk lamp and squinted at it.

I folded my arms and tried to look severe.

"Do I know this person?" he asked himself. "She looks like the old Sharon, in spite of the haircut. She talks like her, too. But McCone Investigations? A separate business checking account? Rent for an office suite? Pretty strange stuff, if you ask me."

"Not nearly as strange as what's going on upstairs in those rooms that you dignify with the word 'suite.' " As if to support my statement, an enormous crash resounded at the front of the big Victorian's second floor. I winced.

Ted rolled his eyes toward the ceiling.

In the long-unused cubbyhole next to my office, a Pacific Bell woman was installing lines for my new phone, fax machine, and computer modem. Jack Stuart, the co-op's criminal law specialist, and Hank Zahn, my former boss, had just gone

7

up there to remove my chaise longue and place it in Jack's van. I wasn't sure whether the crash had to do with the chaise, which Jack had agreed to transport to my house, or my forty-seven-hundred-dollar Apple computer and laser printer, but if one had to be sacrificed, I'd just as soon it was the well-loved but not nearly so costly piece of furniture.

Before I could run up there and check, Jack's blue-jeaned posterior appeared on the stair landing; he was hunched over and gripping the chaise as he inched backwards. In spite of my anxiety over the crash, I took a moment to admire the co-op's acknowledged hunk from this vantage. Ted, the sly devil, noticed and winked. I winked back.

Next Hank appeared at the other end of the chaise, red-faced and scowling. Halfway down the stairs he began performing a series of odd maneuvers that looked as though he'd developed a severe case of Saint Vitus' dance. I watched in alarm, then realized he was trying to push up his thick horn-rimmed glasses, which had slipped dangerously low on his nose; as he passed Ted and me, I reached out and returned the glasses to their proper position. Hank smiled gratefully.

"What fell?" I asked.

"Not to worry."

"What fell?"

Jack said, "One of those stupid rabbit bookends you keep on your desk. It broke."

"Oh." I swallowed hard. The "stupid rabbit bookends" had come from Gump's and cost a minor fortune, even five years ago when a former boyfriend had given them to me for Christmas. Well, I still had one. . . .

A little over a month ago in that high mountain meadow, my plan to establish my own firm and rent office space from All Souls had seemed a stroke of genius—a way of turning down a slightly expanded job as head of their newly formed Investigative Services department while maintaining my connection to the people who for me were more like an extended

8

family than coworkers. But now after weeks of negotiations and reams of legal documents and licensing and bonding applications, to say nothing of a steady stream of outgoing checks, I was beginning to think I'd been quite mad. Still, I was sure that once established, I'd be better off independent of the co-op and certainly better off keeping my distance from Renshaw and Kessell International, the high-tech, ethically bankrupt security firm whose offer of a lucrative position as field investigator had been my other alternative. I'd always have a soft spot for RKI, however: the cash bonus they'd given me last July, prompted by my saving them from a disastrous situation, had put McCone Investigations in business.

I glanced at my watch. Nearly eleven. The chaise was out of my office in time to make space for the new sofa and chair that were to be delivered any minute.

Ted must have sensed that I felt a little down, because he said, "I bet I can glue the rabbit back together so you'll never notice it's been broken."

"Thanks." I smiled fondly at him. He's such an odd combination of aesthete and hardheaded administrator—a goateed gentleman who favors old-fashioned dress and quotes Latin in the course of routine conversations and who also controls a staff of close to a hundred and keeps northern California's largest legal-services plan on track with seemingly effortless efficiency. And now he was laying claim to a talent for repairing broken treasures.

"By the way," he added, "somebody's waiting for you in the parlor."

I glanced over there, saw no one. "Who?"

He checked a scratch pad on his desk. "T. J. Gordon. Said you know him."

The name wasn't familiar. I moved closer to the archway and peered into the room. A man in dark blue business attire stood in the window bay, hands clasped behind him as he contemplated the street.

I blinked. Sucked in my breath. "Suitcase," I said softly.

"What?" Ted asked.

I shook my head, staring.

T. J. Gordon—Telford Junius Gordon, according to his driver's license—had gone by the nickname Suitcase for as long as I'd known him. I hadn't given him so much as a thought in more than fifteen years.

Those years hadn't changed him much. His five-foot-seven frame was still scrawny; his narrow shoulders still slumped; his dark brown hair, now shot with gray, still rose in a cowlick at the crown and flopped limply onto his high forehead. The expensive-looking suit might have been tailor-made, the watch that he now glanced impatiently at might have been a Rolex, but something told me that not too far beneath the civilized facade lurked the Suitcase Gordon of old.

As I stepped into the parlor, he heard me and turned. His gray eyes moved shrewdly over me, and he nodded, as if my appearance matched up to some private expectation. His sharp-featured face was relatively unlined; when he smiled, I found he still reminded me of a friendly rodent. He bent and picked up a handsome leather briefcase that sat on the floor next to his equally handsome shoes, and the past came rushing back to me.

In the old days on the U.C. Berkeley campus it would have been a suitcase he picked up—one of the ancient brown-striped cardboard variety that went everywhere with him. It would have been crammed full of whatever he was peddling at the time: marijuana, term papers on an infinite variety of subjects, amphetamines, false identification, purloined copies of upcoming exams, blank airline tickets, manuals of legal tips for protesters, lists of safe houses for revolutionaries. He'd billed himself as an itinerant purveyor of prefab scams, schemes, and perhaps even dreams, with something for everyone in the shabby suitcase that had earned him his nickname.

Suits, as we came to call him, was a frequent fixture at the big old house on Durant Avenue that I shared with a fluctuating group of other students, including Hank Zahn and his now wife Anne-Marie Altman. He'd suddenly appear on the doorstep, just in from southern California or the East Coast or the Midwest, and we'd find ourselves providing him with food and drink and a place to crash. In return Suits would hand out samples of whatever he was currently selling and regale us with tales of events on campuses in such far-flung places as Boston, Ann Arbor, Boulder, and Austin. Then he'd go about his business, scurrying around Berkeley in his hunched, furtive way, suitcase in hand. One day he'd simply be gone, giving no forewarning and offering no explanation.

As Suits came toward me now, I wondered what he had in that briefcase. And I had a suspicion that I was going to find out fairly soon.

"Lookin' good, Sherry-O," he said, setting the case on the coffee table and holding out his arms for a hug.

Sherry-O! I couldn't believe I used to let him call me that. Smiling weakly, I stepped into his embrace. My body felt stiff and wooden; I extricated myself quickly.

Suits's thin lips still held a smile, but now it was . . . sarcastic? No, ironic. Why?

He said, "Read in the *Examiner* about you opening your own firm. Good going."

A reporter friend had done a long profile of me for last Sunday's business section. "Thanks," I said. "Please, sit down."

Suits shot his cuff and looked at his watch again. A Rolex all right. "Can't. I've got a meeting downtown in twenty-four minutes, so I'll cut to the reason I'm here. I want to hire you."

"To do what?"

"We'll have to talk about that later. I spent damn near half an hour waiting for you."

The remark reminded me of his less-than-endearing habit of making criticisms at inopportune moments. Social graces

11

were not within the realm of his talents. "You could have called for an appointment," I said tartly.

"Uh-uh. Given our history, it was better to just show up."

"Our history?"

"Well, I did dump you."

"You *what*?"

He seemed startled by my response. Then he glanced around as if he was afraid someone might be eavesdropping. "You know, after that Halloween party. I slunk out of town the next morning. Felt guilty about it for years, but that's the way it had to be. I wasn't ready to settle down, not then."

"Halloween party? Oh . . ." Now I remembered what he was talking about, but his revisionist version of "our" history struck me as truly remarkable.

One wine- and dope-saturated night in the late seventies I'd lost all reason and allowed Suits to crawl into my bed. The next morning I woke horrified at what I'd done and relieved to find him gone. On his subsequent visit to campus I avoided him, and within six months I'd fallen in love—or so I thought at the time—and moved in with my new boyfriend. The disgraceful episode with Suits was relegated to the corner of my mind reserved for extreme lapses in judgment, and eventually forgotten.

Apparently not so for him, though—the man who had "dumped" me and "slunk out of town" in order to avoid further romantic entanglement!

He was watching me anxiously, no doubt hoping for absolution. I felt a nasty urge to set the record straight, but quickly suppressed it. No need to rehash an ancient and irreconcilable difference of opinion. No need to bruise his male pride at this late date. Besides, the man was here to hire me.

"Well," I said after pretending to give his words serious consideration, "you probably saved us both a lot of grief by leaving town. God knows, I wasn't ready to settle down then, either. Never have been."

12

He nodded, obviously relieved. "So what do you say, Sherry-O? Will you take on an old friend as a client?"

"Suits, I need to know more about the case before I can say."

He glanced at his watch again. "Later, okay? We'll talk later."

"When?"

"Two o'clock." He reached into his inside pocket, took out a business card, and handed it to me. "The address where I'm living is on the back. You be on time." Then he moved toward the door, glancing from side to side, shoulders hunched, in an odd scampering gait that was vintage Suitcase.

I looked at the card. The embossed side said "Intervention Management, Inc., T. J. Gordon, President" and gave an address on Wilshire Boulevard in Beverly Hills. On the other side he'd scribbled a local address in a very pricey new condominium complex on the Embarcadero in the South Beach district.

So what did this mean? Had Suitcase Gordon become a legitimate businessman? Or had he simply perfected one of his many scams?

I reviewed his unaltered mannerisms and appearance. Discounted the expensive suit, briefcase, and Rolex. Decided he couldn't possibly be legitimate. No legitimate person would act *that* furtive.

* * *

I pocketed Suits's card and went upstairs. The phone-company woman was still installing, the new furniture hadn't yet arrived, and my nephew, Mick Savage, lay flat on his stomach on my office floor doing something to one of the electrical sockets. He looked over his shoulder when he heard me come in and grimaced.

"Wiring must've been put in about the time Noah's Ark sailed," he complained.

I eyed him nervously. "Did you shut off the power?"

"Do I look like an idiot?"

"I won't answer that." In truth, my sister Charlene's eldest could look vacuous upon occasion, but I took that to be typical of many seventeen-year-olds and assumed he'd outgrow it. He was a big kid: sandy blond like his mother; stocky like his father, country-music star Ricky Savage; and he had the same easy, outgoing disposition as both his parents.

Mick had been sent from Pacific Palisades to San Francisco for the month because I needed someone to teach me how to use my computer. In that department my nephew was a genius—had, in fact, been suspended from school during his senior year for getting into the board of education's mainframe and selling teachers' confidential evaluations of students to the highest bidders. The night before she put him on the northbound plane, Charlene had confided over the phone that she was worried about her son: first there'd been the time he ran away to San Francisco at the holidays and I'd had to spend my Christmas Eve scouring the city for him; then there was the business of him changing his preferred version of his given name six times in the past three years; and, of course, there was the disgraceful hacker episode. Since graduation, Charlene said, Mick had been drifting and directionless; he refused to discuss his future plans. Perhaps I could counsel him while he was with me? At least persuade him to give college a try? I said I'd see what I could do.

Unfortunately, Charlene and Ricky were going to be very unhappy with the results of Mick's visit.

I went over to my desk and picked up my mail. Nothing but bills and a large manila envelope. I slit it open and pulled out a thick booklet: "P.I. & Security Mail-Order Catalog, The One-Stop Shopping Source for Your Investigation Business." On the front was a silhouette of a guy in a trench coat; the note attached to it began, "Dear Mr. Savage, Thank you for your interest . . ."

I looked at the address label on the envelope, realized I'd mistakenly opened Mick's mail, and sighed.

During the past couple of weeks, Mick had made up his mind he wanted to become a private investigator. Why, of all possible professions, he'd chosen mine remained unclear to me, particularly since he hadn't seen me do any actual investigating since he'd been here. But he'd decided, and if I couldn't defuse the idea, I was definitely going to be on my sister's blacklist.

First I'd pointed out that he was too young to be licensed. He'd said he would stay on and work for me, learning the trade until he was of age. Then I told him I couldn't afford to pay both him and the assistant I planned to hire. He said he'd accept room and board at my house in lieu of a salary. I insisted that I liked living alone. He said I wouldn't even know he was there. I declared the plan unworkable. He pouted. Since our latest discussion he'd become silent and secretive, but I gathered his studies were moving forward: yesterday I'd found several volumes—including *Advanced Lock Picking* and *Getaway: Driving Techniques for Escape and Evasion*—hidden under the guest room bed. Given Mick's past interest in extralegal activity, those two titles made me distinctly uneasy.

Yes, Charlene and Ricky were going to be *extremely* unhappy with Aunt Sharon's effect on their son. In fact, if Mick persisted in this plan, my sister would kill me.

Mick finished with the socket and stood up, dusting off the front of his jeans and work shirt. He saw the catalog in my hands and started guiltily.

"So what're you going to order from this one?" I asked, paging through the offerings. "*The Hacker's Handbook? Money for Nothing: Rip-Offs, Cons, and Swindles?* Or how about *Counterfeit ID Made Easy?*"

"You opened my mail."

"In error." I handed the catalog to him.

He pushed out his lips in a fair imitation of a bulldog. "Yeah, sure, in error. You're in such an uproar about me

15

wanting to become a P.I. that you've probably tapped the phone."

"Mick—"

"I don't see what's the big deal about it."

"I've told you, it's a tough business. Tough to break into, too."

"Well, yeah, maybe for you, being a woman way back then."

Way back during the Dark Ages. God, there were times when Mick could make me feel *old*! "That's right. But the training—for anybody, even now—is less than thrilling. You work as a security guard the way I did before and during college and hope management'll pick you out of the rank and file, or you sit in a cubicle running endless computer traces, or you go out on auto repos—"

"So? You stuck with it and got your license."

"Only because I couldn't find any other job after getting a B.A. in sociology. Only because I got lucky and ended up with a boss who was willing to train and promote me."

"Well, *I* got lucky when Mom and Dad sent me up here to help you."

"It's not the same, Michael."

"Mick."

"Sorry."

"Why isn't it the same?"

"Because . . ." I hunted for an explanation. "Because you have advantages and prospects that I didn't."

"Like what?"

"Like wealthy parents who are willing to pay your way through college." There, Charlene, I thought, I've talked to him about higher education.

Mick rolled his eyes. "Don't start, Aunt Shar."

The title "aunt" was one of the things that made me feel old. I figured if he could change his name all those times and expect me to remember which was current, I could insist he break himself of a lifelong habit. "Sharon or Shar," I said firmly. "Forget the 'aunt.' "

He frowned. "Uh, okay."

From outside I heard the rumble of a truck's engine. I went to the window, looked down, and saw the van from Breuner's. "The furniture's here," I told him, glad for the interruption. "You want to go down and direct them?"

He went to the door, the one-stop shopping source clutched protectively in both hands. "You know," he said, "if you don't want me working for you, I'll have to go for it on my own. I have a plan."

"What plan?"

He shook his head, grinned evilly at me, and disappeared around the doorjamb. I sighed in resignation.

Oh, yes, my sister was going to *kill* me.

Two

During the 1840s Gold Rush, San Francisco's South Beach was called Happy Valley, and to this day the name applies. Of course, only ghosts of the newly rich miners and their fancy ladies remain; gone too are most of the sailors and longshoremen who used to work the waterfront there; many light industrial firms fled the high rents in the early 1980s. But now the abandoned warehouses and factories are making way for luxurious residential complexes; the crumbling old piers are being reclaimed for non-maritime use; there's a new marina, and an upscale restaurant seems to open every week. Even the big quake of 1989 did South Beach a favor by damaging the unsightly Embarcadero Freeway to its north; when the structure was finally razed, the long-forgotten bay views stunned us all. There's an abundance of attractions in this present-day Happy Valley.

So which of them, I wondered, had drawn Suitcase Gordon?

His condominium complex, Bay Vista, was eight stories of dark red brick whose style reprised that of the nineteenth

19

century. A sign advertising that units were still available boasted of individual terraces facing the waterfront, a health club, two pools, tennis courts, a deli, a grocery store, concierge services, sheltered parking, and a twenty-four-hour doorman. Unfortunately, it was impossible to approach the complex from the Embarcadero because of a thirty-foot-wide open trench where the roadbed was being expanded. I had to go around the block and park behind the building, then cross a vacant lot full of rubble and idle earthmoving equipment.

A doorman was on duty as advertised, but he acted surly until I asked for Mr. Gordon; then he became respectful to the point of fawning. A high-speed elevator—semiprivate, serving only two units—took me to the top floor, where Suits waited impatiently in his doorway. He hustled me inside through a spacious foyer to an enormous room with a glass wall overlooking the terrace. At one end was a marble fireplace, at the other a mirrored wet bar; and in the exact center of the pegged hardwood floor, on an Indian rug that looked as though it had been bought at Cost Plus, stood a cluttered card table and two folding chairs. Three steel file cabinets and a stand holding a phone and fax machine were lined up along the wall perpendicular to the bar. And that was it.

"Nice furnishings," I said.

Suits frowned, then shrugged. "I meant to buy some, but I never got around to it."

"And you've lived here how long?"

"A year?"

"A year."

"What can I say? I've been busy."

"Obviously. But why have a place like this if you're just going to crash here the way you used to in the old days at our house on Durant?"

"Well, I like the dry-cleaning and maid services. And there's a heliport on the roof. But . . . come on." He put his arm around my shoulders and steered me to the terrace. "The view's the real attraction. It's what I need to keep my vision intact."

I was about to ask what he meant by that when a great rumble came from below. Seizing the opportunity to escape his unwanted touch, I went to the terrace wall and looked down. A scoop loader was creeping along the trench, belching nasty black exhaust.

Suits came up beside me and said something.

"What?"

He scowled down at the scoop loader, then motioned for me to precede him inside and banged the door shut behind us.

"I just wish they'd get the goddamn road built and go away," he muttered. "Between the noise and the fumes and those fuckin' beepers that sound off when they back up, I'm going nuts. Guy who invented those beepers ought to be shot."

"How long's that been going on down there?"

"Too long. Look, let's get out of here, go grab a cup of coffee. Then we can talk."

I was just as glad to do that, so I waited while he changed into a hooded sweatshirt, jeans, and running shoes. In them he looked more like the Suits of college days. As the elevator took us down to the lobby, I asked, "Suits, what exactly is it that you do for a living?"

He shook his head, glancing around suspiciously.

Good God, did he think the elevator was bugged? I shrugged and followed him outside, past the still-fawning doorman. Suits skirted the trench, casting a hostile look at an idle workman, then darted across the pockmarked pavement of the Embarcadero, eluding oncoming cars with the nimble-footed skill of a toreador. I waited till traffic cleared before joining him.

"Do you perhaps have a death wish?" I asked.

He didn't reply, merely cut a diagonal course past the Boon-docks restaurant and Red's Java House and struck out southward. I hurried along in his wake, caught up, and tugged at the hood of his sweatshirt. "Where're we going?"

He pulled away and kept on in his curious scuttling gait— working off his irritation with the construction project, I guessed. A fair distance along the waterfront, past the new marina and a few closed-up piers, sat another small eatery, Miranda's. Suits headed for the squat gray clapboard building and held its door open for me. Inside it was your standard longshoremen's diner: no tricking up for the tourists, no pseudo-nautical frills, just a lunch counter with a grill and coffee urns behind it and yellow leatherette booths beneath the windows. I slipped into the one Suits indicated, and he asked, "What'll you have?"

"Coffee, please. Black."

"Nothing to eat?"

"No, thanks, just coffee."

He shrugged and went over to the counter. The cook, a heavyset bald man in a stained white apron, apparently knew him, because he nodded in brusque friendliness and called him T.J. Suits gave his order and sat down on a stool to wait for it.

I looked away, out the grimy salt-caked window. It afforded a view all the way from the Bay Bridge and Yerba Buena Island to the drawbridge at China Basin. A gray view today, typical weather for August, although unusually dour for this area, which enjoyed one of the better climates in a city of many climate zones. I watched a flock of gulls plane north above the water, then pinwheel off in various directions. Farther out, a container ship moved slowly toward the Port of Oakland.

Suits returned in a few minutes carrying two mugs of coffee, then went back for a plate containing half a dozen little hamburgers. Before I finished stirring my coffee to cool it, he'd wolfed down three of them. I'd forgotten that for a skinny guy, Suits could consume enormous quantities of food.

"All right," I said after taking a sip of what turned out to be a particularly nasty brew, "now are you ready to tell me what this is about?"

He swabbed his mouth with a paper napkin. "Do you know what a turnaround man is?"

"One of those people who bring corporations back from the edge of bankruptcy?"

"That's it. And that's me. When they get down and desperate, I rescue 'em."

While he ate the rest of his burgers I remained silent, recalling an article I'd noticed in an old copy of *Fortune* that had been the only thing to read in my dentist's waiting room a few months back. It was titled "Turnaround Pros Sweep the Compensation Ratings," and the lead paragraphs—which were all I'd gotten through before being summoned to the drill— described the turnaround men as a breed apart, white knights riding into battle in private jets and limousines. The image did not fit the Suitcase Gordon I'd known, and the requisite skills were none he'd ever demonstrated.

"How'd you get into that line of work?" I asked.

He shook his head—an abrupt reflexive dismissal of my question. It reminded me of the way the savings-and-loan boys told reporters "No comment" when the indictments came down. "Just fell into it by accident," he finally said.

I hesitated, wondering if I should press for a better explanation. No, I decided, the set of his mouth indicated I wouldn't get one. Come to think of it, in all the time I'd known him, Suits had imparted very little personal information. He was a tireless talker, but his conversational repertoire consisted of inconsequential chatter, aimless bullshit, and largely apocryphal stories. I had not the slightest idea of where he'd been born, grown up, or attended school; I knew his full name only because I'd once glimpsed his Massachusetts driver's license when he wrote a check—which later bounced—at Berkeley's Co-op Market.

I said, "Tell me more about what you do."

23

Suits balled up his napkin, tossed it onto the plate, and belched discreetly. "Okay, here's how it works. Say you've got a company that's about to go down the tubes. They owe millions, their creditors're hounding them. The atmosphere's bad: employees're stampeding out the door, management's pissed off at the board, the board's lost all confidence in management. Chapter Eleven's looming on the horizon, and the stockholders're dumping their shares. What does the board do?"

I raised my eyebrows inquiringly.

"They make a last-ditch stand, send for a troubleshooter. A man who can turn things around." He jerked his thumb at his chest. "Me."

I reached into my bag and took out my minicassette recorder. Might as well have the conversation on tape, in case I decided to take him on as a client. "Do you mind?" I asked.

He shook his head, waved it away. "Nothing I say goes on somebody else's tape. Nothing."

I shrugged, put the recorder away. "Go on."

"Okay, the turnaround man—me—comes on board. There aren't all that many of us—maybe nine, ten, tops, in the country—who're first-rate. The board pays maximum dollar, maximum options and non-cash perks to get me. They agree to let me call all the shots. I'm a dictator with a license to kill—and that's exactly what I do. The first step is the bloodbath."

Interesting how Suits, who had always claimed to embrace the values of peace and love, described his profession with such violent metaphors.

"Okay," he went on, "here's how it goes down. You find a sacrificial lamb. Doesn't have to be the guy responsible for what's wrong, just has to be somebody with high visibility. You find him and you crucify him. Bang! He's gone. You've shown everybody how ruthless you are, and people're nervous now. Hell, you do it right, you've got them running to the can seventeen times a day."

24

"Nice."

"Hey, it has to be done."

"You've changed, Suits."

His eyes met mine, level and candid. "Haven't we all, Sherry-O?" he said mildly.

I acknowledged the implication with a rueful grimace.

"Okay, the bloodbath's over, for the most part. Next you bring in your own people. I've got a permanent staff in my L.A. office, but they're just administrative. For my on-site people I draw on a talent pool from all over the country: a finance guy in Chicago; a marketing guy in Dallas; a statistician in L.A.; an operations guy in Atlanta. These people come in. They've got high visibility, they've got authority. And they show they know how to kick butt.

"Now's the time when you clear out more deadwood. You clean things up, trim things back. You make your deals with the moneymen—the banks and investors. You make your deals with the creditors. People'll cut you any amount of slack if they think they've got a chance of getting their money back. So basically what you do is get things stabilized. That can take about a year."

"Is that why you've been too busy to buy furniture?"

He grinned. "You got it."

I was still troubled by the tone of what he was telling me. The Suitcase Gordon I'd once known had been short on the social niceties and often crassly insensitive, yes. But he'd never been cruel.

As if he'd heard my thoughts, he touched my hand gently with his forefinger. "Sometimes, Sherry-O, you've got to cause pain to accomplish something worthwhile. The people who get hurt in the bloodbath generally're the ones who contributed to how bad things are. Or they're people who'll be better off out of there anyway. And the bloodbath and stabilizing stages lead to what I call the visionary stage. That's when you can really make things happen."

I moved my hand away, reserving judgment and wishing he'd stop calling me Sherry-O. "What kind of things?"

Suits's gray eyes began to take on a glow; his pale skin became suffused with color. My unease deepened. I'd seen that expression before on the faces of zealots—and madmen.

He said, "Revolutionary things. Sweeping changes that reach far beyond the corporation. You can change the course of every life you hold in your hands. You can change the course of a nation. You can completely alter history."

Zealot, I decided.

Suits sat up straighter, fixed his burning eyes on mine. "What I'm offering you," he announced, "is the chance to help me alter the course of the history of San Francisco. But first you'll have to find the bastard who's trying to kill me."

No, I thought. Madman.

Three

Suits waited expectantly for my reaction. He seemed disappointed when I asked, "What makes you think somebody's trying to kill you?"

"There have been incidents." He glanced over his shoulder.

"Such as?"

"Incidents," he repeated darkly. "Here—I'll have Carmen tell you about the latest."

"Carmen?" I looked around, saw no one except the big bald man behind the counter.

Suits beckoned to him. He came around and crossed to our booth, rubbing his palms on his apron and grinning at my puzzled expression. "They got to calling me that back in the sixties when I was offloading Costa Rican banana boats," he said. "Carmen Miranda, you know? Some guy's idea of a joke. It stuck." He shrugged philosophically. "What d'you need, T.J.?"

"Tell the lady about last Thursday night, will you?"

Carmen hesitated, frowning.

27

"It's okay. She's working for me."

Suits's words didn't seem to reassure him. He hesitated some more, chewing on his lower lip. "Well, what happened, I'm locking up. Maybe eleven-thirty. And there's this big splash pierside. I turn on my floods, go out, take a look. And there's T.J. in the water, flopping around like a half-dead sea lion. I toss him a line, but he can't grab it, and I realize he's practically unconscious. So I've got to go in after him, and when I haul him up on the pier, I see he's got the start of a big knot on the back of his head." Carmen patted the back of his own skull. "And before I'm done with him he's puked up about a gallon of water."

I looked at Suits. "How'd you end up in the Bay?"

"Somebody hit me and dumped me in. I'd stopped for a beer with Carmen, left around eleven twenty-five, and started back toward my place. I remember footsteps coming up fast behind me, and nothing much after that until my friend here was pumping the water out of me."

I glanced back at Carmen; his expression was remote. More to this than he's letting on, I thought.

"You see anybody?" I asked him.

He shook his head.

"Hear anything between the time Suits . . . T.J. left and when he hit the water?"

"Nope."

"Was there anybody here in the diner who might have followed him?"

"Hadn't had a customer for nearly an hour."

I turned to Suits. "Was anything taken? Your wallet, for instance?"

"No, and I had a few hundred dollars on me, plus my Rolex."

"So you think this has to do with the other—" I didn't finish, because he moved his eyes from side to side, signaling that he didn't want to discuss the other incidents in front of Carmen.

"Thanks, Carmen," I said. "If you remember anything else, let T.J. know, would you?"

He nodded brusquely and went back to the counter, but not before I glimpsed a trace of indecision clouding his eyes. Carmen wanted to mention something else, but he wasn't sure how it would go over with Suits.

"All right," I said to Suits, "give me the whole story, starting with this current turnaround."

"You know Golden Gate Lines?"

"The shipping company? Sure. They're based in Oakland, aren't they?"

"For now, yes. They called me in a little less than a year ago, after they filed for Chapter Eleven. I've already got them stabilized, and I'm moving into the visionary stage. It's a sweeping vision; like I said before, it'll change the course of this city's history. And somebody doesn't want me to live to make it happen."

"Why not?"

". . . Wait a minute." He got up, went to the pay phone on the wall by the door, and made a quick call. When he finished, he motioned to me. "Come on, I can show you better than I can tell you." Before I could object, he waved to Carmen and hurried outside.

There are times in every investigator's career when it's wise to walk away from a prospective client. I knew instinctively that this was one of those. But did I do it? No. Instead I went after Suits and followed him back toward his building, like a child trailing after a demented Pied Piper.

When we got to Bay Vista, Suits led me to the extreme rear of the complex and into an elevator that had to be operated with a key. As we stepped on, I said, "Where're we—"

"Roof."

"Why?"

He folded his arms and leaned against the wall of the cage, flashing me an irritated look. "You ask too many questions. Can't you just let things unfold?"

"Asking questions is my job."

"There'll be plenty of time for that later."

"When?"

He rolled his eyes. We rode the rest of the way and stepped out onto the roof in silence. It was windy up there, and cold; I zipped my jacket. Suits put his hand to his eyes like a visor and scanned the sky.

"There's the bird," he said. "Record time."

I looked to the east. A helicopter—a big one, probably a JetRanger—was flapping toward us.

"Is that—"

"Mine." He tapped his chest proudly. "JetRanger Three, and I've got a Learjet Thirty-five-A as well. But the bird's my favorite. Pilot's on call twenty-four hours—Josh Haddon. Good man, he—"

The copter was overhead now, its roar drowning out the rest of his words. As it bobbed into position over an X painted on the concrete, Suits grabbed my shoulder and spoke directly into my ear. "Did you catch the identification number?"

I glanced at the copter's fuselage, saw the number was E622T. In aviation radio parlance, it would be pronounced Echo-six-two-two-Tango. Cute.

The copter hovered briefly before beginning its clumsy descent. Wind from its rotors swept my hair from my shoulders, kicked up grit that stung my face and eyes.

I hate helicopters. You're always reading about them getting tangled up in high-tension wires, and when they crash they drop like a stone. After piloting an aerodynamically perfect plane like Hy's Citabria—I'd started taking flying lessons and expected to solo by the end of the year—a helicopter's move-

30

ments felt unnatural and clumsy to me. But now it seemed I was to be treated to a ride in one, courtesy of Suitcase Gordon.

The copter touched down, its rotors slowing; the pilot leaned over and pushed open its door. Suits motioned for me to precede him. I ducked my head and hurried over. The pilot, a big redhead with a generous sprinkling of freckles across his weathered face, extended a hand and helped me on board. Suits shouted introductions and instructions as I belted myself into one of the backseats and put on the headset that would enable us to talk. Then he climbed in next to me, and the copter lifted off.

"All right," I said when he had his headset on, "where're we going?"

"I told you—too many questions."

"Suits!"

"Let me tell you something about Golden Gate Lines."

I shook my head in resignation and settled in for the ride. Josh Haddon turned the copter out over the Bay and angled south along the shoreline, toward China Basin. To our left was Oakland, its downtown spires shrouded by yellowish haze; to our right I glimpsed the white telecommunications tower that crowns the russet hump of Bernal Heights where All Souls is located.

"You ever heard of the Pacific Coast Steamers?" Suits asked through the headset.

"Of course I have." The Pacific Coast Steamers plied the country's western shoreline from Portland to San Diego, beginning in the 1870s. Every good student of California history knows that—and I am a very good one. I hoped to God Suits wasn't about to deliver a lecture on the subject.

"Well, Golden Gate Lines was formed in nineteen sixteen," he said, "when the Pacific Coast Steamship Company was bought out by Admiral Line. Seems one of the principals at Pacific Coast detested the old reprobate who'd built Admiral

Line, so he took the money and started a rival shipping company. Within ten years Golden Gate was a premier ocean-freight carrier, homeported in San Francisco."

"Suits, what does all this have to do with—"

"Context is everything."

Whatever that meant.

"Okay, we move ahead to the mid-seventies."

So much for context. Trust Suits to dismiss six decades with a flick of his hand.

"The line's riding high," he continued. "They've got sixteen container ships, and they're cashing in on the Persian Gulf trade. Money's flowing in—up to three mil a voyage. Those ships're loaded to the max—three hundred and fifty, four hundred containers. But money's also flowing out: cost overruns on crane rentals, astronomical phone bills, high salaries, lost equipment. But nobody notices, because they're not nickel-and-diming."

He paused, shaking his head. "You know, they'd offload those shipping containers to Iranian haulers, and the damned things'd just disappear into the desert. To this day you can see them outside of Teheran, housing entire Bedouin families. But nobody noticed, nobody gave a rat's ass, the line was flying. And when the Mideast trade fell off in seventy-seven and the roof caved in, they all acted shocked."

We were nearing Hunters Point now, where dilapidated housing built for shipyard workers during World War II still sprawls over the hillsides, providing dubious shelter for many of our less privileged citizens. Maybe, I thought, those Bedouins don't have it half bad. A twenty-year-old ocean-freight container must keep out the elements better than those places.

"So what does Golden Gate's board do?" Suits asked rhetorically. "Fire management? Bring in a troubleshooter? No, they do not. Instead they sell off the five best ships they've got, recruit more management at higher salaries, fire the one guy there who's got any sense, and move the line to Oakland, where somebody's cooked up a deal with a moneyman that immediately falls through. And then it's Chapter Eleven time, and a lot of good people—employees, stockholders, creditors—are left holding the bag."

"But that was in the late seventies," I said. "The line survived."

"Yeah, they found an angel. Guy by the name of Harvey Cameron. Big industrialist from Ohio, in love with the sea like a lot of landlocked people are. Old Harve got it into his head to move west, run a shipping line. Bought GGL in seventy-eight, turned it into a modest success. Not the dramatic turnaround I'd have liked, but you've got to give him credit."

"So what happened to bring the line down again?"

"Old Harve died. And then his heirs also got it into their heads to move west and run a shipping line. Trouble is, they're a bunch of dickheads. It took them a year to totally screw up, one more to head the line back into Chapter Eleven."

"And then they sent for you."

Suits started to laugh. I flinched. His laugh was another thing I'd forgotten: a high-pitched explosion, somewhere between a whoop and a cackle.

"What's so funny?" I asked.

"They sent for me because the chief dickhead, Kirk Cameron, used to buy dope, term papers, and acid off me when he was at Ohio State. So you see, those old connections're still paying off for me, Sherry-O, and—"

Now something besides his laugh was grating on me. "Hold it right there!"

Suits frowned.

"I want you to stop calling me by that ridiculous nickname. I'm Sharon. Say it—Sharon."

". . . I didn't think you minded. I like it when you call me Suits. Reminds me of the old days."

"Then I'll continue to call you that. But no more Sherry-O."

33

He shrugged, clearly as puzzled as Mick had been when I'd earlier insisted he stop calling me Aunt Sharon. After a moment he said, "Okay. Now where was I? Oh, yeah—those old connections're still paying off for me, and they can for you, too. Name your fee, I won't even question it."

An investigator's dream, and coming at just the right time. Still, I said, "I need to know everything before—"

"Look down! There it is!"

I looked. We were hovering over the abandoned Hunters Point Naval Shipyard. Over five hundred acres of decaying buildings, pitted pavement, rusted cranes, and weedy rubble-strewn terrain spread below us. The base had been closed since 1974. The federal government had been trying to offload it to the city for years, but had succeeded in transferring only eighty acres that were suitable for conversion to a business district to serve the adjacent Bayview–Hunters Point neighborhood. The rest stood empty and desolate, its sewer system rotted, its facilities outmoded, much of it so contaminated by toxic waste that cleanup seemed an impossibility.

"So what do you see?" Suits asked me.

"A ghost town."

"That's what *you* see. What *I* see is a state-of-the-art inter-modal containerized-freight station. I see piers and truck and railway terminals and a ship-repair facility. I see jobs and prosperity and the renaissance of the Port of San Francisco. And *that* is vision."

"You mean you want to—"

"I'm *going* to. I'm going to relieve the navy of that albatross and turn the entire port around. I'm going to bring Golden Gate Lines back home where it belongs—to its own mega-terminal, right down there."

". . . But the base is contaminated."

"I'm tapping the EPA's superfund for cleanup financing."

"It's out of date."

"I'll bring it up to date. I've already cut my deals with my moneymen."

"San Francisco's got limited rail access. You can't—"

"I can."

"You're crazy."

"I finalized the purchase agreement yesterday. Josh, set the bird down."

"Right, boss."

"Suits, why are we landing? We can see all that we need—"

"No, we can't. I want you to really experience this. Then you'll understand about the tunnel."

"Tunnel," I said weakly.

"Uh-huh."

"What—"

"Too many questions. Let it unfold."

Josh set the copter down. As we thumped onto the ground, I thought of the perfect three-point landing I'd once—quite accidentally—made in the Citabria. And tried not to sneer.

Four

I'd visited ghost towns before. They struck me as sad, even tragic, places, but the strength of their pathos was diluted by many decades. Not so with the modern-day ghost town at Hunters Point. No edges were yet blunted, no ugliness softened. It didn't help, of course, that the wind blew harshly there; didn't help, either, that the afternoon was so unrelentingly gray. But borne on the cold air was a sense of waste and ruin. A sense of forgotten lives spent in largely forgotten toil. A confirmation of the futility of most forms of human endeavor.

Suits and I stood on a knoll near the helicopter, looking down a badly potholed street toward a cluster of crumbling piers and corroded equipment. Seemingly oblivious to both the cold and the emotions that swirled in the void around us, he spoke animatedly, with much pointing and gesturing.

"Over there by the South Basin"—he motioned in the direction of distant Candlestick Park—"that area's so contaminated it'll just have to be sealed—paved over. But the piers there"—he directed my attention to the northeast—"they're fully rehabilitable. The dry dock"—he shrugged—"it'll be costly to bring up to snuff, so I'm saving it for last."

"And this?" I swept my hand over the buildings and parking areas around us.

"Truck and rail freight station." He pivoted slightly. "That land over there where Dago Mary's restaurant and those arts-and-crafts buildings are belongs to the city now. The businesses that'll move in can't help but benefit from my mega-terminal. And I'm planning a hiring and job-training program that'll directly impact the residents of Bayview—Hunters Point."

"You haven't mentioned the tunnel yet."

"Best for last." Taking hold of my shoulders, he turned me until I faced the hilly area to the west. "See those rails?"

They were rusted and weed-choked. "Uh-huh."

"They join the old Southern Pacific line at a tunnel in the Bayshore district. Through that tunnel, south down the Peninsula, then a quick jog east, and it's clear tracks all the way to Chicago and other transfer points."

I stared along the rails, envisioning the journey he described. I'd never seen the tunnel, but I'd been aware of its existence as well as that of another near Potrero Hill, both over a hundred years old. San Francisco's location behind a ridge of hills at the tip of a long narrow peninsula had always made for problematical rail access and, in part, had contributed to our port's decline.

"So what about the tunnel?" I asked.

"Trouble is, it's outmoded. Railways started double-stacking ocean-freight containers years ago—saves time and money—but the tunnel's not large enough to accommodate them. So it seems to me that deepening it is the key to keeping at least part of the waterfront in maritime use. I've worked a deal with the Southern Pacific and the port where I'll match funds and take responsibility for having the work done."

"How much will that cost you?"

"Oh, six mil, give or take."

"My God."

"It's nothing. The return on investment'll wipe out the cost in no time."

It all sounded so plausible—or would have, had anyone but Suitcase Gordon proposed it. Or was I underestimating him?

Finally I said, "Okay, you've filled me in on the history of Golden Gate Lines and your plans for it. But aside from the incident at Miranda's, which could have just been a mugging that got out of hand, you haven't given me much proof that somebody's trying to kill you."

"Come on." He started toward the waiting JetRanger.

I hesitated, then followed. There was a definite danger in associating with Suits: what if he succeeded in training me not only to refrain from asking questions but also to take orders?

* * *

"It happened approximately the way Mr. Gordon described it to you."

I caught a note of reserve in Dick Farley's voice and glanced up at the manager of the Jack London Terminal on Oakland's Inner Harbor, which handled Golden Gate Lines' freight. Under the rim of his hard hat, Farley's weather-browned face was expressionless.

Suits had had Josh Haddon set the helicopter down there half an hour before, then made me don a hard hat and dragged me along a pier to Berth Three, where the office said Farley could be found conferring with one of his longshoremen. Ostensibly the purpose of our visit was so Farley could tell me in his own words about the accident two weeks before when Suits claimed he was almost killed by a wrench falling from a crane offloading GGL's *Napa Harvest*. But Suits hadn't let the man talk, had instead described the incident himself in dramatic detail. He'd just reached the story's culmination—"Only grazed my shoulder, but it hurt like hell for days. All I could think was that it could've been my head, split open like a ripe melon!"—when a beeper in the zipper pocket of his sweatshirt went off and he excused himself to find a phone.

Now Farley and I were walking back along the pier toward the terminal offices. To our left towered the curving white sides of a vessel laden with stacked containers; to our right lay an enormous expanse of concrete where more containers, semitrailers, forklifts, and cranes were parked. The roar of diesel engines and the creak of heavy equipment drowned out all but the loudest voice. I raised mine and shouted, "Approximately?"

Farley nodded.

I waited until we'd come out of the hard hat area, took mine off, and shook out my hair. It fell neatly to my shoulders, just as the stylist who had shorn my former long tresses over a month ago had guaranteed. Farley removed his hat too, passing his hand over an iron-gray military cut. He motioned to me, and we went to stand pierside where the din was less intrusive.

I said, "I suppose the incident wasn't as life-threatening as Mr. Gordon made it out to be."

"Well, any time you have an accident out here it can be damned serious. And Mr. Gordon had neglected to put on his hard hat." He thumped a knuckle on his own. "But the injury to his shoulder was minimal."

A minimal injury that "hurt like hell for days." I was beginning to think my old friend suffered from a touch of hypochondria.

"You investigated the accident?" I asked.

"We conduct a thorough investigation of every accident, no matter how insignificant. And of course Mr. Gordon demanded a full-scale inquisition." Farley smiled faintly, then squinted down at me to see how I'd taken the comment.

I smiled too.

"It was an accident, plain and simple," he went on. "We determined who left the wrench up there, and he's been disciplined. As for it falling, the vibration of the crane caused that. Operator confirms it, and he's one of our most trusted employees."

"So as far as you know, no one connected with the terminal was trying to harm Mr. Gordon."

"As far as I know."

"Is there anyone working here who might have reason to harm him?"

". . . Well, men like him make enemies. He could have stepped on some toes. But as to whose . . ." He shrugged.

"Are you aware of his plans for GGL?"

"Yes, he's been up-front all along."

"Don't those plans pose a threat to the Port of Oakland?"

"Well . . ." Farley thought, placing the hard hat under his arm and balancing it against one lean hip. "There's no doubt that the port's in trouble. Last year APL—American President Lines—chose to expand its terminals at Seattle and L.A. rather than Oakland. That was partly the port's fault; it failed to put together the parcel of land they needed for their expansion. But the Army Corps of Engineers and the EPA are responsible, too; they've delayed their scheduled dredging of Bay channels, and we can't accommodate the new larger vessels."

"I thought the Inner Harbor dredging project was done."

"Only the first phase. Now the EPA's concerned about finding appropriate dump sites for the rest of the silt. Typical bureaucracy—didn't think it through beforehand—and the delay'll cost the city millions of tax dollars and thousands of jobs. But that's got nothing to do with GGL. Fact is, they aren't a power in the industry, haven't been for some time. I'd say their loss will have a negligible effect on the port's income and the city's economy."

"What about its effect on your terminal?"

"Well, naturally we wish they'd stay. It's always hard to lose a major customer. But they're only one of many lines that use our facilities, and like I said, Mr. Gordon's been up-front, given us enough time to work on attracting others."

"Mr. Farley, is there anything else you can tell me about the accident? Or about Mr. Gordon's relationships with your employees?"

He shifted his weight, eyes troubled. "About the accident, no. About your Mr. Gordon . . ."

"You can be frank with me."

"I don't like to carry tales, but . . . he's touchy. Imagines slights. Flies off the handle without much provocation. They tell me he's a smart businessman, but he's not going about his business in a very smart way."

I was about to ask for specific examples when I heard Suits calling me. "Got to get moving fast. They need me at the office."

I took out one of my cards and handed it to Farley. "May I call you to discuss this further?"

"Like I said, I don't want to carry tales."

"Anything you tell me will be held in confidence."

He nodded curtly, pocketed the card, and relieved me of the hard hat.

"Sherry-O, come *on*!"

I took my time getting to the JetRanger, to punish him for continuing to use the hated nickname.

*　　*　　*

Our next stop was the roof of a downtown office building within blocks of Oakland's convention center. The elevator that Suits and I took down, an ancient cage replete with an accordion grille that had to be yanked open by hand, creaked and wheezed and bounced ominously when it reached the fifth floor. Suits hauled at the lever on the grille, pushed open the door, and preceded me into a dingy green hallway with scarred wainscoting and doors with pebbled-glass windows and transoms. I felt as though I'd stepped back into the forties.

"Guess GGL really *was* in trouble before they called on you," I commented.

Suits gave the elevator door a shove; it caught on a curled square of linoleum. He threw his hands up and started down the hall. "They damned well were in trouble. Had three floors of offices at One Kaiser Plaza. Rosewood and Oriental rugs up the wazoo."

"You moved them from Kaiser Plaza to *this?*"

He stopped before an unmarked door at the end of the corridor. "First tenet of turnaround: slash costs. Second tenet: scare 'em. I slashed costs by cutting office rent to a third. And I scared 'em by moving to a slummy building with no carpeting and exposed pipes on the ceiling." He laughed, a whoop that echoed off the bare walls. "The dickhead contingent put up a fuss, of course. 'But our image,' they said. 'What image?' I said. 'Everybody in town knows you're up to your asses in unpaid invoices.' At that point a couple of the dickheads threw in the towel and went back to Ohio. Kirk Cameron stayed, but he's taken to seriously working on his golf game. But most of the admin staff and operations people stuck by me."

He threw open the door and extended his hand toward the room beyond it. I stepped inside, saw two rows of steel desks topped by computer terminals and covered with papers and files. Most of the desks were occupied, and all the occupants were busy. Suits led me down the center aisle toward a cubicle at the rear, calling greetings to people as he passed. I watched their responses, trying to gauge how they felt about him; they ranged from cordiality to wariness.

The cubicle was small, its walls topped with more pebbled glass. Suits motioned at its Spartan furnishings and said, "Not much of an office for the head honcho, huh?"

"It's worse than the closet under the stairs that I used to work in at All Souls."

"Third tenet of turnaround: don't give yourself perks when you're taking them away from everybody else. Besides, I do

43

most of my work in the bird or at the condo." He sprawled in the swivel chair, propping his feet on the desk, and pointed at the straight-back across from him. "Sit."

"I thought you had urgent business to attend to."

"It can wait a minute. First I want to introduce you to a couple of my people."

I glanced at my watch. Almost five. By now, I hoped, Mick would have put my offices in order. No doubt at this moment he was ensconced on the new sofa studying . . . what? *Methods of Disguise? Games Criminals Play?* When I'd seen those two titles in the gym bag he carried, the thought of how he might apply the knowledge had made me cringe.

Suits saw me checking the time, but chose to ignore my concern. "One team member that I asked to stop in is . . . here right now."

A tall woman with closely clipped blond hair stopped on the threshold of the cubicle. Suits got up, indicating she should take his chair. She remained where she was, frowning in disapproval. "They're waiting for you down in Legal."

"On my way. This is the investigator I told you about, Sharon McCone. Sharon, Carole Lattimer, my chief financial officer."

I rose and shook Lattimer's hand, secretly amused that the "finance guy" from Chicago whom Suits had said he called upon was a woman.

Suits squeezed past Lattimer, calling over his shoulder, "I asked Russ to stop in, too. You three can talk about me. Tell Sharon what a terrific guy I am to work with."

Lattimer shook her head and grinned wryly at me. She was young for her position—perhaps in her late twenties—and wore a very short black dress, matching tights, and suede flats decorated with a swirl of amber beading that complemented her jewelry. Hardly banker's attire, I thought, and in a meeting with the moneymen, as Suits called them, it would send the message that she was too confident to be hampered by tradition.

"So are you going to do that?" I asked. "Tell me how terrific he is?"

She sat down on the edge of the desk, crossing her ankles and swinging her legs. "I could. Working with him's a unique experience, and T.J.'s an original, for sure. You've known him a long time?"

"Yes, but until today I hadn't seen him in over fifteen years. I had no idea he'd become such a power in the business world."

"Really? I've always assumed that T.J.'s been wheeling and dealing his whole life."

I commandeered Suits's chair, which looked more comfortable than the one I'd occupied. "Now that you mention it," I said, "I suppose that in his own way he has. How long have you been associated with him?"

"Around five years. I helped him turn Lost Hope, Nevada."

"What's that?"

"A town in the desert between Reno and Las Vegas. It was dying; now it's a thriving midpoint stop on the north-south route."

"Gambling town?" I asked, wondering if Suits had somehow gotten mixed up with organized crime.

Lattimer shook her head. "Some gambling, but it's more tourist- and family-oriented."

"What other kinds of turnarounds has T.J. done?"

"Well, there was a steel mill, and a large financial corporation—wish I'd gotten in on that one. An equipment company that had something to do with the film industry; a firm in Colorado . . . mining? You'd have to ask him about that."

"Isn't it unusual for somebody to walk into an organization or a town that he's got no experience with and know how to turn it?"

"Very. That's one of the things that make T.J. an original.

45

Most turnaround pros stick to an industry or a type of business that they know inside and out—manufacturing, services, finance, whatever. But T.J.'s jumped all over the board. He's an inexhaustible researcher, has a photographic memory, and is an incredibly quick study. And he has an instinctive grasp of nuance."

"Isn't his personality . . ." I hesitated, wanting to phrase the question delicately.

Lattimer grinned. "You mean his stunning lack of tact and polish? His way of stirring people up until they're practically running amok in the streets? Actually you'd be surprised how closely he fits the profile of turnaround pros."

"What's the profile?"

She began to trace patterns in the dust on the desk with her forefinger. "They're top-flight people, of course. Usually well educated, but they've come up the hard way. Generally they're not very . . . attractive. They don't do well at cocktail parties, don't have many friends. Most of them are aware they don't fit in, but they don't want to, anyway. They're insensitive to other people's needs, except when satisfying them will get them what *they* want. They expect excellence of themselves and of the people who work for them; they don't tolerate others' shortcomings, don't suffer fools. And they're very, very focused, to the exclusion of everything but the job at hand." She paused. "Frankly, they're a pain in the ass, and everybody's happy when the job's done and they go away."

Yes, Suits was a close fit for the profile. "So why would anybody—you, for instance—want to work for someone like that?"

"Money. Stock options. The chance to watch somebody who's the absolute best there is do his thing. And the challenge of being part of that thing. But you go into it aware that you have to draw lines."

"Such as?"

"Take the relationship between T.J. and me: He knows

46

I'm tops at what I do. He knows he can count on my total commitment and loyalty. I know I can count on the same from him. I know he'll keep his promises. But that doesn't mean we're friends. It doesn't even mean we like each other. We don't do lunch; I don't invite him to my home. It's business, plain and simple, and it wouldn't work otherwise."

In a cold, practical way, that made sense. "Okay, you've mentioned one thing that makes him an original. What're the others?"

"The major one is vision. T.J. sees possibilities that you or I wouldn't even dream of. He can look at a disaster area like the Hunters Point base and visualize a rebirth of the Port of San Francisco. Initially his concepts may seem skewed, but in the end he makes them work."

A voice from the door said, "Often by force of his own pigheadedness."

I looked over there at a stocky, round-faced man with a mop of black hair. "Nice kudos to T.J., Carole," he added, "but it won't earn you any additional perks unless he's hiding under the desk."

"Ah, Russ." There was an edge to Lattimer's greeting and little warmth as she performed the introductions. Russ Zola, she explained, was Suits's organizational strategist and had been with him "forever."

Zola turned the straight-backed chair around and straddled it, his forearms resting on the crosspiece. Diamond-studded links winked from the cuffs of his white shirt, and a diamond-and-onyx ring gleamed on his right hand. "What're you trying to do, Carole?" he asked easily. "Make me out to be older than God?"

Lattimer didn't reply.

I asked, "What does an organizational strategist do, specifically?"

"I look at the overall structure of the corporation, decide what can be changed to facilitate efficiency. I make recommendations, help implement them, monitor progress, make constant adjustments."

"In short," Lattimer said, "Russ is T.J.'s executioner."

"Thank you, Carole. Such a dramatic job description." He smiled at me and changed the subject. "So you're the investigator who's going to save T.J. from the alleged assassin."

"Russ." Lattimer's voice held a warning note.

"What—we're supposed to pretend we don't know why she's here?"

"I believe that's a confidential matter between T.J. and Ms. McCone." Now her tone was markedly chilly. "When you came in, we were discussing what makes T.J. unique as a turnaround pro. We talked about his lack of specialization and, as you heard, his vision. Since you've been with him so long, I'm sure you have something to add to that."

Zola rolled his eyes, obviously amused at her stiff manner. The subject to which she'd attempted to redirect the conversation seemed to interest him, though; he considered before speaking, his expression thoughtful. "The speed of T.J.'s turnarounds is pretty damned impressive. The average pro will do four or five in a lifetime. T.J.'s been operating for around fourteen years now, and he's already up to half a dozen."

I asked, "You've worked with him on all of them?"

"All but the very first."

"How does he manage them so quickly?"

"Advance planning. He does comprehensive research and goes in with a strong game plan. And he pushes everybody mercilessly, including himself and those of us on his team. He's brutal to the few employees who survive the bloodbath. He's a whiz at getting answers out of the banks and creditors, is even better at getting action out of his investors. To tell you the truth, I've seen no evidence that he's ever slept."

Zola paused again, dark eyes reflective. "Of course, there's a downside to all that. T.J.'s easily bored. Once he's got a firm stabilized, he's itching to get on to the visionary stage. Once the vision begins to become reality, he's already thinking about where he wants to go next, sifting through the offers that've come in."

"So he doesn't see things through?"

"Sometimes. Keystone Steel, company we turned some seven, eight years ago, is a perfect example. Big mill in southwestern Pennsylvania on the fringe of Appalachia. The last one operating in that area, and about to go bust. T.J. had it stabilized, but then he got a vision and jumped ahead too fast. Saved the company, but at an awful human cost. And then there's the problem of his temper; he's just too volatile for his own good. He'll get in a big fight with the board, make it impossible for them to go on working with him."

"How often does that happen?"

"Once or twice a turnaround. He manages to smooth it over but again, at a terrific cost."

"All right," I said, "let's get back to the way he treats his people. Lucrative or not, why do such talented individuals as the two of you come each time he calls?"

Lattimer said, "As I told you, it's the chance of a lifetime to see someone like T.J. do his stuff."

Zola nodded. "When he's good, he's very, very good. That's really something to be a part of. And when he's bad . . . well, it's still damned interesting."

I'd asked the question to see if either would betray hidden resentment or animosity, but both responses seemed genuine. After a moment I said, "I'm wondering how T.J. got to be so good at this line of work. You don't just decide to become a turnaround man and hang out your shingle. What is there in his background that qualifies him?"

Zola looked perplexed. "An M.B.A. from Harvard doesn't qualify him?"

"He attended *Harvard*?"

"Both as an undergrad and as a graduate student."

But how had his cross-country ramblings permitted time for that? "When?"

Zola chuckled. "I'm surprised an old friend like you didn't know. Or maybe I'm not. Man's got a mania for privacy, that's for sure. Anyway, it's a fascinating story. T.J. was one of those child prodigies you hear about: reading at an adult level when most kids are learning their ABC's; fiddling with advanced calculus when the others are still having trouble with their multiplication tables. By twelve he'd finished high school and was taking college courses. Started Harvard at fourteen and earned his degree in two years. A year after that he had his M.B.A."

"And then?"

Zola shrugged. "Time off to grow up, I guess. All I know is that he did his first turnaround about fourteen years ago— something to do with agriculture north of here. Then he contacted me about helping turn Avery Equipment in L.A., and we've been kicking corporate butt ever since. It never occurred to me to question him about the time between Harvard and then; I didn't need to check on his background because I'd seen him in action."

I was fairly sure Suits wouldn't want his associates to know he'd acted as an itinerant peddler of mostly illegal commodities during those years, so I didn't respond to the question implied in Zola's tone. In truth, I was having difficulty digesting this latest piece of information about the life and times of Suitcase Gordon. Finally I forced my attention back to the business at hand and said, "Now I'd like to talk about the reason T.J. wants to hire me. Mr. Zola, earlier you mentioned the 'alleged assassin.' Is that your phrasing or T.J.'s?"

"Mine. I believe he used the term 'hit man.' "

"Ms. Lattimer, has he also commented on the situation to you?"

She nodded. "Same terminology."

"Does either of you have an opinion about what's going on?"

They exchanged glances. "Well," Lattimer said, "*something's* wrong."

"She knows that, Carole. What she's asking is if the hit man theory holds water."

I turned to Zola. "Does it?"

"Only if the hit man's preposterously incompetent. T.J. claims he's made four different attempts by four different means."

Unorthodox as well as incompetent. "So what's happening here?"

He shrugged.

"*Is* somebody trying to kill him?"

Lattimer said, "This may sound strange, but I'd like to believe someone is. If not, T.J.'s becoming a head case, and we're all going to be in trouble."

"Paranoid?"

"Uh-huh. He's exhibiting some classic signs."

"So which is it—hit man or head case?"

Again they exchanged glances.

Zola said, "I vote for head case."

Lattimer nodded.

*   *   *

"It happened right here," Suits said. "You can see where the bullet hit the pillar."

We were standing next to his vintage silver Corvette in the lower-level parking area of his building. On the copter ride back across the Bay he'd told me of two additional attempts on his life: a hand pushing him into traffic while he stood on a crowded street corner in the financial district—shades of an old Hitchcock film, I'd thought—and a shot being fired at him as he parked in his assigned space late one night the week before last. I took a close look at the nick that he indicated on the support pillar. Yes, it could have been made by a bullet. But given its height, it could just as well have been made by a car.

I wondered if Suits had watched many of the dozens of TV movies depicting shootings in parking garages.

"How come the security guard didn't respond?" I asked.

"He wasn't around when I drove in. And it was only a pop—the shooter probably used a silencer."

TV movie, all right.

"You called the police?"

He nodded.

"They find the bullet?"

". . . No."

"What action're they taking?"

"They're investigating." The set of his mouth was turning sullen.

"If you have the name of the officer in charge of the case, I'll check on its status."

"I've got his card someplace upstairs." Suits moved toward the nearby elevator, but I stopped him.

"You've used the term 'hit man' to Russ Zola and Carole Lattimer. Do you think there's a contract out on you?"

He looked down at the concrete floor, scuffed at something with the toe of his sneaker.

"If you do," I went on, "let me reassure you. A pro wouldn't have bungled it. He'd have come to town, made a quick hit, and been long gone. And in the unlikely event that he failed on his first attempt, he wouldn't have used a different method the next time. That's not the way the pros operate."

Suits mumbled something to the floor.

"What?"

"I said, I know how the pros operate. I've resigned myself to the fact that whoever's trying to kill me has a personal reason, may even be somebody close to me."

I ran my thumb over the nick on the pillar, trying to

tactfully phrase what I needed to ask next. "Suits, you've been working pretty hard this past year. Russ Zola says he's seen no evidence you've ever slept—and he was only half joking. You're not using cocaine or—"

"You don't believe me." He didn't sound angry, merely defeated.

"I didn't say that."

"You didn't have to."

"Suits . . ."

He turned his back to me, began walking toward the elevator. "I am not using coke or anything else," he said wearily. "Drugs are a roller-coaster ride that's not worth the price of the ticket. I am not imagining these attempts on my life; I don't have much imagination, except as it pertains to my work. I am not paranoid; paranoid people are not self-aware, and I am—painfully so." He lifted his hand toward the elevator call button, then let his arm drop to his side.

When he faced me, his lips were twisted in a lopsided, self-mocking smile. "You think I don't know who and what I am? Try this, then: Remember that bullshit I handed you this morning about how I slunk out of town after our substance-induced fling because I wasn't ready to settle down? Well, do you know why I really left?"

I shook my head.

"I left because I knew I was a runty, funny-looking guy with a mediocre personality who'd just happened to get very lucky. You were the prettiest, nicest, smartest woman I'd ever gone to bed with, and I knew you'd never let it happen again. And I also knew that if I stayed in town I wouldn't've been able to leave you alone. That would've only made us both miserable. I just plain didn't want to put either of us through that."

"Oh, Suits—"

"No." He held up his hand. "Spare me any kindness at this late date. I don't need it, I don't want it. What I do need and want—" He looked down at the floor again. A shudder passed through his slight frame as he tried to control runaway emotions.

"What I do need and want," he went on after a moment, "is for you to help me." He looked up and met my gaze; his eyes were jumpy with restrained fear; odd pinpoints of light flared in their depths.

I stepped forward and took his hand; it was icy. I looked more closely at his face to make sure he wasn't conning me. His skin was ashen, pulled so tight it seemed brittle.

I said gently, "We'll talk more in the morning."

Five

It was after seven when I got back to the office; Mick had given up on me and gone home. I stood in the little room over the Victorian's entryway, which someday would belong to my assistant, looking over the new equipment assembled there. The lights on the answering machine glowed; the display panel on the fax broadcast the word "standby." After a moment I went over to the computer and ran my finger across its keyboard. Felt something akin to a mild electric shock, even though it was turned off. And realized it was emotional static.

For years I'd resisted becoming computer literate, turning over accessing the databases I routinely needed to my former assistant, Rae Kelleher. I'd told her I wasn't good with machines, that I couldn't even type properly, but the real reason was my fear of becoming trapped in the office, far from the action and interaction I thrive on. Now—at least until I could winnow out a promising assistant from an unpromising crop of applicants—I would have to learn to use the computer in order to keep the cash flowing.

But why not? I thought. I'd once said I wouldn't have a microwave in the house; now I defrosted and cooked entire feasts in record time. While my earthquake cottage was under renovation I'd mastered electrical wiring and become a fair plumber's helper. My stomach had once lurched at Hy's suggestion of piloting the Citabria upside down; now I was impatient to solo and kept pestering him to teach me the fancy stuff. Compared to understanding the circular flight computer, learning the Apple would be a piece of cake.

And all this had come about because of a crazy week last June when I'd undergone a series of severe emotional shocks as well as an ordeal that forced me to call upon resources I hadn't suspected I possessed. After that there was no going back. I'd stepped off the high dive into a new future, and now I was treading water as fast as I could.

I turned away from the Apple and went into my office, noting with approval that my new sofa and chair looked exactly as I'd pictured them when I saw them in the showroom. My rose from Hy had also arrived; it stood in its bud vase on the corner of my desk, and Mick had even thought to add fresh water.

The roses—a single long-stemmed beauty delivered every Tuesday—were Hy's way of keeping us close no matter how long the separation or how great the distance between us. Initially they'd been yellow; after we became lovers he changed their color to an exotic tangerine; but after that harrowing time last June when I'd almost lost him, he changed it once again—to a velvety blackish red. We'd talked about his reasons for the other color choices: yellow because I wasn't traditional enough for red or sentimental enough for pink; exotic tangerine because it described our passion. But this strange deep red? Neither of us had so much as mentioned it.

I went over and touched the flower's soft petals, breathed in its rich fragrance. Red—the color of love, the deeper the better. Red—the color of shed blood, the product of violence.

Which? Both had been components of that tumultuous week. . . .

My fingers tightened on the stem of the vase. Suddenly I wanted to pick it up and hurl it at the wall. Better yet, seize the rose, rip its petals off, and trample them.

After all we'd gone through during that week, after all we'd almost lost, after all the commitment I thought we'd made to each other, Hy was once more out of reach. Had, since he dropped me at Oakland Airport in early July, been off on an uncharacteristic spate of traveling whose significance I failed to understand.

Postcards arrived and phone calls came. The plain white cards—Hy wasn't the picture-postcard type—bore both U.S. and foreign postmarks and messages of no consequence. The calls were brief, filled with superficial chatter: Yes, my business license had come through. No, I hadn't taken on any clients yet. Yes, the weather was hot and muggy in Miami—or rainy in London or overcast in New York. No, he wasn't exactly sure where he'd be going next. I'd filed the cards in order, listed the dates and cities of origin of the calls. Neither gave a hint of an organized itinerary; neither revealed the purpose of his travels.

For some time now Hy had expressed dissatisfaction with his participation in the environmental movement; he felt his confrontational style was outmoded, his fund-raising ability limited. In June he also had been forced to face his past and reassess his future. Like me, he'd opted for change, but so far I hadn't a clue as to what form that change would take. All I knew was that his travels were not the typical idle wanderings of a man with a good deal of money and time on his hands.

I also suspected that somehow his movements were connected to a mysterious nine-year hole in his life—a period that had almost destroyed him and about which he'd told no one, not even me.

I didn't know what hurt more—his refusal to open up to

me or his absence right now when I needed him most. I'd set out on the riskiest venture of my life: for the first time I was working alone without the support of an employer; money was flying out the door, but clients weren't flying in; my sister had saddled me with a teenager with criminal tendencies. And now I'd been presented a first case that was potentially lucrative but riddled with complications. I needed to talk with Hy, my touchstone, but I hadn't the faintest idea of where in the world to reach him.

I eyed the rose malevolently. Plucked it from the vase and fingered a petal, contemplating a perverse variant on the old he-loves-me-he-loves-me-not game, involving atrocities I'd have liked to commit upon my lover. Then I replaced it, straightening its greenery. No sense in trivializing the situation; no need to add childishness to my roster of character defects.

Forcing my attention back to Suitcase Gordon, I decided to go upstairs and see if Rae was home. In the past I'd often benefited from her insights; maybe she could cut to the core of my uncertainty about taking him on as my first client.

Rae lived in a big skylit room in the attic. She, Ted, tax attorney Pam Ogata, and corporate-law specialist Larry Koslowski were the last holdouts from the days when All Souls was a poverty law firm in the strictest sense of the term and offered its underpaid staff free rooms as part of their meager compensation package. The four stayed because they enjoyed the camaraderie, and more often than not many of us who lived elsewhere could be found there after the close of business, sitting in on their poker games or pitching in at their potlucks.

I knocked on the frame of Rae's Moroccan-curtained doorway, and her voice called for me to come in. I swept the curtain aside, ducked my head to avoid a low beam, and entered. The room was dimly lighted; Rae sat cross-legged on the floor under the roof's steep angle, wearing her ratty plaid bathrobe and peering at her face in an illuminated makeup mirror perched atop the trunk where she kept her jeans and sweaters.

She saw me in the mirror and grinned, her freckled nose crinkling. "Hey, I was just thinking about you," she said.

"Really?" I sat down on the mattress and box spring that were all that remained of her treasured brass bed. It had gotten crushed while the skylights were being installed last spring and, true to form, Rae had spent the insurance money on a trip to Tahoe and some clothes. I saw that one of the new outfits, a clingy skirt and tunic in a russet color that complemented her auburn hair, was laid out on the mattress. "Date tonight?" I asked.

"Not exactly. But I'm running late, and that's one reason I was thinking about you. You really ought to curb your nephew."

"What's Mick done now?"

"Cornered me in my office when I was trying to finish up and asked me a bunch of questions about the business, some of which I couldn't answer."

"Sorry about that. He's going home at the end of the month."

"Oh, I didn't really mind." She leaned closer to the mirror and began applying eye shadow. "I just hate having some kid know more about my job than I do."

"So what's happening?" I motioned at the clothing.

Rae groaned, set the eye shadow down, and turned to face me. With only one eye done and a somewhat tremulous expression, she looked like a little girl who'd gotten caught playing with her mother's makeup. "Shar," she said, "I'm going out with some women friends tonight. To a bar."

"The Remedy?" It was All Souls's tavern of choice, down the hill on Mission Street.

"God, no. Would I get made up to go there? This is a nice bar—a club, actually—in the Marina. We're going to . . . look for men."

I waited.

"Did you hear what I said—look for men?"

"What's wrong with that?"

She sighed. "Nothing, I guess. It's just that I feel so . . . inexperienced. I haven't really done that since college."

"This must mean it's finally over with Willie." Since she divorced her perpetual-student husband, Rae had been seeing Willie Whelan, self-styled discount-jewelry king of northern California—to say nothing of former fence of stolen goods. The relationship had fallen apart over some nonsense about a prenuptial agreement last spring, but since then the two had argued on an almost daily basis, and I'd expected they'd eventually get back together.

"It's over," she said, her mouth hardening. "And now I'm getting on with my life. But, God, it's rough. Can't you give me some advice? I mean, you've never had any trouble getting men."

I hadn't, maybe because I'd always met my lovers when I was too wrapped up in something—a case, a cause, a class— to be anxious about my lack of male companionship. In my experience, most worthwhile people are put off by someone who is obviously seeking nothing more than a warm body. But I wasn't about to tell Rae that when she was feeling so fragile, so I said lightly, "Consider the quality of the men I've gotten."

"Hy's terrific, Shar. And you guys have a great relationship—so unconfining."

"Mmm." I thought of the rose petals that had almost littered my office floor. "Well, Hy excepted, I haven't done all that well."

Rae was silent; I could tell she was checking names off a mental list. Then she shrugged and turned back to the mirror. "Well, I just know that if I meet anybody tonight, he'll be horrible. But I'm ready; I've memorized my friend Vanessa's instructions."

"Instructions?" In spite of wanting to talk about Suits, I was curious as to what kind of rules were mandated for present-day barhopping.

"Instructions." Rae nodded. "Don't wear anything too revealing, but try to look subtly seductive. One glass of wine beforehand for courage, but only one, and you travel by cab. Avoid the guys who're scamming at the end of the bar by the door; they're usually nerds or predators, or both. Never go anyplace with a guy the first night; instead, exchange business cards and make arrangements to meet the next week in a public place. But always carry condoms, just in case." She snorted. "The damned things'll probably stay in my purse so long they'll be fossilized. To tell you the truth, I'd much rather hang out and play pinball at the Remedy."

"So why don't you?"

"No, I've got to at least give this a try. Tonight we hit this low-key place in the Marina where a lot of stockbrokers hang out. If nothing pans out there, we'll try a SoMa supper club and this neo-yuppie bar in South Beach next week. And if those don't produce, there's a Eurocrowd café in North Beach that we're saving for the week after that. And the week after *that*, you'll find me in front of the Remedy's pinball machine."

I hesitated, trying to come up with an appropriate response. Actually I felt superior and envious at the same time. For as long as I'd known her, Rae had drifted from one emotional catastrophe to another; this man-hunting scheme was sure to steer her into trouble again. But at least she was sailing forth, out there with her face to the wind. Rae would never dream of hanging around her office after business hours, contemplating mayhem on an innocent rose sent by a straying lover.

She noticed my silence and frowned. "Did you come up here for a reason, or just to chat?"

"A reason. Somebody who could become my first client showed up today."

Rae ran her fingers through her unruly curls and stood up. "Good money?"

"He said to name my fee."

"Go for it."

"I'm not sure I should." As she took the russet outfit from its hanger I began filling her in on Suits and his problem. My voice rose as I talked; I could hear myself becoming unnecessarily strident.

"Dammit!" I concluded. "Why does this have to happen now? I don't *want* my first client to be a weird guy out of my past who has serious potential to drive me crazy!"

"Sounds like he already has," she said mildly, adjusting a scarf around her neck.

"Close to," I admitted. "So what's your take on it?"

"Well, if I read you right, you've got several objections to taking his case. One, you think the whole thing may be some paranoid tic of his."

I nodded.

"Two, you're really still in the start-up phase with the agency, and you don't have time for a complex investigation."

"Right."

"Three, this Suits used to be your lover."

"A one-night stand ages ago doesn't really qualify—"

"But he admitted he had a thing for you. That qualifies. And four—you said it—he's weird."

I waited, aware of Rae's habit of building a case for one side, then arguing for the other.

She studied the hang of the scarf, made a face, and untied it. "Let's address the issues in reverse order. He's weird. Not a valid objection—you *like* weird people. Face it, Shar—you're a little off center yourself."

"*Moi?*"

"*Tu.* Okay, next objection—he was your lover, or whatever. Also not valid. You all but forgot about him years ago. And if he's harboring any feelings, it doesn't sound as if he's going to let them get in the way." She adjusted the scarf one more time, then yanked it off and tossed it on the mattress. "Third objection, you don't have time. Bullshit. Anybody can make time to charge a huge fee for doing something interesting. If you ask me, you're afraid to take this on."

"Afraid? That's ridiculous!"

"Is it? Shar, all this interest in learning the computer, all this haste to get it down pat so you can send Mick home before he gets any more obsessed with becoming an investigator—that's just an excuse."

"For?"

"For not plunging in and getting on with what you set out to do when you quit the co-op."

The words stung. For a moment I wanted to lash out at her, but I couldn't come up with a suitable retort. And, much as I hated to admit it, she had a point.

"Fourth objection," Rae went on, "Suits may be going 'round the bend. Well, maybe he is, but you'll never really know unless you take his case. Can you stand not knowing?"

Again she had me.

"Besides," she added, "if somebody actually is trying to kill him, you can prevent it and become a little chapter in San Francisco history."

I snorted.

"Stranger things have happened." She picked up her purse and headed for the door. "Think about it."

* * *

Before I left the co-op I ran into Jack Stuart, who was clearing out the last of his personal belongings from the room he'd formerly occupied on the second floor. Jack, the latest defector from the live-in contingent, had decided he needed a change of scene after the disastrous breakup of a love affair last spring—a breakup in which I'd played an unfortunate but necessary part. I helped him take his boxes out to his van, and then we shared some wine; I'd hoped he might give me an opinion on the Suits situation, but Jack was more interested in discussing the color schemes he'd picked out for his new condo on Diamond Heights. When I finally said good night to him, it was after nine, and I felt more isolated than ever.

You've got nobody to blame but yourself, McCone, I told myself as I drove toward home. This is the life you chose for yourself; get used to it.

* * *

Most of the lights in my renovated earthquake cottage were blazing. I flicked off the overheads in the guest room and parlor as I went down the hall. A mutter of voices came from the sitting room; I paused, listening. Damned if one didn't sound like a police dispatcher.

I hurried in there. Mick sat at my old card table, which he'd set up against the wall by the fireplace, and on it was the most elaborate radio setup I'd ever seen. Sound-level lights blinked as Mick fiddled with a transceiver; he was so intent on it that he didn't hear me come in.

Neither did Ralph, my orange tabby. He sat on the back of an armchair staring bloodthirstily at W. C. Fields, my crotchety-looking silk parrot, who hung on a perch by the window. I'd bought the parrot for seventy-five-plus-tax big bucks last June in exchange for information I thought might lead me to Hy, and ever since I'd brought it home, Ralphie had eyed it evilly, intent on ripping its throat out. I was equally intent that he wouldn't touch it, and as I crossed the room toward Mick, I swatted the cat off the chair. He thudded to the floor, mowled in protest, and leaped over an empty cardboard carton next to Mick. Alice, his calico sister, was sitting in the box; she and Mick looked up with identical bewildered expressions.

I asked, "What the hell is this?"

Mick turned off the transceiver. "Sorry, I didn't know you were home."

"So?" I asked, waving at the card table. "What is?"

"My radio. I assembled it myself from components I bought up at garage sales and flea markets."

"You assembled it tonight?" I stared incredulously at him.

"Of course not—a couple of years ago. Last week when I talked to Dad I asked him to pack it up and send it UPS. It came this afternoon." His hand caressed the transceiver as if it were a beloved pet. "Look, Aunt . . . I mean, Shar. It's got everything. Here's the police band, and here're the fire calls. This is UHF, VHF, MHz."

"You can listen in on the air traffic?"

"Yeah, at both Oakland and SFO. What's the frequency for Oakland?"

"Ground Control's one-twenty-one-point-nine."

He flipped a switch, turned a knob.

". . . Oakland Ground, this is one-two-one-three-Delta. I'm eastbound to Livermore with Alfa . . ."

Mick said, "Next time Hy flies down, you can monitor the radio, hear him call in to the tower, and be over there before he phones you to come get him. Tell him you're psychic; it'll drive him crazy."

Next time Hy flies down . . . I pushed the thought aside, smiled in response to Mick's delighted grin. His pleasure was so keen that I could hardly bear to blunt it, and yet . . .

Avoiding the obligatory discussion, I went to the kitchen to survey my supply of frozen entrées. Mick followed and crowded in next to me, reaching into the fridge for a can of cola. "You know," he said, "I've been thinking that we really should put together an earthquake preparedness kit."

"A what?"

"I was reading an article last week on how to get ready for the Big One, and I looked around the house and realized you weren't. Prepared, I mean. So I called the state Earthquake Safety Hotline and got a booklet. I figure we could put everything we'd need in one box and store it in the closet of the room you use for your home office."

"That's a good idea, but what if the closet collapses and we can't get at it?"

"Won't. I checked while I was installing the antenna for my radio—there's a main support beam running over it."

He'd installed an antenna on the roof of my house! "Mick," I began weakly.

"I can't believe you never put stuff together," he said. "How'd you survive the quake of eighty-nine?"

"Crawled under a desk." I took a package of creamed chipped beef from the freezer, trying to figure a way to get through to him.

"You know, that's probably not very good for you," he told me, nodding at the package. "It's got a lot of fat and sodium."

My frayed patience snapped. I pointed to his cola. "That's probably not good for you, either. Your mom'll cut you off the stuff as soon as you're home." I opened the package, poked holes in the plastic pouch, and stuck it in the microwave.

When I turned, Mick's shoulders were slumped and his mouth curved down dejectedly. "What?" I asked. Added to myself, I refuse to feel guilty.

He shrugged, avoiding my eyes and scrubbing with a sponge at the already clean countertop. I watched as his lips pushed out in the same belligerent expression that his mother had worn for most of her adolescence.

Yes, I thought, he's determined not to go home. He sends for his radio, he talks about "our" earthquake preparedness kit. God Almighty, what *am* I going to do about him?

I studied Mick thoughtfully, an idea beginning to take shape. What was I going to do about him? Well, why not do to him what had been done to me years before? I'd toss him into the business, give him a dose of hands-on experience, test his mettle. Mick wasn't a child any more; whether his parents liked it or not, it was time he started making his own choices. If he had the makings of a private investigator, we'd find out soon enough.

I said, "I've been thinking—how'd you like to stay on and help me out for a while longer, if your folks are agreeable?"

The transformation in his spirits was tangible: he stood taller and his face shone with pure happiness. For a moment I thought he might kiss me; instead he began scouring the counter with renewed vigor. "They'll agree," he said, "because you'll talk them into it."

The microwave buzzed. I checked the pouch, found it luke-warm. Punched the buttons for a few more whirls. I was hungry and tired and out of sorts. It seemed as if I'd spent most of the day doing things for other people, and now I couldn't even get the damned oven to behave—

"Something's wrong with that machine," Mick said. "If you want, I'll fix it before I go to work tomorrow morning."

Well, sometimes when you did things for others, they gave something in return.

Six

The call from Suits came at roughly one-fifty in the morning. For some reason I'd turned off the bell on the phone in my bedroom, so I heard nothing till Mick—his face showing the alarm of a person who wasn't used to middle-of-the-night calls—tapped at my door. I grabbed the receiver, motioned that everything was under control and he should go back to bed.

Suits's voice was clogged with pain. "Sorry to wake you, but I need—"

The rest of his words were distorted by a siren's wail. I sat up, gripping the receiver. "Where are you?"

"S.F. General. Emergency room. Can you come get me?"

"Of course. What happened?"

"Can't talk now—they're taking me to X-ray."

"Wait—"

He hung up, leaving me with my questions. As I got out of bed and rummaged through my closet I decided that his

69

injuries couldn't be too serious, since he'd been able to make the phone call. Still, the echo of the pain in his voice made me pull on jeans and a sweater all the faster.

* * *

When I arrived at the big brick hospital at the foot of Potrero Hill, the lights of its parking lots were heavily misted. A couple of white-coated attendants leaned against an ambulance near the emergency entrance, but otherwise I saw no one outside. The city's major trauma unit can be a madhouse at any given time, particularly on weekends and holidays, but it can also be as peaceful as a church after services let out. The quiet reminded me of another early morning when I'd waited there for word of Hank Zahn's condition after he'd taken a bullet that I should have shielded him from. The memory still unsettled me, so I pushed it away.

I went straight to the information desk inside the emergency entrance and inquired about Suits. Mr. Gordon, the intake worker said, was still in the examining room. I sat down at the end of the nearest row of chairs, avoiding the glances of the dozen or so people who waited there. Most were minorities, and a few had small children with them. A little boy was curled up asleep on a coat on the floor; an infant cried fretfully. Behind me a woman's voice droned, talking about the quality of care at various Bay Area hospitals; after a moment I realized she was an emergency room junkie.

They're a sad and disturbing type of individual, a nurse friend once told me. They crave attention, so they manufacture ailments, and when their loneliness drives them from their homes, they head for the nearest emergency-care facility. The personnel are quick to spot them; intake workers place them far down on the priority list, hoping they'll give up and go home. But most are content to remain in the waiting room, striking up conversations with anyone who will listen, disturbing people who are anxious about the condition of a friend or loved one, and ultimately driving up health-care costs. When they tire of one facility, they move on to another in a never-ending search for someone who will diagnose what's really bothering them. An age-old problem, chronic loneliness, and one that our system isn't set up to deal with.

One's compassion extends only so far, however, and mine didn't stand me in particularly good stead during the next forty minutes while the woman babbled about her symptoms and how Kaiser Foundation Hospital had treated them the week before. When a maternal-looking blond nurse pushed Suits's wheelchair through the swinging doors, I was more than ready to leave. His left arm was in a cast and bound to his chest by a sling; his pale face was abraded and purpled around the left eye, and his lower lip was badly split. When I came up to them, the nurse brought the chair to a stop.

"What happened to you?" I demanded.

"Long story." He grimaced and flicked his eyes toward the nurse.

She said, "Mr. Gordon had a run-in with somebody who didn't like him." From her tone, I judged she found that unsurprising. She added, "He's given his statement to the police and is ready to go home."

Suits said, "I've asked Ms. Lubbock here if she isn't perhaps related to Nurse Ratchet. She denies any kinship, but you could've fooled me."

Nurse Ratchet—Big Nurse of *One Flew Over the Cuckoo's Nest*. No wonder Ms. Lubbock had spoken so stiffly! I glanced at her. She shrugged and gave me a long-suffering look. Then she began guiding the wheelchair toward the exit. An orderly joined us, I went to fetch my MG, and the three of us maneuvered Suits into the passenger's seat. "Good luck, honey," Ms. Lubbock said to me as she slammed the door.

I went around and slipped behind the wheel. "Why did you

pick on that woman?" I demanded. "Don't you know how difficult her job is, without patients indulging in cheap shots?"

Suits slumped down in the seat. "Sorry. She reminds me of my mother."

That gave me pause. Of course Suits had a mother, but I couldn't for the life of me imagine what she might be like, what the relationship between them might be. He'd never so much as mentioned his family. I let the comment pass, though, and asked, "Now will you please explain what happened to you?"

He pressed his free hand over his swollen eye, pain momentarily stiffening his body. Then he sighed, relaxing some. "I was at a dinner meeting with one of my moneymen. Came home, maybe twelve-thirty. Bastard was in my condo."

"The person who did this to you, you mean."

He nodded. "Beat me up, broke my arm."

"For God's sake, what's wrong with Security in that building?"

The anger in my voice startled him; he glanced at me, one eyebrow raised. After a moment he said, "That's what I want to know."

"You get a look at him?"

"It was too dark. I passed out, came to, called the doorman on the house phone. He got the ambulance."

"Well, obviously you're not safe at Bay Vista. I'd better take you to a hotel."

"Hotel?" He laughed harshly. "No decent place would take me, looking like this. And I'm long past my days of sleeping in fleabags."

"What about an associate's place? A friend's?" As I made the suggestion, I realized its impossibility—and saw what was coming.

"Take me to your place, Sherry . . . Sharon."

"Suits, I have a small house, and my nephew's staying with me. There's no room."

"I'll sleep on the couch, the floor. I've got nobody else to turn to." The admission shamed him; he looked away.

I stared at the back of his head, its cowlick sprouting at odd angles and rendering him curiously vulnerable. Suddenly I was transported back to the night of the infamous Halloween party, so many light-years before.

Suits had come to the party dressed as a troll, but nobody noticed he was in costume. The realization that his usual appearance closely approximated that of a creature who spent most of its time under a bridge depressed him; he took refuge on the stairway of the big house on Durant, watching the others through the balusters of its banister. I arrived late from one of my security-guard gigs, and everybody thought my uniform was a costume; the realization that my on-the-job appearance was something of a joke depressed *me*, and I joined Suits to share a joint. After a while someone—Hank, I think— took pity on us and brought over a jug of Carlo Rossi, which we also proceeded to share; and as the evening wore on, we remained content to view the party through the bars of our self-made prison. When I finally stood to stumble upstairs to my room, Suits looked up at me, and the naked loneliness in his eyes made me hold out my hand. Now I realized with some surprise that I no longer regretted the act, or those that had followed.

And I also realized that I wanted to take on Suit's case.

* * *

I expected Suits to pay little attention to my house; after all, he was in pain and—in spite of his claim to the contrary— probably exhausted. But he looked it over with interest and pronounced it charming. His flattery somewhat warmed me to his presence, and while my innate cynicism told me that had been his intent, I offered to make up the couch and fetch him some of the Percodan I had left over from my last trip to the dentist. He refused the pills, oversaw the bed-making, then asked if he could have some coffee. I started a pot for him. He asked if I had an extra toothbrush. I provided one. Then he asked if he could make some phone calls. By that time the effect of the flattery had worn off; I told him that if any of the calls were long-distance he should use a credit card.

When I went to bed, Suits was sitting at the kitchen table, cordless receiver braced against his cast as he punched out a number. Even though I was very tired, it was a long time before I dropped off, and my fitful dreams were infused with the sound of his voice going on and on into the morning.

*   *   *

I could still hear talking in the kitchen when I woke around eight, only this time there were two voices, both male and neither of them Mick's. I showered and dressed hastily, fleeing up and down the hall between my bedroom and the bathroom so Suits and whatever stranger he'd invited into my home would have only a fleeting impression of a white terry-cloth-clad figure. Then I went to see what was going on.

A fresh pot of coffee sat on the warmer, and Suits and a gaunt man in dark business attire faced each other across the table. When I came in, the man rose. He was very tall, with black hair combed straight back and falling loose at the nape of his neck; the skin of his face was drawn so tight that it looked skeletal. I wondered if he was ill.

Suits remained seated as he introduced his attorney, Noah Romanchek. Romanchek's eyes moved over me; then he shook my hand, nodding slightly, his thin lips unmoving. This, I thought, was a man who owned others' secrets, and he would guard them until he found a way to exploit them.

When Romanchek released my hand from his dry, papery grip, I went to pour a cup of coffee. Suits said, "Sherry—"

I turned and glared.

"Uh-oh," he finished. "Sharon," he began again, "Noah and I're just finishing up some of yesterday's business. Then

74

we're going to take a spin over to the Port of Oakland. You want to come along for the ride?"

"No. If I plan to earn that fee you told me to name, I've got to get moving."

Suit's face brightened; in spite of his split lip he attempted a grin. "Thanks. You won't regret this."

I wasn't too sure about that, but I smiled back. Something in his eyes alerted me that he didn't want to discuss hiring me in front of the attorney, so I changed the subject, asking, "Did my nephew leave already?"

"About fifteen minutes ago. Nice kid. He fixed your microwave for you. Asked me to remind you to call his parents."

"Right." I'd do that from my car phone on the way to a couple of stops I planned to make in South Beach. "Will you let me have the keys to your condo and a note to Building Security saying it's okay for me to have access?"

He took out one of his cards and scribbled on the back of it, then removed a couple of keys from his case and handed them over. Romanchek watched with interest.

"Walk me out, will you?" I asked, setting down my coffee cup and nodding good-bye to the attorney.

With an effort Suits got up and followed me down the hall.

"About my fee . . ." I pulled a jacket from the coat tree in the front parlor.

"Name it."

I did—one that exceeded the biannual salary I'd drawn when I worked for All Souls.

Suits didn't even blink.

"Plus expenses."

"Sure."

"And a fifty percent bonus if I wrap the case up within seven days."

Now he hesitated. "Working or calendar days?"

"Calendar. Every day's a working day for me."

He nodded and we shook on it. I made a mental note to

have Mick draw up a contract. As I went down the front steps, Suits called after me, "You need anything, phone the office, and they'll beep me."

I waved and kept going. I wouldn't call on him unless I absolutely had to; today I wanted to work solo.

* * *

Charlene had no problem with Mick staying longer, particularly when I said I was working on the college issue and had hope he'd come around. I absolved myself of the lie by thinking that the boring day-to-day realities of private investigation probably would drive him into the halls of higher learning, and used the congested traffic near the construction on the Embarcadero as excuse to cut the conversation short. Actually, it was a valid excuse; the car phone, like the computer, was a recent acquisition, and I hadn't quite gotten the hang of simultaneous driving and talking.

The same surly doorman was on duty at Bay Vista. I showed him my identification and Suits's note, and his manner changed. He'd heard about what happened to Mr. Gordon, and wasn't it a shame? Yes, it was, I said. Could he tell me the name and address of the man on the midnight-to-eight shift who had called the ambulance? He'd like to, but he wasn't allowed to give out information about building employees or residents; of course Security would be glad to help me.

The complex's head of security turned out to be Sue Mahoney, a woman I'd occasionally worked with back when I guarded downtown office buildings at night while attending Berkeley during the day. Her job performance had never impressed me; it consisted mainly of reading the tabloids and painting her fingernails mother-of-pearl to match her frosted hair. Now her hair was its natural brown, crisply styled, and her fingernails were plainly polished; there wasn't a tabloid in sight. Still, I couldn't help but wonder if some laxness on her part hadn't contributed to the security breach that had sent my client to S.F. General.

Mahoney didn't act pleased to see me, nor did she like the fact that one of the residents had hired me to look into an incident that had occurred on her turf. At first she refused to give me the phone number and address of either of the other two doormen employed there, told me I could talk with them when they came on shift. I said that Mr. Gordon had given me instructions to speak with them this morning. Mahoney hesitated, probably reminding herself that her salary was paid out of the owners' maintenance fees, then wrote down the information. I thanked her and went upstairs to Suits's penthouse.

The first signs of violence that I noted were bloodstains and scuff marks on the floor of the foyer. I checked the door locks, both an ordinary spring type and a dead bolt, but saw no indication that they'd been breached. In the living room I found the card table knocked over, files and papers fanning out on the cheap rug. The fax machine, an easily hockable item, was still on the stand next to the telephone, tending to rule out the possibility that Suits had surprised a thief. The terrace door, dead-bolted and bar-locked, further argued against it.

I returned to the archway that led to the foyer and acted out what Suits must have done upon coming home. There were no overhead lights in the living room, except for recessed ones over the wet bar, and they operated on a switch at the far end of the room. The foyer light would have been bright enough for him to see the floor lamp next to the card table, so he had gone over there, and the attacker had come from . . . the archway leading to the unfurnished dining room, given the angle at which the card table had fallen.

I went into the dining room and looked around for proof of my theory. Nothing, not even a scratch on the hardwood floor. Feeling very much the intruder, I then began exploring the parts of the unit that I hadn't yet seen: a huge white-and-chrome kitchen that clearly was used for nothing more elaborate than making coffee and microwaving; two bedrooms and a library that were completely bare; two baths that looked as though they'd never been used; a sparsely furnished master suite. Nothing seemed to be out of place; neither the windows nor a service door off the pantry had been tampered with.

Someone, then, had gotten past the doorman and Security and entered with a key. Or gotten *to* the doorman or Security and entered with a key.

As I passed through the empty rooms again, I was struck full force by the strangeness of Suits's life. He had no possessions to speak of, other than an expensive wardrobe and some office equipment; he had no home except for a succession of half-furnished shells in whatever cities his turnarounds took him to. The only family member he'd ever mentioned was his mother, and that hadn't been an especially favorable comment. And when he ended up in the hospital, he'd had to turn to me, a woman he'd seen that morning for the first time in over fifteen years.

It occurred to me now that Suits really hadn't changed all that much, was simply repeating the pattern of his earlier years. He still led a nomadic existence; he still peddled his scams and schemes and dreams, only now his clients were investors and boards of directors. He was still restless, easily bored, and very much alone. Even in college, I'd felt as though a glass wall stood between Suits and the rest of us. Through it he talked, laughed, made glancing contact. But the wall filtered out emotion, shielded him from any intimacy.

Yesterday he had implied that for me he once would have shattered that wall. The admission, I realized, must have cost him a great deal.

When I went back to the foyer, I heard noises outside; a key rattled in the lock. I stepped behind the wall. The door opened and someone came in; a woman's voice made a wordless exclamation of dismay. I peered around the wall, saw a maid in a gray uniform kneeling beside the bloodstains; her cart stood just outside the door. She started when I moved forward, her young Hispanic face alarmed.

"It's all right," I said. "I'm a friend of Mr. Gordon. He's been hurt."

She stood up, brushing her palms over her uniform skirt. "I heard what has happened. He is okay?"

"He has a broken arm, but nothing more serious."

"A terrible thing." She clicked her tongue. "He is home?"

"Not now."

"Then I will clean these." She ran her rubber-soled shoe over one of the stains. "Is there anything else?" Her eyes moved toward the living room.

"Only the table in there, and you'd better leave it for Mr. Gordon, in case the papers are still in order."

"I never touch his papers." She went to the cart and came back with a bucket and a sponge.

"Tell me," I said, "who else besides you has a key to this unit?"

"Security. Building Maintenance. And the concierge, to return the dry cleaning and bring up the packages or flowers that are delivered."

"Not the doormen?"

"No, ma'am."

"Do the keys ever leave the building?"

She glanced down at the steel ring that hung from her belt. "We give them in to Security when we go home."

"What about the concierge and maintenance people? Do they give them in, too?"

"Maintenance, yes. The concierge . . . sometimes I have seen him leave with the keys, when he does special errands for the people."

I thanked her and went downstairs to the concierge's desk in the lobby, but found it unstaffed. When I asked the doorman, he told me that its operator, Sid Blessing, had called in sick that morning. Again he referred me to Security for the man's address.

*   *   *

"What *is* this with the questions?" Mahoney demanded. "First you want the doormen's addresses, now Sid's. Can't you wait till he's back on the job?"

"Mr. Gordon asked—"

"Mr. Gordon is a pain in the ass!" As soon as she said it, she realized her mistake. Color flared on her cheeks, and she bit her lip.

"Mahoney, I'll forget you said that in exchange for the information."

She turned and walked stiff-backed to her desk, where she consulted a card file, wrote on a scratch pad, ripped the top sheet off, and extended it to me. "Here! Is there anything else you require?"

I made a show of thinking, shook my head. "Not at the moment, Mahoney, but keep yourself available."

As I left the office, I realized just how thoroughly I'd disliked Sue Mahoney, ever since the night she bullied me into making her rounds at the Monadnock Building because the polish wasn't yet dry on her fingernails. I'd usually found the settling of old scores not nearly as satisfying as I'd anticipated; this, however, was the exception.

*   *   *

"No kidding—broke his arm?" Carmen set my coffee cup on the counter, then folded his own muscled arms across his apron and scowled fiercely. "Bastard!"

I stirred my coffee, took a sip, and reached for the sugar dispenser. I seldom sugared my coffee, but something had to be done to improve this lethal brew. The diner was half full, the rush for the advertised Stevedore's Breakfast long over.

Carmen scribbled a total on a check, slid it down the counter to a waiting customer, and turned back to me.

I said, "Yesterday I noticed that you didn't quite agree with Suits's . . . T.J.'s version of the night he went into the Bay."

He looked away, moved along the counter to the seat the customer had vacated. After he'd picked up the bills and coins left next to the empty plate and deposited them in the register, he returned to me, his expression conflicted. "Look, Miss McCone, I know you're working for T.J., but a lot of people do, and he don't seem to trust most've them farther than he can throw them. I'm not saying anything against you, but—"

"That's okay." I took out the folder containing my I.D. and flopped it open on the counter. "T.J. hired me to find out who's doing these things to him. If you like, you can check with him."

Carmen continued to equivocate. After a moment he went to pour himself some coffee, then motioned for me to join him in one of the window booths. "All right," he said as he heaved his bulk onto the bench opposite me, "here's how it was. T.J. was drunk that night—shit-faced. I'd never seen him that way before."

"You see a lot of him?"

"Most days he eats here at least once, comes in a few times a week around closing to have a beer and some conversation."

"What do you talk about?"

"The port. How it used to be." Carmen's gaze grew remote.

I knew what he was picturing: the waterfront in its heyday. The seamen's taverns and hiring halls; the jazz joints and flophouses and rescue missions; the freighters offloading coffee from Brazil, tea from China, spices from Ceylon, rice from Thailand. Last spring in San Diego a retired professor had spoken to me of that port's glory days with the same bittersweet wistfulness I now observed on Carmen's rough features; despite the obvious differences between the two men, I couldn't help but liken them.

"Anyway," Carmen went on, "most nights T.J. would've been out walking for hours, stopping at the cafés, talking with the old-timers. He said he was trying to soak up the past, get in touch with the waterfront's ghosts, find out how it really was." He shrugged. "I figured he was a little cracked on the subject, but pretty much harmless."

"So on that night . . . ?"

"Like I said, he was drunk as a skunk. Bourbon—you could smell it. Surprised me. I never seen him drink more'n one beer, and mostly he just nursed it. But that night he was plastered to the gills and not making a whole lot of sense."

"How so?"

"Well, he started out talking about the port, like usual. And then he was rambling on about some old-timer he'd gotten friendly with who's living out of his van down around Mission Bay. And he just kept on rambling. He was talking about the port, but it wasn't the port—you know what I mean? There was something about a railroad overpass and two people, or maybe it was three. And something else about heat lightning on the water. When I asked him if by railroad overpass he meant that tunnel he's always telling me about, it snapped him out of it. He blinked and looked around like he'd woke up from a trance, and then he got real quiet."

I thought about that for a moment. Carmen reached across the table and put his big hand on my wrist. "Miss McCone, those fellas who took too many drugs back in the sixties? They flip in, they flip out. Does T.J. . . . ?"

Suits's words of yesterday, when I asked him if he was on coke, replayed in my mind: "Drugs are a roller-coaster ride that's not worth the price of the ticket." In the old days he'd smoked plenty of grass, but now that I thought about it, I couldn't recall him using anything more potent. "I doubt it, Carmen."

"Then what the hell was all that about?"

"I don't know. Did he say anything else after he . . . came out of the trance?"

"Yeah, but that didn't make much sense, either." He closed his eyes in concentration. "He said . . . that even when you work hard at forgetting things and think they're behind you, they've got a way of coming back. You get reminded when you least expect to, and then you realize what your own stupidity has ruined."

I considered his words in light of what I knew of Suits's life, shook my head. "And that's it?"

"That's it. He left then, and next thing I know, I'm hauling him out of the Bay. I figured he fell in because he was drunk, and then he made up the story about being mugged because he was embarrassed."

"And what do you think now?"

Carmen spread his big hands on the table and studied them as if their lines and scars might contain the answer. "Well, I'd say either T.J.'s having a run of real bad luck or else somebody *is* out to get him."

Seven

A railroad overpass, two—or maybe three—people, heat lightning on the water. The key elements of Suits's drunken ramblings played in my mind as I drove south toward Pacifica, where Bay Vista's concierge lived. Something Suits had tried to forget, a memory that refused to die. But was it related to his current problem? And if so, would he tell me about it?

I'd ask him, but I wouldn't count on him confiding in me. Suits, I'd realized, was an intensely private man; if the memory was painful, he wouldn't share it with anyone, for whatever reason. Better to turn my attention to finding out how last night's intruder got into his penthouse. If I knew that, there was a good chance I could identify him and wrap this case up. Then Suits could get on with the business of changing the history of the Port of San Francisco, and I could collect my obscenely large fee and get on with the business of attracting a stable of steady clients.

I took the Pacifica exit from the 280 freeway, crested the hill, and glided down toward the flat gray sea.

Pacifica is a town of many disparate areas: tracts that sprawl across the hills; commercial flatlands by the water; residential neighborhoods of all types that crowd deep into the canyons. Because of this diversity it hasn't ever forged much of a cohesive identity, unless you count the fact that it's odd. Things are done differently there than they are in the more mainstream Peninsula communities east of the hills. Pacifica, for example has a Fog Festival to celebrate its dreary, socked-in summer climate; a few years ago, in a fit of previously unheard-of political activism, its residents recalled the entire city council. As I exited Route One at Paloma Avenue, I reflected that I kind of liked the town—proving, perhaps, Rae's contention that I myself was a little off center.

Carmel Avenue, which I'd earlier pinpointed on my Rand McNally StreetFinder, was a narrow strip of eucalyptus-shaded pavement whose houses crowded up against a hill on which someone had built a castle. Not so much a house that looked like a castle as the real thing: stone walls and battlements and slits of windows at which to stand watch in case the enemy invaded by sea. I'd glimpsed it many times from the coast highway and vowed that one day I'd drive up there and have a close look; now there was no time, and I reluctantly bypassed the lane that led to it.

The homes on Carmel ranged from 1950s tract houses to architecturally improbable structures that were only a level above shacks. Cars and trucks and boats on trailers clogged their driveways or stood along the edge of the pavement next to a treacherous-looking drainage ditch. The address for Sid Blessing was a dilapidated cottage that had been added on to without any definite plan: clapboard painted a blistered electric blue, with a broken and taped front window where several crudely executed stained-glass pieces hung. An assortment of flowerpots containing half-dead plants cluttered the front stoop; the lawn, if ever there was one, had gone to weeds.

I pulled the MG into the driveway next to a rusted-out van whose rear axle was propped up on concrete blocks. The cottage's wooden steps swayed ominously as I climbed them. When I rang the bell it played a familiar tune that I couldn't immediately place. Then the lyrics "You can't always get what you want" came to me. Appropriate.

No one answered my ring. I tried a second time, then went back down the steps and checked the sides. A fence to the left, too high to see over; a padlocked gate to the right; no window in the garage door.

The neighboring house was more conventional: brown wood and stucco, well kept up; a late-model Chevy with an infant carrier in the backseat sat in the drive. I skirted the drainage ditch and went up to the door of the house, noting the words "Welcome to Our Happy Home" stenciled in green paint on the concrete sidewalk. A more promising sentiment than the message delivered by Sid Blessing's bell.

The sweatsuit-clad woman who came to the door was young, Asian, and looked as cheerful as the words on her front walk. "The people in the blue cottage?" she said after I showed her my I.D. and asked my question. "I don't know much about them. They're kind of . . . well, nobody ever told them it isn't nineteen sixty-eight anymore."

"Old hippies?"

"Not exactly; they probably were just babies back then. Maybe they get it from their parents. All I can tell you is that their kids are called Ariel and Ariadne, and when the parents think we're not looking, they throw their trash in our can because they're too cheap to pay for pickup."

"The man has a job, though?"

"Oh, yeah. Goes off every morning in this maroon-and-gray uniform. They're just cheap about the trash, is all. I'm glad they're moving."

"Moving? When?"

"They may already be gone. A guy I see visiting there sometimes came in a Ryder truck yesterday and took away most of their stuff." She glanced over at the blue cottage. "Maybe they decided to stick the landlord with that dead bus. But her stained glass is still in the window, so they might come back for one last load."

"What time did the guy with the truck come yesterday?"

"Noon? Yeah, 'All My Children' had just come on."

"And you didn't talk to him? Ask him where the Blessings were going?"

"I didn't care. The whole time they lived there, I kept wishing they'd go away."

I got out my card with the office and car-phone numbers and scribbled down my home number as well. "If they come back, will you call me?"

"Sure." She took the card, fingered its raised lettering. "Look, you want me to try to find out where they went? I could ask the people on the other side when they come home from work tonight. I think they're the only ones on the street who had much to do with the Blessings."

"I'd appreciate that, and I'd pay—"

She shook her head. "No, it'd be my pleasure. I'm kind of fascinated by P.I.'s. On 'All My Children,' there's this guy, Tad? He used to be a P.I., but then he got amnesia from falling off the bridge and came back two years later thinking he was somebody else. The new P.I.'s, Charlie and Hayley, are okay, but they don't have Tad's—" She clapped a hand over her mouth, eyes wide. "Sorry! My husband *hates* it when I do that."

I smiled. "Doesn't bother me. Speaking of Tad, it's noon. I don't want to make you miss your program."

*   *   *

I'd just passed the turnoff for Skyline Drive on my way back to the city when the car phone buzzed. I picked it up and heard Suits's agitated voice. "Dammit, Sherry-O, I've been trying to get you for an hour!"

"My name is Sharon, and I've been out of the car—on your business."

Suits ignored the comment. "I need you—now."

I sighed. "Where are you?"

"My Oakland office."

"I can be there in forty-five minutes."

"No, go to Bay Vista. That second key I gave you works the elevator to the roof. I'll have Josh pick you up in the bird."

"Suits, I'd rather—"

"Josh'll be waiting. Hurry, please. The goddamn butchers're trying to cut me down." He broke the connection.

I replaced the receiver none too gently. Butchers—good God, he could be dramatic! But this latest crisis might be relevant to the case. . . .

I drove to Bay Vista.

*   *   *

"Shut that thing down and come talk to me!" I shouted at Josh Haddon.

He frowned and pointed to his ear.

I ducked under the JetRanger's rotor and shouted again. He nodded and turned off the engine. The rotor whiffled to a stop.

I moved away and perched on the wall, nine stories above the ditch where construction workers and equipment toiled. Josh came over and leaned beside me, taking out a cigarette and lighting it in cupped hands. "T.J.'ll be furious if we don't get to the office ASAP," he said.

"Too bad. I need to ask you some questions."

He glanced at me, lines around his eyes crinkling. "You don't take any shit from him."

"No. Do you?"

He shrugged. "Man's got a lot of power." Paused to drag

on his cigarette and added, "But it's easy to tune him out when I fly."

"You've been piloting for him how long?"

"Thirteen years. Things sure have changed. At first all we had was my little patched-up Cessna." His mouth tightened—something unpleasant about the memory.

"So you've been with him during all his turnarounds?"

"Knew him before he did the first. Back then I was flying for the . . . company."

"What company?"

He smiled slowly. "Actually, it was a dope farm up near Garberville."

"He turned a *marijuana farm*?"

"Uh-huh."

"And you were their pilot?"

"Yeah. Those were great days." His freckled face softened, the way a child's does when recalling a special Christmas. "Was a terrific spread, way up in the hills. Belonged to a guy named Gerry who'd made some money down in Hollywood and sunk it all into the land. He was growing class stuff; you could smell it for miles. I was flying it all over the country in my Cessna. We were distributing incredible quantities, getting top dollar. Trouble was, Ger wasn't making any profit, and nobody could figure out why."

"So Suits . . ."

"Suits." He shook his head. "Jesus, it's been a long time since anybody called him that. Remember the suitcase? What a piece of shit. Yeah, Suits was one of our customers. Used to make a run up there every month or so. Liked to hang around, get stoned with Ger. One night they were solving the world's problems like usual, and Ger starts telling Suits about *his* problem—namely, no profit. And Suits says, 'Hey, what'll you give me if I fix that?' And Ger—he's really stoned by now—Ger goes, 'A million dollars, cash.' And Suits tells him, 'Done deal.' And they shake on it."

"So how did he fix it?"

"Same way he has ever since. Fired everybody, including me. Posted armed guards to keep us off the land. Sent Ger on a long vacation. Brought in people who needed the work and didn't blow weed. The problem was simple, see: everybody from Ger on down had been smoking the profit."

"Did Suits get his million?"

"Yeah. Ger turned it over to him in four installments— each time in the rottenest old suitcases he could find. First thing Suits did was bail my Cessna out of hock—I'd gotten behind on the payments—and hire me as his pilot. Plane belonged to him after that, but I still got to fly it. Then Ger sent him to one of his doper customers in L.A. who owned a film-equipment company that was in trouble. That guy sent him to Colorado, and then we went to Texas, Pennsylvania, and Nevada. And the aircraft just kept getting better."

"So all this time you've been pretty close to Suits—"

A beeping sound came from Josh's windbreaker. He reached into its pocket, grimaced. "That means T.J.'s getting seriously impatient."

*   *   *

Suits was waiting for us on the roof of the office building, uninjured arm semaphoring wildly, as if he thought Josh couldn't set the JetRanger down without his help. When we landed, he rushed forward so heedlessly that I feared for his head. Josh opened the door, gave him a hand up, and he slumped beside me, panting.

Josh glanced back for instructions. I motioned for him to shut the copter down. Suits, struggling with his headset, overruled me by pointing toward the sky. I helped him adjust the earphones, then said into my mouthpiece, "Let's not go anyplace till we've talked."

"No." Again he pointed upward. "Just fly, Josh."

"Suits, you're wasting money—"

"It's my money, dammit! Some people take tranquilizers or drink when they're stressed. Others work out or run to their shrinks. I fly."

Expensive stress-management technique, I thought. But he had a point: it was his money. "So," I said, watching the building grow smaller beneath us, "what's happened now?"

He sank lower in his seat, cradling his cast with his good hand. "Noah and I took a run over to the Port of Stockton. Noah . . . what'd you think of him?"

"I didn't get a chance to form an impression, other than that he looks ill."

"He is—heart trouble. Could pop off any minute." Suits's mouth curled disapprovingly; he seemed to take Romanchek's illness as a sign of weak character. "Looks like the perfect corporate lawyer, doesn't he?"

"Yes."

He laughed. "Not with his checkered past. Used to be a drug lawyer, defended some of the biggest names in the business—successfully. Proves appearances can deceive even you."

"I've been fooled a time or two. You said you and he went to Stockton?"

Suits's smile faded. "Yeah. Noah'd prepared the final contract for the guy who was going to be my terminal manager. All I needed was his signature. I wanted to bring him on board right away; this terminal's going to be state-of-the-art, and I need its manager to work with the architects and contractors from the first. But the guy backed out on me."

"Why?"

"He said word had gotten out about our deal, and his present employer had gone me one better. Bullshit. I know the operation he works for; they couldn't've topped my terms. I think somebody bought him off."

On the surface, his reaction to this business reversal seemed extreme. "But you don't have any proof of that," I said.

"No, but I've got a hell of a lot of coincidence. After

Stockton I went back to the office. There was a message from the head of my architectural firm; I returned the call. He said they've run into some snags on their current project that'll cause a delay in getting started on mine. He suggested I should think about getting somebody else."

"When was he supposed to start on the terminal?"

"Next week."

"He didn't give you much advance notice."

"No, and I happen to know he's already wrapped up this current project."

"You confront him about that?"

"Sure. He said I must've been misinformed and if I wanted I could verify what he told me with the client whose project supposedly got bogged down."

"Did you?"

"Why bother? If he's telling me to verify it, it means the client's backing him up."

"All right, I can see why you feel that—"

"You don't see anything yet. You know the old superstition about disasters coming in threes?"

I nodded.

"About ten minutes after that conversation, I get *another* call. This time it's one of my moneymen. He's mumbling about unanticipated losses and shortfall in cash flow—all that kind of vague bullshit that I know's bullshit because I've slung it a thousand times myself to cover up the fact that I've decided to pull out of a deal that I'm not yet legally committed to. The gist of what he's saying is, he's out. You still think this is simple coincidence?"

"No," I admitted, "I don't."

"You've got to make these guys talk. Find out who's doing this to me."

"I am trying to find that out. But I doubt I can *make* any of them talk. If they're stonewalling you, they're certainly not going to open up for me."

Suits's eyes narrowed and a muscle began to tic in his right cheek. "Then find out some other way. Tap their phones, plant bugs in their offices. What the hell're you in business for?"

Calm, McCone, I told myself. Keep calm. "Suits, what you're asking is illegal. I don't work that way. I suppose I could maintain legal surveillances on them, but I doubt that would be productive."

"Then what the fuck *are* you going to do for me?" The words came out high-pitched and shrill.

I looked away, giving him time to compose himself. Realized we'd been circling above the Bay off Alameda Island the whole time. As the copter turned lazily, I noted bridges: the San Mateo, the Bay, the Richmond. Farther away, draped in mist, were the Golden Gate and the twin spans at the Carquinez Strait.

When I turned back to Suits, he still looked aggravated, but seemed calmer. I said, "I'm not going to waste my time and your money maintaining useless surveillances. I do have a couple of leads on the person who attacked you last night, and I'll pursue them. But I'm also going to have to look at some background information."

"On what?"

"Your turnarounds. Your present associates, people you fired from GGL, people who don't want the line moved from Oakland, people who don't want the line moved to San Francisco. Your past associates on past turnarounds, people whose toes you stepped on back then. You."

"Me? Why the hell—"

"Because someone's out to get you, and it feels personal. You *are* the central figure here."

"Forget it."

"Suits, I know you're a private man—"

"You don't *know* anything about me."

"More than you think, perhaps. For instance, I know that you went to Harvard."

94

A flash of surprise, followed by a scowl. "Who told you that?"

"Russ Zola."

"Jesus Christ!"

"And I know you got your start by turning a dope farm."

He included the back of Josh's head in his scowl. Josh hadn't reacted to his earlier agitation, and he didn't react now. As he'd said, he tuned Suits out when he was flying.

I asked, "Why didn't you tell me about any of those things?"

"I didn't think you needed a rundown of my life."

"But even in the old days you didn't mention about Harvard. None of us knew."

"I didn't like to talk about it. I still don't."

"Why not?"

He sighed. "Look, that was an awful time. Really awful. When I started there I was just a kid who should've been out trying to talk to girls at the Dairy Queen. Hell, I couldn't even drive yet. And when I got my M.B.A. I was still just a kid—seventeen, the age when most people *start* college. I had acne and dandruff; I'd never had a friend, I'd never had a date, much less gotten laid. I was a genius; I was a freak. And that's all you need to know about my life."

"But—"

"Uh-uh. Strictly off-limits. I'll talk about the turnarounds and my associates, but nothing else."

I wanted to ask him about his drunken ramblings to Carmen—the railroad overpass, the people, the heat lightning on the water—but I knew this wasn't the time. There might never be a time for that. Instead I said, "Is there anyone in your organization whom you trust completely?"

The promptness of his reply surprised me. "My executive assistant in my L.A. office, Dottie Collier."

"And does she have files on your people and your turnarounds?"

"Yes."

"I'll need them faxed to me today—as much of them as possible."

The request didn't faze him. "Dottie'll manage it."

"Good. Now will you ask Josh to drop me at Bay Vista? I want to follow up on those leads I mentioned."

"You'll be in touch later?"

"When I know something more."

"About tonight, I need a place to stay—"

"No."

"You yourself said my condo's not safe. If whoever attacked me could get to me there, he can get to me in a hotel."

And at my house, I thought. I wasn't concerned for myself so much as for Mick. "Then I'll find someplace where no one will think to look for you." As I spoke, inspiration struck. I turned my face toward the window so he couldn't see the beginnings of my wicked grin. "Pack whatever you need and meet me at my office this evening," I added.

The hiding place I had in mind was perfect. In fact, the only drawback I could perceive was that after one night on the lumpy old sofa bed in Jack Stuart's former quarters at All Souls, Suits would be begging the homeless shelters for a space.

*   *   *

I spent what was left of the afternoon tracking down Bay Vista's doormen. The man on the midnight-to-eight shift didn't want to talk with me; after I paid him ten dollars, all he would tell me was that he'd answered Suits's cries for help and called the ambulance. His counterpart on the four-to-midnight shift wasn't at his apartment in the Inner Sunset; when I finally located him at a bar on Irving Street that his landlady said he frequented, a shot of scotch bought me only the information that he'd admitted no unauthorized persons to the building the night before and had seen no strangers take the semiprivate elevator to the penthouse.

I arrived at my office at a little after five. By then Mick

had made himself at home at the desk in the room over the entryway—had forted himself up there, actually, as if building a wall of his books and pamphlets would make it impossible for me to oust him. The fax machine whirred as it disgorged a long, curling roll of paper.

Mick looked up from the stack of cut pages he was tapping into alignment. "Did you talk to my mom?"

"You're here for as long as I need you."

"Yeeesss!" He raised his fist exultantly.

"Is that"—I motioned at the fax—"from Dottie Collier in L.A.?"

"Yeah. This, too." He patted the stack on the desk. "She's already used up almost two rolls of paper."

"That's okay; we'll bill the client." I took the stack, glanced at the top sheet, and nodded.

"There're a couple of other things. A lady called from Pacifica, said you'd talked to her this morning." He studied scribblings on a scratch pad, then went on. "She saw the guy in the Ryder truck again, asked about the Blessings. He told her he bought everything in the house from them. They came into some money and left the area, but the guy didn't know where they went. Does that make sense?"

"Uh-huh." Someone had probably paid Bay Vista's concierge to deliver copies of the keys to the building and to Suits's penthouse; by now Blessing and his family would be untraceable. Unless . . . I looked speculatively at Mick's bent head.

He added, "A Claudia James from DataBase messengered over some job applications; she wants background checks run on the people." He extended a manila envelope to me.

I was so deep in thought that I stared uncomprehendingly at it. Then I took it and removed the apps. Claudia James used to own my former answering service; when machines threatened to render that business obsolete she sold out, went into computers, and now had her own firm—whose function

I'd yet to figure out. The formal announcement of McCone Investigations' opening that I'd sent her last week had already paid off. I looked the applications over: strictly routine.

"Well, let's get started." I handed them to Mick.

He looked down at them, blinking. "These're . . . mine?"

"Yes." I pulled a straight-backed chair close to the desk. "I'll explain what you need to do with them, and tomorrow morning you're on your own."

"On my own," he said.

"Uh-huh. And after that, how'd you like to try your hand at a skip trace?"

* * *

"Sherry-O?"

"Yes?" The tartness had long ago gone out of my voice; Suits's plaintive queries, addressed to me from the door of my office, had worn me down. It was all I could do to keep my burning eyes on the pages in front of me.

"Are you sure it's okay to hang my towel just anyplace in there?" The towel he referred to was one Ted had earlier loaned him; "there" was All Souls's second-floor communal bathroom.

"Anyplace, Suits." I highlighted a phrase and read doggedly on. He was still in the doorway, though; I could hear him breathing. "What else?"

"I need to make a call."

I motioned toward my phone.

"Privately."

"My nephew's office." I waved toward the door.

"Thank you." It was as humble a tone, I was sure, as Suits had ever managed.

I read on.

From the other side of the wall I could hear the drone of his voice. I pressed my palm to my ear and leaned on my elbow; it helped, but not much. Suits droned. I read. And suddenly he was quiet. I stretched my arms, looked at my watch. Ten-thirty. Another page and I'd be finished with this stack. I'd bundle up the other, take it home to go over in front of the fire.

Suits's voice started in again, this time through the wall that separated my office from Ted's Baroque cubbyhole. Probably checking again on towel-hanging proprieties, I thought. Ted's voice responded, but only briefly. Suits said something else, went on and on.

I gathered the other papers, crammed them into my brief-case. Put on my jacket and tiptoed into the hall. Ted's door was open; as I flicked off my lights, I heard him say, "Well, how do you feel about that?"

No reply from Suits.

Ted remained silent, waiting him out.

My God, I thought, he's practicing therapy on him!

For quite some time now Ted, a gay man who had lost many friends and two former lovers to the AIDS epidemic, had been severely depressed. In July I'd referred him to a therapist friend, who in turn had referred him to a grief counselor. While there had been no dramatic change in Ted's emotional state as yet, he suffered from fewer of what he called his black-and-blue days, and occasionally I caught a glimpse of the cheerful, quixotic man of old. An unnerving side effect of his counseling sessions, however, was his tendency to play amateur psychologist to anyone who confessed to having so much as a hangnail.

"I think—" Suits began.

"No, how do you *feel*?"

I stood quietly outside the door, hoping that Suits might open up to Ted and tell him something that would give me insight into the side of himself he kept so carefully hidden.

Suits said, "I feel like I ought to go to bed now."

Before he could step into the hall, I hurried past the door and down the stairs.

Eight

Cold fingers and a dull headache and cramped limbs. And the smell of coffee. I opened my eyes as a hand set a mug on the table in front of them. Mick's hand. He said, "Wake up—it's after eight o'clock."

I struggled to sit, flailed, and watched a stack of papers slither off the couch and across the carpet like my childhood Slinky toy. I'd fallen asleep here in the sitting room. Mick must've covered me with this quilt, an old one made by my sister Patsy in her artsy-craftsy phase.

Mick started picking up the pages; the slick fax paper slid neatly into order. I disentangled myself from the quilt, set my feet on the floor, and reached for the coffee mug. After taking a swallow, I asked, "What time did I doze off?"

"Don't know. You were still reading when I went to bed around midnight. I got up to take a pee at five, and you were sacked out good, so I covered you."

"Thanks. And thanks for the coffee." I warmed my fingers on the mug and looked toward the window. The light that

101

filtered into the walkway between my house and the Curleys' next door was drab, promising another foggy day. Ralph was perched on the back of the chair again, hungrily eyeing W.C. "Don't even think about it," I told him.

The cat regarded me with slitted eyes. When he did that, I could never be sure whether he was glaring or just near-sighted. In case it was the former, I added, "And don't give me that look." Ralph jumped to the floor, stretched noncha-lantly, and sauntered toward the kitchen, batting my leg with his tail as he passed.

Mick was putting on his down jacket. "You off to work?" I asked.

He nodded. "I want to get cracking on those DataBase apps and the Blessing skip trace."

"Well, if you have any questions and can't locate me, ask Rae."

"Yes, ma'am." He saluted me and hurried down the hall, a jaunty bounce to his step.

Oh, to be seventeen again and have such enthusiasm for small tasks. . . .

* * *

When I got out of the shower, I found a message from Suits on my machine: "I'm off to Long Beach today, got to talk to my number two choice for terminal manager. Sherry-O, I *like* it here at All Souls. Reminds me of the old days."

Terrific, I thought grimly as I rewound the tape. He'll want to live there and pester me for however long this investigation takes.

I went to the kitchen, poured another cup of coffee, and noticed a stack of mail on the table. Yesterday's: phone bill, white-sale notice from Macy's, reminder that the cats' shots were overdue. And a postcard from Hy.

Just a few words in his bold hand: "Dinner and dancing at Zelda's on your birthday?" I turned the card over and examined the postmark. Zurich. Good God! He was back in Europe.

Zelda's on my birthday. It wasn't until September twenty-eighth. That meant he'd probably arrive in the Bay Area the day before and expect me to meet him at Oakland Airport, where the Citabria was tied down, for the flight to his ranch in Mono County. Zelda's was a big old-fashioned roadhouse on the shore of Tufa Lake in the high desert country. We'd first danced together there, and I assumed sentimental reasons had prompted Hy to suggest it for our celebration.

But what was he doing in Zurich? I turned the card over and over, fingering it as if it could provide some tactile answer to the question. What had he been doing in Miami, New York, and Taipei? These trips were costing plenty. Who was paying for them? Hy had money—a great deal, made in those nine missing years—and he'd inherited even more from his wife, Julie Spaulding. But still, there were limits.

God, the man could be exasperating! There were times—such as today—when I wished him out of my life for good. No matter that he was tall, lanky, and handsome in a hawk-nosed, shaggy way. No matter that he had a lively mind, lively interests, and a lively manner in bed. So what if he possessed a wonderful off-the-wall sense of humor and could fluently speak English, French, Russian, and Spanish—and was currently getting practice in all of them, as far as I knew? He was also frequently secretive, occasionally violent, and sometimes emotionally stingy.

It didn't help my mood any to remind myself that I, too, was frequently secretive, occasionally violent, and sometimes emotionally stingy. . . .

I balled up the postcard and hurled it across the room. It came to rest in a puddle next to the cats' water dish. Lay there as sodden as my hope of ever figuring Hy out.

The hell with it, I thought, and went to get dressed. Afterward I sat down and finished reading and making notes on the stack of papers I'd started in front of the fire the night before. I thought for a while, went back over all my notes, then made several phone calls. My day arranged practically to the minute, I set off for downtown and the Transamerica Pyramid, where Charles Loftus, one of Suits's major financial backers, had his offices.

*   *   *

Six in the evening, and Suits still hadn't returned from Long Beach. I called his office, was told that the JetRanger had taken off some fifty minutes ago but was delayed by unseasonably bad weather off the central coast. Maybe that was just as well, I thought. It would give me more time to prepare for the conversation I needed to have with him. I'd just finished going over the tapes of the interviews I'd conducted during the day and had come to a disturbing conclusion.

Outside my office's bay window the fog had thickened to a heavy mist, almost a rain. I swiveled and stared at the peaked roofs of the buildings across the triangular park out front. Two of those buildings were now leased by All Souls; what had begun as a renegade band of idealists out to aid their fellow humans had evolved into the largest legal-services plan in northern California. Fortunately the concept of quality representation regardless of income level had not died with the installation of the 800-number hot line. To one degree or other we all still . . .

Not we. *They.* I was only a tenant here.

The thought made me feel a little disconnected, but not for long. On its heels came other, more pleasant ones: I no longer drew a pitifully small salary for the extensive hours my investigations entailed. I would no longer fall victim to the often unreasonable whims of the partners. And should a complicated case come their way, they'd call me in. I still had the support and friendship of the people I cared about most.

I turned back to the desk and began replaying selected passages of the tapes, getting my facts straight so I could present a strong case to Suits.

Charles Loftus, billionaire venture capitalist and real-estate developer, who had backed Suits on two previous turnarounds: "I don't know of a single developer who was whoring after that

Hunters Point base. Too many problems there. Too many hurdles. You've got the federal and the city governments to deal with. Even if they like a project, you've still got to go up against agencies like the Bay Conservation and Development Commission. T.J. is the only one who's willing to work with all of them *and* put that land back into maritime use. Frankly I think they should give him a medal for his vision."

Dana Wilson, Suits's liaison at the city's Port Commission: "No one, absolutely no one, is opposed to Mr. Gordon's plans for the mega-terminal. They fit perfectly with the current mixed-use scheme for the port. Both the city and federal governments are grateful to him for coming up with a solution for Hunters Point. . . . Enemies? I'm sure he has plenty, but not where this project is concerned. To tell you the truth, I'm a very nosy woman; if anyone wanted to stop him, I'd have found out."

James Lewis, Oakland Port Commission: "Let's face it, our port's in trouble. Nobody wants to see GGL leave. But if Gordon's successful with the Hunters Point project, it'll mean a boost for the whole Bay Area economy. If the new mega-terminal draws business from other West Coast ports, we're sure to siphon off some of the overflow."

Noah Romanchek, Suits's chief counsel: "I don't think that what's been happening to T.J. has anything to do with GGL or either of the ports. . . . Why? Because the person knows too much about his organization: how much to offer a guy to go back on what's practically a done deal, which moneyman's on shaky enough ground to be bribed. Hell, he even knows T.J.'s personal habits: where he stops in for a beer at night, how to get into the place where he lives. You look closely at T.J.'s associates and you'll find your man."

Russ Zola, Suits's organizational strategist: "Noah's right, but I'll take it a step further. What's going on doesn't have a damn thing to do with this current turnaround—or maybe with business at all. . . . I can't say why; I don't have that good a grasp of it. But whoever's doing this to him has put a lot of energy into it. It feels personal, like you said. A grudge that's been nurtured a long time. You go back into his past, his personal life, and then you'll be on the right track."

Carole Lattimer, Suits's chief financial officer: "What Noah and Russ told you strikes me as right on target. You're going to have one tough time shaking anything out of T.J., though. He'll protect that sacred privacy of his to the grave, and there'll be hell to pay for any of us who violate it."

There was more, but those were the best-taken and most convincing points. I switched off the tape recorder. Lattimer's voice saying "to the grave" had put a chill on me. I got up and went downstairs, looking for companionship.

The first floor was deserted. In the foyer, Ted's desk was tidy, his lamp turned low. The parlor was dark, the evening news flickering soundlessly on the TV screen. As I moved toward the back of the house, past the law library and Hank's and Rae's dark offices, I belatedly remembered this was the co-op's softball night. They were playing another firm down in San Mateo, where the sun was probably shining.

In the kitchen I went to the fridge, poured myself a glass of jug wine, and marked my initials in the IOU column of the sheet taped to the door. Then I sat down at the table by the window to wait for Suits, listening to the old house creak and groan around me.

Softball night, I thought, and nobody'd reminded me. I'd never been a regular on the team—my schedule was too erratic for that—but when possible I'd gone along and dusted off my high school cheerleading skills. But today there hadn't been any reminder notice of the game on my desk, and of course I no longer had a mailbox by Ted's workstation for somebody to slip a note into.

Was it possible, I wondered, that the members of the co-op harbored resentment because I'd turned down what they all considered a handsome promotion? Did they take my need to be my own boss as a personal rejection of them? If so, the partners had masked their feelings well when I'd appeared at their mid-

July meeting and informed them of my decision; they'd seemed genuinely pleased when I asked if I could rent office space. But now that I thought of it, tonight wasn't the first time I'd been left out of their activities: nobody had told me about last Thursday's poker game; nobody had invited me to go in on the pizza that several of them had ordered while working late last Friday; my office no longer seemed to be a stop on the route for people collecting people for a trip downhill to the Remedy.

Maybe all these years I'd mistaken what were essentially business relationships for friendships. Maybe now that I no longer worked for the co-op those relationships would cease. Sure, old friends like Hank, Ted, and Rae would still come around, but what about the others—Jack, Pam, Larry, Gloria, Mike? I didn't regret my decision to fly solo, but it saddened me that it might involve such a big trade-off.

*　　*　　*

Suits arrived at twenty to seven; I could identify him by the sound of his odd gait. "Back here in the kitchen," I called.

A few seconds later he appeared in the doorway, his bruised face drawn, his suit rumpled, his shoulders sagging.

"Are you okay?" I asked.

"It's been a long day." He came over to the table and slumped into the chair next to mine.

"Drink?"

"I could use a beer."

I went to the fridge, got one out, and again marked the IOU column. When I handed the bottle to him, I asked, "So how was Long Beach?"

"A pisser. My second-choice guy blew me off." He sipped beer, set the bottle on the table. "Believe me, I know what his deal is down there. It doesn't come close to what I'm offering. He has to've been bought." He leaned back in the chair, massaged his temples with his thumb and forefinger.

"Suits, I talked with a number of people today. There's

something of a consensus about what's going on." Then I set forth the theories, quoted from the tapes. "I need to spend some time with you, go over the information on your associates and turnarounds that Dottie Collier sent me. And I need to talk with you about your personal life."

He shook his head.

"Suits, isn't it worth talking if we can stop this person?"

He got up and went around the table to the window. Stood with his back to me, looking out at the misted cityscape. How many times in the years I'd worked here had I done the same? I'd brooded, analyzed, planned, suffered, and rejoiced at this window.

Finally he said, "It's not that I'm hiding anything."

"I know."

"But I've never been able to talk about personal stuff, except to . . ."

I waited.

He turned and stared at me, intense eyes moving over my face. After a moment he stepped toward me and touched my cheek. His fingers were dry; their effect on me was nothing more than the brush of autumn leaves. When he withdrew his hand, he frowned down at it, as if he'd experienced the same sensation—one that he hadn't expected. Then he nodded, a decision made.

"Let's go," he said.

"Where?"

"There's somebody I want you to meet."

"Who?"

"We'll go to your place first. Pack a bag—weekend clothes. Better be prepared for rain and cold, if what we ran into coming up the coast is any example."

"Suits—"

"Come *on*."

"*Where?*"

"Too many questions. Just let it unfold."

Nine

As the JetRanger crossed the Bay and sliced through the airspace above Marin County there was enough daylight left so that I could see thick fog masses boiling through the hollows of the coastal hills. Josh set the copter on a northwesterly course above the Point Reyes National Seashore; ahead, the lights that ringed Bodega Harbor glowed faintly through the mist.

Somewhere between my house and the landing pad on Bay Vista's roof I'd made the conscious decision to give in to what Suits called letting events unfold. Not an easy concession for a person like me, who felt a constant need to be in control, but now I found curious comfort in my self-imposed passivity. Perhaps it was the gathering darkness or the rhythmic throbbing of the engine and the flap of the rotor; maybe I was just tired. Whatever the reason, I felt cocooned. Besides, my failure to ask questions was bugging the hell out of Suits.

By the time we passed Fort Ross, flying parallel to the shoreline above the sea, night was falling. I took a last look inland, saw the tops of sequoias piercing the fog cover, and thought of miniature Christmas trees on a spun-cotton backdrop. Soon after that there was nothing but blackness.

Suits kept glancing at me, mystified by my silence. He'd undoubtedly expected me to pepper him with questions the whole ride—and had also expected to amuse himself by fending them off. After a while I smiled serenely at him. He frowned and looked away.

Soon drops of rain began to speckle the windows. Josh's voice came through the earphones. "Looks like we're in for more weather like we saw down south. I'm going to take her up higher, try for smoother air."

Suits didn't reply, leaving it to the expert.

The air wasn't any smoother at the higher altitude; the copter hit a crosscurrent with a bump. "Sorry about that," Josh said. In the distance lightning flashed.

"What *is* it with this weather?" Suits asked. "It's August, for Christ's sake."

I'd flown in far worse, but that had been on commercial carriers or with Hy, whose abilities and instincts I knew and trusted. The cocoon of comfort I'd spun began to unravel; my fingers tensed against the seat edge. I glanced at Suits, but he seemed sunk in private thoughts.

Another jarring crosscurrent. Josh took the copter even higher. Wind buffeted it, driving us farther out to sea; rain made slash marks on the windows.

"Boss, I think we better bypass the cove and set down at the county airport. That pad's dangerous when it's wet, and I don't like landing that close to the cliff in this wind."

"Okay, ask Ground Control at Little River to call that cabdriver down at Elk, see if he'll run up and fetch us."

"Right."

Suits stared at my face, waiting for a barrage of questions. I looked back silently, taking pleasure in torturing him. I already knew as much about our destination as he'd tell me, anyway: one of the many small coves that scallop the coast south of Mendocino.

Suits turned his head toward the window again. For the tense remainder of the flight he broke the silence only once, suddenly sitting up straighter and peering downward. He said, "There it is—we're right over Bootlegger's Cove."

Josh had veered inland; I had to lean across Suits to see the coastline. A faint scattering of lights lay below; one of them blinked green. "Pretty," I said and settled back in my seat.

Suits frowned and waited. I smiled.

"You're getting a kick out of this, aren't you?" he demanded.

"Out of what?"

He made a disgusted sound and began drumming his fingers on his knee.

Several minutes later we touched down at the county airport at Little River. The wind lashed the rain into stinging torrents; Josh had to steady me against its force when I stepped out. Then Suits grabbed my arm—more for ballast than to assist me—and we ran for the tiny terminal. Under the overhang of its roof we shook off water like dogs, stamped our cold feet, slapped icy hands together. Josh hurried up a minute later with the bags, his hair plastered to his head.

Suits asked, "You coming along to the cove with us? It's been a long time—"

"Can't. There's a sound in the engine that I don't like. I'll bunk in with my buddy in Albion, come back first thing in the morning and work on it."

"Whatever." Suits shrugged. "We'll drop you off, if that cab— Here he comes now."

A brown sedan with a light on top that inexplicably said "Yellow Cab Company" was pulling in to the terminal parking lot. Suits motioned to me, and we ran for it, Josh following with the bags. The cab's interior was musty with old cigar smoke, but the driver, an elderly man in a hooded army surplus slicker, had the heat on high, so I could forgive any noxious odor. Suits and Josh greeted him familiarly, and we set off south, stopping to let Josh out at the foot of a road on the coast highway below the hamlet of Albion. As we continued, Suits began to hum tunelessly, fingers of his right hand splayed and pressing hard against his thigh.

Nervous, I thought. Something to do with the person he's taking me to meet.

I didn't ask, though. Just let it unfold.

* * *

When the cab turned off the highway some ten minutes later, its headlights washed over a high stake fence. Suits got out and ran through the rain to a wooden box mounted next to the gate, used a key, and the gate swung open. The driver pulled the cab forward, and Suits got back in. They'd done this before, I thought.

The property beyond the fence was heavily forested in cypress; a blacktop drive cut through the trees, then climbed a steep rise. After the cab crested it, I saw rocky land falling away to the sea cliff and, on its edge, the lights I'd glimpsed from the air. Wind buffeted the cab as it crossed the unsheltered land; beside me Suits leaned forward, staring at a house whose outlines began to emerge from the sheeting rain.

I leaned forward too, saw two long, low wings of fieldstone and timber connected by a peak-roofed glass gallery that resembled a greenhouse. The lights in either wing were masked by drawn curtains, and smoke from one of the chimneys was caught and swept inland by the gale. As the cab stopped in front of the glass section, spotlights flashed on inside; they shone on a profusion of palms and yuccas and vines, casting complex shadows through which a silhouette moved.

Suits's earlier tension flowed out in a sigh. "It's called Moonshine House," he told me, "after the liquor they used to offload down at the cove." His voice was light now, almost boyish.

I turned toward him, but already he was opening the cab's door and scrambling out. While I located my purse and brief-case and pulled the hood of my parka over my head, he dealt with money matters and hoisted one of the bags with his good hand. I climbed out and grabbed the other, and we ran for the house. The door swung open, and I skidded through it, dropping the bag on a slick tile floor. A strong, slender hand steadied me. I looked into the face of the woman who waited there.

Suits said, "Sherry-O, this is my wife, Anna."

She could have been my sister, we looked that much alike.

* * *

At first I could only stare, my eyes moving from Anna to Suits and back again. Then he let fly one of his alarming whoops of laughter and the spell was broken.

Anna Gordon—taller and more slender than I, with waist-length black hair like mine before I had it cut—looked sternly at her husband. To me she said, "I don't suppose he mentioned the resemblance."

"No."

"The man does love a surprise." She shot him one more stern glance, then urged me to our left, into a long wing where kitchen, dining area, and living room flowed into a single open space that was dominated by a pit fireplace and a westward-oriented window wall. Instead of the sea, I saw our images—Anna's and mine—reflected on the black glass. She touched my arm and pointed; we studied ourselves and each other.

There were differences, of course: Her height, accentuated by slim jeans and a loose silk top the color of clover honey. Her features, more strongly Native American than mine, which are a genetic accident, a throwback to the Shoshone blood that traces to my great-grandmother, Mary McCone. Her manner-isms . . . I couldn't quite pinpoint it, but already I sensed a contentment . . . no, a self-containment that I didn't have, probably never would have.

But the likeness, given the circumstances, was unsettling.

Suits came in behind us. He'd removed the raincoat he'd worn draped over his shoulders and was still chuckling.

I turned and glared at him.

He held out his good hand as if to fend me off. "Sorry," he said. "The devil made me do it."

Really? I wondered. A practical joke, or an omission prompted by nervousness about how I would take the fact that he'd married a woman who looked a great deal like me? I thought of the way he'd stared at me in All Souls's kitchen before making the decision to bring me here; of his brooding silence on the JetRanger and his edginess in the taxi. In either case, I'd misread Suits once again, imagining him to be a loner whose life was played out in a series of half-furnished places in cities that weren't home. It convinced me that I would never read him accurately, would never do anything more than scratch the surface of his persona.

Anna took my purse and briefcase, helped me out of my wet parka, and loaded them onto Suits's good arm. "Make yourself useful," she told him. Then she led me to one of the sofas that surrounded the fire pit. "Take off those boots and put your feet up," she said. "I'm going to fix us some food."

I sat holding my hands out toward the warmth of the flames. The rain whacked down on the roof, smacked mercilessly against the glass wall behind me. After a moment I pulled off my boots, wriggled my toes, and propped them up to toast on the fire pit's edge.

Anna had gone to the kitchen at the far end of the space— rich wood and copper and earth-toned tiles, warm on a night like this. Suits came in from wherever he'd taken my things and joined her. She stood at a counter that faced out into the room, arranging food on a plate; he moved behind her, cradling her body with his good arm. Anna paused in her work, turned for a kiss, touched his cast gently with her fingertips. When she resumed what she'd been doing, he rested his chin on her shoulder; she was a few inches taller than he, and his head fit nicely into the curve of her neck. As I watched, his weary face underwent a transformation: lines smoothed; his eyes closed; a smile curved his lips.

My work has made me something of a voyeur, but even such an accomplished one as I knows when to stop intruding on a private moment. I looked away at the fire pit. In spite of the many questions that nagged at me, the flames soon had me mesmerized. I heard soft conversation and rattling of dishes in the kitchen, the repetitive beeping of a microwave oven. My limbs sagged against the soft cushions, and my eyelids grew heavy. . . .

The conversation was louder now, something to do with wine. I jerked my head up; I'd been dozing. Anna crossed the room and set a tray laden with glasses, plates, and utensils on the fire pit wall. "Hope you don't mind eating informally," she said. "That dining room table? We've had it five years now and never once used it." Then she went back to the kitchen, and I removed my still-damp feet from next to the tray. She and Suits returned with two additional trays and took seats on either side of me.

"Okay," Anna said, "you can eat fancy or plain, or both. We've got duck liver pâté and another kind—I think it's pork and beef—with some of those designer mushrooms that Suits likes but I find suspect. There's Brie and Stilton"—Suits growled in appreciation—"and caviar and anchovies"—she made a face—"and crackers and sourdough. Now, over here"—she indicated the tray closest to her—"is the kind of stuff I live on when he's not home, which is most of the time. All microwavable."

I stared. It was a junk-food fancier's dream: egg rolls, tiny pizzas, little tacos, pot stickers, chicken wings, White Castle burgers, chips and dips and pork rinds. "This is *wonderful*!"

Anna smiled triumphantly at Suits. I gathered they'd made a wager over which kind of cuisine—if either could be so termed—I'd go for. She reached for a taco and said, "We have such a crazy setup here that I haven't cooked a meal except for big pots of chili and soup in years. I'm not sure I'd even know how any more." Then she looked at Suits, who was plunging his knife into the Stilton cheese. "The wine?"

"Oh, right." He picked up a bottle and glanced at its label. "The Cabernet is a nineteen eighty-five Spottswoode—very crisp and lively. The Chardonnay is a nineteen ninety-three Sanford Barrel Select—spicy, complex—"

"Just ask her white or red and pour, would you?" To me, Anna added, "It's that damn photographic memory of his; he reads a wine magazine and the descriptions stick in his head."

To my surprise, Suits grinned widely. "She keeps me honest," he said.

I opted for the Cab—a perfect choice for a cold, rainy night—and loaded my plate with junk-food tidbits. As a concession to Suits, I also sampled some caviar and Brie.

Suits was working seriously on the Stilton, as if he was afraid Anna or I might decide we wanted it and leave him only a chicken wing. "So, Sherry-O," he said, "I guess you're pissed at me."

"I will be dangerously pissed if you don't stop calling me Sherry-O."

"It's only a nickname."

"I hate it."

"Sorry, Sherry-O."

Anna leaned around me, frowning severely at him.

Suits looked at her, rolled his eyes, and said, "Okay, I won't use it again."

I smiled at Anna, shook her hand. To Suits I said, "You're not off the hook yet. You might at least have told me you were married."

He shrugged.

I asked Anna, "Was the resemblance a shock to you, too?"

"Well, I'd known about it for years. The first time he laid eyes on me he told me about you. I used to be jealous. It's not easy, thinking you've been chosen not for who you are but for who you look like."

"What changed that?"

She glanced at him, the corners of her eyes turning down in amusement. "Oh, one time when he was throwing a fit over something and screaming at me, all of a sudden I thought, Hey, this guy really loves *me*. Those're my faults he's criticizing, nobody else's."

Suits smiled complacently.

I told him, "You must realize how many questions I have."

"Yeah." He looked at his wife.

And then I knew why he'd brought me here: Anna would be his voice; through her, he would tell me the things he couldn't bear to discuss himself.

She dusted pork rind fragments from her hands, picked up her wineglass. "First I should tell you about Suits and me. To do that I've got to go into my own background."

I poured myself more wine and snagged another pot sticker.

"I'm a Kashia Pomo," she began. "Grew up on the reservation in the hills above here, off Ridge Road. You know about it?"

I shook my head.

"Not many outsiders do. It's tiny—maybe a dozen families left by now. There's a school, three or four telephones, a graveyard. Even though it's part of Mendocino County, it's about as far removed from the rest of it as the moon. My parents . . . they left for a number of years, saw something of the world, but they weren't prepared for it, and it wounded them. They went back, became very insular, very committed to keeping the family on the land. Naturally, I rebelled. Turned out really wild."

Surprisingly Suits picked up the narrative. "When I met

Anna, she was living at the dope farm outside Garberville—the main reason I kept going there to make my buys. The guy she was with is—" He glanced at Anna, then shook his head. "Well, that doesn't matter anymore. When I started to turn the place around, I threw him out, told him Anna didn't want to go with him. A lie, but she stayed; she had no place else to go and was too strung out to care. Just about the time I realized how bad off she was, she disappeared. I spent nearly a year looking for her and finally found her in a Santa Rosa rehab house. She was doing fine."

"And I didn't want anything to do with him anymore," she said. "I'd put all that behind me, and I wasn't about to get mixed up with a guy who was trying to turn a dope farm into a profit-making proposition. But he was persistent, and when he got his first installment on Gerry's million, he made me an offer I couldn't refuse."

I looked questioningly at Suits.

"I bribed her to marry me. I told her she could have half the million and do whatever she wanted with it."

Anna said, "I knew a good deal when I heard one. We got married, and he put half of what he had into a separate account of my own. Looking back, I realize I was pretty cold, but I'd been through a lot and had grown fond of the guy, anyway. By then I'd graduated from high school and been accepted at college. Suits went back to finish turning the farm; I went to San Jose State. By the time he was done turning the film-equipment company in L.A., I was well on my way to a degree in psychology. By the time he was through with the Colorado turnaround, I'd fallen in love with him. But I still went back to the reservation."

"Why?" I asked.

"To make peace with my parents and my ancestors. To take a long look at my people. The young people in particular concerned me; I knew the reservation wasn't going to be able to hold them, but they weren't any more prepared for the outside than I'd been. Naturally, there wasn't anything I could do for them up there; their families didn't want me to encourage them to leave. So I hunted up and down the coast and found this house. It's got a lot of rooms, plus the guest cottage where you'll be staying. The kids from the reservation know they can come here anytime, stay as long as they want. While they're with me, I help them develop their survival skills—and their talents. The only reason we don't have two big teenagers hanging around tonight is that they're down in Sausalito, where a Native American gallery is exhibiting their crafts this week."

"My wife," Suits said, "is one of those women who do good works. On my money."

Anna gave him another of her stern looks. "The marriage," she told me, "is not without its flaws." Then she broke down and smiled at him. "The worst of them is that I don't get to see enough of the guy, although we talk on the phone for hours every night."

So that was who he'd been droning on to in the late hours.

Suits and Anna were smiling at each other across me. I realized that they would probably like to spend some time alone. "So what's on the agenda for tomorrow?" I asked.

Suits said, "We'll go over the background information Dottie Collier sent you. And you can ask your other questions."

"Then I'd better get some rest." I stood up, stretching. "You said something about a guest house?"

"Moonshine Cottage, it's called." Suits stood up too. "I'll take her there, Anna. You don't want to go out in this weather."

The cottage sat on a bluff above the south end of the cove, secluded in a cypress grove. Timber and stone like the main house, it contained two rooms, a bath, and a tiny kitchen. Suits showed me into the bedroom, lighted the logs that were laid on the small hearth, and departed with awkward formality. Away from Anna, he'd become ill at ease with me; I sensed that allowing me to intrude on his carefully guarded private life had cost him—and perhaps our relationship—more than he'd bargained for.

By now weariness had a strong hold on me. I stripped off my damp clothing and slid between maroon-striped sheets under a goose-down comforter. Turned off the light and watched the fire. Rain beat on the roof; wind baffled around the chimney; and under the storm-noises lay the constant crash and ebb of the sea. I thought of Anna and Suits, together in the big house. I thought of Hy, wherever he might be.

Was this going to be my life—sleeping alone while others slept together? Waiting for Hy while he ran from—or toward—his demons? At first our relationship had seemed nontraditional and unconfining to me; now it seemed odd and uncommitted. At first I'd felt a connection to him that transcended time and distance; now more often than not that connection short-circuited.

Tufa Lake on my birthday? I'd go, see how things were with us. I owed Hy that much. But if they were as I suspected, I owed it to myself to tell him it was over.

Ten

"Okay, we've eliminated all but two." I consulted my notes. "Russ Zola, a longtime associate. Goes all the way back to when you turned the film-equipment company in L.A."

Suits closed his eyes, pinched the bridge of his nose between thumb and forefinger. "As I said, under that amiable exterior there's a cruel streak. We call him the executioner, and he likes his work. But I can't think of any reason . . . Ah, well, we've been over that, too. Motives aren't always logical or apparent."

I nodded. "Now, Noah Romanchek. Another associate of long standing. Goes back to the beginning in Garberville. Former drug lawyer. You admit you can't get a handle on what makes him tick."

"I have no idea what goes on inside his head. But that doesn't mean he's plotting against me."

"But both of these men have access to the information that the person responsible for these attacks on you would need."

"Each of them has access to *some* of that information. And both of them pointed out to you that the responsible party would need it. Why would either—"

"Covering. A person who volunteers the information can't possibly be guilty, now, can he?"

Suits shrugged.

I dropped my notepad on the table between our low-slung chairs and swiveled toward the window wall. It was nearing three in the afternoon; we'd been going over the data on Suits's organization and turnarounds since eight-thirty that morning. I'd drunk so much coffee that my fingertips tingled. He'd been eating aspirin tablets as if they were snack food.

Overnight the storm had blown out to sea, leaving behind a rain-washed day whose brilliant light defined every branch on distant cypress trees, every crease in the offshore rocks. Even the waves looked sharp-edged. Anna was walking along the cliff, wearing a hooded crimson cape. A sudden gust of wind whipped the hood from her head; strands of her long hair blew free and trailed out behind her. Suits's breath caught. I glanced at him, saw he was staring at his wife with frank admiration.

I said, "She must be very lonely here when you're away."

"Anna, lonely? I don't think she's had a lonely moment in her life."

"Still—"

"Look, Sharon, what do we really have here?" He motioned at the papers on the table. "Two guys who've been with me a long time, who have access to information, who know more about my personal habits than the others. But so what? Neither's got it in for me, as far as I know. Neither strikes me as the kind who would lurk in my parking garage or condo."

"Each of them has the wherewithal to buy off people such as your architect and to hire someone to shoot at you and beat you up."

"That just doesn't compute, though."

I suspected he was right. "Then let's look at those turn-arounds again. Keystone Steel and Lost Hope, Nevada."

"Tough ones, caused a lot of resentment. Keystone wasn't totally successful. But again—so what?"

I didn't necessarily agree with him on that. "Still, I think it would be a good idea if I visited the sites in Pennsylvania and Nevada, tried to find out what some of those . . . what do you call them? Sacrificial lambs?"

He nodded.

"Find out what some of them are doing now."

"Do whatever you feel you have to."

"Which brings us to the next order of business: we need to talk about your private life."

His mouth tightened.

"You said I could ask my other questions."

"I know what I said, but not now. Look, why don't we break for a while? You go outside, take a walk with Anna. She'll show you the cove; it can be interesting after a storm. Things wash up—bottles, even, from a bootlegger's boat that was wrecked out there in the twenties."

"Suits, these diversionary tactics won't help us—"

"Go on, now. We'll talk more later. I'm not feeling so great." He stood up and crossed toward the glass gallery that connected this wing with the one where the bedrooms were. Maybe he did need a break; he held himself stiffly, as if he was in considerable pain.

After a moment I put the papers into order on the table and went out to the gallery. Anna was just coming inside, her cheeks rosy from the wind, but when I told her what Suits had suggested, she readily agreed to show me the cove. The parka I'd worn the night before was still damp, so she offered me one of hers. As I was putting it on, I complimented her on her cape.

"One of the young women from my reservation, Franny

Silva, designed and wove it," she told me. "Look—it tells a story, a modern-day one."

I examined the fabric more closely. From a distance it had appeared to be all one color, but there were actually shapes and figures interwoven in subtle shades of orange and purple. "What does it say?"

"It talks about a woman such as Franny coming down here from the hills and finding hope."

"You give a lot of yourself to your people."

She shook her head. "Not so much. I've been fortunate and I believe in passing it along, that's all."

We went through a door on the sea side of the gallery and followed a series of terraced rocks through the gorse and ice plant to the edge of the promontory. A redwood platform with built-in benches stood there, a gate giving access to a stairway that scaled the cliff face. Anna opened the gate with a key and led me down the steps. They were interrupted halfway by a landing, then switched back; we stopped there so she could point out the shape of the sand beach below.

"It's like a hand reaching out of the water and clutching at the land," she said. "Like a drowning person who knows he's got to hang on."

"Do you always come up with such cheerful images?"

"I'm not a naturally cheerful woman, I'll admit that. I spend too much time alone."

"Suits claims you've never had a lonely moment."

"Well, what would he know? I swear he says things like that to convince himself, so he can salve his conscience about being gone so much. It's true that there're usually people here, but they're protégés and I'm the mentor. The situation doesn't make for true companionship."

"Have you talked to Suits about that?"

"What good would it do?"

I nodded, thinking of her husband: so self-absorbed, wrapped up in his pursuits to the exclusion of everyone else's needs and feelings. Thought then of Hy, and realized that in a way Anna's situation mirrored my own. "Does he refuse to let you go along with him?"

"Not exactly." She turned and led the way down the rest of the steps. As we struck out across the soft sand toward the tide line, she added, "Being apart is the lifestyle we've grown into. At first it wasn't possible for me to be with him; then I tried going along. It . . . didn't work well, so we made the mutual decision not to do it again." Her eyes clouded—an unpleasant memory?—but then she brightened. "Hey, it's no big deal. This place is where we relate best, and when you've got money and aircraft at your disposal, distance isn't a factor."

"I noticed that you have a security gate but no alarm system, and your fences look as if they'd be simple to get around. Aren't you ever uneasy living alone in an isolated house?"

"Not really. I considered an alarm system, but they're always malfunctioning and sending you into a panic. I also thought about a guard dog, but they're smelly critters. I'm a good shot, though—when I was a kid on the reservation, we used to hunt—and I own a couple of handguns. A three-fifty-seven Magnum and a Beretta ninety-two-F that I carry in my purse. They're my security."

In spite of the fact that I'm an excellent shot and enjoy practicing on the range with my .38, I try to avoid carrying it unless it's absolutely necessary. And I've always been uncomfortable about people owning handguns when they don't have a professional need for them. I asked, "Would you actually use one of your guns against an intruder?"

She hesitated, the set of her mouth becoming grim. Then she turned the question aside, saying, "Let's walk south. I'll show you the cave where the bootleggers used to stash their hooch."

She quickened her pace; I did the same. Why, I thought, did I feel she'd been on the brink of telling me something important at some point during the conversation, then decided against it?

"Anna," I said after a moment, "did Suits send me on this walk so you could answer my questions about his private life?"

"He didn't specifically ask me to, if that's what you mean. But it's possible that was in the back of his mind."

"This mania about his privacy seems to have been a lifelong preoccupation. I've known him for over fifteen years, and I wasn't aware he went to Harvard until one of his associates told me just the other day."

"I suppose it has to do with all the attention that was focused on him when he was a child prodigy. Those early years weren't a good time for him."

"There's another thing that interests me: why, when he had a Harvard M.B.A., did he choose to roam all over the country peddling stuff like dope and term papers?"

"Suits never had a childhood or an adolescence. Rather than start on a high-powered adult career at seventeen, he decided to catch up on what he'd missed."

Ahead of us the cliff face curved toward the sea, then disintegrated into a tumble of rocks that extended into the water, forming a natural jetty. I stopped walking, my eyes drawn to the top of the sandstone; a feeling had stolen over me—that of being watched. I scanned the cliffs, but saw no one.

"This way," Anna called.

I shrugged the feeling off and followed her around a jagged mass of barnacle-encrusted stone to an A-shaped opening in the cliff's wall. "Our smugglers' cave," she said.

Inside, the cave was damp and echoing, noticeably colder than the beach. Deep shelflike hollows gouged its walls, suitable caches for crates of illegal liquor. I went over to one and ran my hand across its mossy surface, then perched on a reasonably dry rock that protruded from the pebbled sand. Anna came over and leaned beside me.

I said, "Suits and I could only pinpoint a couple of people

in his organization who have access to enough information to have planned these attacks on him—Noah Romanchek and Russ Zola. Do you know them?"

"Not well enough to hold an opinion on what they're capable of."

"We also isolated a couple of turnarounds that may be at the root of the trouble—Keystone Steel and Lost Hope, Nevada."

She nodded slowly.

"I have the files on those," I went on, "but I'd like your impression of how things were for Suits personally during those periods. You talk on the phone every night, so you probably have insight—"

"Unfortunately, I don't."

"Why not?"

She pushed away from the rock and began to walk restlessly around the cave. "Last night when I said the marriage wasn't without its flaws? Well, I meant it as a joke, but there's a good deal of truth in it. Suits and I weren't getting along around the time he went to Pennsylvania, and we agreed to a trial separation. It wasn't until after he finished Nevada that we worked things out and got back together."

"All together how long was that?"

"Four years, give or take."

"And you had no contact the whole time?"

"Very little."

"Didn't you ever discuss those years with him?"

She shook her head. "We decided to start over from the day we got back together. That meant no dwelling on past problems, no delving into what went on during the years we were separated. Those years were hard on both of us; I think Keystone would have been more successful if he hadn't had the breakdown of our marriage on his mind. And I . . . There were things I would have done differently, too, if I'd been safe in the marriage."

Anna interested me; I wanted to ask her about those things, but they really weren't any of my business. I said, "Suits has made a lot of enemies over the years. Can you think of any who might go to this extreme?"

She considered the question thoughtfully, drawing a pattern in the pebbles with the toe of her sneaker. "No one comes to mind."

"This next question may seem offensive, and I apologize in advance, but I have to ask it. Have you ever known Suits to do drugs?"

"I'm the ex-druggie in the family. He hardly even drinks; you saw how little wine he had last night. Why do you ask?"

"A number of people have described him as paranoid, and even though I believe someone really is out to get him, I've noticed paranoid behavior, too."

"Suits has always been on the paranoid side of the scale, so I know what you mean. Frankly, I'm worried about him. A few weeks ago he admitted that he's had his phones wired with recording devices. He keeps tapes of his conversations and examines them for sinister connotations. And he's taken to conducting most of his business meetings in public places or on the helicopter. He says they can't get to him there."

"They?"

She nodded. *They.*

"Not good. Do the people he's talking with on the phone know they're being taped?"

Anna shook her head.

"He's committing a crime."

"I know that. I'm the only one he's told about it, so don't you let on to him."

"I won't. There's another reason I asked about drugs, though: a man he knows in the city described him as having what sounds like a flashback." I explained what Carmen had told me. "A railroad overpass, two or three people, heat lightning on the water," I repeated. "Do those images mean anything to you?"

She became very still. I could see her hug herself beneath the folds of her cape. "Did you ask him about them?"

"I wouldn't have gotten a straight answer. Might even have damaged our rapport."

Anna's face was pale now, her gaze turned inward. Finally she said in a flat voice, "Well, I don't know what they could possibly mean."

Maybe she didn't understand their exact significance, but I was sure she'd recognized something in the images. Before I could ask more, she moved outside the cave and began walking toward the tide line.

I went after her, but it was obvious that the subject was closed. As soon as I caught up she began to chatter, trying to divert me with tales of bootleggers and shipwrecks, with a skill that her husband would have admired. As we walked, the feeling of being covertly watched came over me again; I scanned the beach and the cliff tops, but saw no one.

* * *

When Anna and I got back to Moonshine House, the Jet Ranger was idling near the edge of the cliff on a flat cleared area. Suits met us halfway up the slope, turned me around, and pointed me toward the cottage. "Get your things together," he said.

"What's going on?" I asked.

"Trouble. We've got to go back to the Bay Area. I'll meet you at the copter."

"Suits—"

He was already heading toward the house.

I glanced at Anna; her lips had pulled tight and her eyes were stormy. She looked at me, shrugged, and started toward the cottage.

I remained where I was, my brimming annoyance with Suits spilling over onto her. What was wrong with her, anyway? She wasn't going to protest, wasn't even going to ask the reason for his abrupt departure! After a moment I followed, gathered my things in silence.

When I'd zipped my travel bag, I saw that Anna was staring out the window at the sea, arms wrapped around herself under the cape. She turned—mouth dejected, eyes bleak now—and my anger deflated. I touched her shoulder. "Why don't you let me help you pull the sheets off the bed."

She shook her head. "I'll take care of them after you leave. I'm expecting a young friend from the reservation—Franny Silva, the woman who wove this cape. Getting the cottage fixed up for her will give me something to do."

When we got back to the house, Suits met us in the gallery and handed me my briefcase, looking haggard. He whispered his apologies to Anna during a quick embrace. Then he hurried out the door, motioning to me.

I slipped out of the borrowed parka, pulled my own damp one from the hall tree, and turned to Anna to give my thanks. She hugged me, then enfolded me in her lovely handwoven cape.

"Anna, I can't take this—"

"I want you to have it. It's special to me; so are you. In a way I feel like we're sisters. And now you'll excuse me if I don't come outside to say good-bye."

I hugged her in return, pulled the cape's hood over my head so she could see how it looked, then ran after Suits. He and Josh were impatient to be off; they helped me aboard the copter quickly. After I put on my headset I looked out the window toward the greenhouse gallery, but saw no sign of Anna.

As the copter lifted off, I asked Suits, "*Now* what's happened?"

He hesitated a moment before replying. "It's Carole Lattimer. She was mugged and beaten in the garage across from our building, where she parks her car."

"She's alive?"

"Barely. We don't know the full extent of her injuries yet."

"When did it happen?"

"Middle of this afternoon. Noah—he's at the hospital—Noah says they're afraid there's brain damage." Suits slumped in his seat, chin on his collarbone. "The police . . . they say it's the neighborhood. They say she should've been more careful. They say . . . ah, hell! I know there's more to it than that."

"You can't be sure."

"I can. It's just more of the same." He put his hand over his eyes. When he spoke again, his voice rasped with emotion. "Sherry-O, I hate this. I just plain *hate* this. The goddamn butchers can do what they want to me, but why do they have to hurt my *people*?"

* * *

Later that day the Mendocino County authorities would tell us that we must have just cleared the ridge of coastal hills on our inland journey when Moonshine House exploded, fragmenting everything and everyone inside.

Touchstone

September 28

Black smoke belching from a helter-skelter heap of wood and stone. Orange flame licking at its edges. Firefighters scurrying like frightened insects, leaving a spoor of hoses across the charred vegetation.

Wind sweeping the smoke higher, buffeting the copter; Josh crying so hard he was having trouble setting it down.

Suits's hand in mine—limp as the corpse of a small animal. Face a rigid plaster-of-Paris mask, and just as fragile. His eyes . . . no, I can't look into his eyes.

Hot tears now. Whose? Mine. Burning tracks on my face.

Suits couldn't believe it when the Oakland P.D. met us on the roof of the building and told us. Insisted we fly straight back. He believes it now.

Sob catching in my throat. I believe it, too.

Close to the ground. Closer. Visibility nil. A bump. Door open, smoke billowing in. Filling my lungs, I can't breathe. And the smell . . .

Smell of countless things incinerated, shattered, ripped apart, ru-ined. And, faintly, the smell of charred human flesh—

I'm strangling on it. Trying to scream, but the sound won't come. Straining harder, and now it does—hoarse, raw. And I'm falling—

Arms catching me, folding me close. A voice, Hy's voice. Over and over he's saying, "No, no, McCone, no. . . ."

*   *   *

After I'd fought free of the nightmare that was more a memory than a dream, I told Hy I needed to get some air. September was a hot month here in the high desert; Hy's ranch house had been closed up since early July. Perhaps it was the lingering heat and stuffiness that had suggested flame and smoke.

Who was I trying to fool? The nightmare had recurred on an almost daily basis in the cool, fog-washed air of San Francisco.

We dressed and went out into the gray dawn. Sheep huddled in their fenced pasture; they moved restively as we went by. Hy led the way across rough sagebrush-dotted ground to a grove of gold-leafed aspen. A dry creek bed meandered through the trees; we bridged it on well-worn stones. On the other side of the grove, the land dropped off sharply in a series of ridges to the volcanic plain where Tufa Lake nestled. As we sat on the cliff's edge, our feet dangling, I could see the landing light at the nearby Vernon airstrip wink green.

Hy said, "Can't just be thirty-ninth birthday nerves."

"No."

"And it can't just be your friend Anna getting killed. You hadn't known her all that long, and besides, you've dealt with worse things."

"Dealt with them better than I am with this, you mean."

"Uh-huh. Your friend Suits—"

"Is being a total *asshole!* I *hate* him!"

The vehemence of my response surprised both of us. Hy

frowned and waited. When I didn't go on, he said, "McCone, talk to me."

My fingers clenched together. I bowed my head. So far I hadn't been able to relate more than the surface details about the explosion, certainly hadn't been able to describe my feelings. The feelings only crept forth in the night, in my dreams. Otherwise they lay buried as deep as what few fragments they'd been able to find of Anna. To look at me as I dealt with clients and conducted interviews and instructed Mick, you'd never have known that I was only part there—that the greater portion of me was lost in the smoke and the smells at Bootlegger's Cove.

I thought of the many things I hadn't told Hy: Of the framed photo of Anna and Suits that I'd come upon near the helipad, miraculously thrown free and unharmed by the blast that had destroyed all else. Of Josh's anguished cry when he saw me holding it. Of Suits talking with a sheriff's deputy and the fire captain, then growing more and more still, as if he were flipping a series of internal circuit breakers to disable all human connection. And of the suspicion that had grown in my mind during this past month, that was the worst thing of all. . . .

Hy couldn't possibly know what I suspected, but when he tugged at the cape I wore, I started and glanced up at his face to see if somehow he'd guessed. The cape was Anna's, the one she'd given me immediately before the explosion, the one I'd worn from the house to the JetRanger, its hood raised. When I'd thrown it on to go meet Hy at Oakland Airport the previous evening, I'd done so as a symbolic act—a declaration that I was committing to a risky and possibly ruinous course of action.

On September 6, Suits had terminated his contract with me. A check signed by Dottie Collier arrived at my office, accompanied by a brief note thanking me for my efforts on her employer's behalf. A check for the full amount of my fee, plus a fifty percent bonus—buying me off, buying me out of Suits's life.

I hadn't deposited the check; I hadn't earned it. And I couldn't be bought, especially not in this instance.

Hy gave up on me initiating a conversation and asked, "Did you go up to Mendocino County last week, like Gordon's lawyer wanted?"

"Yes." Suits had refused to return to the Bay Area with Josh and me after the explosion. Moonshine Cottage had survived intact, and it was there he took up residence—had remained in residence to this day.

The week before, Noah Romanchek had called me. "It's about T.J.," he said. "He's in terrible shape, won't deal with the business. GGL's hanging on, but just barely. Decisions have to be made about the Hunters Point base. The Port Commission and the Southern Pacific want to get moving on deepening that tunnel. A lot of people are depending on this project. Christ, Carole Lattimer had brain surgery, and she's pitching in from her hospital bed. If she can do that, T.J. ought to be able to pull himself together."

"Have you told him this?" I asked.

"Of course. I went up to the cove to talk with him last week. He threw me out of the cottage."

"Well, I don't know what I can do. I'm not working for him anymore."

"T.J. once told me that he respects your opinion. Please go up there and try to get through to him. We'll pay whatever your usual rate is."

For reasons of my own, I'd agreed and flown north in the JetRanger with a somber Josh Haddon. Had left the pilot walking among the charred ruins on the clifftop and gone to the cottage.

Now I told Hy, "I found pretty much the kind of deteriorating scene Romanchek described. Suits is wallowing in grief; he seems to enjoy it."

"Drinking?"

"No, no drugs, either. He's just . . . shut down, doesn't give a damn about anybody or anything."

"Well, maybe he'll snap out of it. We all handle our grief in different ways. When Julie died, even though I'd known for years that the disease would eventually take her, I went crazy for a while. Drank, self-destructed all over the map. Went berserk at whatever protests the movement was staging, hoping some cop would blow me away and put me out of my misery."

"But that kind of behavior was in character for you. Suits's isn't. After the explosion there was a lot of speculation in the press, particularly the tabloids: had he been responsible for the explosion? No one ever went so far as to suggest he actually blew the place up himself or hired someone to do it, but there were allusions to Anna's and his 'unusual lifestyle.' And they dredged up about him turning the dope farm, and her addiction, as well as their four-year separation and the story of how he bribed her to marry him."

Hy grimaced. "Fuckin' vultures."

I nodded. "The man I knew would have reacted just that way. He'd've come out swinging at the tabloids, slapped them with huge lawsuits. But as it was, he didn't even issue a press release. And here's what makes me angriest of all with him: he doesn't care why Anna died, doesn't want to find out who set that explosion."

I paused, thinking back to August. "You know, Suits said something once, to the effect that the butchers were trying to cut him down. At the time I thought he was being overly dramatic, but that's exactly what they did. They—his enemies and the press—butchered his wife, and they butchered him."

I pictured Suits lying listlessly on dirty blue sheets in the room I'd occupied at Moonshine Cottage. Trash had clogged the fireplace; soft-drink cans and plates full of half-eaten food sat everywhere. I'd tried to persuade him to get up, clean up, come out for a meal or at least a walk, but he refused. I'd tried to give him Anna's cape, so he would have something of hers, but he wouldn't take it.

"Keep it, Sherry-O," he'd said. "I don't want it. I don't want anything."

It was the ultimate rebuff, of both his dead wife and our dead friendship. I left the cottage a few minutes later. When I got back to the helipad I found Josh standing next to the JetRanger, fingering a piece of blackened stone and crying, as he had on the day of the explosion. His eyes rested on the cape that I held over my arm; he turned and angrily hurled the stone into the sea. We hadn't spoken since then; I wasn't even sure if he was still in the Bay Area.

Hy asked, "Do they have any leads on who set the explosion?"

"No. It was plastic explosives, but the blasting caps and wiring devices don't tell them anything. They figure the charges were laid earlier that week when Anna was down in Sausalito helping a couple of her protégés set up a crafts exhibit, and detonated by remote control." My voice quavered; I breathed deeply, steadied it before I continued. "They've got little enough to work with; the only way they got an I.D. on Anna was that the dentist who takes care of the people from her reservation recognized a couple of fillings as his work."

Hy didn't speak for a moment. I looked at him, saw he was staring toward distant Tufa Lake. Its waters were turning pinkish gray now, the towers of calcified vegetation that gave it its name taking on definition.

He said, "All right, now let's talk about what's really bothering you."

The old nonverbal connection that I'd feared lost was still in place. Thank God I'd come up here with a wait-and-see attitude regarding Hy and me; maybe things would be all right between us after all.

"Okay," I said, "I don't think the explosion was intended to kill Anna."

"No?"

"No. I think that initially it was supposed to be more of the same—an attempt to intimidate Suits but not hurt him, or anybody else."

"You said you felt like somebody was watching when you and Anna walked on the beach that afternoon. Whoever detonated those charges knew who was at the house."

"Right."

"So what went wrong?"

"Okay, I've got to back up a bit. In my conversation with Romanchek before I went up to Mendo last week, he told me that one of the reasons Suits went to Moonshine House that night was to ask Anna to move to the city. It wasn't a snap decision; several people on his staff knew. He planned to surprise Anna with it just before he left, get her to come along on the return trip."

"Would she have done it on such short notice?"

"Romanchek claims yes. If Suits asked her in advance, Anna would've come up with all sorts of reasons not to. But she liked to act on impulse, and Suits felt getting her to the city and then persuading her to stay was his best shot."

"And then what happened to Carole Lattimer made him put off asking. But I don't see——"

I plunged ahead, cutting him off. "Ripinsky, I think we can assume that whoever was responsible for that explosion had access to all of the information that the people on Suits's staff did. Including the fact that Anna was supposed to return to the city with him. And that he'd hired me."

Hy nodded. Waited.

"What would a watcher have seen when Suits and I boarded the JetRanger?"

He thought, shook his head. "You tell me."

"Suits and a woman who looked like Anna. A woman of around the same height, with black hair, wearing this cape with the hood raised." I pulled the hood over my head, looked up at him from under its edge.

Hy's jaw clenched. "So that's it."

"That's it. I was supposed to be the one who died at Bootlegger's Cove. What better way to stop the investigation that Suits had initiated?"

For a moment all I could hear was Hy's breathing, as fast and hard as my own. Then he said, "But he didn't put a stop to it, now, did he?"

"No, he didn't."

"McCone, you take Route Three-fifty-nine east out of here to Hawthorne, Nevada, and then it's a clear shot south on Ninety-five to Lost Hope. My Land Rover needs servicing, but you borrow it, get that taken care of, and you could be there by nightfall."

I'd been thinking the same thing, since putting on Anna's cape the previous evening.

The sun was spilling over the mountains behind us now, turning the mesquite to spun gold, chasing shadows deep into the creases of the ridge. In the distance Tufa Lake glowed in violent hues, its surrealistic towers obsidian monuments against its flat surface.

"Happy birthday, McCone," Hy said.

Part Two

Lost Hope, Nevada

September

Eleven

The lights of the town shone far across the desert. I'd been moving toward them for what seemed to be hours.

Coming south out of Hawthorne the landscape had been rugged: unrelenting brown interrupted occasionally by the deceptive water-slickness of dry alkali lakes, surrounded by the wild Toiyabe National Forest and the jagged peaks of the Monte Cristo Range. At a junction with a dirt road that cut through sagebrush toward the mountains stood a collection of trailers and a bar-café; a neon sign advertised Mimi's Massage, a euphemism for brothel in this state where prostitution was legalized. After that I saw nothing but an occasional car or truck and more barren land.

The highway was a good one, two straight lanes of asphalt ascending into the hills so slowly that I had to glance in the rearview mirror to tell that I was climbing. I let the Land Rover's speedometer drift near eighty; when dusk came on, I eased up some. Even at sixty-five I felt as if I were barely moving. And out of the dusk the lights of Lost Hope appeared:

143

just over the next rise . . . just atop the next hill . . . just out of reach. . . .

I turned on the radio but could get nothing but static. Snapped it off in annoyance. The tires hummed on the asphalt; headlights flashed behind me, and a pickup went past in a rush of speed, red taillights winking good-bye. The desert sky was wide and clear, shot with ice-chip stars.

As I watched the town's distant lights I thought of Hy. He was at his ranch house, comfortable among his books and his memories of our time together. But out here in this lonesome land, my memories didn't suffice. In just one night, my body hadn't gotten enough of his; my spirit hadn't gotten enough renewal from the strong emotional connection that seemed to be working for us once more. For company and reassurance I replayed our parting conversation.

He'd leaned into the window of the Rover, kissed me lightly, and said, "You know, before last night I had a suspicion you might be coming up here to break it off with me."

"It had crossed my mind."

"Is that what you want?"

"No."

"Then?"

"From here on out, it's up to you."

His lips tightened and he looked away. "McCone, I'm working toward being up-front with you. That's not easy, given that deception's been more or less my way of life."

Deception, his way of life. Was that a life worth sharing?

He added, "I want this—us. Give me a little more time. That's all I'm asking."

And so he had a little more time. Till the end of the year, that's what I'd give him.

I'd have no choice, anyway. Tomorrow morning he'd be gone again. To San Diego in the Citabria, where he had to talk with some people. Then he would catch a commercial flight to an unspecified destination on the East Coast.

TILL THE BUTCHERS CUT HIM DOWN

I suspected who the people were: Gage Renshaw and Dan Kessell, principal owners of RKI, and figures out of Hy's dim past. Last June they'd engaged his services in an attempt to lure him into partnership in the firm. He'd turned them down, but perhaps he'd had a change of heart. Perhaps he'd begun to crave more of what Gage Renshaw called "the old action." Risk-taking, danger—that was Hy's métier, even more than it was mine.

Well, no use speculating. Maybe I would do well, as Suits had repeatedly told me, to just let it unfold. . . .

*   *   *

The highway ran straight through the town, its speed limit abruptly cut to twenty-five. At first there were gas stations, fast-food drive-ins, and inexpensive motels; after about half a mile the old-fashioned central district began. High concrete curbs bordered the pavement, and beyond them stood stone and wood buildings that harked back to the teens and twenties. On the slopes behind them more lights shone, revealing a sprawl of small dwellings.

This was silver-mining country, the information from Suits's files had said. Lost Hope had been a boomtown during the teens, nearly died in the thirties, and languished for years after that, its residents eking out a living from travelers driving between Reno and Vegas and tourists headed for Death Valley or Yosemite. Four years ago the city government had been bankrupt, as were most of the businesses.

The town's salvation had come in the form of a gambler pal of Suits's, stranded there by car trouble on his way to a high-stakes poker game in Vegas. During the day it took for his car parts to come by bus from Reno, he and the old man who ran the La Rose Hotel had discovered a mutual fondness for gin rummy, and in the course of their conversation across the card table, the gambler had mentioned that he knew a miracle worker who could transform the place into a profit-making

145

enterprise. When he left the next day, the old hotelier was several hundred dollars richer and in possession of T. J. Gordon's phone number.

Transform the place Suits had. Yes, he certainly had.

Miner's Saloon and Casino, Boomtown Museum, Montezuma Mining Company Tours, Sagebrush Bed and Breakfast, Rock and Mineral Shop, T-shirts, T-shirts, T-shirts! Esmeralda Steak House, Old West Barbecue, Kiddie Korral, the General Store, Antiques, Native American Crafts Outlet. . . .

The neon signs blinked and shimmered. Motels sported No Vacancy signs. Tourist families strolled. Couples window-shopped. At the central intersection two mule teams waited to take customers on hayrides.

Once again the town had it all. But did it really want its newfound hope?

I'd made a reservation at the La Rose Hotel; now I had mental reservations as well. But I was pleasantly surprised when I found the four-story granite building at the far end of the strip: no neon flashed there; no banners advertised all-you-can-eat buffets. A doorman in conservative livery met me and summoned a valet parking attendant and a bellman. Inside, the lobby was tastefully restored in dark wood and brass; the reception desk and pigeonhole mailboxes looked to be original. To the left I spotted an old-fashioned bar; through an archway to the right came the familiar burble of computerized slot machines.

As I registered, I asked if any faxes had arrived for me. They were there—copies of my notes on Suits's turnaround files that I'd requested Mick send when I'd called to check on how things were at the office. As the clerk handed them across the counter, he gave me a curious look that made me suspect he'd glanced over them, maybe even read them. I wasn't sure how I felt about that; on the one hand his interest might be harmless enough, but on the other. . . .

My room was also a pleasant surprise: large, comfortably furnished in pseudo-antiques, decorated in Laura Ashley prints. Overly warm, but that was to be expected; while desert people are a hardy breed, they seem to think that we city types are hothouse flowers. I unpacked what little I had brought along, hung my toiletries case in the bathroom, and went over the notes. Then I freshened up and took myself downstairs for a drink, dinner, and perhaps some conversation.

The old man whose acquaintance with Suits's gambler friend had sparked Lost Hope's renaissance had died during the turn-around—of shame, perhaps. The new owner was Marty McNear, the old man's nephew. I stopped at the reservation desk, gave the clerk my card, and asked if Mr. McNear was available. He went into the office, came back, and said the owner would meet me in the lounge in ten minutes. Before I went there, I checked out the slot machines.

All were of the new computerized variety rather than the noisy one-armed bandits with the pictures of cherries and oranges and watermelons that had first piqued my mild interest in gambling. I dropped a quarter into one. After I pressed the play button, it informed me that I had a credit of two dollars. Did I want to cash in or keep playing?

I kept playing.

Two bucks, four bucks, ten bucks, three-fifty. Three-fifty, two twenty-five, seventy-five cents, nothing.

They'll get you every time—watermelons and cherries or not.

Marty McNear met me at the door to the lounge. He was perhaps in his early fifties, although it was hard to judge. His skin had the brown toughness of an outdoorsman who doesn't bother with sunblock; his dark hair had receded to a curly, low-slung halo. He wore western garb and a big smile that told me he wasn't the least bit wary of meeting with a private investigator. By the time we were settled on a red velvet banquette with our drinks, I knew why.

"I've got to admit it, I'm nosy," he told me. "I looked over your faxes. Didn't intend to, but the name Gordon caught my eye, and then I couldn't help myself." His smile faded and he took a sip of beer. "I heard about what happened to T.J.'s wife. Pretty grim."

"You know T.J., then?"

"Sure. I came out here a few years ago after my uncle died. Planned to fix up the hotel so I could sell it, then go back to Baltimore. T.J. and his pilot were staying in the worst ratholes in the building. His other people were at a motel out by the highway. You get to know a man when you're living under the same roof—particularly one that leaks."

"Would you say you and he were friends?"

McNear frowned, fingering a book of matches that was propped in the ashtray. "I don't know as I could lay a claim to friendship. But we were good companions, and seeing his enthusiasm for the town gave me the idea to stay on."

"So you're happy with the way the turnaround affected Lost Hope?"

"Well, sure. Oh, I know it's kind of tacky, but you should've seen it before."

"How do the natives feel?"

"The merchants're happy."

"And the others?"

"Well, there're always people who resent progress."

"Anyone in particular?"

He hesitated. "Ms. McCone, exactly why are you here?"

"I'm an old friend of T.J. I was a friend of his wife, too, although I only knew her briefly. T.J. hired me last summer because someone was trying to sabotage a turnaround he was working on in San Francisco. What was happening didn't seem to have much connection to that, so we went over his past projects and pinpointed Lost Hope as a possible trouble spot."

"Was Anna Gordon's death connected to that sabotage?"

"Yes, I think so. I'm here because I want . . . no, I *need* to find out who killed her."

"Well, I can understand that. She was a wonderful lady."

"You knew her, too?"

"Sure. She visited T.J. for about two weeks shortly before he left here."

Why hadn't Anna mentioned that to me? Oversight? No—an intentional omission. "What do you recall about her visit?"

He shrugged. "Not a whole lot. I liked her. They seemed to be having a good time. We spent a few pleasant evenings together."

"Can you think of anybody who could tell me more?"

"You might try Brenda Walker over at the Indian crafts shop. She and Anna hit it off, spent time together. In fact, Brenda took on some of the crafts from Anna's reservation. Did real well with them, she said."

"Is the shop open tonight?"

McNear smiled. "No moneymaking enterprise in Lost Hope ever closes early."

*　　*　　*

The Native American Crafts Outlet contained an eclectic assortment of merchandise: Zuni pottery, Navajo weaving, Hopi kachinas, Plains tribes beadwork and quillwork, even Eskimo carvings. A short, round woman with close-cropped gray hair whom I took to be Brenda Walker was helping a customer decide among a trayful of silver earrings; I began to browse, stopping at a display of Shoshone basketry.

Recently I'd developed a curiosity about my Shoshone great-grandmother, Mary McCone—natural, I supposed, since I was the only member of the family whose appearance mirrored our one-eighth Indian heritage. I'd done some reading on her people and learned that they're one of the many Plains tribes, now scattered from the Wind River Reservation in western Wyoming to settlements in Idaho to small enclaves in Nevada. Their reputation as peaceable people is largely derived from their arms-open welcome of the white man—an acceptance prompted less by fondness for their Euro-American brothers than by their violent hatred of the Sioux. The white man rewarded them with some forty-four million acres in Wyoming, Utah, Idaho, and Colorado, then recognized the value of that land and proceeded to take it all back. The Shoshone ended up sharing the Wind River land with another old enemy, the Arapahoe—referred to by all good members of the tribe as "dog eaters." The Arapahoe don't even dignify their fellow reservation dwellers with an epithet, merely turn up their noses and call them "non-Indians."

I'd read many amusing tales about the odd-couple tribes of Wind River Reservation, but none of them told me the things I really wanted to know. Such as what sixteen-year-old Mary had been doing in Flagstaff, Arizona, when my great-grandfather Robert McCone passed through in 1888 on his westward journey from Virginia. Such as what made her take up with a much older Scotch-Irishman and turn her back forever on her people. I wondered what her life had been as the Indian bride of a white man in turn-of-the-century California. I wondered why we had only one photograph of her—a faded and browned formal studio shot that showed her in her Sunday dress, rosary in hand, looking for all the world like a good Catholic matron. I supposed I'd be searching for the answers to my questions till the day I died.

The gray-haired woman had made her sale, and the customer was leaving. I went over to the counter. "Ms. Walker?"

She had her back to me, was doing something with a credit-card slip. "Yes, may I help you?" She turned and glanced at me; her round face paled. Her eyes moved from my face to the cape I wore and back again. When she frowned, I realized that for a moment she'd thought I was Anna Gordon.

I identified myself and explained that I wanted to talk with her about Anna. She relaxed somewhat, pressing her hand to her breastbone over her heart. "That cape," she said, "it was woven by the same girl who made Anna's?"

I nodded, unwilling to tell her that it actually was Anna's;

150

the explanation of how I came to have it was one I didn't care to go into with a stranger. "Can we talk about her?" I repeated.

"Why?"

I took out one of my cards and handed it to her. "Anna's husband is my client."

She studied the card, then set it on the counter. "He hired you to find out who killed her?"

"Not exactly. The authorities in California are investigating that. Mr. Gordon hired me before Anna died, to look into some problems he was having with his current turnaround. I'm here because of them."

"So why are you asking about Anna?"

"She was a friend of mine. Her death may be connected to those problems."

"Are you licensed to work in Nevada?"

Oh, lady, don't give me trouble! "Generally one jurisdiction honors a license issued in another."

"Aren't you supposed to check in with the local law?"

"I plan to do that."

"The sheriff's substation is at the south end of town opposite the truck stop. Deputy in charge is named Chuck Westerkamp."

Why such strong resistance to talking with me? "Ms. Walker, I was with Anna Gordon the day she died. If we could talk about the time she spent here—"

She picked up the receiver of a phone that sat under the counter.

"Who're you calling?"

"Westerkamp. I'll either tell him you're on your way to check in, or make a complaint about you harassing me. Which will it be?"

* * *

"Brenda's a little cracked, but she means well."

Chuck Westerkamp slouched in his creaky swivel chair. His

tiny office was chilly, cold air leaking so badly around the aluminum window frames of the prefab building that it stirred the venetian blinds. The Esmeralda County Sheriff's substation was housed in three such prefabs on a windblown mesa at the very edge of town. Across from it sprawled an enormous truck stop, where semis hulked in shadow like slumbering mastodons. Others huffed at the gas pumps, then growled away into the ancient desert darkness. When I'd arrived there, I stood beside the Land Rover for a minute, watching a convoy lumber onto the highway and crawl south; as the night swallowed it I began to feel lonesome, and I wrapped Anna's cape closer for comfort.

Now I perched on the metal folding chair that Westerkamp offered me and asked, "Why do you suppose Ms. Walker's so sensitive on the subject of Anna Gordon?"

The deputy, a wiry sunbrowned man with thinning white hair, shrugged. "Lots of folks in the town've got cause to be sensitive on the subject of the Gordons."

"But I understand Ms. Walker was a friend of Anna's. She and I are—should be—on the same side."

"Like I said, Brenda's a little cracked. Watches too much TV, if you ask me. A week doesn't go by without us getting a call from her about some heinous criminal she saw on *Unsolved Mysteries* who's holed up right here in Lost Hope."

"Tell me about Lost Hope, Deputy. What kind of town is it?"

He took a paper-wrapped toothpick from the pocket of his uniform shirt and unwrapped it. Stuck it in his mouth and chewed on it while he considered the question. "First word that comes to mind is 'greedy.' Was greedy way back during the silver boom; was greedy during the Depression when the people in Washington more or less forgot we existed; has gotten *real* greedy since your T. J. Gordon performed what some folks call his miracle."

He paused, pale eyes thoughtful. "It's a rowdy town, too:

152

Miners back when. Nowadays it's drunks. What this department mostly does is keep them off Main Street, out of their pickups, and from beating each other up." He took the flattened toothpick from his mouth, contemplated it, and returned it. "Nasty town as well."

"In what way?"

"Goes hand in hand with the greed. Oh, you could say everybody's got a nasty secret or two: man doesn't want the wife to know about the girl he's got on the side; woman doesn't want the husband to know about the booze she puts away when he's not home. But that's garden-variety nastiness. I'm talking about the kind when folks do despicable things for pure profit."

"Such as?"

"There's a lot at stake in this little town, always has been. Maybe not fortunes by Vegas or California standards, but fortunes to the kind of people who've settled here. That desert out there's been an unholy graveyard since the first vein of silver was uncovered back in the teens. If you knew where to look, you couldn't go more'n a mile without stumbling over a grave—some of them fairly fresh, too."

"This is on the level?"

He nodded, gnawing the toothpick.

"I thought you said your department mainly dealt with drunks."

"I should've added missing persons. People who're missing because they want to be, others . . . who knows? Folks have a habit of flat-out disappearing around here."

"So what do you do?"

"Depends on how bad somebody wants them found. We take reports, make helicopter sweeps. One time we even had a psychic come out, looking for her client's rich husband."

"She find him?"

Westerkamp smiled. "What do you think?"

"To get back to the Gordons—did you know either of them?"

"Never met her; she wasn't here long enough. Knew T.J. and the rest of the crew. Him, you couldn't help but. He had a habit of prowling around town, talking to folks at all hours of the day and night. Trying to get in touch with Lost Hope's past, he said. It's a wonder he didn't get himself shot."

"Does anyone specific come to mind—somebody who might have a serious grudge against him?"

"Only half the town."

"A serious enough grudge that the person would've recently started a campaign of harassment?"

One corner of the deputy's mouth twitched; my question had touched a memory—or a nerve. "I can't name names, Ms. McCone. Wouldn't be right, certainly wouldn't give you the whole picture. In my job you can't help but hear gossip, but you never hear all of the story. Folks're leery of letting the sheriff's deputy in on things they wouldn't tell their best friends. I make a practice of not repeating what I do hear."

I couldn't fault him for that. "Well, I guess that about covers it. Do I have your okay to look into the history of the Lost Hope turnaround? Talk with some of the citizens who were involved?"

He grinned wryly. "Nice way to put it—makes you sound like a researcher for the state historical society."

"The turnaround *is* history, Deputy."

"Yeah. I just hope it stays that way."

"Meaning?"

He shook his head and got to his feet. "No hidden meaning, Ms. McCone, just a bad feeling I've had lately. Tell you the truth, I'm kind of twitchy tonight. Maybe it's that wind that's building up on the flatlands to the south. Whatever, I'm going to be glad when my shift's over and I can go get me a beer."

"When's that?"

"Midnight. You got any more questions, or want to stand me to a round, I'll be at Joker's on West Street. In the meantime, ask all the questions you want of our illustrious citizenry."

* * *

It was close to ten when I wedged the Land Rover into a parking space across from the Native American Crafts Outlet. One glance told me that the shop was closed. I thought of Marty McNear's words: "No moneymaking enterprise in Lost Hope ever closes early." By that I assumed he meant drinking and gaming establishments, which as a rule operate around the clock in Nevada, but the shops on either side of Brenda Walker's were still open and doing a fair business. I crossed the street and checked the hours on the card posted in the window: eleven to eleven.

The mule-team hayride stand was only a few yards away. A driver in western wear slumped on the wagon box, smoking a cigar. I went over and asked him if he knew Brenda Walker. He nodded, exhaling and appraising me through the smoke.

"How come she's closed early?" I asked.

He glanced at the darkened shop and shrugged.

"Did you see her leave?"

He just looked at me, dragging heavily on the cigar.

I moved closer to the wagon, took a five-dollar bill from my bag, and extended it to him. "When did she leave?"

He looked down at the bill and scowled.

I put another five on top of it.

The driver took them. "Fifteen minutes ago."

"Going which way?"

He averted his eyes.

I put my foot on the wagon's bottom step. "You know, I just spent some time with Deputy Chuck Westerkamp. He tells me this is a greedy little town."

The man's eyes flicked toward me.

"Was Brenda Walker alone?" I asked. "With someone?"

". . . Alone."

"And?"

"Going home, I guess."

"Where does she live?"

He gestured to his right.

"What's the address?"

Now he looked at me, eyes glittering hotly. "Yellow house on the corner of Sixth and B Streets."

"Thank you." I began walking back toward the Land Rover. The wagon driver spat on the sidewalk, narrowly missing my feet. "Greedy little town, my ass!" he called.

*　　*　　*

The intersection of Sixth and B Streets was halfway up the slope on the western side of town. The pavement there was narrow and potholed, crumbling away at its edges; most of the streets were little more than alleys bordered by high fences. Behind them stood a mix of old wood-frame cottages, newer prefabs, and mobile homes. Their dirt yards contained cactus gardens, assortments of junk, and hostile-sounding dogs.

Brenda Walker's yellow house looked better kept up than most of its neighbors. It stood back from the corner, tucked in among tall yucca trees; the trees' spindly trunks swayed in the wind, the motion of their leaves setting shadows to dancing over the pale walls. As I pulled the Land Rover to a stop at the opposite corner, I saw Walker moving back and forth past the lighted front window. She was pacing and talking on a cordless phone; her left hand gestured emphatically, and several times she raked her fingers through her short gray hair. After a few minutes she hung up, walked to the window, and jerked the draperies closed. Then the lights behind them went out.

I slouched behind the wheel, peering at Walker's front door. In seconds it opened and she hurried out, clad in a down jacket. She climbed into a blue Ford pickup that sat in her yard; its engine roared, its headlights flared, and she turned around, heading uphill. I gave her a little lead, then started the Land Rover and followed without lights for a few blocks. When a third vehicle came out of a side street, its brights blinding, I used the opportunity to switch on my own lights.

Walker drove at a steady twenty-five through increasingly shabby houses and trailers to an unpaved road that climbed steeply in switchbacks. Once we were in open country, I dropped back some. The pickup crested the hill, and its taillights disappeared; I sped up and cut to parking lights at the top. On the other side, the road descended through rocks and sagebrush. The pickup was already far below, where a glow backlit a thick stand of brush. The truck stopped next to the brush, its headlights went out, and Walker jumped down and disappeared into the darkness.

I coasted down the road until I found a place to pull off behind a clump of greasewood. There I left the Land Rover and continued on foot, the full moon lighting my way. When I reached Walker's pickup I skirted the stand of vegetation— more greasewood, gone wild and rangy, with sage and yuccas mixed in—until I found a flat outcropping. Crept onto it, keeping low, and peered over its edge.

Below lay a wide rock-strewn wash. At one end, where it backed up into a box canyon, the lights that I'd glimpsed from above glittered in a multitude of colors and shapes, refracted at a thousand angles. Crystal, amber, green, and brown formed a disorderly kaleidoscopic pattern. Among them chaotically fragmented shadows moved: an elongated one to the right, a smaller one to the left. The shadows seemed to fall to pieces and disappear, then regroup themselves.

I squeezed my eyes shut, opened them. Still could make no sense of the crazy sight in the wash below me. I moved my gaze to the periphery of the pattern and concentrated on its outlines. After a moment the shape of a house emerged against

157

the surrounding darkness. But when I glanced back at its center I lost all sense of form and again was sucked into the fractured light and fragmented shadows.

After a moment I slid off the outcropping and down the rocky slope. Now I could make out a peaked roofline; corners took on definition. At the bottom of the incline I came to a low stone wall. Peered over it, steadying myself with one hand. My fingers touched something smooth and polished embedded among the stones. I looked down and made out a circle of glass, the bottom of a bottle. Feeling around, I found dozens more, held together by stones and mortar.

I looked at the house again; at this distance the varicolored lights appeared circular—some large, others quite small. The house's walls seemed to be constructed of more bottles and mortar, the bottoms of the bottles turned outward, as if to form lenses. They trapped the light from within, refracted it, distorted whatever moved behind them.

What kind of maniac had created such a structure, here at the bottom of an isolated wash in the desert?

The shadows inside began to move again. After a moment I heard a door open and the sound of voices—a woman's and a man's, their words indistinguishable. A short figure that I assumed was Walker appeared at the left side of the house and hurried uphill toward the pickup. As the truck's engine caught, I watched the taller shadow cross behind the rows of bottles.

The pickup toiled up the hill, the sound of its engine gradually fading. The night grew very still. No one moved inside the bottle house now, and after a bit the refracted lights began to go out. I remained where I was awhile longer, then crept uphill to the Land Rover.

* * *

The tavern called Joker's stood on a short commercial block that paralleled Main Street—a block that gave a fair indication of how the rank-and-file citizens of Lost Hope lived. The bar was sandwiched between a small offset-printing shop and an auto-parts store, across from a tiny branch of the county library. Unprepossessing on the outside, it was more so on the inside: just a row of wooden booths and some tables, with a bar on the left and a pool table at the rear. The table was in use, and a few of the booths were occupied; the jukebox played a dirge about deception and depravity, like the box in every such tavern where I'd ever set foot.

Deputy Chuck Westerkamp hunched on a stool midway down the bar, apart from his fellow drinkers, hands limp around a nearly empty mug of beer. From the droop of his head and the sag of his shoulders, I gathered he wasn't enjoying his after-shift brew as much as he'd anticipated. He perked up some, though, when I slipped onto the stool next to his.

"So you decided to stand me to a round after all."

I nodded and held up two fingers to the bartender.

"Been out asking your questions?"

"Damned few of them, considering I've already paid ten bucks for information."

"Told you it's a greedy town."

The bartender set two mugs in front of us and took away the bills I placed on the plank. Westerkamp drained what was left in his mug, pushed it aside, and reached for the fresh one. "Who relieved you of the ten-spot?"

"Cigar-smoking hayride-wagon driver with shifty eyes."

"Robbie, my sister's boy. The little shit."

That explained the driver's reaction to my mention of Westerkamp; when you're the nephew of the sheriff's deputy, you watch your step—but you don't necessarily like it. "You're a native?" I asked.

"Lived here damn near all my life. My daddy came out from Missouri as soon as the news of the silver strikes traveled back there. He never found silver, but he opened a saloon, which in those days was just as good. Daddy married late, was dead by the time I was grown. I got out for a while—Korea—and then I was a cop in Reno, but I came back when my mama got sick. Then . . . I don't know." He shrugged, his shoulders frail under his uniform shirt. "The years just went by. Couple more and I'll retire."

"And do what?"

He looked bleakly at me. "Tell you the truth, I don't know. Find some way to pass the time, I guess."

The years just went by. Like Westerkamp, maybe someday I'd look back over decades of wasted years. Here it was, my thirty-ninth birthday; tonight I should have been with Hy at Zelda's, drinking champagne and dancing to a—probably—egregiously bad country-and-western band and later going home to make love. Instead I was holding down a stool in a decrepit desert tavern, drinking watery-tasting beer and chatting up a melancholy lawman. Good God, was this going to be my *life?*

I'd asked myself the same question while lying alone in bed at Moonshine Cottage the night before the explosion; now it took on greater meaning. I glanced at myself in the streaky mirror behind the bar, saw the furrow between my brows, the quizzical and somewhat alarmed expression in my eyes.

On the one hand, it wasn't such a bad life: I answered to no one; I went where events took me; if I failed, I had only myself to blame. But on the other hand, it had its drawbacks: long stretches of loneliness, downright boredom, and—as I'd repeatedly found out—danger.

The thought of danger reminded me why I was here. This was no routine investigation; I'd come to the desert because I was bent on finding the bastard who'd killed Anna—who'd actually meant to kill me. Revenge? Yes. My lifelong obsession with getting at the truth? That, too. It had always ruled me, always would. And if that meant my life would consist of nights like this, so be it.

I sat up straighter, raised my mug to my mirrored image in a happy-birthday salute, and drank. Then, feeling a little silly, I glanced at Westerkamp to see if he'd noticed. The deputy still slouched over the bar, contemplating his beer in silence. From the jukebox my brother-in-law's voice began complaining about the shadows in the house where love once lived. I blocked Ricky out and said, "I came across something curious tonight."

Westerkamp raised an eyebrow and waited.

"A house built out of bottles, down in a wash to the west of town."

"Leon Deck's place." He nodded. "What the hell were you doing way out there?"

"Following Brenda Walker." Briefly I explained. "Who's Leon Deck?"

"Lord knows. Artist of some kind. Showed up here four, five years ago. Started going through everybody's trash for bottles and built that damn thing. Given where he put it at the bottom of the wash, we all figured he'd get flooded out and go away, maybe even drown in a flash flood. But he's still there, and folks've gotten used to him."

"You say he's an artist?"

"Who else would build something like that? Don't know if he actually works at it, but he pays his bills. Stays out there most of the time, only comes to town for groceries and his mail."

"Is he a friend of Brenda Walker?"

Westerkamp thought. "Doubtful."

"What about T. J. Gordon? Did they ever have dealings?"

"Not that I heard of, but the way Gordon wandered all over the place, he might've run across Leon."

"So what do you suppose Walker's visit to Deck was about?"

The deputy regarded me, eyes as bleak as when he'd talked about retiring. "Damned if I know, but that bad feeling I've been having lately is coming on strong."

Twelve

A red-tailed hawk circled above me, its wings sketching perfect arcs against the desert sky. The light had a filtered quality at nine in the morning; the crunch and clatter of stones beneath my feet as I made my way along the wash to the bottle house shattered a heavy silence. Although the day promised to warm quickly, I could feel and smell autumn in the air. Autumn, and then a hard, cold winter.

I was dressed in hiking clothes and had my old Nikkormat slung around my neck. I'd brought the camera from home in order to take some color shots of Tufa Lake, in hope of getting a good enough one to enlarge and hang in my front hall. Now I was using it as I often did: to appear a harmless tourist while actually on a surveillance. When I was some twenty yards from the bottle house I stopped, removed the lens cap, and sighted on the peculiar structure.

By the light of day it looked wildly eccentric: rough mortar and odd-sized stones holding the circles of glass in their random

163

arrangement. The peaked roof was of overlapping sheets of corrugated metal; a rusted stove chimney leaned lopsidedly. The door, which faced toward me, had been fashioned of clumsily nailed planks and crosspieces. The low stone wall surrounded the house, and protruding from the ground behind it were strangely shaped masses of the same materials as the house—free-form sculptures, perhaps. I pressed the shutter a few times and resumed walking. When I reached the wall I leaned over it and snapped one last shot of the largest of the sculptures.

Sounds came from inside the house now: a wordless high-pitched singing. Some classical melody that I knew but couldn't put a name to. The door opened and the singing grew louder, then cut off abruptly as a man peered out at me. He was so tall that he had to stoop to avoid hitting his head. His tank top and shorts revealed spindly legs and arms; dark matted curls fell well below his shoulder blades. He squinted into the sunlight, frowning.

"Mr. Deck?" I called. "Leon Deck?"

After an initial hesitation he nodded.

"I'd like to talk with you about your house. May I come inside?"

He nodded again.

There was no opening in the wall, so I climbed over it. When I got closer to Deck I caught sight of his eyes: dark and curiously clouded. Drugs, I thought, if not now, too many at some point in his life.

Deck continued to lean in the doorway, his vague eyes on my face. I could smell him now: not so much rank as musty, as if he needed an airing. After a moment he turned and motioned for me to follow him inside. Confusion and delayed reactions, more evidence of drug-induced damage.

Once inside I felt as if I'd sunk to the bottom of a dirty fishbowl. Murky green and brown light shot by occasional crystalline flashes surrounded me. A flickering oil lamp sat on a makeshift table in the middle of the long room. I looked around, saw other furnishings that looked to be castoffs: a sprung armchair bleeding its stuffing; a scarred bureau with two missing drawers; a filthy and torn mattress with a ragged sleeping bag thrown over it. In one corner hulked a grease-encrusted woodstove; dirty pans and dishes sat on top of it. No electrical or phone service out here; no running water, either, although as I'd driven in, I'd spotted a clump of tamarisk trees that indicated a spring.

Leon Deck had not yet spoken. He turned the flame of the oil lamp higher, went to the armchair, and sat. I spotted a broken-down wicker stool and moved it closer. As I sat, Deck watched me incuriously.

I said, "I'm interested in your house, Mr. Deck. How long did it take you to build it?"

It was a moment before he spoke. Then, in a voice as high-pitched as his singing, he said, "The bottoms of the bottles? They let in the light. The necks? They keep everything else out."

It wasn't exactly an answer, but at least he'd said something. "You mean they keep out the cold? The heat?"

He frowned, as if he found the question exceedingly stupid. "I see things, you know."

"Yes?"

"They must not be allowed inside."

"What musn't?"

"Warping and distortion."

"What about it?"

"It weakens their power."

"Whose power?"

"I see things."

"Mr. Deck—"

"I have secrets, you know." Now his eyes were clearer, as if some relay switch in his consciousness had kicked in. They gleamed slyly.

165

"What kinds of secrets?" I asked.

He shook his head, a smile revealing gapped and broken teeth. "It is said that a thief in red will come to steal my secrets."

"Who says that?"

He just kept smiling.

"Who says—"

"I have secrets."

"Mr. Deck—"

"I know who you are, you know."

"And who am I?"

"The thief in red."

I glanced down to assure myself that I actually was wearing my tan T-shirt. The conversation—if it could be called that— threatened to make me as loony as Leon Deck.

"It is said that a thief in red will come."

"I'm not wearing red."

"Today."

"I'm not a thief."

"To steal them."

"Mr. Deck, I don't want to steal—"

"I am to guard against her."

"I'm not here to—"

"You can't have them!" He jumped up, agitated now, his breath becoming ragged.

I stood quickly, braced against an attack. Deck's hands were fisted; he was close to hyperventilating. "Keep your secrets, Mr. Deck," I said. "Keep them."

The words failed to calm him. He came toward me, fists raised. I sidestepped and backed toward the door.

"You'll come again," he panted. "In the night. Wearing red. For my secrets."

I pushed the door open, stepped outside. Leon Deck stopped a few feet away.

"Food for the coyotes," he said.

"What?"

"I see things, you know."

The crazy conversational loop was beginning again. "*What* do you see?"

"I see things."

"What do you see?"

"I see the coyotes feeding on the August man's flesh and bones."

"Who—"

Deck shut the door. From behind it I could hear him panting.

*   *   *

As I drove back to town I went over Deck's ramblings again and again. Repeated them aloud, as if sound could impart meaning. And found that there *was* meaning of a sort—once I broke his crazy code and placed the information beside what facts I already knew.

Back at the hotel I hurried up to my room and checked my notes on the turnaround. It had been completed and Suits had left here in September of last year. I put the notes in my bag, then went downstairs and asked at the desk for Marty McNear. The clerk directed me to the lounge, where I could see the hotel owner going over some invoices with the bartender. He poured me a cup of coffee, and I sat down at the same table we'd occupied the night before to wait till he finished.

There were plenty of questions I could ask McNear, but as I waited I decided to move cautiously. Although the hotelier had seemed candid, he'd also admitted to having read my faxes, and I had only his word that he'd been fond of the Gordons. Maybe he'd steered me to Brenda Walker because he knew she wouldn't talk with me; maybe he was the one she'd been on the phone with before she paid her visit to Leon Deck. Far-fetched reasoning? Probably. A touch of paranoia? Sure. Even so, I'd limit my questions.

When McNear joined me, I asked him only one thing. "Do you recall exactly when Anna Gordon visited her husband?"

He thought, shook his head. "Shortly before he left here."

"Would your guest register show the dates?"

"No. We weren't in operation yet, so neither she nor T.J. had to register."

"Was it in August, perhaps? September?"

"August, I think. By the way, how'd you get on with Brenda Walker?"

"I didn't."

"Oh?"

"She refused to talk with me and sent me directly to Deputy Westerkamp."

It didn't seem to surprise him. "What'd Westerkamp tell you?"

"Not much, just gave me permission to investigate in his jurisdiction."

McNear nodded, and then we ran out of conversation. I thanked him and went upstairs to call for an appointment with Lost Hope's town manager, Boyd Briggs. Briggs, an urban administrator who had been hired to ensure that Suits's master plan didn't go haywire, could see me in half an hour.

*   *   *

The swamp cooler on the roof above Byron Briggs's office rattled and burbled. Briggs—a short, chubby, bald man with a funny nasal voice, who was a dead ringer for the cartoon character Elmer Fudd—kept glancing nervously at the ceiling. Suits's files had said that he was one of the most talented city managers in the western states, and so far his responses to my preliminary questions about the turnaround had exhibited a keen intelligence, but I couldn't get past the Fudd image and kept smiling inappropriately.

". . . remained stable for a year now. In another year I'll be out of here."

I forced my attention back to what he was saying. "What about resentment among the townspeople who opposed the turnaround?"

"That's been tempered by steady paychecks."

"There must be some people who haven't benefited."

"Well, of course, every town has its disaffected citizens, but they're usually all talk and no action. I doubt any of ours could conceive an intricate plan of harassment such as you describe."

"Mr. Gordon gave me the names of three people who created serious disturbances during the turnaround." I consulted my notes and read them off to him. "Have any of them left town in the past few months?"

"Not to my knowledge. The first's too busy running his Burger King franchise; the second's campaigning for county office; the third's applied for liquor and gaming licenses."

"Okay, I'd like to return to a year ago last August. Mr. Gordon's wife came to visit."

He nodded. "Charming woman. A great loss—"

"Yes. She was here for two weeks?"

"Two and a half, actually. She'd planned to stay until Mr. Gordon was ready to leave for California, but she went home suddenly."

"Why?"

"I wasn't informed as to her reasons. She was here one day, and the next she was flying out on that Learjet of his."

"Was there some sort of trouble?"

"Not that I'm aware of."

"Do you recall the exact date of her departure?"

". . . No, but . . ." He pressed a button on his intercom; when his secretary answered he asked, "Will you check your files and see on what date last August Nevada Bell completed their installation of the new system?" To me he added, "I remember because Mr. Gordon needed to sign off on it, and he was out at the landing strip."

Briggs held the line for a moment, eyes dramatically raised toward the roof, where the swamp cooler had begun to wheeze and gargle. "August twenty-sixth? Thanks." He looked at me and repeated, "August twenty-sixth was the day she left."

*   *   *

The night before, I'd noticed a little branch library across the street from Joker's tavern. I drove over there and asked about the local newspaper. The town had none, the librarian told me, only a weekly ad sheet aimed at tourists. The sheriff's calls? They were printed in the Tonopah paper. I checked their microfilms for the dates surrounding August 26 of the previous year and found an interesting item.

A woman had phoned the Lost Hope substation, claiming that a fugitive from justice who had been featured on a recent edition of *Unsolved Mysteries* was staying at the Aces and Eights Motel. Deputies investigated, but the man had apparently left town without paying his bill.

I suspected who the woman caller was.

*   *   *

When I finally located Deputy Chuck Westerkamp at quarter to two, he was doing his laundry. He sat in a molded plastic chair at an establishment called Suds 'n' Duds, staring morosely at his clothes as they flopped in the dryer. I'd tracked him down through his neighbor, who said she'd seen him walking along the street "with a full pillowcase slung over his shoulder like a goddamn Santa Claus." Westerkamp didn't act particularly surprised to see me, just nodded and patted the chair next to his.

"You do get around," he said mildly.

I sat. "You wouldn't believe the half of it."

"Probably not. What d'you need?"

"On August twenty-sixth of last year someone phoned in a

tip to your substation about a fugitive staying at the Aces and Eights Motel. That would have been Brenda Walker?"

"Yeah. We followed up, went to the Aces. He'd cleared out—sort of. Stuff was still there, so was his old van. Never did find him, though we searched real good."

"The van—"

"Was stolen in Colorado. No fingerprints—wiped clean. So was his motel room."

"Odd. And the personal stuff?"

"Is in our property room."

"May I see it?"

"Why?"

I hesitated.

Westerkamp's pale eyes regarded me with more than usual interest. He waited.

I felt the same wariness as with Marty McNear. Westerkamp was a law officer, but I'd known enough crooked cops to realize that law-enforcement powers didn't necessarily go hand in hand with a law-abiding attitude.

"Okay, Ms. McCone," he finally said. "Neither of us has taken the full measure of the other, but I sense you've been straight with me, and I hope you feel the same about my dealings with you. So—supposing I let you look at the stuff in my property room, and supposing it means something to you. What're you gonna do then?"

Good question.

"You gonna tell me what it means, or you gonna leave me guessing?"

If what I suspected was true, ethically I'd be bound to tell him. "I won't leave you guessing."

"Then I'll see you at the substation when I come on shift at four."

I looked impatiently at my watch.

"That's only two hours, give or take a minute," he said. "I'm sure you'll find some way to amuse yourself in the meantime."

* * *

I decided to pass the time by finishing up the roll of film in my Nikkormat. I'd left my big camera bag and assorted lenses—bought back in the days when I'd fancied myself a budding professional photographer—at home and carried only the camera body itself, outfitted with a 28-millimeter wide-angle lens. The wide-angle suggested that I should try some panoramic shots of the town, so I drove into the hills on the road that led to Leon Deck's place.

As I drove, I thought back to the time when I'd taken my photography seriously. I'd enrolled in every course I could fit into my college schedule and, later on, in others at the U.C. Extension campus in the city; I'd toiled in the darkroom for what must have added up to years. And when I finally emerged for the last time from the chemical fumes and the glow of the safelight, I'd been forced to admit that my efforts were merely competent. Competent, and somewhat trite.

After that disappointment I put the Nikkormat away for a while, then brought it out to use in my surveillances. But one day, while photographing a kayaking insurance-company defrauder from a nearby sailboat, I realized that handling the camera still gave me a great deal of pleasure. Now, freed from my self-imposed standards of excellence, I produced commercially processed color photos that pleased me, and damned if they weren't getting better and better. Soon the cracked walls of my front hallway would be covered with enlargements, and they would eventually spill over onto the walls of my sitting room.

I reached a good vantage point, got out of the Land Rover, and set the camera on its hood. Removed the lens cap, adjusted the f-stop and shutter speed. The light meter needle behaved strangely—probably it needed a new battery. I focused, studied what was in the frame, then pressed the shutter.

That would be a good shot; sometimes you just could tell. But given the erratic behavior of the light meter, shouldn't I take one more? I altered the speed, thumbed the film-advance lever—

Something wrong here.

I pressed the shutter, thumbed the lever again. No resistance —slack, actually. As if there were no film in the camera . . .

I repeated the process, tried to rewind the film. Still slack. Picked up the camera and pressed the catch to open its back. Empty. Someone had removed the film containing the shots I'd taken that morning at the bottle house.

When? I thought back to where the Nikkormat had been since I'd taken those pictures. Around my neck as I talked with Leon Deck. Around my neck as I walked back to the Land Rover. Under the driver's seat the rest of the time while I was inside the hotel, the town hall, the library, and the Suds 'n' Duds.

Had I locked the Rover? Hard to say. Locking a car was a reflex action, conditioned by many years of city living. But the failure to perform such actions often went unnoticed.

But who would have stolen my film? And why?

Impossible to say. Yet, anyway.

*　　*　　*

There was only one quick-service photo developer listed in the town directory, on Main Street not far from my hotel. The young woman behind the counter confirmed that someone had brought in a partially exposed roll of 35-millimeter color film containing pictures of Leon Deck's bottle house that day, but when I asked for the customer's name, she refused to give it. A five-dollar bill undermined her business ethics considerably; the customer, she told me, was Mrs. Walker, who owned the Native American Crafts Outlet. She'd brought the film in around eleven and had picked it up a little over an hour ago.

Prior to eleven I'd been in the hotel, and the Land Rover had been in the custody of valet parking.

*   *   *

"Sure, I let her into your Rover," the parking attendant said sullenly. "Mr. McNear told me to."

I whirled around, leaving him openmouthed in the fenced lot back of the hotel, and went inside to see his boss. At first the desk clerk told me McNear wasn't available, but when I said—loudly—that I wanted to talk with him about the theft of personal property from my vehicle while it was in valet parking, he summoned the hotelier from his office. McNear looked nervously at two other guests who were watching with interest, and ushered me into the room behind the reception desk.

Without offering me a chair he asked, "Now, Ms. McCone, what is this?"

"You tell me. I've already spoken with your parking attendant; he says you okayed letting Brenda Walker into my Land Rover. She took a partly exposed roll of film from my camera."

McNear turned away, looked out the window at the parking lot. "Why would she do that?"

"The film contained pictures of Leon Deck's bottle house; I think she saw me taking them. But you know this."

McNear's posture had stiffened at my mention of Deck. "No, I don't."

"Then what excuse did Walker give you for wanting to get into my vehicle?"

He was silent for a moment, fingering the cord of the raised venetian blinds. "Did it ever occur to you that the attendant's lying?"

"Yes, but only for a moment. The kid doesn't look dumb enough to try to shift the blame onto his boss."

McNear sighed and faced me. "All right. Brenda suspected

you'd been to the bottle house, and she wanted the film to confirm that."

"Bull. In order to know about the camera, she would have needed to see me using it out there."

He shrugged. "All I know is what she told me."

"I think you know a good bit more. Why did she have to confirm that I'd been there?"

"She was worried about Leon."

"What's he to her?"

McNear looked uncomfortable. "This won't go any further?"

"That depends on what it is."

"Well . . . Leon's Brenda's brother. Half brother, actually. You've seen him?"

I nodded.

"Then you know. He's a badly damaged man. Came out here to be near her after many years in an institution back in the Midwest. Brenda's very protective of him."

"Then why doesn't she acknowledge him? Have him live with her?"

"Leon's like a wild animal; he can't be domesticated. He's better off out there with his bottles and his strange dreams. As for Brenda not acknowledging him"—he shrugged again—"I suppose she's ashamed. Fancies herself a pillar of the community and doesn't want people to know she's got a crazy ex-addict brother. But she looks out for him."

I thought for a moment. It still didn't explain why Walker had wanted my roll of film. She knew I'd been out there and talked with Leon. So why take the film?

Unless there was something in that wash that she was afraid might show up in the photographs . . .

* * *

The crafts outlet was closed again. I barely slowed as I drove past it, just kept going and turned uphill toward Walker's house. No pickup in the yard there, no answer to my repeated knocks. I stepped off the porch and tried the strategy I'd earlier used to locate Deputy Westerkamp: ask a neighbor.

"Brenda?" the pleasant-faced woman who was hanging wash on her line said. "Saw her a while ago loading her backpack and sleeping bag into her pickup. She does that sometimes— just takes off into the desert for a few days. Says she's an old desert rat at heart."

"Where would she go?"

The woman made a wide gesture with the hand that held a clothespin. "That's a big desert out there, honey. Brenda never did mention any one place."

* * *

The door of the bottle house stood open. I climbed over the wall, calling Deck's name.

No reply, just the creak of the door moving in a light breeze.

I stepped inside, allowed my eyes to get accustomed to the murky light. The room was empty, the oil lamp turned off. Deck's sleeping bag no longer lay across the tattered mattress.

Coincidence that he'd decided to take off at the same time as his half sister? Hardly.

On my way down the wash to the Land Rover, I studied the surrounding terrain, trying to see anything that would have made my undeveloped photographs damaging to Deck or Walker. But it just looked like any other rain-and-flood-sculpted gully—wider than most but essentially uninteresting and barren.

Nevertheless, I suspected it wasn't nearly as uninteresting as it seemed.

* * *

The property room of the sheriff's substation was a walk-in closet off Westerkamp's office. The deputy went inside, thumped around, cursed some, and emerged red-faced and dusty with a cardboard file box. He dumped its contents uncer-emoniously on his desk.

Small blue travel bag with a United Airlines logo. Contents: three changes of underwear, two T-shirts, one pair of jeans, two pair of socks, toiletries; two paperback westerns; half a six-pack of Coors, two packs of Winstons, unused book of matches from a restaurant in Ely, Nevada; handful of tokens for free drinks from a casino in the same town, Triple-A road map of the state, set of lockpicks. I held up one with a serpentine probe and looked questioningly at the deputy. He grinned and shrugged.

"No wallet or identification?" I asked.

"No."

"Keys to the stolen van?"

"No keys. It was towed to the county impound lot."

"No other keys?"

He shook his head.

"Was the personal property also wiped of prints?"

"There were a few partials. Not good enough to run through NCIC."

"How'd he pay for his room?"

"Cash for the first two nights. For the other two, Aces was glad to carry him."

"Not a class establishment, then."

"They're doing better now, thanks to your Mr. Gordon."

I picked up the paperbacks, thumbed through them; nothing tucked inside. Set them down and began examining the inside of the travel bag for hidden pockets. There weren't any, but I felt something slender caught beneath the bottom lining. I worked my fingers in there and pulled it free. It was a ballpoint pen; I looked at the printing on it: Keystone Steel Company, Monora, PA.

I stared at the words. Silver against black. They seemed to shimmer.

"Nobody saw him leave town?" I asked Westerkamp.

"Uh-uh."

"And the fugitive Walker saw on TV?"

"Was apprehended later on in South Carolina."

"Figures." I kept staring at the pen, rolling it between my thumb and forefinger.

"I see things, you know. . . . It is said that a thief in red will come to steal my secrets. . . . I am to guard against her. . . . I see the coyotes feeding on the August man's flesh and bones. . . ."

I looked up at Westerkamp: *"First word that comes to mind is 'greedy'. . . .* Nasty town as well. . . . That desert out there's been an unholy graveyard since the first vein of silver was uncovered. . . . some of them fairly fresh. . . ."

"Ms. McCone, you all right?"

Not really. Problem here, a big one. I could be hurting the person I set out to help.

"Ms. McCone?"

"I'm okay."

But I couldn't keep what I suspected to myself; I'd never been one to circumvent the law in matters like this.

"Then what—"

"Deputy, I think I know where you can find your missing man."

He raised an eyebrow.

"He's somewhere in that wash where Leon Deck built his bottle house. In one of those unholy graves you were telling me about."

178

Thirteen

"I hope you're right about this," Chuck Westerkamp said, watching two of his officers fan out along the wash in front of us. He was obviously thinking about budgetary constraints and overtime. I, on the other hand, had been worried about him making an illegal search of Leon Deck's property until he informed me that Deck was merely squatting on county land.

"Hope you're right," he said again.

"I'm right."

"Okay, this fellow comes out here from Pennsylvania looking to get revenge on Gordon for something that went on back there. Would a person really go to all that trouble just because of bad business dealings?"

"We don't know if his motive was business-related or personal. But, yes, I think in either case he would. Gordon calls the Keystone turnaround 'less than successful,' but I've read the files, and taking into account the human factor, I call it a disaster."

"All right—he gets here and what happens?"

We'd been over this at the substation, but I sensed it comforted him to rehash it. If a body turned up in the wash, this promised to be the biggest case of Westerkamp's career; if one didn't, he'd have to explain to his superiors why he'd pulled two men off their regular duties on only the word of an out-of-state private investigator with a bizarre theory.

I said, "There was some sort of confrontation, and the August man, as Deck calls him, was killed."

"By Gordon."

"We don't know that, either. It could have been Gordon"—God, how I hoped not!—"or one of his people or one of your townspeople with a vested interest in the turnaround. But whoever killed him, Brenda Walker got involved in disposing of the body."

"She probably thought she could confuse us with that tip about him being a fugitive; she thought we'd figure he'd skipped out because she'd made him, and not look real thoroughly. But burying him near her crazy brother's house? I'm not sure I buy that part of it, not with a whole big desert out there, and Brenda knowing it better than most of us."

"The farther the body was moved, the more risk was involved. With it here, she could keep an eye on the grave, make sure it wasn't disturbed."

Westerkamp shrugged, and we began walking toward the house. So far neither of his men had covered much ground or come across anything remotely resembling a grave. After a moment he said, "You don't think Leon buried the body?"

"He might have, although I doubt she'd trust him with a task like that. More likely he saw it being buried or found it afterward. The grave could have been disturbed by animals; he made that comment about the coyotes feeding on the August man's flesh and bones. But no matter how he knew, Brenda persuaded him to keep her secret. And last night after I went to her shop asking about the Gordons, she hurried out here to warn him against telling me."

"The thief in red." Westerkamp tugged at Anna's cape, which I'd put on against the late-afternoon chill.

"Right. There's something that bothers me, though: before Walker left her house last night, she made a phone call, looked fairly agitated while she was talking. To whom?"

"Well, if we find a body out here, we'll subpoena the phone-company records. *If* we fin ` ` body."

"We'll find it."

We reached Deck's low wall and stopped beside it. It was close to six by now; the light was fading fast down here in the wash; soon Westerkamp would have to abandon the search or bring in artificial illumination.

He folded his arms across his chest, looking at the bottle house. "What d'you suppose ever possessed him?"

"Deck? To build this house? Well, one of the things he told me is that the bottles let the light in but keep everything else out by warping and distorting it. I suppose by 'everything else' he could have meant evil."

"Evil spirits?" The deputy looked skeptical.

"Maybe. He's an ex-addict and probably paranoid. His fears don't have to be rational."

"Whose do? Me, I'm deathly afraid of getting peanut butter stuck to the roof of my mouth. All I've got to do is see a jar of Skippy and my palms start to sweat. Go figure."

"I used to be afraid of birds."

"How'd you get over it?"

"It just went away of its own accord." I propped one knee on the low wall, stared over it at the strange stone-and-bottle sculptures.

Westerkamp said, "You know, it strikes me as stupid of Brenda to take off that way. I mean, what could Deck really tell anybody? Who would believe him?"

"She panicked. There must've been something in the photos that I took out here that made her think I knew more than I really did." I thought back to the shots I'd snapped: two as I came along the wash, another one of that sculpture—

Damn!

"Deputy," I said then, "I think I know where the grave is."

*   *   *

The bottles glittered in the headlights of the two off-road vehicles that Westerkamp had had his men drive into the wash and position so their high beams focused on the sculpture. Static and occasional voices crackled from the radios—"I didn't copy that. . . ." "Sorry, eleven-four-four, what's your ETA for Tonopah?" Westerkamp and I leaned against his Jeep, watching the deputies pry the glass and stone apart with pickaxes. By the time they began digging up the ground underneath, it was full dark. By the time they uncovered the remains, the moon rode high.

One of the deputies climbed out of the hole and signaled to Westerkamp. "Wait here," he told me and went over there. He stood looking down into the grave for a moment, then came back, his face somber. "He's down there, all right, what's left of him. Must've been buried shallow at first, because it sure looks like the coyotes got to him." He reached into the Jeep and radioed in for the county medical examiner and crime-lab personnel, then—almost as an afterthought—put out a pickup order on Walker and Deck.

When he finished, I asked, "How long will it take your people to get here?"

"Half hour."

"You need me any longer?"

"For a statement later. Maybe by then we'll know who he is. Why?"

"I need to go back to my hotel and call my office."

"And your client?"

I shook my head. "I doubt I could reach him, but even if I could, I wouldn't. I realize you have to talk with him first."

Westerkamp studied my face, nodded. "Okay, go make your call. Come out to the substation when you're done. And Ms. McCone? Don't talk to anybody in town about this. Word'll get out soon enough—there're an awful lot of scanners in trucks and homes around here—and I don't want more of a crowd than we can handle."

* * *

Back at the hotel, I reviewed my options, made a quick decision, and placed a credit-card call to my house. The machine answered. I left a message for Mick, then dialed my office number. Was surprised when my nephew's voice said, "McCone Investigations."

"Why're you there so late?"

"Shar, where are you? I tried calling Hy's, but nobody was home."

"I'm in Nevada. Why're you still at the office?"

"I'm working on something. Are you in Lost Hope?"

"Yes. What're you working on?"

"The Blessing trace."

"I thought I told you to give up on it."

"You did, but things've been slow here and I got bored, so I started tinkering. And I've got something. Yesterday afternoon I borrowed Rae's car and drove down to Pacifica. You know that old van the Blessings ditched in their yard?"

"What about it?"

"Well, they took the plates off it, but I copied down the VIN, just in case the registration was current. Ran it by the DMV, and they gave me a name."

"A name's all they're allowed to give out, and it's not much to go on."

"This one was: Enid Tomchuck. Unusual. So I started thinking, what if this Enid Tomchuck was Sid Blessing's wife? I called that neighbor lady you talked to back in August, and she said, yes, Mrs. Blessing's first name was Enid. Now, last summer when you asked me to try to trace those people, I ran a Dataquick statewide real-estate search and came up with nothing. But I couldn't get out of my head what the neighbor woman told you about the family coming into some money. I mean, what's the first thing most people do when that happens? They buy a house. But if they got the money illegally, they're not going to want to call attention to themselves, are they? So I ran another search, on Enid this time, and found out she bought a house in Modesto on August fifth."

Right around the time the harassment of Suits began, and a few weeks before Moonshine House blew up. Had the money Sid Blessing came into been a down payment on those acts?

Mick went on, "There wasn't any phone number on the property detail, and when I called Information they said it was unlisted. But I ran Tomchuck's name through Mortgage Leads and got it. Then I called and asked for Sid."

"And?"

"He's dead. Got killed by a hit-and-run driver on September tenth."

Two weeks after the explosion. "Where?"

"In Modesto. You know how those fast-growing valley towns are? One minute you're in tracts, the next you're in an orchard? Well, Blessing was found by a construction crew that was framing in some houses in this half-built tract at the edge of town. Very isolated place. He was . . . kind of squashed in the street. The autopsy showed he was run over late the night before."

"Mick, you seem to know a lot about the accident."

Silence.

"Mick?"

"Okay, I borrowed Rae's car again this morning and drove out there. The wife wouldn't talk to me, but I got some information from the cops who're assigned to the case."

"You're not licensed to—"

"I didn't represent myself as a licensed P.I. But the cops were impressed that I'm working under your license; the one in charge had read that newspaper story about you opening the agency."

"How did you convince them you were working for me?"

". . . Well, last week, you know? I, um, took the liberty of having some business cards printed up."

"McCone Investigations cards with *your* name on them?"

"Uh, right."

"Who paid for them?"

". . . McCone Investigations. But listen to this, Shar!"

"I'm all ears," I said sarcastically.

He ignored my tone. "I gave the cops a story about working a missing-heir case and needing to get in touch with Blessing's wife. And while the one was looking up the phone number in the file, I sneaked a glance at it and got Sid's Social Security number."

"Mick, do not use that number to request anything we can't legally access!"

Silence again.

"And just forget what it says in *The Hacker's Handbook*."

When he spoke, his voice was pained. "Do you want to hear the rest of this or not?"

Curiosity got the better of me. "All right, what's the rest?"

"Through various means, I found out that Sid was once in the service. Army."

"Various means?"

"Mostly legal."

"Mostly?"

"Mostly."

I sighed. "Okay, what's done is done. Send a Form One-eighty to the National Personnel Records Center—"

"I already faxed it."

"Good work."

185

"Does this mean you're not too pissed at me?"

I hesitated, not wanting to send the wrong message. But he *had* done good work, mostly legal means or not. "I'm not *too* pissed at you. But, Mick, don't make any more unauthorized expenditures like the business cards, or I'll have to dock your pay."

"My pay? All I'm getting is room and board!"

"As of today you're on salary. Until I can hire a real assistant."

I hung up on his surprised exclamation, checked the directory listings for airlines, and called to find out about flights east from Las Vegas. Then I dialed Noah Romanchek's number. The attorney told me that as far as he knew, Suits was still at Moonshine Cottage.

"We're about to pack it in at GGL and turn the operation back to Kirk Cameron," he added. "No point in going on without T.J. Carole Lattimer was released from the hospital and went back to Chicago last night."

"How is she?"

"Fair. The surgery was a success, and psychologically she feels somewhat better now that the man who mugged her is behind bars."

"When did they pick him up? Who is he?"

"Oakland P.D. picked him up on an unrelated charge yesterday. He's a maintenance worker at one of the buildings near the Convention Center. Confessed to a series of muggings in the area, and insists he's never heard of T. J. Gordon or Golden Gate Lines. As far as anyone can tell, it's the truth."

"Random violence, then. Does T.J. know about this?"

"Not yet."

"He should."

"I'm not sure he'd care. And frankly I've given up on trying to get through to him."

"Noah, would you try one more time? I would, but I'm out of town right now. I'll need to talk with him when I get back, though, and some other people want to contact him as well. Will you go up to Bootlegger's Cove and ask him to come back to San Francisco?"

"It sounds important."

"It is."

Romanchek waited for me to elaborate. When he realized I wasn't going to, he said, "All right, I'll get hold of Josh and fly up tomorrow."

"Thanks. By the way, how's Josh doing?" I recalled the pilot's tears and anger at the ruins of Moonshine House when he'd ferried me to the cove, and his withdrawn silence on the trip back.

"Not very well. He was fond of Anna, of course, and her death hit him hard. He's camped out in T.J.'s condo at Bay Vista—the company okayed it, since his lease was up at the beginning of September on the place where he was living, and given the uncertainty of the situation, he didn't want to renegotiate it. But without Suits, Josh has got nothing to do, just rattles around there and makes an occasional run over to North Field to check on the aircraft."

"Then maybe it'll do him good to take you up to the cove."

"Maybe." Romanchek didn't sound too sanguine.

I said good-bye to the attorney, packed, checked out of the hotel, and headed for the sheriff's substation.

* * *

No identification had been found with the August man's remains, and Westerkamp was prematurely discouraged. He would, he told me, query Monora, Pennsylvania, as well as surrounding jurisdictions for reports of missing persons; if any seemed probable matches, they'd try to get an I.D. through dental charts. But that was a long shot, and the deputy knew it. His investigation was stalled until he could send someone to question Suits and his associates.

I made my statement and gave him the information on

Suits's whereabouts, hoping Romanchek would be able to bring our mutual client back to the city, where he could monitor the official questioning. Then I said, "You know, if I were to go to Monora, I might be able to help you."

Westerkamp smiled cynically. "More historical research?"

"Well, look what I turned up here."

"Yeah, a case that's probably going to plague me in my declining years."

"Not necessarily. And you've got to admit, it'd be a lot more cost-effective for you if I went there on my client's money than if you had to send somebody or go yourself."

He shrugged. "You want to make the trip, I'm not gonna stop you." Then he scribbled on a scratch pad and passed the sheet across his desk to me. "That's the name of Monora's chief of police. I'll let them know you're coming."

I glanced at the paper. The chief was a woman, Nancy Koll. "Thanks."

"No, I thank you. Heading out now?"

"If I hurry, I can catch a red-eye east from Vegas."

"Well, Godspeed."

For a long time as I drove south across the dark desert I could see the lights of Lost Hope in my rearview mirror.

*   *   *

I just made the last red-eye to Chicago. It would put me into O'Hare with forty minutes to spare before my connection to Pittsburgh. The flight was nearly empty; after we reached cruising altitude, I pulled a blanket and pillow from the overhead bin, raised the armrests of the adjacent seats, and curled up to sleep.

For about an hour I dozed, but then I came wide awake. After shifting around for a while, trying to get comfortable, I sat up again, propped the pillow between my head and the window, and willed the plane's vibrations to lull me. Finally I accepted the fact that I wasn't going to sleep any more and sat up straight. Stared fixedly at the black window and thought of Hy. By now he'd finished with his business in San Diego, might even be flying east himself. Briefly I fantasized about running into him at O'Hare, then pushed the thought from my mind. I'd never had that much luck.

At a little after eight in the morning I'd arrive in Chicago. Another time change, and I'd land in Pittsburgh before noon. Grab a rental car and a map, get some breakfast, and plan my route. Sleep for a few hours in a motel near the airport. And then I'd be off to Monora, down on the Monongahela River, halfway to the West Virginia line.

With every air mile, I was closer to learning the identity of Anna's killer. My would-be killer. He wasn't in Pennsylvania, though; I'd have to return to California to bring him down. But even as the distance between us lengthened, I was beginning to sense the outlines of his persona.

The jet engines thrummed as the plane sped across the continent toward the dawn that now streaked the sky. I watched the shifting light and shadow and felt a curious sense of inevitability. My client was a man out of my past; we'd reconnected, and it had almost proved fatal. Whatever set those events in motion had begun in Monora; now I was going there to uncover it. The sensation both discomfited and excited me. I'd always resisted the notion of fate, but never failed to respond to its pull.

Again, I decided, I would just let events unfold.

Part Three

Monora, Pennsylvania

Early October

Fourteen

The road paralleled the railway tracks that ran along the edge of the Monongahela. On the river a barge heaped with coal moved slowly north. To my right were steep hills covered with sagging wood-frame and brick houses, their walls blackened by soot. The late-afternoon light did nothing to relieve their dinginess; the only cheerful spots were big orange garbage bags with jack-o'-lantern faces crayoned on them, put out early for Halloween.

After a while the pavement jogged away from the river and climbed some. A small sign that said Monora appeared; the population figure had been painted out and not replaced. The road dipped down into a commercial section, its buildings soot-blackened like the houses on the hill above: Mellon Bank, Dutch Boy Paints, Rexall Drugs; defunct movie theater, McGlennon's Pub, U.S. Post Office; Steel City Pizza, state liquor store, defunct dress shop. Every third business, including the Monora Hotel and Frank's Department Store, was dead; the town had a curiously empty feel, in spite of it being only four-thirty on a Friday afternoon. Cars lined the curbs, but I saw no pedestrians except for a couple of cops crossing a side street from the police station to a doughnut shop.

I kept following the road past more boarded-up and abandoned buildings until it curved again and ran downhill toward the river. And there on a flat plain that bowed out into the Monongahela lay what I'd traveled thousands of miles to see.

The enormous shut-down steel mill stretched for nearly a mile. Huge corrugated metal buildings, corroded and stained red-orange. High catwalks and covered walkways spanning weed-choked railroad tracks. Rows of tall smokestacks that emitted nothing; finger piers where no barges were moored; paralyzed cranes, tumbledown sheds, and cracked pavement; heaps of coal that would never fuel the now-cold blast furnaces. All of it rusting away.

I made a U-turn, got out of my rental car. Crossed a debris-filled drainage ditch to the high chain-link fence and stood peering through it. The wind blew strongly here at the river's edge, cold and crisp with autumn. Above me metal clanked monotonously; I glanced up at a nearby walkway, saw a lattice work of corroded iron dangling and banging against a support. Otherwise there was no sound and nothing moved.

I felt the same sense of desolation and futility that I'd experienced when Suits took me to Hunters Point. Wondered if his plans to revitalize the old naval base had roots in guilt over what he'd done here. If so, it would be small atonement; the closing of Keystone's Monora mill had not only taken away livelihoods but also ended an era.

In the 1950s the mill had been one of the largest in America, rolling over five million tons of steel a year. Its products—building beam and plate and rail and rod and wire—could be found from coast to coast: in the skyscrapers of Manhattan, in the cars rolling off Detroit's assembly lines, in the train yards of the Midwest, in the freeways of California. But after 1957 production dropped off in an alarming series of cyclical swings. Management blamed the federal government for failing to protect the industry from foreign competition; they blamed the steelworkers' union for demanding high wages and imposing inefficient work regulations. They blamed everyone but themselves.

When management could have invested in new technologies, they clung to outmoded open-hearth furnaces. When they could have investigated new product lines, they devoted little money to research-and-development. When they could have worked productively with labor, they adopted an adversarial stance. In 1959 the entire industry was crippled by a major strike that ended only when President Eisenhower invoked the Taft-Hartley Act, forcing workers back to the mills.

Keystone's worst misstep came in the late seventies, when a new two-hundred-million-dollar blast furnace—installed only after baffling technical problems, interminable delays, and cost overruns that sent their accountants reeling—proved, as many would have predicted, to be a white elephant. The company plunged further into the red. Management's response was to raise prices and send senior executives, board members, and their wives on an all-expense-paid "fact-finding" junket to such hubs of heavy industry as Tahiti, Hong Kong, and Australia. In 1982 the layoffs began in earnest. In the late eighties the frightened board finally threw nearly seventy years of deeply entrenched tradition to the winds and sent for Suits.

No one, I thought as I gripped the cold links of the fence around the corpse of what had once been a mighty, vital mill, could blame Suits for what had happened here. By the time he was summoned, there had been little left to work with.

I recalled his description of what he'd found upon his arrival in Monora: "Fifty-five hundred of the most depressed steelworkers on the face of the earth; they'd taken pay cut after pay cut, and relations had deteriorated so badly that management was afraid to walk down the same side of the street with labor. Railroad tracks that a locomotive didn't pass over but twice a week. Whole buildings shut down, others only half used.

The open-hearth sheds were just shells, but Keystone couldn't afford to demolish them. Most of the blast furnaces had been dynamited and were just lying in pieces, waiting to be hauled away. There were virtual graveyards of abandoned coke ovens and equipment. And *this* they expected me to turn around?"

But he *had* turned Keystone. He sent the board on an extended vacation and fired management. He negotiated as best he could with labor. Then he pulled the plug on the mill and sold off every asset that could possibly be liquidated. With the proceeds he built three mini-mills—small and efficient, each offering a single product at below-market cost—in Alabama, where land and labor were cheap and steel was in short supply. Keystone now returned a small but respectable profit to its shareholders.

Suits had saved another company. But to do so he'd destroyed a mill, a town, a way of life. Now that I'd seen this place I was sure that what he'd done here was sufficient grounds for harassment—and ultimately murder.

* * *

It took me less than a minute to realize that the Monora Police Station was a former tavern. Its brick and glass-block facade and double doors with small diamond-shaped windows gave away its previous incarnation; even the framework for a neon sign remained. Amused, I pushed through the doors and found a familiar precinct-house setup. The desk sergeant told me that Chief Nancy Koll was at the doughnut shop across Cop Station Alley, and motioned toward the side street where I'd earlier seen the two uniforms crossing.

Koll was a strong-featured woman in her fifties, a little under six feet tall, with a cordial if somewhat abrupt manner. When I introduced myself, she recognized my name, dismissed the subordinate she'd been conferring with, and asked me to join her.

"Coffee here's okay, but I don't recommend their dough-nuts," she told me. "We use the shop as our conference room; it's better heated than the station."

I ordered coffee and asked her if Deputy Westerkamp had explained why I was coming to Monora.

"He did. Smart man to use you. Saves his department money." Then she launched into a tirade about budget cuts for law enforcement, and I started to like her—as most of us do when we meet someone whose opinions are a near match for our own.

I asked, "Have you turned up anything on who West-erkamp's dead man might be?"

She shook her head. "I've got a man going through our missing-person files right now, but it's a slow process. A lot of people up and went around the time we're talking about. Husbands went out for a pack of cigarettes; wives took up with traveling men; kids ran off to escape another drunken beating. Happens that way when your livelihood's taken from you."

"The town's in bad shape since the mill closed."

"The town's dead. It just doesn't know it yet."

I took my notebook from my bag. "My client . . . Did Westerkamp mention I'm working for T. J. Gordon?"

The web of lines around Koll's eyes deepened. "He did. Can't say as I have much sympathy for Gordon, considering what he did to us, but it's still a tough thing to lose a wife that way. And unlike a lot of people around here, I understand that he just did what he had to."

"There's active resentment of him, then. Can you think of anyone who would go so far as to follow him west to get revenge?"

"No one in particular. Is that what you think the dead man was after?"

"If so, he wasn't the only one. He died over a year ago, but somebody else began harassing Gordon this past August, a few weeks before his house blew up." I flipped through the pages of my notebook, then handed it to her. "This is a list of people who Gordon thinks could have been responsible."

She read it, nodding a couple of times. "The first name you can scratch—he's dead. Suicide. The second was one of the husbands who went out for smokes. I suppose he might've headed west, but he never had enough ambition or brains to stick to any one course of action. This one"—she pointed—"Herb Pace. He's a sorry case."

"How so?"

"Pace was CEO at Keystone before Gordon fired him. Lived high, had one of those trophy wives. She divorced him, took what was left of his money. Now he lives on River Road across from the railroad tracks and spends most of his time at McGlennon's Pub. Pace really hates your client, but I know for certain that he hasn't left town in the past few years. You might want to talk with him, though, to get background on the years when Gordon was here. And he might know of somebody who *has* left town with revenge on his mind. Just be sure to catch him before noon while he's still lucid."

"Anyone else on that list who's a possible suspect?"

"No." She shook her head and handed back the notebook. "The rest are still here, and none of them're devious enough for what you're talking about."

I asked for and wrote down Herb Pace's address. "Is there anyone else you can think of who could give me some insight into the time of the turnaround?"

Koll pursed her lips thoughtfully. "Well, there's Amos Ritter. He's a writer. Big fat paperback historicals that you buy for long plane trips. Has quite an interest in local history, too, so he might be helpful to you. Lives in a big brick house on top of the hill—Raymond Lewis's old place, he was one of the founders of Keystone. I can't give you the exact address, but it's on Crest Avenue; anybody can point it out."

TILL THE BUTCHERS CUT HIM DOWN

I noted the writer's name. "One last question, and I won't take up any more of your time. Is there a motel in town?"

Koll smiled pityingly at me. "Not anymore. I recommend you try Schmidt's Guest House in Pearl Alley." She gave me brief directions. "Jeannie Schmidt keeps a clean place, and it's cheap. Plus she's a notorious gossip. Who knows?" She winked. "You might learn something I don't know."

*　　*　　*

The town, I noticed, had a lot of little unpaved lanes that ran between the regular streets, and each had been given a name. I found Schmidt's Guest House on one of those, set back a ways and screened by two big maple trees. I approached the old-fashioned frame house on a carpet of fallen leaves; a seedpod came spinning down and lit on my shoulder. In college I'd had a friend from Vermont; she called the two-winged seedpods "helicopters."

Jeannie Schmidt—a tiny, birdlike woman with a quick, breathy voice and a thick braid of blond hair hanging down her back—told me I was her first customer that week. She showed me to a large front room furnished in what looked to be good antiques. The bathroom was down the hall and had a very rudimentary shower; Jeannie—as she insisted I call her—apologized twice for the inconvenience. She seemed to have an exaggerated idea of what amenities Californians were used to and was astonished when I told her that for the first year I'd lived in my house I'd put up with a toilet located in a cold cubicle on the back porch. We settled on a very reasonable rate for the room, and then I asked to use the phone, promising to put long-distance calls on my credit card.

First, Mick. My nephew wasn't at home or at my office. I left the guesthouse number on both machines.

Next, Noah Romanchek. His secretary at GGL told me he'd flown up to Bootlegger's Cove that morning and hadn't yet returned. I also left the number with her.

Finally, Amos Ritter. The writer had a soft voice with a touch of the South in it; he readily agreed to see me and gave me directions to what he called his "Gothic horror."

* * *

It *was* a Gothic horror: dark red brick, with turrets and arched windows and stained-glass panels depicting rather violent religious scenes. The slate roof was topped by elaborate ironwork that resembled angry fists raised at the heavens; marble steps led up to a double front door with more stained-glass insets, these depicting the Crucifixion. As I rang the bell I half expected Lurch the butler to answer.

The man who greeted me was in pleasant contrast to the house: slight, blond, with a receding hairline and a fine-featured sensitive face; clad in jeans and a blue velour pullover and shod in plush-lined moccasins. His easy manner made the enormous, high-ceilinged foyer less forbidding. He led me to a parlor whose walls were covered with built-in bookcases, seated me on a leather sofa, and poured two glasses of sherry from a crystal decanter.

I complimented him on the room while warming my hands in the heat from the fireplace.

"In a house like this," he said, "one has to create oases of comfort. In a sense, I suppose I bought it to prove that anything can be turned into a home."

"It was built by a founder of Keystone Steel?"

He handed me one of the wineglasses, took his to an armchair, and propped his feet up on a hassock. "Raymond Lewis. Old man Lewis was a religious fanatic—hence the gory stained glass—and a compulsive spender—hence everything else. There're six bedrooms, six bathrooms, all with hand-painted tiles, a ballroom on the top floor, and a bowling alley in the basement."

"Amazing. You live alone here?"

"I am, as they say, between relationships, and finding a new

200

partner poses a bit of a problem. I'm gay, and few men of my orientation hang out in dying steel towns—unless they're fond of drunken unemployed mill-hunks. But I'm quite happy rattling around here by myself; I have a great many books and hobbies. My firearms collection is considered one of the best in the state, and I'm also into restoring antique furniture."

"Local history is also one of your interests, I'm told. Are you from the area?"

"Biloxi, Mississippi."

"Then how and why . . . ?"

"How and why did I end up here?"

I nodded.

"Well, like many a southern boy, I spent my adolescence in the closet. And also like many, I later headed west to your town. S.F. State, to study creative writing. My parents came to visit during my freshman year; it didn't take them long to catch on to certain nuances of my lifestyle. They stopped sending money, and I started going to school part-time and working odd jobs to get by. Six years later I was still in the creative writing program and living with a man who was offered a teaching position at the state university at California—that's a little south of here. When he moved, I went along."

Ritter paused, eyes contemplative. "The trouble with San Francisco was that I hung out in bars and coffeehouses with other young writers more than I wrote. And when any of us did write, we all sounded the same. I decided that if I got away to a place that was completely foreign to me, I'd eventually start sounding like myself. And I guess I do—I sure as hell don't sound like anybody else. Some people call my books potboilers, and to a certain extent they are; but writing them pleases me, and they pay to keep this Gothic horror up, so who am I to complain?"

He raised his glass in a toast, and I responded in kind.

I said, "I assume because you're not from this area, you have a certain detachment about what goes on here."

"In a way. You said on the phone that you're interested in the Keystone mess. T. J. Gordon's your client?"

"Yes." I explained Suits's present circumstances.

"I heard about the explosion," Ritter said. "It made the national news and, of course, the tabloids. People here couldn't stop speculating."

"Speculating that someone connected with Keystone might be the responsible party?"

"Uh-huh. Very few people in Monora really understand what happened with the mill. The Keystone board and management were a bunch of shortsighted fuckups who didn't realize how far into the ground they'd run the company until it was way too late. Most of them—Herb Pace, the former CEO, is a good example—still don't get it."

"Tell me about Herb Pace."

"He was the first to be fired. Your client arrived in town, and before he'd unpacked, Pace was out on his ass. To add to that humiliation, his marriage fell apart as soon as the big salary he'd been paying himself stopped."

So Pace had been Suits's sacrificial lamb. "What about the other Keystone execs?"

"The ones who're still in the area are retired and living off their investments. Others found jobs elsewhere. People like them do a lot of damage and still manage to land on their feet." He paused, thinking. "Labor didn't play a much loftier part in the Keystone debacle, though. The USWA local made extreme demands, and when they weren't met, they used dirty tactics. Your client arrived at a crisis point, and for a while it looked as if he might have a strike or even a riot on his hands. Then the head of the local, Ed Bodine, was caught dealing drugs and sent to prison. After that, union leadership more or less collapsed."

"When was Bodine arrested?"

"Shortly after Gordon took over. He was dealing cocaine.

Claimed he was framed, but some very reputable people, including a member of his own union, testified to the contrary."

"Can you name names?"

Ritter thought, shook his head. "I can't recall any."

I made a mental note to ask Chief Koll about the arrest and trial.

Ritter got up to pour more wine. "The way I see it," he went on, "Gordon was a man with a tough job—a near impossible job—to do, and he went ahead and did it. Unfortunately, he's not particularly likable, certainly no diplomat, and neither are the people he surrounds himself with. Their tactics struck everybody as excessively heavy-handed and insensitive. I always thought he should have used his wife in a community-relations capacity; apparently she was charming and might have been able to do him some good. But as it was, she wasn't here long enough—"

"Wait a minute—Anna Gordon came to Monora?"

Ritter looked surprised at the sharpness of my tone. "For a couple of months right at the beginning, but then she went back to California. There were rumors that the marriage was in trouble."

I replayed my mental tape of Anna's and my conversation on the beach at the cove the day she died. What had she said about accompanying Suits to his turnaround sites? That she'd tried but it hadn't worked well. And I'd had the impression that she was about to tell me something important but decided against it. Later she'd claimed she could give me no insight into either Lost Hope or Keystone, because she and Suits had agreed to a trial separation at the time he went to Pennsylvania and hadn't worked things out until after he finished in Nevada. But now I found she'd lied about going to both places.

Anna had also said something that struck me as interesting, but that I didn't pursue because I felt it was none of my business: there were things she would have done differently if she'd been safe in the marriage. Now I wished I'd asked her what she meant.

*   *   *

Ritter insisted I stay to dinner—an elegant caviar-and-lox omelet and a salad—so it was after ten by the time I got back to the guest house. The writer had handed me no further surprises about Suits's time in Monora, although the stories he told affected me strongly. He told of grown men and women crying when they received their layoff notices; of workers begging to take a pay cut to five dollars an hour if they could keep their jobs; of union food-and-clothing drives; of families piling their possessions in trucks and of leave-takings reminiscent of those of the Great Depression. Jobs at the new mini-mills in Alabama had been offered to the workers with the most seniority, but few took them; it was hard for older people to pull up roots that went back in some cases for generations. Militant young workers spurned the offers, too, because the wages were below scale; currently none were making what they could have had they relocated.

As I drove back to the guest house I wondered what I would have done had I been in Suits's position. Save a company, but destroy its employees' lives? Return a profit to the shareholders, but let the men and women who had labored for it go hungry? The concept went against my idealistic grain, but my practical side recognized a certain necessity and inevitability in his actions. Possibly after having been in his line of work so long, he hadn't even considered the human side of the equation.

Jeannie Schmidt's big frame house was dark except for a porch light and sconces in the hallways. A small lamp glowed on the bedside table in my room; the covers had been turned down and a note lay on my pillow. Noah Romanchek wanted me to call him.

I left the room and tiptoed down the hall to the stairway, trying to avoid squeaky floorboards and instead hitting every one. The stairs creaked loudly, and I had to grope around to find the light switch for the alcove off the parlor where the phone was. Romanchek had left his home number, and he answered on the first ring.

"I went up to Mendocino County this morning. T.J. is missing."

"What?"

"He's not at Bootlegger's Cove. The cottage is empty. Josh and I called that cabdriver T.J. sometimes uses; he hasn't seen him since he drove him to a clinic in Fort Bragg a week ago to have the cast removed from his arm. We had him come get us and take us into Elk; someone from the grocery store there dropped off supplies at the cottage last Wednesday, but nobody's had any contact with T.J. since. Nobody's seen him in Albion, Little River, Mendocino, or at the airport."

I thought of Moonshine Cottage: its loneliness; its view of the blackened rubble on the cliff top; the nearby precipitous drop to the rocks in the cove. "You don't suppose he killed himself?"

"There was no body, no note, no other evidence of that."

"You contacted the sheriff's department?"

"Filed a report. Sharon, what is it you want to talk with him about?"

"There're a few details I need to clear up."

"Anything I can help you with?"

"No. Where do you suppose he went? And how?"

"God knows. Hitchhiked, maybe. By the way, I couldn't help but recognize the area code you called from. You're in Monora?"

Damn! I should have called back instead of leaving the number. Even though Romanchek had been very cooperative with my investigation, I didn't trust him, sensed Suits didn't really trust him, either. "Yes," I said grudgingly.

"These details you need to clear up—do they pertain to the Keystone turnaround?"

"No, they're personal."

"I see. How long have you been in Pennsylvania?"

"Only the day."

"And have you found anything promising there?"

"No. I'll be coming back to California soon. Noah, has T.J. indicated to you at any time since the explosion that he was planning to leave the cove?"

Romanchek was silent.

I repeated the question.

"Sorry, I was thinking. There *is* one thing, and in light of his disappearance I don't like its implications one bit. The last time I went up there he said there was only one reason he'd leave—if he figured out who had set the explosion. Then, he told me, he'd go after the bastard and kill him."

Fifteen

After talking with Romanchek for a few more minutes and coming to no definite conclusions, I went to bed but couldn't sleep. The night passed slowly as I repeatedly changed position on the too-soft bed. The old house groaned and creaked; a wind kicked up around four in the morning, causing a tree branch to scratch against the window glass.

So Suits had finally shaken off his apathy, I thought. Walked away from the rubble of his life. To where and to what purpose? The unanswerable question nagged at me. Without Anna to anchor him, and fueled by rage over her death, my client was a loose cannon, dangerous both to himself and to anyone his paranoid psyche might focus on.

The thought of the damage he might do made me want to get up, drive straight back to Pittsburgh, and catch the next flight west. But what sense was there in that? Sure, I could go to Mendocino County, repeat Romanchek and Josh's inquiries, but it sounded as though they'd been thorough. Still, given my distrust of the attorney . . .

At five-thirty I got up and pulled on my jeans and sweater. Tiptoed through the silent house to the phone again and, not caring that it was only two-thirty there, called home. Mick answered on the sixth ring, his voice a groggy croak. "Wake up," I said. "There's something I need you to do."

". . . Shar, do you know what time it is?"

"Get used to this, kid. Rotten hours and calls in the middle of the night are what private investigation's all about."

Grunt.

"Mick!"

"Okay, I'm here. I was trying to find a pencil and paper."

He was nothing if not willing—I had to give him that. Briefly I explained the circumstances of Suits's disappearance. "I want you to go up there and verify what Romanchek told me. Ask as many people as you can if they've seen or spoken to Suits. Keep detailed notes and call me here as soon as you're finished."

"Shar, how am I supposed to get there? I don't have a car, and I doubt Rae'll lend me hers if I wake her up at three in the morning."

"Good Lord, you don't have to leave yet! The trip'll only take you three, three and a half hours."

"I still don't think she'll let me take the Ramblin' Wreck on a weekend."

Now that I thought of Rae's appropriately named old Rambler American, I didn't want Mick driving it on the narrow, winding coast highway. "You can use mine. It's parked at the general aviation terminal at Oakland Airport. Extra keys are hanging on the hook on the fridge."

"I can see them from here." Now Mick sounded fully alert— even excited. "Shar, I waited all day, but there was nothing from NPRC on Sid Blessing."

"They're a bureaucracy. We'll be lucky if we hear in a week."

208

"Listen, I won't be able to sleep any more tonight. I could go into the office and tinker—"

"No! Every time you pull something illegal you're putting my license in jeopardy."

"I won't get caught."

"Oh, yeah? Remember what happened with the board of education?"

". . . Right. Well, maybe I'll just run up to Mendocino now, get a head start."

"Yes, why don't you do that?"

It wasn't until I was back in bed that I realized he would have one hell of a time getting to Oakland Airport at three in the morning.

*　　*　　*

At some point before dawn I fell into a heavy, dreamless sleep and woke woolly-mouthed and disoriented at a little after nine. I dragged myself along the hall for a cold shower, dressed, and followed the smell of coffee downstairs to a big 1950s-style kitchen that reminded me of the one at All Souls. Jeannie had told me to help myself; I filled the cup she'd set out and took it to the backyard, where I found her raking leaves.

"Hope I didn't bother you going back and forth to the phone last night," I said.

"Not at all. I sleep like a *Murmeltier*. Always have." She leaned the rake against an elm tree and wiped her brow with the back of her hand.

"Like a . . . ?"

"German for marmot. *Schlafen wie ein Murmeltier.* It's an old saying I picked up from my mother. So where are you off to this morning?"

"I have to see a man named Herb Pace. Do you know him?"

"Only by sight, poor man. What do you want with Mr. Pace?"

Up to now I'd been candid about my reasons for coming here with the Monorans I'd encountered, but Nancy Koll was the chief of police, and Amos Ritter something of an outsider. It wouldn't do to let the town gossip know the purpose of my trip. "Oh," I said, "I work for an insurance company; it's one of those routine matters."

"I see." Jeannie looked faintly disappointed.

I sat down on a weathered wooden bench that wrapped around the trunk of a maple. "Why do you say 'poor man'?"

She began raking again, speaking above the whisk and rustle. "Well, he had such a big job with the mill, was really somebody. Then overnight they threw him out, and he was nobody at all. Now you see him around town, walking up from that dump of his by the river to the state liquor store and McGlennon's, and he looks like any other pathetic soul with too much time on his hands. Just waiting it out till he dies—helping it out, too, with the liquor." She paused, leaning on the rake. "Not that I've got any use for Keystone management. That mill ate people up for generations. Ruined a lot of lives."

"How so?"

"Happens that way in company towns. Take my ex-husband, Al. When we were in school, he wanted more than anything to become an engineer. Had the talent, too. But Al's dad was a steelworker, and the philosophy was that children of steelworkers should follow their parents into the mill. When Al wanted to apply to college, the teachers put him off, said he wasn't smart enough. For a while he went to classes part-time down at California and worked night shift at Keystone, but that's a hard life and eventually he gave up on it. Afterward he was a broken man."

"What happened to Al?"

"When the mill closed, he turned down a chance to go to Alabama. Said maybe it was for the best, he'd go back to school. But it's hard to start over at thirty-nine. Al just sat around the house drinking, and one day he left town." She said it matter-of-factly, but her lips pulled tight with pain. "I like to think that wherever he is, he might be realizing his ambitions."

"You should hold on to that thought." It was the only comfort she was ever likely to get. I'd seen hundreds of Als on the streets of San Francisco and other cities: sleeping on benches, huddled in doorways, lining up in front of the shelters.

"Oh, I will. No matter what's happened to him, he's better off out of here. Should've gone years ago. That mill"—she looked to the south, where its smokestacks were visible above the treetops—"the ordinary people of this town were only fuel for it. As far as management was concerned, our lives weren't worth more than a ton of coal. Were certainly worth less than a ton of ore."

* * *

I left my rental car at the guest house and walked downhill to River Street. The air was crisp this morning; Anna's cape, which had kept me overly warm in Nevada, afforded scant protection here. Leaves from the maples and elms fluttered down and crunched under my feet—flame, burgundy, and a gold that was the exact color of candlelight. Up on the hill by Jeannie's, the houses were large, with wraparound and upstairs sleeping porches; although many had been broken up into apartments and were in need of paint, they were reasonably well maintained. But as I descended, they became smaller, poorer; all were in bad repair, and some had been abandoned and vandalized. It occurred to me that if you walked from Amos Ritter's Gothic mansion to the river, you would have traversed the town's entire socioeconomic spectrum.

Herb Pace's house was little more than a shack facing the railroad embankment. It was covered with ancient soot-stained aluminum siding; a faded striped awning shaded its front window; a tattered sofa sat on the porch. I went up there and rang the bell. It echoed inside, loud enough to wake a badly hungover man, but no one answered.

After I rang a few more times, I decided to walk up to Main Street. Jeannie Schmidt had mentioned that Pace was a habitué of both the state liquor store and McGlennon's Pub; perhaps he was starting his drinking day early.

McGlennon's didn't open till eleven, but two blocks away the state liquor store was doing a brisk business. As I walked over there, five people came out with shopping bags; inside, six other customers browsed. I asked the grandmotherly woman at the cash register if Pace had been in that morning. She motioned at the door. "He just left."

"What does he look like?"

"Gray. Gray hair, gray face, gray overcoat. Glen plaid scarf. Fifth of Kessler's in his canvas tote bag; it won't last him the day." She made the comment blandly, but there was malice in her eyes. The people of Monora might hate Suits for what he'd done to their town, but some at least understood Pace's role in Keystone's downfall.

I thanked her and hurried out of the store. A man in a gray overcoat with a trailing plaid scarf was turning onto a side street leading downhill. I went after him, called his name.

Pace didn't hear me at first. When I called again, he looked around, annoyed. I asked him to wait, and he stopped, resting a hand against a utility pole. Under his too-loose overcoat, he looked frail; his hair was unkempt, his cheeks were stubbled, his eyes were reddened and vague. He frowned as if he knew me from somewhere and was trying to place me.

I reached him and gave him my name, said I was writing a book about the Keystone Steel turnaround. Pace's lips curled down, but before he could speak I added, "I've learned that many people, you included, were treated shabbily by T. J. Gordon. That's to be my focus. Can we talk?"

For a moment I was sure he would refuse me. Then he shrugged and resumed walking downhill. I fell in beside him.

After half a block Pace said, "The word 'shabbily' is inadequate." His voice rasped as if he had a bad cold; he began coughing spasmodically.

I asked, "Are you okay?"

Pace got his coughing under control. "Do I look *okay*, young lady? Does this town look *okay*?" He gestured extravagantly and staggered.

Drinking already, I thought, and more than one. "No," I replied, "the town's in bad shape."

"And why? All because of T. J. Gordon and his executioners. From the turn of the century, Keystone Steel was both mother and father to the people of this area. Monora was their home, and a damned fine one, too. Keystone provided for their every need. Then Gordon came here and destroyed our mill. In effect, he orphaned every one of those workers. They can't fend for themselves; they never had to. The mill took care of them, their parents, their grandparents, even their great-grandparents, from the cradle to the grave. The phrase 'in bad shape' is also inadequate."

If it hadn't been for my earlier conversation with Jeannie Schmidt, I might have taken Pace's words as indication of a limited sort of compassion for his former workers. As it was, I realized they were merely indicative of Keystone management's paternalism and arrogance.

"What about you, Mr. Pace?" I asked. "Do you feel as if you've been orphaned?"

He stopped walking, pulling himself more erect. Glared down his nose at me. "No, young lady, I do not. In truth, I feel as if I've been destroyed. For forty-one years Keystone Steel was my life. I ran the mill; I guided the company. I made every major corporate decision. When they killed that mill, I lost my soul."

"But as CEO, you must also have made the decision to bring Gordon on board, give him a free hand."

Pace's lips compressed; his glare faded, and he began walking again. After a moment he said, "I was wrongly overruled by my board of directors. I tried to tell them that the corporation was not in that bad a condition, that we'd ridden out worse slumps before. They refused to listen."

I remembered Suits's description of the situation he'd found upon his arrival here. A slump? No way. Amos Ritter was right about Pace: he still didn't get it.

We rounded the corner of River Street. Pace quickened his step—eager, no doubt, to get on with his drinking.

I asked, "What about labor relations, Mr. Pace? I understand the USW local was talking strike before Ed Bodine was arrested."

"The local was always talking strike, even in the good years. Bodine was a professional agitator who never put in an honest day's work in his life."

"And apparently he was also a drug dealer."

Pace snorted derisively. We'd reached his house. He negotiated the porch steps with difficulty, clutching at the railing and breathing hard. He dropped his keys while trying to fit them into the lock; I retrieved them and opened the door for him. He didn't thank me, just shambled down the hallway. I shut the door and followed.

The small kitchen where Pace led me horrified even an indifferent housekeeper like me. Its counters were littered with dirty plates and glasses, and most of the plates were covered with substances that I supposed once might have been food. The source of the overpowering odor that was trapped there was too awful to contemplate; sticky patches on the floor seemed to have designs on my shoes.

Pace set his tote bag on the counter and pulled out the fifth of Kessler's. He located a glass, then remembered his manners and looked questioningly at me; when I shook my head, he seemed relieved. Without rinsing the glass, he poured a good three fingers of liquor, drank it off, and refilled.

I tried to keep my expression neutral, but Pace saw through

me. "Yes, I am an alcoholic," he said. "And, yes, I've quit trying to hide the fact. I simply don't give a damn anymore. My kitchen offends you?"

"Does it matter?"

"No." Abruptly he moved past me. "However, out of respect for your sensibilities, we'll sit on the front porch."

When we were settled at opposite ends of the old sofa, Pace asked, "Now, what were we discussing?"

"Ed Bodine. Specifically, his arrest for dealing cocaine. I understand it weakened the local considerably."

"Finished it, for all practical purposes. Meek as lambs they were, after Bodine went to prison." Pace stared down into his glass, swirling the liquor. "Bodine had been a thorn in my side for over a decade. Months before his arrest—even weeks— I would have rejoiced to see him taken down. But by then I was gone from Keystone. Nothing mattered."

"Bodine's defense was that the arrest was a setup?"

"Of course."

"Was it?"

"Yes. Know thine enemy—an important precept of business. I knew mine enemy, and Ed Bodine was no drug dealer."

"So who set him up?"

"Who else but T. J. Gordon?"

Once it would have been hard for me to believe, having known Suits in the old days, but as I'd observed last August, he'd changed. Besides, Suits was a former dealer himself; wouldn't the plan of framing an adversary with drugs have come naturally to him?

I remembered sitting in Miranda's diner with him. Saying, "You've changed, Suits." And he'd acknowledged it. "Haven't we all, Sherry-O?" he'd said.

But had Suits changed that much? By extension, had I?

Suddenly Pace started laughing, and the laughter turned into another coughing fit. When he got control of it he drank off what was left in his glass and went into the house for a refill. He was gone a long time, probably having several extra snorts to tide him over. When he finally returned, he was still amused.

"What were you thinking before?" I asked.

"About Ed Bodine. He may not have dealt drugs before his arrest, but he certainly adapted well to life as a convict."

"Meaning?"

"He learned to play the system like any good con. Ingratiated himself, acted the true repentant. Within a few years he was transferred from Western Pennsylvania to a minimum-security facility at Greensburg. And one day he simply walked away. Hot-wired one of the guards' cars and disappeared. The car was abandoned in Ohio. And Ed Bodine has never been seen or heard of since."

"When was this?"

"A year ago this past Fourth of July. I remember well, because I was sitting right here on this sofa watching the fireworks over the river when the news came on my transistor radio. Bodine took advantage of a heavy crowd of holiday visitors at Greensburg."

"A year ago this past Fourth of July. You're sure of that?"

Pace scowled and drained his glass. "Young lady, I may be a drunk, but I am not senile."

Last year, July Fourth. I stared at the humpbacked railroad embankment, trying to put together a logical progression.

Ed Bodine, a man supposedly framed by Suits for a crime he didn't commit, walks away from prison on Independence Day—a nice ironic touch. His stolen car is later abandoned in Ohio, to the west. A little over a month later, a van is stolen in Colorado, also to the west. The same van is abandoned outside the Aces and Eights Motel in Lost Hope weeks after that. And two days ago, the August man's remains are exhumed by the Esmeralda County Sheriff's Department.

Coincidence? Maybe. Maybe not.

Either way, I knew how to find out.

Sixteen

After I explained my theory to her, Chief Koll sat me down at an empty desk in the squad room with the files on Ed Bodine's arrest and went to her office, the former tavern's poolroom, to call the state department of corrections. I tuned out the ringing phones and voices around me and began to wade through the thick stack of documents. By the time I'd read the last one, I was convinced that the Bodine bust had been a setup.

The police had been alerted to the alleged cocaine deal late on a Friday night by an anonymous caller who said something interesting was going down in one of the empty open-hearth sheds at Keystone. There they found Bodine and Jim Spitz, a fellow union member and rival for its local leadership. Spitz readily admitted that they'd met so he could buy a quantity of coke from Bodine, and produced an envelope containing a large amount of cash. Bodine denied everything, claiming Spitz had requested the meeting to discuss confidential information he'd stumbled across concerning management plans that would seriously weaken the local, but when he submitted to a body search, packets of cocaine were found in the lining of his jacket. Bodine said he didn't know how the packets got there and that any number of people could have gained access to the jacket in his locker at the mill. When the police searched his apartment, however, they turned up more coke.

When the case came to trial neither the defense nor the prosecution had a preponderance of evidence. No one had been with Bodine when he received the alleged call from Spitz requesting the meeting, and he hadn't mentioned it to anyone. On the other hand, Spitz, who testified in exchange for immunity from prosecution, claimed he'd financed the drug buy on his own, even though he was known for being chronically short of funds. It seemed suspect that a shrewd man like Bodine would agree to meet a rival in the isolated open-hearth shed in the middle of the night, but he was also streetwise and capable of taking care of himself. The anonymous phone tip to the police department weakened Spitz's contention that he'd acted alone, but he had a reputation for talking too much, so it was possible he might have bragged about the deal to the wrong person.

In the end, it all came down to which man the jury believed. Spitz came across as attractive, articulate, and remorseful; Bodine came across as unattractive, poorly spoken, and defiant. The jury believed Spitz.

I closed the file, pushed back from the desk, and went to the door of Koll's office. The chief sat in her swivel chair contemplating a studio portrait of two little girls that hung on the wall. I knocked on the doorframe, and she started, then motioned me inside. "I'm waiting for the department of corrections to get back to me," she said. "They're checking to see if Bodine had any dental work done while he was in prison."

"Care to answer a few questions while you wait?"

"Sure." She waved at the chair across from her.

I asked, "What happened to Jim Spitz?"

"Left town right after the trial. Hastily, and driving a new Buick. I hear he's living down at Charleroi now, has set himself up as a small-time dealer." She laughed harshly. "They say he siphoned off some of the coke that was meant to be used to frame Bodine and used it as a stake for his business."

"So you knew all along that Bodine had been telling the truth?"

"Of course," she replied calmly. "I said as much to Bodine's lawyer, but he never did anything with it. Guess they bought him, too."

"And you didn't bother to investigate any further?"

Annoyance flashed in her eyes. "Ms. McCone, this is a poor town. We don't have the funds or the manpower to conduct that kind of investigation—particularly when a big-money fix is in."

"I see. Another question: if a person were to make a major drug buy here, who would he contact?"

"Back then, you mean? Ray Wilmer."

"Where can I find him?"

"You can't—he's dead. Somebody blew him away. Most folks think it was a drug burn, but my opinion is that the KKK was responsible. Wilmer was black, came over from Wheeling. His gaudy lifestyle brought him a dangerous kind of attention."

"I didn't realize the Klan was active in this area."

"God, yes. Has been for decades, but it's even more open now, ever since whites started to lose ground economically. The race hatred goes all the way back to the thirties when blacks were brought in as strikebreakers. Now it's part of the culture. Ironic thing is, most of the haters don't even remember how it got started." Her eyes moved back to the portrait on the wall.

"Who're the little girls?"

"My grandchildren. Their father was one of the ones who

up and left after the mill closed." She shook her head. "It's a hell of a legacy we're leaving the next generation."

I nodded in agreement. "To get back to Jim Spitz, you say he's dealing around someplace called Charleroi?"

"Yes—town on the river midway between here and California, where the college is."

"Can you find out his address for me?"

Koll's eyes narrowed. "You want to talk with him?"

"Yes."

"He won't admit anything."

"Maybe not, but he's been bought once, and I suspect he can be bought again."

She hesitated, then shook her head decisively. "Ms. McCone, I probably could get an address for you, but I'm not even going to try. You came here as a representative of the Esmeralda County Sheriff's Department to get a lead on the man they turned up in the desert out there. You've accomplished that—maybe—and it's time for you to go home."

"But—"

"No buts. Talking to Jim Spitz would only stir up a lot of trouble that this town doesn't need. We've got enough problems, and I don't want to top them off with a scandal about political and judicial corruption."

The phone buzzed. Koll looked distractedly at it, then picked up the receiver. "Chief Koll here. . . . You do. That's good. Here's where you send them—Fed Ex, please." She reached for a scratch pad, read off the address of the Esmeralda County crime lab. As she hung up, she said to me, "Bodine's dental charts're as good as on the way. I'll call Deputy Westerkamp, let him know." She dialed, held a brief conversation with the deputy, then handed the receiver to me.

From his tone I could tell that Westerkamp was having difficulty containing his elation at the news. "Ms. McCone, thanks for your help with this."

"Well, nothing's solved yet. Has the autopsy on the August man been completed?"

"We're not backlogged the way they are in your city; report was on my desk this morning. Was shot in the heart once, nine-millimeter weapon. Our killer was either very lucky or a very good marksman."

"Have you picked up Walker and Deck yet?"

"Nope. We're dealing with a great big desert."

"What about Walker's phone-company records? Did you subpoena them?"

"Now, there's a problem. Couldn't get the judge to issue the subpoena or a search warrant for Walker's house. He said we didn't have any evidence she was involved in that body getting buried on the land where her brother's squatting. And he's got a point."

"I suppose."

"Are you planning on coming back to Lost Hope?"

"I'm not sure." I glanced at my watch. After three, and I hadn't even eaten yet. "With luck, I may be able to wrap things up here and catch a late-evening flight. Why don't I check in with you when I get back to the coast? Will you be around?"

"I'll be here until this thing's wrapped up and tied in ribbons."

"Then we'll talk later." I said good-bye and handed the receiver back to Koll, who had been listening with interest.

"Get things wrapped up here?" the chief repeated.

"Well, I have to pack, and I promised Amos Ritter I'd stop by before I left. The two of us hit it off very well."

Her skeptical expression made it clear that she didn't believe my plans were so innocent.

"Really," I added, "you're right: my business here is finished. I'm going home."

"You mean that?"

"Of course. I have an open reservation, so I'll drive up to Pittsburgh and see if I can get on a westbound flight."

Koll nodded, still looking skeptical. "Well, have a good trip."

*   *   *

The first person Koll would check with to verify that I'd left town was Jeannie Schmidt, so I went back to the guest house and told the landlady I would be leaving. Jeannie, who was on her way to the market, expressed dismay until I said she should keep the money I'd prepaid for that night's rent. Then she perked up some, said she was sorry we'd had such a brief acquaintance, and went down the hill toward town, her aluminum shopping cart trailing in her wake. I threw my things into my bag and made a quick call to Amos Ritter.

I cut through the writer's questions about what I'd been doing all day with a question of my own. "Where do the drug dealers hang out around here?"

Ritter didn't even hesitate. "River Park."

"How do I get there?"

"It's right off River Street, three blocks south of Herb Pace's place. If you follow Elm downhill, you'll come to a railroad trestle on the embankment. Cross under it and you're in the park."

"Thanks."

"Wait—are you going there now?"

"Yes, but if Chief Koll calls and asks where I am, tell her I've left for the airport."

"Sharon, I don't think you should go to the park alone, even during the day. That's a pretty rough crowd down there. Let me go with you."

"Thanks, Amos, but that won't be necessary."

"At least don't go unarmed. You can borrow one of the guns from my collection."

"I'd rather not, but I may need the use of your phone later on. Okay to stop by?"

"Any time. I'll be here. And be careful."

*　　*　　*

Long afternoon shadows were falling when I reached the foot of Elm Avenue. The weed-covered railroad embankment blocked my view of the river, and a black iron trestle spanned a sloping dirt track that looked to be a boat launch. I followed it under the trestle, avoiding discarded cans and bottles, to a narrow beach. The river was fairly wide at that point, the opposite bank forested in brilliant fall colors. A flock of ducks immediately noticed my presence and swam toward shore, making expectant little noises.

Monora's version of a riverside park wasn't much: a flat dirt area fringed to the north by a grove of willows. Somebody's abandoned bicycle lay half submerged in the water; trash overflowed onto the ground from a metal drum. I saw no evidence of the rough crowd Ritter had warned me about, only two men sitting at a broken-down picnic table. When they noticed me, one stood up, spoke briefly with his companion, then moved along the beach, hands stuffed in the pockets of his shabby denim jacket. The other—thin, with wispy white hair and pale skin—watched me silently. As I walked toward him, he pulled his blue knitted cap down low on his forehead.

I stopped opposite him, the picnic table between us. "Nice afternoon," I said.

He hesitated, still sizing me up, then nodded curtly.

"You come to the park often?"

Shrug.

"The reason I ask is that I'm looking for somebody I'm told hangs out here—Jim Spitz."

Flash of recognition, followed by another shrug.

"He lives down at Charleroi. You know him?"

"If he lives down at Charleroi, why'd he be hangin' here?"

"Business reasons."

The man's eyes narrowed. "You got business with him?"

"I might."

He studied me some more. "You're not heat."

"No."

"Not buyin', either."

"Not what Spitz usually sells, no."

"What, then?"

I shook my head. "That's between him and me."

"Well, I can't help you."

I took a twenty from my bag and showed it to him. "This is yours if you get in touch with Spitz and ask him to call me at the number on this piece of paper."

He glanced at the twenty, then looked away.

I took out another. "And this'll be waiting for you with the bartender at McGlennon's Pub after I hear from Spitz."

He ran his tongue over his upper lip, focusing on the twenties. Then he held out his hand. I gave him one bill and the piece of paper on which I'd written Amos Ritter's phone number; he stood up and stuffed them into his jeans pocket.

"Can't guarantee Spitz'll call you," he said.

"I know that, but there's a good chance he will if you tell him that I work for T. J. Gordon."

"T. J. Gordon," he repeated. The name didn't seem to mean anything to him. He turned without another word and walked toward the dirt track that led under the trestle.

I watched him go, then looked back toward the river. An empty barge was passing, churning the water; waves moved toward shore and lapped softly at the pebbled beach. I remained there until the barge moved around the bend where the defunct mill sprawled. This place was completely foreign to me, and yet it felt familiar. . . .

A railroad overpass . . . two people, or maybe it was three . . . heat lightning on the water . . .

Impossible.

Why?

Too much of a coincidence.

Coincidences happen.

I had asked Anna about those images, and she said they didn't mean anything to her. But Anna was here in Monora.

And she lied about that.

Yes, she did.

I ran back under the trestle to my rental car and headed for Amos Ritter's.

*   *   *

"You the one who was talking to Whitey at River Park?" The voice was wheezy, the question ending in a cough.

"Yes. Mr. Spitz?"

"What's this about T. J. Gordon?"

"I'm working for him. He wants to send some money your way."

"What's he need me to do this time?"

"I'd prefer to explain that in person. Can we meet?"

Another spasm of coughing; it reminded me of Herb Pace. No wonder people here had respiratory problems, though: for decades they'd had to contend with serious pollution from the steel mill.

Spitz finally asked, "How much're we talking about here?"

"How much money? Two hundred dollars."

Rasping laugh. "Gordon's got *millions*. Couple of hundred's nothing to him."

"But it's something to you, Mr. Spitz."

Silence.

"Mr. Spitz?"

"Look, how do I know you're on the level?"

"You don't, but what have you got to lose?"

"Plenty."

"I'm not a cop, if that's what you're afraid of. Ask Whitey—

he knew that right off. And I'm working for the man who fronted your original merchandise for you."

Spitz's breath wheezed. "Okay, make it five hundred, and it's a meet."

"Done. Where and when?"

"River Park, eight tonight. I'll be at the picnic table where you talked to Whitey. Come alone."

"I'll see you then." I replaced the receiver.

Amos Ritter came up behind me, frowning. "That was him."

"Uh-huh. I'm meeting him at the park at eight."

"I don't like that."

"I'll be okay." I hesitated. "Seems I keep asking you for favors, and now I need a couple more. Spitz wants five hundred dollars, and I don't have that much cash. My ATM card's good for two hundred; can I write you a check for the balance?"

"Sure. What else do you need?"

"I want to take you up on your offer of the loan of a gun."

My appointment with Spitz wasn't for two hours, so after Amos had given me the cash and I'd chosen a small, light-weight Smith and Wesson .38 from his collection, I borrowed a phone book. In reading the files on the Bodine case, I'd noticed that Ed's father had also lived in Monora; he was still listed, and I decided to pay him a visit. When I left Amos's house, he was standing in front of one of his gory stained-glass windows, shading his worried eyes from the setting sun.

*   *   *

Ed Bodine Sr. lived in a five-story brick retirement home on the hill above the abandoned steel mill; an inscription over its door indicated that it had once been the Sisters of Mercy Hospital. As I stepped off the elevator at the third floor, I caught a glimpse of the mill through the window—sprawling, dark, and unpopulated in the fading light. The residents of this home, Amos had told me, were mainly former steelworkers; I wondered how they could bear to look at the mill's ruins day after day. For me, that would have been a constant reminder of life's failures and my own impending death.

The man who answered my knock at the door of unit three-seventeen was bent and frail, supported by an aluminum walker. When I gave him my card and asked if I could talk with him about his son, anxiety clouded Bodine's eyes. He ran an arthritically swollen hand over his thin white hair, and for a moment I thought he would refuse to let me inside. Then he moved back, almost shying away from me; I sat in the place that he indicated at the end of the sofa, and he took a chair opposite, warily positioning the walker between us.

"Mr. Bodine," I said, "I know the last few years have been very difficult for you, and I understand that you don't want to relive unpleasant memories. But in the course of a related investigation I've found some facts that may help to clear your son's name."

Bodine's fingers tightened on the walker.

I went on, "I understand that before his arrest Ed was afraid that management was plotting to get rid of him." Bodine had said so in the statement taken immediately after his arrest.

The old man dipped his chin in acknowledgment.

"Did he ever talk about his fears with you?"

He cleared his throat and spoke in a deep voice that was at odds with his frail appearance. "Eddie didn't talk much about union business. Child protecting the parent; he didn't want me to worry about him. Why, I don't know. I'm a union man myself. Walked the picket line at Keystone during the strike of fifty-nine. Was dangerous then, just like in Eddie's time. Hell, the work itself's dangerous. Just a fact of life; you learn to live with it."

"But you knew he feared for his safety?"

"Well, sure. Not just his safety—his life. He knew Gordon's kind, and the gang he brought in to do his dirty work. The local was one of their main problems, and the best way to weaken labor was to do away with their leader—my Eddie."

"Had Ed taken any precautions against that? Made any preparations in case they went after him?"

"Sure. Three weeks before he got arrested, Eddie left this canvas bag with me. Said it was full of extra clothes and cash, in case he needed to get out of town and hole up someplace."

When I'd begun to suspect that Ed Bodine and the August man were one and the same, a detail about the United Airlines bag left in the room at the Aces and Eights Motel had bothered me: the Keystone Steel pen caught in its lining. I doubted that Bodine would have carried the pen to prison with him, but if the bag had belonged to him before his incarceration, the pen's presence made more sense.

I asked his father, "What happened to the bag?"

He looked away. "I got rid of it after Eddie went to prison."

"What did it look like?"

". . . I don't remember."

"It wouldn't have been blue, with a United Airlines logo?"

Slowly he looked back at me. "You've seen it?"

"Yes."

"You've seen Eddie?"

"No." What had been exhumed from the desert grave was not his son—not anymore.

Bodine nodded, as if I'd confirmed something for him.

"When did Ed pick up the bag?" I asked. "The night he walked away from Greensburg?"

"He didn't pick it up."

I waited.

Bodine sighed, let go of his walker, slumped in his chair. "All right, he called that night and asked me to bring it to him. That was before my arthritis got so bad, and I was still driving. I met him at a rest stop over on the turnpike—New Stanton."

"Have you heard from him since?"

228

He shook his head.

"Are you sure of that?"

"All right—two postcards, that's all."

"From where?"

"One from someplace in Illinois, the other from Omaha. No message, really, just the usual tourist stuff, and not in Eddie's true hand. After that, nothing."

"Did he say where he planned to go when you met him on the turnpike? What he planned to do?"

Again the old man looked away.

"Mr. Bodine?"

"Doesn't matter anyway."

"I'm sorry?"

"Can't hurt Eddie now. He's dead."

"Why do you say that?"

"Because if he was alive, he'd've been in touch. I know my boy. He went after Gordon, and Gordon finished him."

"He told you he was going after Gordon?"

Bodine closed his eyes, nodded. "Yeah. We was sitting in my car that night at New Stanton. Eddie said he'd make Gordon pay for what he done to him and Keystone. I told him Gordon was too powerful. I begged him to let it go. But my Eddie never listened to me."

I thought again of the desert grave, of the dental charts that were now speeding toward Nevada.

"Nothing matters now," Bodine said.

I had no words to comfort him, and none were expected. Bodine had lost his son, he knew it, and very soon—perhaps as early as tomorrow morning—a police officer would knock on his door and deliver the news that the old man already felt in his brittle bones.

* * *

I dropped off the twenty-dollar bill I'd promised Whitey with the bartender at McGlennon's Pub and was parked near the railroad embankment on River Street by seven-fifty. A harvest moon hung high, streaky clouds scudding across it; the night was so chill that I could see my breath. Lights shone behind curtains and blinds of the shabby houses facing the river. A jack-o'-lantern leered prematurely from a porch railing.

I watched the railroad trestle, but no one entered the park. A police car rounded the corner and began to prowl toward me; I ducked down until it had gone past and turned uphill. Then I got out of my car and walked toward the trestle.

From the south came the blare of a train's horn. I glanced up, saw its headlight moving slowly around the bend by the decaying mill. Long freight, picking up speed on the straightaway. I started down the dirt track to the beach, and then the train was overhead, engine thundering, wheels pounding, steel squealing against steel. I was prepared for the noise but not for the vibration; it nearly threw me off-balance, and I stopped walking until the train passed. Finally, when its sound began to fade thin and plaintive in the distance, I moved to the far side of the trestle and peered out at the darkened park.

No one there. Just the metal drum surrounded by trash and illuminated by a dim spotlight. The rickety picnic table slumped in shadow.

Spitz might have changed his mind, I thought, but more likely he was biding his time, checking things out, just as I was. I decided to wait under the trestle a few minutes more. The gun I'd borrowed from Amos was in the side pocket of my shoulder bag; now I transferred it to the waistband of my jeans. Anna's cape concealed it, gave me plenty of room to maneuver if necessary.

Men's voices on the beach now. I pulled back, listened. Two of them, coming this way. Talking loud, slurring their words. Then a clank as a tossed can hit and bounced off the trash drum. The men kept walking past the trestle and south along the shoreline.

I relaxed some, then heard more voices, this time on River Street. Tensed all over again, hoping whoever it was wouldn't come under the trestle. A car door slammed, and an engine started up. Going away.

After that the night became very quiet. It was black and damp under the trestle. Cold, too. The Monongahela lay wide and still, the moon's path scarcely rippling. I stared at it, in danger of becoming hypnotized. And heard a suppressed cough coming from the grove of willows.

Jim Spitz, checking out the park from the shelter of the trees.

Spitz waited. I waited. Finally I decided it was a standoff and stepped out onto the beach. Stood close to the trestle, hand resting on the gun's grip.

After half a minute a man came out of the grove: medium height, clad in a navy pea jacket and jeans. I couldn't make out his features, only the paleness of his face, the darkness of his hair. He stopped, looking toward me, then went over to the picnic table and sat down.

I went over there, too. Stood on the table's far side, as I had earlier with Whitey. In the moonlight I saw a face that had been handsome before age and hard experience set in. Now the eyes were pouched, the once-chiseled nose skewed by a break that hadn't healed right. Discontented parentheses surrounded Spitz's mouth, and in its set I caught a touch of uncertainty. I took my hand off the gun; I had nothing to fear from this loser.

Spitz studied me in return, began to cough, then asked, "So where's Gordon's five hundred?" The question was supposed to sound tough, but it came out a whine.

"Two hundred now," I told him, "three later."

"When, later?"

"After we talk."

"About what?"

"How you set up Ed Bodine."

". . . I thought you said you were working for Gordon."

"I am."

"Then you ought to know all about it."

"I wasn't working for Gordon when that went down, and he's not talking about it. He's not talking about much these days. You heard what happened to his wife?"

Spitz nodded.

I took one of my cards out, slid it across the table toward him. "Gordon hired me to find somebody who was harassing him, but before I could, the explosion happened. I think it was set by the same person, and I also think the whole thing started here in Monora, with the Bodine bust. I want to know everything about it—who approached you, who figured in the arrangements."

He held the card up, squinted at it. Fingered the lettering as if he were reading Braille. I watched, waiting for him to make up his mind. Far away a car backfired, and then a dog began barking.

After a while Spitz asked, "You going to make trouble for me?"

"No. As far as I'm concerned, the Bodine bust is history. You give me the information, I'll pay you and leave you alone from then on."

"But how do I know you won't take what I tell you to the cops, the D.A.?"

"This is how." I took out two hundred dollars and set it in the middle of the table. "This taints any evidence I could pass along to them."

Spitz looked at the money for a moment; then his hand snaked forward and grasped it. As he stuffed it into the pocket of his pea jacket, he was seized by a spasm of coughing. He got it under control, took out a handkerchief and spat into it. "I got TB," he said. "You believe that? Nobody gets TB any more."

"I've heard there's been a rise in the incidence of it."

"Yeah, well, leave it to me to be on the cutting edge of a trend." His lips twisted bitterly. "I got this fuckin' disease, I got no wife any more, I got two little boys to raise. Kids, they need things. Otherwise I wouldn't touch your goddamn money."

I doubted that, but I merely said, "Why don't you tell me about the Bodine bust?"

"Yeah, okay. First person who talked to me about it was this gofer on Gordon's staff, I forget his name now. He said word had come down to take care of Bodine, and did I want to earn some extra money? I didn't mind; Ed'd screwed me over more times than I could count."

"Who bought the drugs? You?"

"Nah, I wasn't into this dodge then. I just steered them towards Ray Wilmer. The guy who delivered the blow to me was Gordon's pilot, that Josh Haddon. I snagged Bodine's jacket while he was on shift and had my wife sew the bags into the lining. Then I made the call to Bodine and set up the meet. It was easy to sell Ed on the idea I was on to some confidential management plans. He knew they were going to get him; it was just a matter of time. What he didn't figure was that they'd use a union brother to do it."

"Who planted the coke in Bodine's apartment and tipped off the cops?"

"Haddon or the gofer, I suppose. Haddon was the one I let know about when the meet was coming down."

"And for this they paid you . . . ?"

"Not nearly enough." His mouth tightened, and he looked away.

"Weren't you concerned that the prosecutor's office might not grant you immunity?"

"No. They told me the fix was already in."

"Did you have contact with anyone in Gordon's organization besides the gofer and Haddon?"

"Well, Russ Zola's name came up a couple of times, but I

never talked to him. The way I figure it, word came down from Gordon to Zola, then to Haddon, who sent the gofer to make the first contact."

It was, I thought, a perfect example of limiting accountability, a concept that had been developed to a science under the last few political administrations. Corporate specialists like Suits had now perfected it to an art. God knew to what new heights the rest of us would take it in the future.

"Okay, Mr. Spitz," I said, "you steered them to Ray Wilmer. Do you know who made the buy?"

"Haddon, I think. He was pretty damn streetwise—already knew about Wilmer, knew he kept regular business hours here in the park."

"And who paid you off afterward?"

"Haddon."

"What were the conditions of the payoff?"

"The what?"

"Did they tell you not to talk about the frame to anyone? Did they tell you to leave town?"

"Both." Spitz began to look anxious. What if this was a test of how well he continued to comply with the first condition?

"Don't worry, Mr. Spitz." I reached into my bag for the remaining three hundred dollars, held the bills up for him to see.

Spitz's greedy eyes focused on them. "That all you want to know?"

"Almost. Did Gordon's name ever come up in connection with the frame?"

"Not really."

"What about Noah Romanchek, his lawyer?"

"No, although I figured he was the one fixed it with the D.A."

"But basically it was just Haddon, the gofer, and a few mentions of Zola?"

"Yeah."

"Anything else you can tell me?"

He shook his head, eyes still on the money.

I set it on the table, watched as he grabbed it and tucked it away without bothering to count it. He stood up, hesitated, then started around the table toward me, a swagger in his step now that he'd collected.

"Something else I can do for you, lady?" he asked. "I got pills, crystal, blow. Or maybe you want something more interesting?"

Suddenly my emotions boiled over: rage at Suits and his cohorts, disgust at the greed and corruption that had ended Anna's life, had almost ended mine. I took it out on this pathetic loser, brought the gun between us before he could come any closer. My finger played with its trigger; I had to force myself to ease off.

Spitz's eyes widened. He made a strangling sound, took a step backwards.

I breathed in deeply, calming myself. Said, "Get the hell out of here."

Spitz turned and ran for the shelter of the willows.

*　　*　　*

"Why not stay over?" Amos Ritter said. "It's late, you'll never get a direct flight to San Francisco. I've got plenty of room—"

"No, it's better I leave tonight. Thanks for the loan of the gun. Thanks for everything." I hugged him and started down the steps of his Gothic horror.

"Come back sometime," he called. "Any time." Then added, "I wish you'd reconsider."

I shook my head, waved, and ran toward my rental car. Amos's suggestion made sense, but I couldn't take him up on it. I was afraid that if I paused to rest I'd interrupt the momentum that had begun as my plane streaked toward the rising sun yesterday morning. I needed that momentum more than ever now, needed it to combat the heavy weight of the knowledge I'd gleaned here.

River Park, Monora, Pennsylvania: scene of a drug buy.

Keystone Steel, Monora, Pennsylvania: scene of a drug frame.

The buy and the frame were, I feared, the proverbial tip of the iceberg. God only knew what further crimes and corruption I'd uncover before I was through delving into Suits's life and organization. I could see a conflict brewing ahead, between my loyalty to my old friend Suits and my loyalty to my old friend the truth. And deep down I knew that when I resolved it, my client might take a fall from which I couldn't—and wouldn't—save him.

This was one of those days when I hated my work. I wished I'd never heard of Ed Bodine, never seen his unmarked grave in the Nevada desert. I wished I'd never seen Monora and River Park. I wished I'd never seen the ruins of Keystone Steel and Moonshine House.

Most of all, I wished that Suitcase Gordon had never walked back into my life.

Touchstone

October 3

The pay phone's slot swallowed my credit card, and I punched out eleven digits. Thousands of miles and two time zones away, the bell rang in an empty ranch house. I didn't expect Hy to answer, but this slight link would help me get through what promised to be a long, lonely night. I slouched lower in the booth, counting rings, picturing the dark house and the stark, moon-shot landscape surrounding it.

And Hy's sleepy voice said, "Hello?"

"You're there!"

"Uh, yeah. Where're you?" He was alert now; he had that ability to come awake quickly and fully.

"Dallas—Fort Worth Airport."

"Good God, why?"

"Because the only flight west that I could get from Pittsburgh was here. Now I can either hippety-hop all over, to Denver to Salt Lake to L.A. to San Francisco, or wait for the first direct flight at eight-forty in the morning."

"So you went to Pennsylvania, too. Thought you would.

But what about flights to Reno? If you can get there, I could pick you up in the Citabria."

"I checked on Reno and Las Vegas. Won't work. How come you're back home so soon?"

"My business in San Diego turned out to be more profitable than I expected, so I canceled out on the East Coast. Was your trip profitable also?"

"Uh-huh." There was an edge to my voice now; his failure to elaborate on what he'd done in San Diego annoyed me.

Hy ignored it. "What'd you find out?"

"Plenty."

He waited. When I didn't go on, he asked, "So what'd you do with my Land Rover?"

"It's in long-term parking at McCarran Field."

"Good place for it."

"Look, I'll return it as soon—"

"No problem, McCone. I got a buddy owes me a favor; we can fly down there and he'll drive it back. So what's up?"

Because he'd resolved the problem of the Land Rover, I relented and filled him in on the details of the past few days, concluding, "I really need to get to San Francisco and locate Suits before he does himself or somebody else serious damage."

"What makes you think he's there?"

"Facts, plus a dash of instinct. He may not be in the city itself, but I'll bet he's somewhere in northern California."

Hy was silent, thinking it over. "When does the Denver flight leave?"

I glanced over at the gate. "It's about to board right now."

"So what're you waiting for?"

My lips curved in a slow smile. "I'll call you from Salt Lake if I get lonesome."

Part Four

Northern California

October

Seventeen

"Shar? God, what're you doing up this early on a Sunday?"

"I could ask the same of you." Rae had a hard time rising on a work morning, let alone a weekend; it was only eight-twenty, but over the phone her voice sounded curiously alert.

"I've been up all night," she said.

"Working?"

"No."

"You finally meet somebody?"

"Well, sort of. I've been having the most incredible . . . um, sensual experience."

"Who is he?"

"It's kind of hard to explain. Listen, why are you calling?"

"I'm trying to locate Mick. I just got into SFO, and he has my car, so I want him to pick me up. I called both my house and my office, but I got the machines. Have you seen him?"

". . . Not since around eight last night. He came in while I was fooling with your computer—I'm thinking of getting

241

one like it and knew you wouldn't mind if I tried it out—and took off again."

"He say where he was going?"

"No, we only talked for a minute. I told him I was on line to Wisdom and thanked him for letting me know about it. He said something . . . let me think. Yeah, he pulled a fax out of your machine and said he'd just received some information that he wouldn't have gotten so fast if it hadn't been for a contact he'd made through the bulletin boards. Then he took off in a hurry."

"What's this about bulletin boards and . . . Wisdom, is it?"

"Wisdom's a computer network. You remember a few weeks ago when I gave up on the bar-and-club circuit and started hanging around the Technomat?"

"The . . . oh, right." The singles scene hadn't worked out for Rae; she'd met what she described as two total nerds, innumerable alcoholics, a guy who was into handcuffs, and an attorney who was well known to clerks in the lingerie departments of various downtown stores. Next her friend Vanessa had told her about a place to do her laundry in Noe Valley that was hooked into a citywide computer network; while you waited for your clothes to wash and dry, you could drink coffee and communicate with other similarly occupied people in other laundries via computer terminals that were set into little café tables. No romance had developed from that, either, but for a while there Rae had the cleanest clothes in town.

"So," I said, "Wisdom's another of these networks?"

"Nationwide. You yourself subscribe to it."

"I do?"

"Well, I guess Mick does."

And I knew on whose nickel.

"Anyway," she went on, "there're various bulletin boards

where you can post messages, and people reply to them, and eventually you get a dialogue going. I met two guys through the Frank Conversations board, and I've got this thing going with them."

In spite of my concern with what Mick was up to, I couldn't help but ask, "Separately or together?"

"Uh, together."

My God, what would she get into next?

"It's not anything sleazy like phone sex, Shar!"

"Did I suggest that?"

"You didn't have to; I know how your mind works. But it's really . . . like all the barriers to total communication are removed. You mesh intellectually, and then you just . . ."

"Yes?"

"I can't explain."

"Come on, Rae, remove the barriers to total communication and tell me." Needling her was often irresistible.

"I *knew* you wouldn't understand. Why did I ever mention it in the first place?"

"Okay, we'll drop the subject—for now." I got back to business. "Will you do me a favor?"

"Sure." She sounded relieved.

"Thanks. Go to my office and see if the fax Mick got is still there."

She set the receiver down, and I heard her footsteps patter away. In her absence I tried to conjure up an image of what incredibly sensual experience one could have with two men via computer terminal. Nothing materialized. Well, I wasn't going to worry about it; Rae was a big girl, and it was time I started treating her as an equal—even if she did manage to get herself into the damnedest situations.

There was a rustle of paper and Rae said, "Looks like the right one—at least the date matches. It's something to do with a military service record."

"Sidney Blessing's?"

"Uh . . . right." She read me the details. Sid Blessing had been an explosives technician in the army.

When she finished, I said, "I need another favor. Will you see if Mick has a file on Blessing?"

"Will you promise not to nag me to tell you more about the guys I met through Wisdom?"

"Yes," I lied.

"Okay." She went away, came back. "Got it."

"There should be a Modesto address in there."

Pages rustled. "Seven-oh-four Cassie Court."

"Thanks, Rae. I'll talk to you later."

"Wait—any message for Mick, in case I see him?"

"No. I have a feeling I'll be seeing him soon."

*　　*　　*

Altamont Pass is the gateway to the Central Valley for those approaching from the Bay Area. The 580 freeway cuts through barren, rolling hills that are dotted with hundreds of science-fictional wind turbines. On a good day their appendages whirl against the sky, giving off flashes of silver; on a bad day they drag or remain stubbornly still. This morning was one of the good ones; the mills spun briskly, and I imagined they were waving in greeting as I drove by in the compact I'd rented at the airport.

Maybe it was an omen that everything would turn out okay, I thought. Maybe Suits wouldn't kill anybody or get himself killed. Maybe I'd reach him in time. . . .

Once over the pass, I was into level brown-and-green land, stretching fifty miles toward the Sierra Nevada. Most outsiders think of California as Los Angeles and San Francisco, or perhaps Yosemite and Big Sur; few realize that a vast portion of our state is farmland, as fertile and flat as the Midwest. In recent decades the farmers of the four-hundred-mile-long Central Valley have been hard hit by tough economic conditions and persistent droughts; farms have been sold off piecemeal to developers, and some of our best agricultural land is now under asphalt and concrete.

Once-peaceful little valley towns have swelled to tract-rimmed bedroom communities for commuters from the Bay Area. Families move there for the relatively low home prices, the schools, the crime-free atmosphere, the small-town life. But too-rapid growth has brought much of what the newcomers are seeking to escape: crime, higher prices, racial tension, and resentment from longtime residents. If future growth isn't planned and controlled, one day the motto on Modesto's town arch—Water, Wealth, Contentment, Health—may describe nothing more than a memory.

Cassie Court was in an older tract on the far north side of town. All the surrounding streets bore women's names; it made me wonder whether the developer had been paying homage to female friends and relatives or if he'd merely picked them out of a what-to-name-the-baby book. Enid Tomchuck Blessing's house stood at the far end of the cul-de-sac where the tract backed up on a walnut grove; light yellow with dark brown trim, its single-story design repeated that of every third dwelling. I glanced around, half expecting to see my old red MG parked at the curb, but if Mick had come here, he'd already departed.

The young woman who answered the door of number 704 was very pale; dark smudges underscored her eyes, and strain lines marred her oval face; her long, straight hair looked dry and brittle. When she saw me, her fingers tightened reflexively on the doorknob.

I introduced myself and handed her my card, asked if I could talk with her about her husband's death. She barely glanced at the card before crumpling it and dropping it to the floor.

"First the others, now you," she said. "I told the blond kid I didn't want to talk to him when he called a few days ago, so he showed up anyway, and—"

"Mick Savage was here?"

"Last night. Real late. The bell woke Ariel, and she cried for hours. She misses her father."

Dammit, Mick! "I apologize for my assistant's intrusion. I hope he didn't make trouble."

"You don't call a screaming kid trouble? That was enough for me. I ran the son of a bitch off with Sid's old hunting rifle. And don't think it wasn't loaded!"

My God, what if she'd shot him? I'd better do something about Mick—and the sooner the better.

Tomchuck added, "I suppose the other one was with your agency, too."

"Describe him."

"Skinny little guy, looks kind of like a rat. *Total* asshole." She grasped her wrist, exposed the underside of her forearm; it was purpled in a series of bruises that looked like finger marks.

"He did that to you?"

She nodded. "You really ought to rethink your hiring policies, if you know what I mean."

Suits, getting violent with a young woman. Not good, not good at all. "He's not affiliated with me," I said, "but I know him. When was he here?"

"Yesterday morning. I'd just gotten the girls off to play with the neighbors' kids. That's not easy these days; all they want to do is hang around the house; I guess it makes them feel safe. And then this guy comes pushing in here, demanding to see Sid, and all the time Sid's dead. When that finally sank in, he started asking me a lot of questions, and when I wouldn't answer them, he twisted my arm." Her hand moved over the bruises.

"What kinds of questions?" I asked.

"About what Sid was doing the week he died."

"You answer them?"

"What choice did I have? I answered them, and then he went away. And that's when I got out Sid's old rifle and loaded it."

"Has the man tried to contact you since?"

She shook her head.

"Well, I wouldn't worry about him. He got what he wanted, and I doubt he'll be back."

"Who *is* he?"

"Someone who knew your husband in San Francisco."

She tensed, drawing her lower lip in under her teeth.

"Ms. Tomchuck, can we talk?"

"About Sid? What's the use? He's dead and never coming back. And don't call me Ms. Tomchuck. It's Mrs. Blessing. Sid made me use my maiden name for legal things because of his . . . activities."

"What activities?"

Silence.

"Mrs. Blessing, don't you want Sid's killer arrested?"

". . . Of course I do. I want to see him sitting in the gas chamber."

"Then why not talk with me?"

"What good'll it do? The police haven't done anything."

"I think I know some things that may help them."

"Why do you want to? What's in it for you?"

"Talking with you will help me with a related case."

She hesitated, still massaging her forearm. "Look, it's not that I don't want . . . It's just that I'm scared."

"Of what? Of whom?"

She glanced over my shoulder, as if she was afraid someone was listening. I used the opportunity to suggest, "Why don't we talk inside?"

". . . I guess it wouldn't hurt. I'm alone; the kids're at my sister's."

Inside, the house had the impersonal feel of a place that the occupants hadn't yet made their own. It didn't help that there was scarcely any furniture. Enid Blessing started toward the living room, which contained only an entertainment center and a scattering of big flowered pillows, then detoured to the adjacent dining area and motioned for me to sit at a white plastic table that was better suited to a patio.

"Sid and I ordered new furniture," she said as she sat down across from me. "When he died, I had to cancel, and I lost the deposit. Couldn't help it, though; I've got those two little girls and no job, so I need to save the money we . . . I've got left."

"I understand you came into quite a bit of money last summer."

Her eyes narrowed. "Who told you that?"

"Your friend who bought the contents of the Pacifica house mentioned it to one of your former neighbors."

"Craig? He's got a mouth on him! That's nobody's business but ours."

"Where did the money come from?"

". . . I don't know."

"Come on, Enid."

"It's God's truth! Sid didn't tell . . . Look, don't you people sometimes pay for information?"

"Sometimes."

"How much would you give me if I told you everything I know?"

"That depends on what you have to offer."

"I'm supposed to tell you *before* we set a price?"

"I won't know what the information's worth until I hear what it is. Besides, is anybody else offering?"

She thought about that, drumming her fingertips on the tabletop. I noticed that the nails were bitten to the quick. "Okay," she finally said, "this probably isn't worth all that much, anyway. But money's money, and I've got my kids to think about. Last July, the first week, Sid came home all excited. Brought a bottle of champagne for us and ice cream for Ariel and Ariadne. He'd taken on an important job for somebody he met at Bay Vista, and he said we could go looking for a house. It had to be away from the Bay Area, though."

"Why?"

"I guess because of whatever he had to do for this job. We moved a lot because of his . . ." She looked down at her hands. "Sid was into things, you know?"

"Things?"

"Scams and stuff. That's why we sort of hid behind my maiden name, so people couldn't check public records and catch up with him."

"I see. So you found this house . . ."

"My sister, who lives here, knew the people who were selling. I loved it right off; I'd always wanted a house of my own. We got a fast escrow, and it closed early in August."

"But you stayed in Pacifica until late that month. Why?"

"Sid needed to be at Bay Vista for a while, to do whatever it was he had to do. And anyway, the girls had day camp and stuff. So I picked out the color schemes and drove out here a few times to paint and wallpaper, and we ordered the furniture and . . . oh, God!" She leaned forward, pressing her palms against her eyes.

This was another of those days when I hated my work. I looked away, waited until she calmed herself, then asked, "Do you know what Sid was doing during those last weeks at Bay Vista?"

"Uh . . ." She took her hands from her eyes, brushed away tears with her fingertips. "Well, he was gone a lot of nights, and he never worked nights at the condo complex. Was gone once on his day off. The day we moved in here, he drove our van out with the stuff we were keeping, offloaded it, then turned around and went right back to San Francisco, and was gone all night. I was mad at him for leaving me alone with the unpacked boxes. Now I'd give anything . . ."

"I know." I touched her hand. First she looked surprised at the gesture, then pathetically grateful. I asked, "You moved here when?"

"The last Tuesday in August."

And that night Suits was attacked in his condominium. "What happened after that?"

"Two days later Sid left here again, in the morning, and stayed away all night and most of the next day. I guess he didn't get back till ten or eleven."

The night he'd stayed away was the one Suits, Anna, and I had spent together at Moonshine House—the night before the explosion.

"How did Sid seem when he got back?"

"Seem?"

I began to feel impatient with her. "Was he upset? Happy? What?"

"Well, more excited than anything else, I guess. He told me he'd taken care of the final thing he had to do to get us the rest of our money."

The final thing. Damned right it was final. He'd ended Anna Gordon's life.

It was a moment before I could ask, "He gave you no idea at all about what this final thing was? Or of what the job was?"

She shook her head, ashamed. "Sid was real secretive about the . . . stuff he was into. He said it was safer if he kept me out of it. I should've made him tell me; I know that now. But then . . . I knew that what he was doing was wrong, but I couldn't've stopped him. And knowing what it was and not being able to do anything about it . . . well, that would've been worse than not knowing at all. You see what I mean?"

I'd never had the desire to shield myself from reality, no

matter how bad it might be, but I could see a certain logic in what she said. "I think so. Did Sid get the rest of the money?"

"Oh, yeah, he had it with him when he came back. Twenty-five thousand dollars, cash. It sounds like a lot, but it isn't, really. We . . . I've got an awfully big mortgage on this place."

It also wasn't a lot when you measured it against the worth of Anna's life. "Okay," I said, "what happened on the night your husband died?"

Her gaze blurred with fresh tears, but she blinked them away. "He got a phone call. Around ten, I guess. He said it was the person he'd done the job for, that there might be more money in it for us. A couple of hours later he went out to meet whoever it was that called. And he just . . . never came home." Her head flopped forward and she clutched the edge of the table with her fingertips.

"And he never told you anything about the person, not even the smallest detail?"

She shook her head; a tear dropped to the tabletop.

I took one of my business checks from my wallet, filled it in for a generous amount, and laid it in front of her. She didn't even look at it. I touched her arm, got up, and let myself out of the house.

Enid Blessing, I thought, had deliberately blinded herself to what her husband was doing, and in a way that made her equally culpable. Still, I sensed a vein of strength in her that might prove valuable, at least to her little girls.

It was warm outside, the autumn temperatures in California's Central Valley being a far cry from those in southwestern Pennsylvania. When I got to my rental car I took off Anna's cape, which I'd worn all the way across the country since my extended thirty-some-hour day had begun in Monora.

So the killer I'd traveled all those miles to find was dead and, anyway, nothing more than a hired technician. I'd suspected as much, but behind him I'd already sensed the outline of a second person. The person who had ordered the explosion at Moonshine House and suggested that there might be a way to take me out in the process.

I needed to fill in that outline before Suits compounded the tragedy.

Eighteen

Suits's silver Corvette was no longer parked in its space in the Bay Vista garage. I went to the complex's security office and, to my surprise, found Sue Mahoney at her desk.

"How come you're working on a sunny Sunday afternoon?" I asked.

Mahoney scowled. "My assistant's wife picked today to have her damn baby. Ruined my plans to go sailing."

"That's tough," I said insincerely.

"What d'you want, McCone?"

"What happened to T. J. Gordon's car?"

"I guess he took it when he was here Friday."

"He was here at Bay Vista?"

"Friday afternoon. Man sure has gone downhill since his wife got killed."

"How so?"

"He looks like hell—shaggy hair, bloodshot eyes, stubbly chin. Must've been sleeping in the same clothes for weeks. Personality's the same, though—lousy."

"The man's wife died, Mahoney."

"So?"

"Compassionate, aren't you?"

"There's nothing in my employment contract that says I have to be."

I let that conversational thread go. "You talk with him?"

"Yeah. He wanted the current address of our former concierge, Sid Blessing. I don't have it, but Payroll does, so I sent Gordon to them. Blessing's a nervy bastard; he walked off the job without giving advance notice in August, then had the gall to call up Payroll and tell them where to send his final check."

So that was how Suits had found Enid. "Blessing's dead, Mahoney."

She raised her eyebrows. "Who killed him?"

"How come you know somebody killed him? I didn't say that."

"It's a joke, for Christ's sake."

"Hilarious."

"You know, McCone, I've never liked you."

I smiled. "There's nothing in your employment contract that says you have to."

* * *

Josh Haddon answered my knock at the door of Suits's penthouse. The pilot had lost weight since I'd last seen him, and his freckled face was more lined.

"You're back from Monora," he said.

"How'd you know I went there?"

"Noah Romanchek told me." Josh stepped aside and motioned for me to come in. The bloodstains and scuff marks had been cleaned from the foyer, and the card table and papers had been straightened, but the place had a desolate feel in spite of the sunlight that slanted through the glass wall.

I asked, "Have you seen T.J.?"

He shook his head.

"He was here at the complex on Friday, spoke with Security, and took his car. He didn't come up?"

"No, and I was around all day. Wonder why not?"

"He seems to have gone underground. Josh, why're you still staying here?"

"Waiting on T.J., just like always. I've got no idea what he's going to do, so I decided I'd better camp out for a while."

I glanced around the room. With the exception of a couple of folding chairs on the balcony, Josh had added no furnishings. It was as if he had tried on Suits's lifestyle and decided it fit him. "Camping out is a good description," I said.

He shrugged. "Doesn't bother me. I've never cared much for creature comforts. T.J. pays me this huge salary for being on call twenty-four hours, and all I've done for years is bank it. Look, why don't we sit outside?"

I followed him to the balcony and took one of the chairs, propping my feet on the lower crosspiece of the railing.

"So what'd you think of Monora?" Josh asked.

"It's grim."

"You find out anything interesting?"

"I talked to a lot of people—Chief Koll, a writer named Amos Ritter, Herb Pace. Jim Spitz."

Josh grew very still. Waiting for the other shoe to drop, I thought.

"Of course you knew all those people," I added.

"I didn't really know Ritter, but I've heard of him. The others—well, sure."

"And you knew Ed Bodine."

". . . Yeah. You see him, too? I thought he was in prison."

"He escaped."

"No kidding. When?"

"A year ago last July."

"He didn't go back to Monora, did he?"

"No, he didn't go back to Monora."

Josh didn't say anything. I let the silence lengthen. Finally he sighed. "All right, you know about us setting Bodine up."

"Yes. I want to hear your version of it."

"Why? It's over and done with."

"I still want to hear your story."

"What're you going to do? Go to Koll, get the case re-opened? And why're you nosing around in it, anyway? I thought you were done working for T.J."

"I'm no more done working for him than you are. As for Koll, she's not going to open what she regards as a political can of worms. So it's all right to tell me about it."

He hesitated a while more. Fished out a cigarette and cupped his hands to light it. "Okay," he finally said. "You know Bodine was a troublemaker. He'd used some damned dirty tactics and was impossible to negotiate with. Word came down—get rid of him. I'm a good little soldier; I obeyed orders."

"Whose orders?"

"Russ Zola's. They don't call him the executioner for nothing."

"Why'd you decide on a drug frame?"

"First thing that occurred to Noah and me. Noah used to be a drug lawyer; they've got the same mentality and connections as dealers. Me . . . well, you know about that."

"So Romanchek was in on it, too."

"He was the one who fixed it with the prosecutor's office and the defense attorney."

"And T.J.?"

Josh shrugged.

"Did he know?"

"Sometimes people know things without really knowing them."

The old lack of accountability again.

"I've watched the way T.J. operates," Josh added. "He'll kick a problem around with someone—Noah, Carole, Russ.

It's a problem with a solution that's pretty obvious and pretty unsavory, only T.J. acts like he can't see it. Next thing you know, the person he's been talking to is taking action, only they don't tell T.J. what they're up to because they've convinced themselves that if he knew he'd stop them." Josh's lips twisted cynically. "Me, I never fooled myself. I knew I had T.J.'s full approval for all my dirty dealing."

"There was a lot of it?"

"Enough." Josh got up and moved to the railing. Ground out his cigarette and kicked it over the edge.

"Why'd you go along with it?"

"Why not? I flew T.J. around, did whatever he told me. In exchange, he paid me well, bought great aircraft. That was all I cared about."

"Past tense?"

"Maybe. Things're different now."

"How?"

"We all change."

"Have you changed because of Anna's death?"

He glanced over his shoulder at me, surprised. Then he scowled and looked away. "I don't want to talk about Anna."

"Josh—"

"No. You better go now."

His back was stiff, resistant; I'd get nothing more from him today. "We'll talk another time, then. Before I leave, do you mind if I make some phone calls?"

"Be T.J.'s guest."

*　　*　　*

For privacy's sake I used an extension I'd noticed in the kitchen to call my house. Mick answered. I asked him if he'd found out anything on his trip up to Mendocino County, and he said he'd located a man who'd spotted Suits hitchhiking south on the coast highway early Friday morning. Then he started to tell me about Sid Blessing's service record, but I cut him short and had him dig up and read to me a list of phone numbers Suits had given me last August. There was only one home number on it, that of Nate Evans, the architect who had pulled out of the Hunters Point project. I copied it down.

Mick said, "I think you ought to know about this Blessing business."

"We'll discuss that when I get home."

"But, Shar, I went—"

"I can't talk about that now." I hung up before I wasted valuable time laying into him for harassing Enid Blessing.

At first Nate Evans was reluctant to interrupt his Sunday for me. I told him my business was urgent and I'd be glad to meet with him at any time. He hesitated, consulted with someone in the background, then agreed to see me at eight-thirty that evening and gave me directions to his Woodside home down on the Peninsula.

Next I called Lost Hope and spoke with Chuck Westerkamp. The remains they'd exhumed from the wash, he told me, had been positively identified from Ed Bodine's dental charts. Walker and Deck still hadn't been apprehended.

I said, "You know, I've been thinking about your problem with getting hold of Walker's phone records."

"Yes?"

"When I was watching from outside her house before she went to see Leon Wednesday night, she was talking on a cordless that looked a lot like mine. Now, on mine there's a redial button; the phone stores the last number called, and when you hit that button, it automatically dials it again."

"And?"

"It would be interesting to know the last person she talked to before she and Leon took off."

"Would be." Westerkamp hesitated. "Small towns like this, it's customary to leave a spare house key with a neighbor. I happen to know that Brenda is very close to our postmistress, who lives across the street. Maybe I'll have a talk with her. You going to be home later on?"

"Until around seven-thirty."

"I'll call you if anything interesting turns up."

*   *   *

When I walked into my living room, my calico cat, Alice, was sitting on the back of the chair near W. C. Fields's perch, left paw reaching toward the silk parrot's tail. "Not you, too!" I yelled.

Allie leaped down, ran halfway across the room, then turned and mowled indignantly.

"That parrot is not for you!"

She mowled again and galloped toward the food bowl.

"And don't talk back to me!"

Then I dropped my weekend bag on the floor, ashamed that I was taking out my anger with Mick on the cat.

The true object of my anger chose that instant to emerge from the hallway leading to the bathroom, his hair wet and slicked back, his face scrubbed and rosy. He saw my glower and stopped.

"At last we meet again," I said.

Mick crossed the kitchen and came into the living room, arms folded defensively.

I asked, "Just where the hell did you go last night after you woke up Enid Blessing's little girl and almost got yourself shot?"

". . . That gun was loaded?"

"Damned right it was." I took the keys to the rental car from my pocket and tossed them to him. "I want you to deliver that Geo that's parked out front to the airport. And don't have an accident; I'm the only one who's supposed to be driving it. After that, you get your ass back here and start packing."

"Shar—"

259

"Mick, you're very bright and talented, but you've displayed incredibly bad judgment. I can't afford to keep you around any more. I can't afford another incident like the one with Enid Blessing."

"How did you find out—"

"From her. You not only put yourself in jeopardy, but you endangered the agency. What if she'd filed a complaint? Did that ever occur to you?"

He bit his lip, looked down at the floor. Mumbled something.

"What?"

"I said, I was only trying to help."

"I know that. But the kind of help I needed from you was in the office, on the phone, or at the computer." I thought about mentioning that I didn't appreciate having the agency's money spent for such items as a Wisdom subscription, but decided enough was enough.

"I'm sorry," he said.

He sounded so crestfallen that I almost weakened. Almost. "Apology accepted," I told him. "And now I've got an appointment down on the Peninsula. You get dressed and return the Geo."

He nodded and started toward the guest room, then stopped and turned. "Shar?"

"Yes?"

He started to say something, shook his head.

"What, Mick?"

"Nothing, really. I just wanted to tell you—I changed the oil in the MG this afternoon, and the gas tank's full."

Nineteen

The affluent, horsey community of Woodside has managed to remain countrified in spite of the urbanization of most other Peninsula towns. It helps that property values are prohibitively high, that many of its humans and animals are pedigreed, that much of it is far off the beaten track. Mountain roads wind high into heavily forested hills, and smaller lanes branch off them into the shadow of redwoods and eucalyptus. The houses are often acres apart and range from ostentatious statements of their owners' financial condition to personal expressions of resident artists. Nate Evans's home fell somewhere in between.

Set high above the narrow pavement, it was three stories of gray wood and glass; tall arched windows spilled light onto the branches of surrounding oak trees. A long wooden stairway negotiated the hill from the road to the front door. Evans had cautioned me that there was no driveway; the garage was set into the hill at street level. I should be careful not to park on the curve, he said, as teenage drivers tended to use the road as

261

a racecourse. I left the MG a fair distance away near the mailbox of another house built into the opposite downhill slope, then walked up and climbed the stairway.

After I reached the front door and rang the bell, I turned and took in the view: dark hills rolling away to the west, where their tops were draped in coastal fog; small lights winking here and there among the trees. The air was chill, laden with the heavy scent of redwood; nothing moved to disturb the silence. Not a good place, I thought, for a person unaccustomed to solitude.

Behind me the door opened. The woman who looked out was young, blond, clad in a leather jacket and jeans. She said, "Himself's in the living room, go right in," and hurried past me, jingling car keys and leaving a trail of exotic perfume.

I stepped into a tiled foyer and shut the door. The living room—yards of white carpet with redwood-paneled walls and jungle-patterned furnishings—lay two steps down. A man rose from a sectional couch in front of a stone fireplace and came toward me.

He said, "If you haven't already made the mistake, never have children."

"I'm sorry?"

"Teenagers are a pain in the ass. My daughter just caught me in a weak moment, borrowed the keys to my Porsche, and ran out of here on some errand that I wish I could believe was innocent. Ms. McCone?"

"Yes. Mr. Evans?"

My host nodded and motioned toward the short section of the couch. As I sat down I studied him. Tall, athletic, gray-haired with a youthful face, he was a casting director's image of an architect who would live in such a house and have a pretty daughter who would wheedle away the keys to the Porsche.

"You have a lovely home," I said. "Did you design it?"

He shook his head. "My area of specialization is strictly

industrial. I wouldn't know how to go about designing a house like this, but fortunately a talented friend of mine does. May I offer you something. Coffee? A drink?"

"Nothing, thanks. I understand from T. J. Gordon that you're one of the best marine-facility architects in the country."

"He overrates me. Considerably." But he smiled, pleased.

"It's natural, then, that he was very upset when you pulled out of his Hunters Point project."

Evans frowned, sitting on the other section of the couch and taking a cigarette from a pack in his shirt pocket. "He didn't send you to ask me to reconsider? No, he wouldn't need a private investigator for that."

"No. Mr. Gordon hired me back in August to investigate what appeared to be a pattern of harassment."

Nate Evans rolled the cigarette between his thumb and forefinger, then picked up a lighter from the end table. "You mind if I smoke?"

I shook my head.

He lighted the cigarette, then said, "Could you be more specific about this harassment?"

I explained, stressing the part about him and two other people pulling out of the project on the same day.

When I finished, Evans put out his cigarette, looking thoughtful. "You know, I've been uncomfortable about pulling out of that deal ever since Gordon's wife was killed. I should have been up-front with him about my reasons. Maybe . . . Well, that's neither here nor there now."

"Exactly what were your reasons?"

He hunched forward, elbows on knees, eyes clouded. "I began to have doubts about the project when a letter came to my office. In essence, it said that the Golden Gate Lines turnaround was going badly; Gordon was overextended, underfinanced, and had personal problems. That gave me pause, but the writer didn't identify himself, and I don't like to react to rumor, so I tossed it out and didn't mention it to T.J. Next there was a phone call from a friend, a venture capitalist whom I respect."

I named the investor who had also pulled out of the project.

Evans nodded. "He'd been hearing similar things at his club. He asked if I knew anything. We agreed to ignore the rumors, but we kept hearing them. People were saying GGL was shakier than ever. I ran into Dick Farley, manager of the Jack London Terminal; he said Gordon was acting strangely. I'd noticed it, too. I had another project in the works, so I backed off."

"It strikes me as highly coincidental that you, the venture capitalist, and the terminal manager at the Port of Stockton whom Gordon hoped to hire all backed out on the same day."

"I won't lie to you: we'd talked, and I suppose the old domino effect was in operation."

"And not one of you confronted Gordon about the rumors."

"By the time we began accepting them as fact, T.J. was acting very strangely. He was paranoid, flew off the handle at the slightest provocation, was often verbally abusive. In short, not a man you'd care to confront. Perhaps if we'd known about the attempts on his life, we'd have acted differently. But as it was, he'd become so strange that when his wife was killed in that explosion, I thought . . . Jesus." He shook his head.

"You thought he'd had her killed."

"A lot of people did. Still do."

"Do you recall anything about the note you received or the rumors you heard that might indicate who was behind them?"

He thought. "Only that it had to be someone who was very knowledgeable about GGL. At least at first; after a while the rumors took on their own momentum."

"Let me ask you this: if Gordon somehow gets it together and revives the Hunters Point project, would you consider working on it?"

"Well, I've taken on another long-term project, but . . . yes, I'd at least consider it."

"May I tell T.J. that?"

"Of course. By the way, how's he doing?"

"Better." And maybe he was. He'd left his self-imposed exile at Moonshine Cottage, set off on a course of action. But was that course of action wholly rational? I'd know when I caught up with him.

If I caught up with him . . .

*   *   *

The night seemed colder and darker as I walked down the stairway from Nate Evans's house. The coastal fog had crept farther in and lay low in the folds of the hills now; a pocket of it surrounded the home on the far side of the road, muting its lights. Up above, an engine droned, and then a small car sped around the sharp curve; its brake lights flashed as it fishtailed into the switchback. Evans hadn't been exaggerating when he said kids used the road as a racecourse.

I stuffed my hands deep in my jacket pockets and walked along the pavement toward the MG. Another car's engine boomed to life above, and I automatically moved over to the road's edge. Headlights flared behind me. I glanced back.

The lights seemed to be coming straight toward me.

Momentarily I froze, waiting for the driver to correct his course. The lights kept coming, faster now. Fear surged through me as I realized he intended to run me down.

Blindly I leaped sideways off the road, twisting my body, my arms out for balance. I felt a rush of air; gravel spurted up and peppered my back. Pain seared my left calf as the car's bumper grazed it. I pitched forward, fell hard, and slid down the incline on a scratchy blanket of pine needles.

I pushed myself to my feet, gritting my teeth against the pain. There was a shriek of tires, a clash of gears. Then the headlight beams splashed over the branches of the trees above me.

Coming back.

I ducked, fumbled my way into a clump of pyracantha bushes. Their spines tore at my clothing, scratched my face. I batted at them, burrowed deeper—heart pounding, mouth dry.

On the road above, the car stopped.

I eased forward, saw a paved driveway on the other side of the bushes. Parted the branches so I could peer up its length.

The car idled at its top—light-colored, low-slung, the make unidentifiable at this distance. After a moment it moved on, but slowly and only for a few yards. Then its engine shut off, its headlights went out.

Coming after me on foot—and not to ask if I was okay.

He'd find me all too easily here.

I broke from the bushes and ran down the driveway, ignoring the pain in my calf. Toward the muted lights of the house where there were people, a phone. . . .

As I ran, I scanned the ground for something to use as a weapon. Nothing. Just a line of pyracanthas and, beyond them, fog and darkness. Why, I thought, was my gun always locked away at home when I needed it! I had a carry permit; I should get over my aversion to keeping the .38 with me—

From high above came the sound of pursuing footsteps.

I ran through a parking area in front of a garage, around the garage, over a decked walkway to the front door. The lights I'd seen were exterior fixtures; the house's interior was dark.

I pushed the bell anyway, pounded on the door. No response.

The footsteps slapped behind me, in the parking area now. Whirling, I saw a stairway leading to a big deck at the side of the house. I plunged down the steps two at a time, grasping the railing for balance.

The deck was huge, illuminated by photoelectric security spots. Beyond it, a pool area was as bright as noonday. I veered off the stairs, slid down a brushy slope to one of the deck's support beams, then ducked under its planking. There was only about four feet of clearance there; I hunched low, worked my way back into the darkness.

I could hear footfalls on the stairs now.

Blood roared in my ears. My leg throbbed. Fear clogged my throat, threatening to burst forth as sound. I clamped my lips together, held my breath.

My pursuer stopped. Moved onto the deck. Stopped again, briefly, then walked more quietly toward its perimeter.

I remained still, my back hurting from the bowed position, my leg throbbing harder now. The terrain sloped steeply here; I had to lean backward and dig in my heels to keep from sliding. My eyes had adjusted to the blackness; I thrust my head forward turtlelike and peered around. Support beams, a drainage pipe, coils of what looked to be sprinkler tubing. And there, by the outermost supports—

A chain-link fence.

Trapped.

He was still moving around overhead. A man—I could tell by the way he walked. Coming back toward me. Coming closer. Tap. Tap. Tap . . .

Directly overhead now. Stopping.

Don't breathe.

He breathed. Softly.

Don't move.

He moved. Purposefully.

Don't look up.

He was looking around. Carefully.

I couldn't hold my breath much longer. My balance felt shaky; at any second I might slip, give myself away. I wanted to look up, try to identify him. Couldn't risk it.

The man began moving again.

Across the deck. Pause. Turn.

Back toward me.

Over my head and toward the stairway.

Stop. Go.

And then he stepped off the planking onto the slope. Heading toward the place where I'd gone under.

Slowly I turned my head. Saw a pair of feet shod in athletic shoes. Legs clad in jeans.

He was big, if foot size was any indication.

Armed?

Impossible to tell.

Dammit, why don't I have my gun!

A sports car's engine raced on the road above; the car turned into the driveway. The owner of the house coming home?

My pursuer's feet pivoted. He was looking up the slope.

The car stopped in the driveway. A garage door began going up.

The man turned again and moved downhill fast. I glimpsed a formless dark figure that blended into the shadows by the chain-link fence. He glided along toward the far boundary—quiet, controlled. He'd done this kind of thing before—and that made him all the more frightening.

The sports car drove into the garage. The garage door shut again. Silence.

Moments later another engine started up on the road—my pursuer's car. I heard it turn and drive downhill. Sedately.

I tried to leave my cramped hiding place, but my legs had begun to shake—delayed reaction, like you have when you've barely missed a collision on the freeway. My foot slipped on the rocky earth and I went down on my ass. Pounded my fists on the hard-packed earth and cursed the man who had forced me to cower here.

After a moment I reined in my rage and, for safety's sake, sat quietly under the deck, hugging myself against the chill for five minutes. Then I eased over to its edge and checked out the house. Dark, except for faint lights on its upper story; the exterior spots were off. Keeping close to the pyracanthas, I dragged myself uphill to my MG.

The night was tranquil once more. In Nate Evans's house

only the entry light shone. Chances were, the architect hadn't taken much notice of the earlier wailing of tires and clashing of gears. Had probably put it off to rowdy teenagers.

Unless he was the one who had alerted my pursuer to the fact I'd be here on this lonely, dangerous curve tonight. Evans had seemed straightforward enough, but I'd long ago learned not to take anyone involved in my investigations at face value.

I locked the MG's doors and sat behind the wheel until I felt fit to drive. It took longer than I expected—and that made me all the more angry.

Twenty

Before I pulled into my driveway, I circled the block a couple of times, looking for cars that resembled the one that had nearly run me down. I spotted a few low-slung, light-colored models, but none were close enough to allow an occupant to easily watch my house. Still, I tucked the MG safely into the garage and hurried inside, turning on lights and looking for signs of an intruder. No one was there, not even Mick. Before I could decide whether his absence was cause for a different kind of concern, the phone rang. I hurried to pick up, thinking it would be Gage Renshaw returning the call I'd earlier placed from my car phone to the emergency number at RKI's La Jolla headquarters.

Chuck Westerkamp's voice said, "Thanks for the tip on the redial button."

It was a few seconds before I realized what he was talking about. "You got inside Brenda Walker's house?"

"Uh-huh. Not exactly legal, but turns out the end justifies the means. I recorded the dial tones, ran them by one of my deputies who's got an ear for that sort of thing. Number was in your area code. I talked to Pacific Bell, and guess what? Belongs to your client."

Not good. "Which number is it?"

Westerkamp recited it. "Address is on the Embarcadero in your town."

"His condominium. Walker couldn't have talked with him, though. He wasn't there—hasn't been for some time."

"Well, she tried to get him, anyway."

"Maybe right before she and Leon took off. I don't suppose there's been any sign of them since we last spoke?"

"No, but we're doing our damnedest to find them."

During the next ten minutes I packed my briefcase and replaced the dirty clothes in my bag with clean ones. Took my .38 from its lockbox in the linen closet and put it in my purse. Mick still hadn't returned; his absence both annoyed me and made me edgy. I went to the guest room and threw some things into a bag for him, too. Allie appeared, saw the bag, and slunk out to her pet door. Both cats hated suitcases more than anything else, even the neighbors' Rottweiler; the appearance of baggage signaled lonely times ahead.

The phone rang, and this time it was Gage Renshaw. "If you're looking for Ripinsky," he said, "he's back at the ranch."

"I know. It's you I want to talk with. I need a couple of favors."

"I told you last spring that if you need anything, it's yours. The offer stands. Will continue to stand."

I pictured Renshaw pacing around wherever he was calling from: tall, thin body restless as usual; longish black hair disheveled, its startling white forelock hanging in his eyes. He'd be wearing hopelessly rumpled clothing, and the glasses that perched on his Abe Lincoln nose would more likely than not be repaired with tape or wire in at least two places. "Thanks, Gage," I said. "At one point either you or Dan mentioned that

272

you've got a hospitality suite here in the city for clients with security problems."

"Right. Top floor of our building on Green Street."

"Is it in use now?"

"I don't know, but I can check. I take it you want to stash someone there?"

"I want to stash *me*."

"Sharon, Sharon. What kind of scrape have you gotten yourself into now?" He sounded amused.

"Nothing very serious, but I need to keep a low profile for a few days."

"Starting off your career as an independent operative with fireworks, are you?"

"Nothing too explosive." I hope.

"Well, let me get back to you."

"Thanks," I said again, listening to a key turn in the front door lock. I replaced the receiver in its base unit as Mick came down the hall. "Where have you been?" I demanded.

"Returning your rental car."

I looked at my watch. "It took you five hours?"

"No, I was with a woman friend. I met somebody, okay?"

"Tonight?"

"Last month."

"You never mentioned her."

"You never asked. You've been kind of . . . preoccupied."

Come to think of it, except when I was giving him orders or he was giving me computer lessons, I *had* been ignoring him. Now I was beginning to understand why he'd made a play for attention by following up on the Blessing lead.

I started to ask what the friend was like, but as Mick came closer I caught the scent of wine on his breath. "You've been drinking."

"A glass of wine with dinner; no more than I have at home. Maggie cooked me dinner at her condo."

"Her condo? How old is Maggie, anyway?"

"Forty-five."

"*What?*"

He smiled slyly. "Gotcha. She's nineteen. And it's actually her folks' condo; they've retired to Palm Springs and are letting her use it." He hesitated, seemed to be gearing up for something. "Shar, I'm moving in with her as soon as her roommate can find a new place."

"You're . . . ?"

He nodded, serious again. "I know you don't want me at the agency or in your life any more, but I'm not going home. Living in a place where I'm generally considered a fuckup and where they're watching me all the time to see what hideous thing I'll do next isn't going to help me learn, as you put it, to exercise better judgment."

"And you think living with a woman will?"

He smiled again. "You're starting to sound like Grandma. I bet it was all you could do not to say 'living in sin.' "

"But you're only seventeen."

"How old were you when you and the captain of the swim team—"

"Okay! You've made your point. How'd you know about that, anyway?"

"It's kind of a family legend."

"Oh, no! Still, Mick, are you prepared—"

"You don't have to give me The Talk," he said in a sarcastic tone. "I've been sexually active and prepared since I was fifteen."

"Oh."

"And to get back to your question—yes, living with someone I care about, getting a job and contributing my share, maybe going to school part-time *will* help me learn to exercise better judgement, because it'll help me get my life together."

Suddenly I was so proud of him that I could have kissed him, but I didn't because it would have embarrassed both of us. Instead I said, "You're starting to sound like a pretty mature seventeen. And you don't have to get a job yet; for the moment, you still have one with me."

He blinked and looked down to cover his relief and pleasure. "Thanks, Shar." Then he nudged my travel bag with his foot. "So what's happening?"

"Plenty, and I don't have time to explain. We're getting out of here tonight."

"Why? To go where?"

"Somebody's been . . . following me; I don't think it's safe for either of us to stay here. You're going to All Souls. Camp out in the office or sleep in Jack Stuart's old room, if you like."

"I can stay at Maggie's—"

"Mick, in this business you don't jeopardize people you care about. Ever. Remember that."

He nodded—filing it away, I thought.

I went on, "I'm going to make it look as if I'm going out of town; you can come over here to feed the cats, bring in the mail, check the answering machine, just the way Ted does when I'm really away."

Mick's face had grown concerned. He sat down on the couch. "Shar, did this person try to hurt you?"

I hesitated, then sat down too. He had a right to know. Briefly I explained what had happened in Woodside, concluding, "It's the same M.O. as in the Blessing murder—isolated place, run the victim down with a car. I doubt he'll try that again, at least not in a congested area, but you never know. Anyway, I don't want to put you in danger, and I can't operate with him watching me."

"So where're you going?"

"I'm trying to get the loan of a secure place, one where he won't know to look for me."

"Shouldn't I go with you? I can help—"

"No, I need you in the office. There's something I want you to do—"

The phone rang again. Renshaw. "It's okay for the suite," he said. "See the guard in the lobby; he'll give you a visitor's badge and a key card that operates the doors and the parking-garage gate. Combination's changed every day, so you'll find a new card under your door in the morning. You mentioned you need a couple of favors; what's the other?"

"Is there a possibility of one of your operatives running some computer checks for me?" I glanced at Mick; he was sitting up straighter, very interested. "No," I told him.

"What?" Renshaw asked.

"Sorry, I was talking to someone else."

"Well, no problem about the checks. See Charlotte Keim on the second floor; she'll arrange for it."

"I owe you, Gage."

"No, you don't—not yet. But someday you will."

When I hung up, Mick was frowning. "That was Gage Renshaw, the guy from RKI?"

"Yes."

"Why're you dealing with him?" Mick had heard enough about my brief history with the security firm to know how strongly I disliked their methods.

"Because he has access to what I need, and he's indebted to me."

"These checks you want done—it's wrong for us to run them ourselves, but it's okay to ask RKI to do it? I don't get you."

"It's not okay, but it's what I'm going to do."

"Aren't you being kind of hypocritical?"

I sighed and sat back down. "In some ways, I am. That's what this business, any business . . . hell, it's what *life* does to you."

"But does it have to?"

I hesitated, unwilling to trample his youthful ideals, but also unwilling to lie. "Yes and no. I guess what we have to do is set limits. Decide when and how far to bend the rules—

our own as well as society's—and try not to exceed that."
Unfortunately, as the years passed I'd found my own ethical
boundaries expanding at an alarming rate.

Mick thought for a moment, looking somewhat deflated.
Then he asked, "Okay, what was it that you were going to ask
me to do right before the phone rang?"

"I need a current photo of Suits. Call GGL and see if they
have one; if not, there's probably one on file at one of the
newspapers. We'll meet someplace tomorrow after you get
hold of it. Otherwise, just keep on with the routine work.
And remember—I'm out of town to everybody. You don't
know where I went."

"What if Gordon calls? What do I tell him?"

"If I know Suits, he won't. But on the off chance he does,
try to find out where he is or get him to come in to the office
and keep him there. Use force if you have to." I picked up a
scratch pad and wrote down RKI's city number. "This is where
I'll be, in case."

Mick pocketed the paper, still looking down.

"Maybe you don't like the business as much as you thought
you did?" I suggested.

He shrugged, forced a grin. "Like you said, that's what life
does to you."

*   *   *

I made no effort to conceal my movements as I drove south
toward SFO, left the MG at the Park 'n' Fly lot on the frontage
road, and took the shuttle bus to the American Airlines terminal. As I crossed from the island where the bus dropped me,
I kept alert for a low-slung light-colored car. There were at
least three, none in a position to do me damage, and the glare
of their headlights concealed their drivers' faces. Of course, the
man didn't necessarily have to be following me now, but I
suspected he was. He'd need to keep tabs on me, watch and
wait for another opportunity.

Well, I thought as I stepped through the automatic door to the lobby, good luck, buddy. First you'll have to find a place to leave your car in the white zone.

I hurried across the lobby as if I were going to the security checkpoint, then veered to the right into the book-and-gift shop. Brushed past browsers at a table of hardcovers, my bag catching on a postcard rack and sending it spinning. Exited again and doubled back to the escalator to the baggage-claim area. I ran down it two steps at a time, across the lower lobby, and outside to the taxi stand. This time of night there was no line; I jumped into the first waiting cab and gave its startled driver RKI's address on Green Street.

I hoped I'd been tailed to the airport. I hoped my tail was now searching the departure gates for me. I hoped that when he got back to his car he'd find a ticket.

* * *

RKI's building was a renovated warehouse at the foot of Telegraph Hill near the Embarcadero. Its exterior—dark brick, ironwork, tall arched windows, and projecting cornices—was merely a shell for a stark modern interior that had been stripped for efficiency. An armed guard in a gray business suit sat inside the lobby door at a console equipped with TV monitors. He buzzed me in, checked my I.D., and consulted a clipboard. Then he took my purse, bag, and briefcase, and had me walk through a security gate—something new since the last time I'd been there.

"You'll have to check the gun with me, ma'am," he said after going through my belongings. I noticed he didn't ask if I had a carry permit for it; RKI wasn't interested in legal formalities.

"Okay with me," I said.

Next the guard gave me a key card, took an instant photograph of me, and laminated it onto my visitor's badge with a device that looked like a flat waffle iron. The photo badge was another innovation.

"Careful, it's hot," he told me, handing me the badge. "Your key card operates the elevator; we've put you in suite C on the third floor, end of the hall. You have a car?"

"Not till tomorrow."

"Mr. Renshaw says if there's anything you want, you're to have it."

I thanked him and went to the elevator.

Suite C was pretty damned luxurious, but I'd expected no less. RKI did everything on a grand scale: state-of-the-art computers; mobile units with the latest in surveillance gear; offices in forty-six U.S. and foreign cities—although some of those were rumored to be little more than mail drops. Their specialty was corporate contingency services, with the emphasis on hostage recovery and counterterrorism; their operatives were tough, some with CIA and FBI backgrounds, and many, including Renshaw and his partner Dan Kessell, had a murky past. They were high-tech and unscrupulous all the way, with many illegal and useful connections—some of which I'd take full advantage of in the morning.

The morning . . .

It was already well after two; I knew I ought to get some sleep. Four nights now since I'd really rested, four days since I'd eaten well or on a regular schedule. No sense in wearing myself down.

But I was too keyed up to sleep. Instead I wandered through the suite, checking out the monitors that allowed me to see the hall outside, the elevator, the lobby door, the garage entrance. Checked for listening devices, although I knew I couldn't locate them; they were there, but too cleverly concealed for me—RKI's installers were that good. The amenities were impressive: Kitchenette with microwave and fully stocked fridge and freezer; fully stocked bar in the living room; TV,

VCR, and CD player; enormous Jacuzzi and shower; phones with panic button everywhere, including the bathroom and the walk-in closet. With the exception of room-service menus, the suite had everything you'd find in a good hotel—more, in fact—and I suspected that if I called downstairs and said I wanted a pizza or a gourmet dinner, they'd deliver it within the hour.

Even so, I sensed a wrongness trapped within these walls—desperation, maybe. I wondered how many people had hidden here because stepping onto the street was a sure death sentence. I wondered how many had been held against their will in this luxurious prison. And how many others had, like me, been waiting out an adversary who thought he was clever but just wasn't clever enough?

The thought of that adversary made me more restless. Where was he? What was he doing now? And where was Suits? What was his game plan? My briefcase lay on the coffee table, stuffed with the information on Suits's turnarounds and associates. I'd been over and over it, but now I took the piles of slick fax paper out and began rereading, searching for something I'd overlooked that would give me the answer to my questions. It was after three-thirty when I concluded they held no answer and went to bed.

Before I put out the light, I whispered good night to whoever had pulled surveillance duty that shift. Gage Renshaw had been generous, but that wouldn't prevent him from eavesdropping on my activities, if for no reason other than curiosity. It didn't bother me, though; we might not be playing on the same side, but I was no longer afraid of Renshaw.

Twenty-one

"This job's an absolute no-brainer. Check with me at noon, I'll have it for you."

"This job's an absolute no-brainer. Check with me at noon, I'll have it for you."

Charlotte Keim was a young, attractive brunette who looked far too innocent to be working for an outfit like RKI. The scantiness of the data I'd provided didn't faze her in the slightest; if anything, she seemed bored.

I left Keim in her cubicle with her computer, went downstairs and reclaimed my .38 from the security desk, then stepped out into a beautiful autumn morning. The weather had invigorated the pedestrians who hurried by; tables were already being set out on the sidewalks in front of the cafés that served workers from nearby decorators' showrooms, antique shops, and offices. I glanced around, saw no suspicious-looking people, no evidence of anyone watching me. Only somewhat reassured, I walked over to a Bank of America branch on Montgomery Street and deposited into my business account the check from Suits that I'd been holding since September.

By now I'd more than earned it. Then I flagged a cab for the Park 'n' Fly lot near the airport.

Once I'd retrieved the MG I headed back toward the city, calling my office on the way. Mick's voice was subdued, somewhat wary.

"Everything okay there?" I asked.

"Sort of. I got GGL to messenger over a photo of Gordon."

"But?"

"I don't know, Shar. A guy called asking for you. When I said you were out of town, he hung up. Somebody else called a little later, same question. He said 'No message' and hung up. It sounded like the same person disguising his voice."

My pursuer—or Suits? No way to tell. "Well, don't worry about it," I told Mick, then made arrangements to meet him and pick up the photo in the parking lot of the Safeway down the hill on Mission Street. Half an hour later I was on my way back to RKI, checking for a tail the whole time.

*　　*　　*

"Your guy *believes* in credit," Keim said. "Look at this." She pointed over my shoulder at the TRW report on the desk in front of me. "Every card ever issued, I swear. And he uses all of them." She ran her index finger down the column showing the account numbers; under each was the notation "lastpay" and a recent date.

Pulling a credit check is illegal for private investigators in California, but very profitable. RKI had somehow devised a way around the law that wouldn't trigger an inquiry from the state board that licenses us. I didn't know how they did it; I didn't want to know. If I yielded to temptation and tried it, a red flag would go up for sure, and in thirty seconds max a representative of the Department of Consumer Affairs would be at my door. That's the kind of luck I have.

"Of course, that's only a start," Keim said, crumpling the

report and pitching it at her wastebasket. She pulled a sheaf of printout from a folder and spread it on the desk. "This gives you the real skinny on your guy, straight from the credit-card companies. He's been buying big-time the last few days. See here—American Express, what looks to me like an entire wardrobe from Eddie Bauer. And then there's Shell Oil, Modesto, on Saturday. Chevron in Benbow on Sunday. Shell again same day, Lombard Street."

Lombard Street was motel row. "Any charges for lodging?"

"Only one: Red Lion Hotel, Modesto, Friday night. From the size of the tab, I'd say he ate there. And he also ate at a place in Cloverdale on Saturday and in Petaluma on Sunday."

Petaluma, Cloverdale, Benbow: all on Highway 101 north of the city.

Keim added, "He even charged his *groceries*, for God's sake. At Petrini's in Stonestown on Sunday. Same day, he used Visa at a big sporting-goods outlet in the same shopping center."

Sporting goods? What the hell was he doing—taking up golf while I sweated over him going underground so he could kill someone? "Does it show what he bought there?"

"No, but if you need to know, I can have the tags pulled."

"Would you, please?"

"Sure, but it'll have to wait till after the lunch hour."

"Go ahead, then, and I'll check with you later. What about his bank account? Any activity there?"

"Daily withdrawals up to the limit on his ATM cards. Your guy likes to spend."

"He can afford to. Anything else?"

Keim shook her head, glanced at her watch. "I've got a lunch date in ten minutes. You want to check with me around three, I'll have your information."

I thanked her and went downstairs, my ethical boundaries pushed several feet farther toward the wrong side.

* * *

I sat in my MG in the parking garage and opened my state road atlas. Traced Highway 101 north to Petaluma, through Sonoma County to Cloverdale, then through Mendocino County and over the line into Humboldt. Benbow, where Suits had bought gas the day before, was only a short distance south of Garberville. I picked up the receiver of the car phone and called Suits's condominium.

Josh answered, sounding surprised to hear from me so soon after yesterday's abrupt dismissal.

I asked, "The guy who owned the dope farm in Garberville—what's his name?"

"Gerry Butler."

"Does he still live up there?"

"Yeah, but it's not a dope farm any more. Gerry got out when the CAMP search-and-destroy missions got serious. Now he's a gentleman farmer and lives off the profits Suits made for him." He laughed hollowly.

"Do you have his phone number?"

"T.J. must, somewhere here." He rummaged, read it off. "Why d'you want to talk to Ger?"

"Just a routine question." I ended the call before Josh could ask more.

When I identified myself to Gerry Butler, he recognized my name and didn't seem surprised to hear from me. "Suits told me when he came up here on Saturday that you worked for him for a while."

"So he did visit you."

"Uh-huh. Dropped in out of nowhere, like he used to back when. Spent the night and took off before I got up the next morning."

"What did he want?"

"Just to touch base, I guess. We sat around, got stoned, reminisced about the old days. Talked about Anna and Josh.

284

Noah. The way we were." Butler laughed. "Jesus, that sounds like a song on the easy-listening station."

"How did he seem?"

"Very intense at first. If I didn't know Suits, I'd've thought he was on something. After we'd smoked a few numbers, he relaxed, and around the time I sent him off to bed, he was downright out of it. Not that I blame him; he thinks it's his fault Anna died, and in a way he's right. You make enough enemies, shit like that happens."

"Did he say anything about knowing who set the explosion?"

"No."

"Or about getting revenge?"

"Well, sure. But I thought that was just the dope talking. I tried to tell him that getting revenge wouldn't bring Anna back and that he had to let go."

"Did you get through to him?"

"Hard to say. He must've felt better in the morning, though, because he left a note thanking me for clearing up loose ends for him."

"What loose ends?"

"Damned if I know." Butler hesitated. "D'you think you and Suits'll get back together now that Anna's gone?"

"What?"

Butler sounded taken aback at my sharp tone. "Well, before Anna, you were the love of his life. I just thought—"

"I was never the love of his life," I told him. "Even Suits doesn't believe that any more."

*　　*　　*

When I got to Miranda's pierside diner the lunch trade had thinned. I sat down at the counter and ordered a burger and coffee from a waitress, caught Carmen's eye as he slapped the patty on the grill. "Hey," he said, "where've you been keeping yourself?"

"Here and there. You have a minute?"

"Once I get these last few orders out. Hang around awhile, coffee's on the house."

I accepted his dubious gift, ate my burger, and was eyeing a piece of chocolate cream pie when Carmen motioned for me to join him in a booth he'd just cleared—saving me from a severe dietary error. As I sat down, he asked, "You seen T.J.?"

"No. Have you?"

"Not since Friday afternoon. He came in around four-thirty, had his usual order of sliders."

"Did he say what he's been doing, where he's been staying?"

"Nope. Was awful quiet, for T.J." Carmen's face grew solemn. "'Course, that's natural, considering what happened to his wife. I tried to offer my condolences, but he just brushed them off, said he didn't want to talk about her."

"So what did the two of you talk about?"

Carmen looked away. "Oh," he said in an overly casual tone, "the weather. He asked me if I thought the rains might start soon."

"What else?"

"I told him that nobody can predict the weather any more, what with these crazy patterns—"

"No, I meant, what else did you talk about?"

"Well, he asked if his pilot'd been in. He hadn't."

"And?"

Carmen studied the window beside the booth, pulled a paper napkin from its dispenser, and carefully removed a ketchup smear from a corner of the pane.

"Hey," I said, "I'm on T.J.'s side—remember?"

"Yeah, I remember." He hesitated. "Okay. The reason he came in was to ask where is a good place to buy a gun without a waiting period."

Not good at all. "What did you tell him?"

"I sent him to Howie Tso."

TILL THE BUTCHERS CUT HIM DOWN

"My God, Carmen!" Howie Tso was the biggest dealer of illegal firearms in northern California; both state and federal authorities had been trying to get something on him for years, but up to now Tso and his legion of runners had been too clever for them.

"Ah, Howie's all right," Carmen said. "At least he don't overcharge his customers."

"How come you know him?"

"We go way back to when he was just a kid hanging around the piers."

Probably waiting to take delivery on a shipment of Uzis, I thought. There was no way I'd ever find out if Suits had actually contacted Tso, because even if the dealer would speak with me—which was extremely doubtful—he wouldn't ever reveal the details of a transaction. Unless . . .

"Carmen," I said, "can you set up a meeting with Tso for me?"

"You want to ask him about what T.J. bought? He won't tell you nothing."

"Still, I'd like to ask."

"Well, I can try. Call me later on, I'll let you know what Howie says."

The waitress shouted from the back room; there was a problem with the Coors delivery. Carmen stood up.

"Wait," I said, "one last question. The old-timer T.J. said he'd been talking to the night he got drunk and ended up in the Bay—do you know who he is?"

"Some old guy who's living in his van up and down the waterfront. Knows all the places to park overnight and moves around a lot so the cops don't hassle him. Kind of an interesting guy, I'm told. Used to be captain of a Matson liner, dines out on his stories."

"You know his name?"

"Uh-uh."

"The van—have you seen it?"

"It's white, newish." He shrugged. "But what with all these makes and models they're coming out with now, I couldn't tell you what kind it is."

* * *

I drove up and down the waterfront from the Ferry Building to Islais Creek, but didn't spot a newish white van driven by anyone who could be described as an old-timer. Near the Mission Rock Terminal, in a weedy lot across from a burned-out pier, sat several old cars that looked as if people were living in them. I pulled the MG over there, bumping across the rusted tracks of the defunct Belt Railway. A woman slept on the front seat of an old sedan crowded with boxed and bagged possessions, and two little kids played in the dirt nearby. The place reminded me of the hobo jungles that had sprung up during the Great Depression—had sprung up again in this era that nobody wanted to call another depression.

I looked around, spotted a trio of men fishing off the wreckage of a pier beyond the chain-link fence and the warning signs. One segment of the fence had been knocked down and flattened; I went over there and stepped across it. The men glanced at me, then returned their attention to their lines.

As I picked my way through the broken concrete and rubble, though, the men's posture altered subtly. They looked at me again, not with hostility—it wasn't time for that yet—but with wariness. Then they exchanged glances, and one of them stood, handing his pole to the man next to him. When I reached the edge of the broken planking, he faced me, arms loose at his sides, blocking access. He was big—around six-three—and a long scar cut a jagged path across the deep brown of his left cheek. His eyes met mine, cold and unyielding.

"Lady," he said, "you can get hurt out here."

"I won't go any farther." I motioned at the water. "You catching anything?"

He hesitated, glanced at his seated companions, who were silently watching. "Just a few bluegills. Enough for supper."

I jerked my head at the weedy lot behind me. "You staying over there?"

"Why, you gonna roust us?" One of the other men snickered at the question; their spokesman glared at him.

"I've got no problem with where you stay."

"So what you want?"

"I'm looking for somebody—an old man who lives along the waterfront in a newish white van. Used to be captain of a Matson liner—"

"What you want with Cap?"

"I've heard he tells good stories."

"Oh, shit, man." Spokesman looked at his companions, laughed. "Don't tell me this is another take-a-homeless-to-dinner week! You rich bitches sure're crazy for Cap and his stories." The others joined in the laughter.

It was the first time in my life that I'd been mistaken for a society matron. I blinked, astonished, then said lamely, "Well, they tell me he's got some good ones."

Spokesman looked at the others. "We don't want to deprive Cap of his free dinner, now, do we?" he asked. "What you do," he told me, "is look for him up at Aquatic Park."

I hadn't thought to search the touristy northern end of the waterfront. "What's he doing up there?"

"Cap, he's got this schedule. Knows where and when they won't hassle him for sleeping in his wheels. Mondays, that's where he's at."

I thanked him and started back toward the pushed-down fence. Spokesman didn't reply, just reached out for his fishing pole. When I got to the vacant lot, the kids were still playing in the dirt and the woman was still sleeping in the sedan. I glanced back at the men on the pier; they sat with their heads bowed over their lines, and beyond them the burned pilings loomed above the water, their shadows shivering and rippling on its slick surface.

* * *

I called Charlotte Keim while waiting for the drawbridge at China Basin to close, thinking that I'd really gotten the hang of this car-phone business. McCone was hurtling into the twenty-first century faster than the speed of light. Pretty soon I'd—

The car behind me honked. I saw that the one in front was already halfway across the bridge. I popped the clutch, stalled the MG, and Keim's voice repeated, "Hello? Who is this?"

Well, hell.

After I got things under control, Keim told me she had the information I'd requested. Suits's purchases at the sporting-goods outlet consisted of a sleeping bag, air mattress, tarp, cook set, and Coleman stove and lantern.

"Sounds like your guy's gone camping," she commented.

It would have sounded that way to me, too, if I hadn't known Suits was looking to make an illegal gun buy.

* * *

I took North Point across town to Aquatic Park, bypassing the congestion near Pier 39 and Fisherman's Wharf, and turned downhill at Ghirardelli Square. At the foot of Polk Street stood the nautical-style Maritime Museum building, a former bathhouse and restaurant constructed in the mid-thirties as a WPA project. It's been a long time since bathers flocked to the protected cove behind it; about the only ones you see nowadays are members of the Dolphin swim club—hardy but, to my way of thinking, somewhat demented souls who daily brave the icy waters. The streamlined Moderne building now houses both the museum and the San Francisco Senior Center, and the park has been incorporated into the Golden Gate National Recreation Area.

I wondered how Cap dodged the park-service patrols when he slept there in his van.

The van wasn't in evidence now, though. I checked the parking area at the end of Beach Street, circled Ghirardelli, then continued along North Point to the big parking lot by the fishing pier at the foot of Van Ness. Still no van.

So, had the fisherman lied to me about Cap's whereabouts? Or had the old-timer simply not arrived yet? Either way, things weren't going well at all, and my sense of urgency about locating Suits was making me tense and edgy.

I pulled into a parking space, contemplated my options, then called Carmen at the diner. Howie Tso had agreed to see me, he said, but not till seven o'clock.

"Where?"

"Here. Howie says he's been lusting after my chicken-fried steak."

I'd seen one of those passing by on its way to an unwary customer. If Howie Tso was making a special trip to the diner for something that looked like that, he was not only a criminal but also insane. "See you at seven," I told Carmen.

Now what? Nearing four o'clock, hours to kill. Go back to suite C and further frustrate myself by poring over the documents in my briefcase? Go back to suite C and take a luxurious bath in that enormous Jacuzzi? Go back to suite C and get seriously into the vintage wine? The latter courses of action were tempting—and definitely uncalled for. There must be something—

The phone buzzed. I snatched it up. Mick.

"A nurse from U.C. Med Center called," he said. "Noah Romanchek's in intensive care and wants to see you."

"What's wrong with him?" Visions of a violent confrontation between Suits and the attorney flashed through my mind.

"Heart attack. From the way the nurse talked, I guess it's serious. She said for you to hurry."

I hurried. Across Van Ness to Fell Street, then a quick jog through Golden Gate Park past Kezar Stadium to Arguello, where I left the MG in Willie Whelan's driveway. Rae's former love owned a 1904 Edwardian just down from the med center parking structure; it would be faster to leave the MG there than to brave near rush-hour traffic on Parnassus Heights. I scribbled a note to Willie and stuck it under the windshield wiper, slipped a spare key through his mail slot in case he needed to move the car. Then I rushed uphill to the parking garage on Frederick Street, took the elevator to the Parnassus level, and—with the help of several kind strangers—finally located the intensive-care heart unit.

Romanchek was in a private room, his right arm connected to an I.V. bag, his left to a heart monitor. His face was gray and even more skeletal than I remembered, and I realized with some surprise that, although I'd spoken frequently on the phone with him, I'd only seen him twice—once at my kitchen table and once in his office at GGL. His eyes were closed when I entered, but as I hesitated some feet from his bed he opened them.

With an effort he said, "Thanks for coming."

"How are you?"

"Bad one." His mouth twitched. "Monitoring me. Irregular activity, they'll make you leave. We'll . . . talk . . . fast."

"Okay." I moved closer and waited.

"Been thinking . . . why it all happened. At the farm . . ."

"Garberville?"

"T.J.'s first mistake. Anna . . . never loved . . . But he was . . . obsessed."

"With Anna?"

He nodded. "Dangerous . . . all that brooding. In Monora . . . another mistake. T.J. didn't understand."

"About what?"

Romanchek didn't reply; his strength was flagging, his breath ragged.

I said, "You're talking about the Bodine frame? I found out that Bodine followed T.J. to Lost Hope and went after him."

"No . . . Anna."

"He went after Anna, and so—"

"He would've . . . done anything for her. Went back to him. Left him. Lost Hope . . . must be when . . . he decided—"

A nurse came in, saw me, scowled, and said, "Out."

I backed into the hallway, still looking at Romanchek. He was even grayer now, his lips white. His eyes followed me, frantic; he seemed to be struggling to finish what he'd started to tell me. Another nurse hurried into the room, then a doctor. Romanchek's heart monitor must have gone off out at the nursing station. They shut the door, and an orderly pointed me toward the visitors' lounge.

I went in there and sat down. It was empty, but the TV was playing. I stared blankly at the tail end of a rerun of "Matlock." Asked myself what the hell I was doing and turned it off. Then I went over my conversation with Romanchek, trying to make sense of it.

Anna had never loved Suits. Well, maybe not at first, but later? On the night before she died? The day she died? You could have fooled me.

"Dangerous . . . all that brooding." Which of them had brooded? Suits? That didn't strike me as in character. More likely Anna, who had told me she wasn't a naturally cheerful woman. But why had it been dangerous?

Suits hadn't understood about the Bodine frame? That didn't wash, not after what Josh had told me yesterday about the way he operated. Had something else happened in Monora that he hadn't understood about?

But there was no question that allowing the frame to go down had been the second mistake that Romanchek alluded to. And I was sure there had been a third mistake: Suits had killed Bodine after the former labor leader went after Anna in Lost Hope.

Lost Hope—an apt name for the place.

Still, my disjointed talk with Romanchek had raised more questions than it answered. I was beginning to suspect that we'd been operating from entirely different sets of facts and assumptions. There was something, perhaps, that the attorney knew and thought I knew, too. Something that would have made it all explicable. . . .

It was close to six o'clock when a doctor came to the lounge. Was I a member of Mr. Romanchek's family?

A representative of his organization, I told her. How was he?

She was sorry to inform me that Mr. Romanchek had passed away.

I stood, put my fingertips to my lips. As if I were holding in words. That didn't make sense; there *were* no words for this.

The doctor was saying something about contacting the family. I told her to get in touch with Dottie Collier in L.A., provided the phone number. Then I moved past her to the door. She stopped me, hand on my arm. "He would have died within a few hours anyway," she said. "And talking with you was very important to him."

I realized she was trying to absolve me of any guilt I might be feeling for somehow having hastened his death. Did I feel any? I honestly didn't know. Nodding, I went out to the elevator.

I supposed I should feel guilty. Our conversation had been very important to Romanchek, and I hadn't even understood it.

Twenty-two

The windows of Miranda's diner glowed yellow against the surrounding darkness. They would have seemed inviting under other circumstances, but I stood on the sidewalk for a long moment, steeling myself for the upcoming encounter with Howie Tso. Romanchek's death had left me drained; now I was here to talk with a criminal whose particular scam I flat-out hated. In order to get the information I wanted, I'd need to handle Tso with finesse.

As I started across the sidewalk, a man stepped through the diner's door: slender and on the tall side, attired in a long brown leather coat. A shock of dark hair fell onto his forehead, and below it his eyes were lively and intelligent. He surveyed me in the light from Miranda's neon sign and said, "Ms. McCone? Howie Tso." Before I could reply, he grasped my upper arm and guided me to the right, into the shadows. "We'll take a walk. You have exactly four minutes."

I shook his hand off and moved a few steps away from him.

Placed my own on the .38 inside the flap of my purse. "Why four minutes?" I asked.

"Because my wife and I are due at a gallery opening, and I plan to be on time."

"Why did you agree to see me at all, then?"

Tso began walking south along the shoreline. I matched his pace, keeping my distance. "Two reasons," he said, ticking them off on slender fingers. "One, Carmen was good to me when I was a kid scrounging odd jobs around the piers. He doesn't often ask a favor. Two, I was curious about you."

I read the papers; I knew who Tso was. Presumably that worked both ways.

He added, "We've wasted nearly a minute on nonessentials. What do you want?"

"Carmen sent a man to you about buying a gun. T. J. Gordon."

"Neither confirmed nor denied."

"Gordon is my client. You may have heard of him; his wife was killed in an explosion last summer. He's bent on avenging her death. I want to know what kind of weapon he bought and anything else he may have said to you."

Tso stopped under one of the pierside security lights. It cast long shadows on his features, made his small eyes glitter.

"Carmen warned me that you don't reveal anything about your . . . transactions," I went on, "but in this case you will. I'm the only one who can stop Gordon from killing somebody with the gun you sold him."

Tso looked bored. "I imagine," he said, "that if I *were* dealing in firearms—which I certainly do not admit to—any number of them would be used to kill people. That's what they're for. And illegally obtained firearms can seldom be traced."

"Mr. Tso, I'm not working for any of the law-enforcement agencies that are interested in you, if that's what you're concerned about. All I want to do is prevent a murder."

He shrugged, looked at his watch.

"Of course," I added, "if a murder occurs, there will be serious repercussions. T. J. Gordon is very high profile. Things could become difficult for you."

His eyelashes flickered—just a fraction.

"As I said, Mr. Gordon is my client. And as an investigator licensed by the state, I have to cooperate with law-enforcement agencies in the event of a crime. I'd have no choice but to tell them everything I know about Gordon. Everything."

"Tell them all you want. You have no proof I sold him anything."

The four minutes were up by now, but Tso hadn't looked at his watch again. I said, "No, *I* don't have proof. Of course, there's always Gordon. He's on a self-destructive path right now, but once he gets his revenge, he's going to snap out of that and start thinking of saving his own ass. The various agencies who're interested in Howie Tso will look favorably on a plea bargain in exchange for getting something on you that'll stick."

Tso was silent, eyes calculating.

"You see what a mess it could be, Mr. Tso? Even if you're not indicted, think of the publicity, the disruption of your day-to-day activities. And it really doesn't have to get messy. Just tell me what I want to know, and I can stop it."

He began walking back toward Miranda's, head bent, steps measured. Again I matched my gait to his, waiting.

Finally he said, "This one time, Ms. McCone, I've decided to break my rule of client confidentiality."

"Wise decision."

Tso's voice roughened, anger simmering under its surface. "Mr. Gordon bought an AR-fifteen semiautomatic rifle."

"When?"

"This morning."

An assault rifle, combining heavy bullet impact and firepower. The thought of how much damage Suits could do with that made me shudder. I controlled it, asked, "Did he indicate where or when he planned to use it?"

"No. He struck me as a man of few words and great focus."

"So he said nothing at all out of the ordinary?"

Tso considered. "I wouldn't call it out of the ordinary, but he did say he was going bird hunting. Then he laughed. He has a very strange laugh."

"And that's all?"

"Yes."

"Thank you, Mr. Tso." I motioned at my watch, added, "I'm afraid I've made you late for your opening."

His lips tightened and his eyes narrowed. He turned abruptly and strode away.

Not smart to make an enemy of a man like Tso, but I didn't regret it. At one time I might have tried to forge an uneasy rapport with the arms dealer, but not any more. There was no longer room in my life for that sort of compromise.

* * *

I still couldn't find Cap's white van in the Aquatic Park area. I checked the quiet end of Beach Street near the Maritime Museum, circled Ghirardelli Square, widened my search, drove past the parking spaces at the foot of Van Ness again. Then I rechecked the museum and spotted a driveway entrance to the left of the building. Coasted down it toward the beach.

The van was tucked into a parking slot behind the Senior Center's lower-level quarters; flickering light showed through its rear windows. I stopped the MG at the foot of the drive and got out. The ground floor of the building was dark, although some function was going on upstairs; voices and laughter came from the long open-air gallery that overlooked the water. As I approached the van I kept close to the wall where I couldn't be seen from above; went up to it and knocked softly on its back door.

A man with white military-cut hair and silver-rimmed

glasses peered out at me. He was clean-shaven, tidily dressed, and smelled faintly of bourbon. A TV played in the background—some sort of travelogue.

"Are you Cap?" I asked.

"That's what they call me."

I identified myself and asked if we could talk. Cap took my card and examined it, then nodded and extended a hand to help me into the van. It was a custom model, with front seats that swiveled like easy chairs; the small TV sat on a table leaf that dropped down from one sidewall; around the carpeted rear space were what looked to be built-in storage bins. Not the home of any ordinary street-sleeper.

Cap turned the passenger's seat around so I could sit there and offered me a drink. When I declined, he poured himself a finger of bourbon from a bottle next to the TV and took it to the driver's seat.

"Glad you came by," he said. "I've seen this special before, and I was getting bored with it." He picked up a remote control from a console between us and muted the sound; the images continued to flicker—animals on a faraway veldt.

For someone who illegally lived in his van, Cap seemed curiously at ease and trusting of a stranger. I asked, "How do you get away with parking here?"

"I have an overnight permit from the Senior Center. They're understaffed. I help them out on Mondays in exchange for the permit."

"And on the other nights?"

He smiled, pleased at my interest. "I have similar arrangements along the rest of the waterfront. It's the most free existence I can manage now that I'm too old to go to sea."

"I understand that you and my friend T. J. Gordon had some interesting conversations about how the port used to be."

Cap frowned; it was clear the name meant nothing to him.

I slipped Suits's photo from my bag and passed it over. He held it up to the TV's light. "Oh, fascinating fellow. I never did get his name." He handed it back to me, added, "Haven't seen him in quite a while. How is he?"

"Not very well." I told him what had happened to Suits since last summer.

The furrows on Cap's forehead deepened. He drank off his bourbon, poured another finger. "Even if I'd known his name, I wouldn't've heard about any of that. I avoid newscasts and the papers; at my age you can't take too much gloom and doom. But I did know that he—T.J., you said?—was in trouble, and when he stopped showing up on Thursdays, I guessed things might have gone badly for him."

"You saw him on Thursdays?"

"Well, most. Down at Mission Rock, where I have an arrangement with a small ship-repair facility."

"When did you last see him?"

Cap thought. "August. Second to last Thursday. That was the only time he talked in detail about his problems."

And later turned up at Carmen's drunk on bourbon. I looked at Cap's bottle. "Curious," I said, "considering he's such a private man."

Cap rubbed his chin thoughtfully. "Well, it's been my experience that even private people need to confide their troubles, and for most of them it's easier to confide in a stranger than in someone they're close to. Myself, I confide *only* in strangers. And your friend T.J. had a load of problems weighing on him."

"He told you about the attempts on his life? The business reversals?"

He nodded.

"Anything else?"

". . . I don't like to break a confidence."

"Cap, T.J.'s set out on a very self-destructive course this past week. You may be able to tell me something that'll give me some idea of how to help him."

"Well, I don't know. Most of what he said had to do with the wife that died."

"And her death is exactly why he's self-destructive. He plans to kill the person who set the explosion. What you tell me could prevent another murder."

Cap was silent a moment—shocked, I thought. Then he slouched lower in his chair, sipped reflectively from his glass. "All right; it's not that original a story, anyway. Your friend described the living arrangement he and his wife had. Said he was tired of a long-distance marriage. He wanted to bring her here to the city, have her with him from then on. He realized how lonely she was, but he didn't know if she'd be willing to move that far away from her people; I gather she was Indian, working with the young folks in her tribe. And he also was afraid he'd mess up again."

"Again?"

"Like I said, it's not that original a story. Happened the same way to me. Did you know I was captain of a passenger liner?"

"Yes."

"Matson Lines. Wonderful ships in their day, sailed the Pacific routes. As captain, I could bring my wife aboard. At first I did, but my jealousy . . ." He set his empty glass on the console, spread his hands before him and stared at their age-swollen joints as if he wondered how they'd gotten that way. "My wife was a very beautiful woman, much younger than I. I couldn't stand the way other men, both passengers and crew, looked at her. Finally I told her it wasn't working out, her coming to sea with me, and made her stay at our apartment in North Beach while I was on my voyages. I left her alone far too much."

"What happened?"

"I couldn't control my jealousy on land, either. Every time I returned home I'd accuse her—falsely, I now know—of having affairs. Finally she couldn't bear any more accusations, and she left me. I told your friend my story, asked him to try again with his wife."

"So T.J. had accused Anna of sleeping around?"

"No." Cap shook his head. "It had to do with the drugs. . . ."

It happened in Monora, Suits had told Cap, on a stifling July night. Heat lightning had been dancing on the Monongahela for hours, and he couldn't sleep. As was his habit, he slipped out of the now-defunct motel where he and Anna and his people were staying and prowled the town—along the main street, up and down the side streets, and finally to the railroad embankment by the river. He hadn't noticed the dirt track under the trestle before, so he followed it. Stopped when he heard voices on the beach. Peered out at the park.

And saw Josh Haddon making a drug buy.

Cap said, "Your friend was certain his pilot was buying cocaine for his wife. He knew she was hooked again. At least he *thought* he knew that. Anna's drugs were to T.J. what my wife's secret lovers were to me."

Suits didn't confront Josh. Instead he rushed back to the motel and confronted a sleepy Anna. She denied his accusations, tempers flared, a violent argument ensued. And in the morning she was on the corporate jet with Josh, bound for home and the beginning of a four-year separation from Suits.

I said to Cap, "I can't understand how he could have had so little faith in her. She'd been drug-free for years. She'd graduated from college—"

"He realized his error later, when he found out that the cocaine was meant for an entirely different purpose. But the damage was done; your friend's wife would have nothing to do with him for years."

"I still don't understand why he'd think that the drugs Josh Haddon was buying were for Anna."

"Haddon? Is that the pilot? Well, to get back to your question, I suppose it was the nature of the relationship."

"How so?"

"He would've done anything for her."

Noah Romanchek had used the identical words—practically his dying words—but he'd been speaking of what happened in Lost Hope.

"Odd way of showing it, accusing her of being hooked again—"

"No, I don't mean your friend; I mean his pilot. Your friend claims his wife never really loved Haddon, but Haddon never stopped loving her."

I closed my eyes, taking it all in. Understanding, finally, what Romanchek had been trying to tell me.

Josh: the chameleonlike man in Suits's organization, who heard through his pilot's headset every detail that Suits and his associates discussed while conducting business in the air.

Josh: who banked the large salary that Suits paid him; who obeyed orders like a good little soldier and did Suits's dirty work; who had brooded dangerously ever since Suits banished him from the dope farm and took away his woman.

Who would have been in a better position to bring his boss down?

Twenty-three

Josh Haddon drove a gold Trans Am, the doorman said.

Low-slung, pale in color: my first real piece of evidence against him.

"Is he up there now?" I asked.

The doorman hesitated; probably Sue Mahoney had cautioned him against talking with me. Then he shrugged, perhaps remembering the shot of good scotch I'd bought him at his neighborhood tavern back in August. "He left around fifteen minutes ago."

"On foot?"

"No, he parks back on Steuart Street. Mahoney keeps 'forgetting' to have a garage key card made for him; she thinks he's not classy enough for Bay Vista, but Gordon's company owns the penthouse and their L.A. office okayed him staying there, so there's not a damned thing she can do about it."

"I don't suppose you remember Haddon's license-plate number?"

He grinned. "Just the letters—SHT. How that one got by the censors, I don't know. I kidded Haddon about it once, and he said 'SHT happens.' "

I laughed, more to keep the doorman on my side than because I found the remark amusing. "Tell me, when Gordon was still living here and Haddon would pick him up in the helicopter, did he have anything to do with Sid Blessing?"

"Sure. The two of them hit it off; they're both ex-army types, although Haddon was 'Nam and Blessing did a stint in the Gulf. If Haddon was waiting around for Gordon when Blessing took his break, they'd go up on the roof, sit in the chopper, smoke, and gas about the good old days. To hear them, you'd've thought those were the best times of their lives."

"I guess for some people they were."

But for Josh the real best times had been at the dope farm, before he lost Anna. I pictured him—amiable and laid-back on the surface, with all that rage simmering just below—trading war stories with Blessing until he was sure of him. And Blessing, the former explosives expert who was into small-time scams, must have leaped at the chance to grab on to the money Josh eventually offered him. To a man like Blessing, it would have seemed like big money, while to Josh it was just savings for which he had no use.

The doorman was still shaking his head, trying to figure out how wartime could be the high point of someone's life. I took out my card, circled the car-phone number. "If Haddon comes back, don't tell him I'm looking for him. And if you call me at this number, it'll be worth a couple of shots of scotch at the Wishing Well."

* * *

So where would Josh Haddon go at close to nine o'clock on a Monday night? I sat in the MG, trying to put myself in the pilot's place, reviewing his options. If he'd followed me to the airport last night, he probably thought I'd gone out of town, and the anonymous calls to my office would have reinforced that. But I'd phoned him that afternoon to get Gerry Butler's number. Would he have assumed I was calling long distance, or would he have checked to see if I'd come back?

I headed for my own neighborhood.

The block-long tail end of Church Street was quiet, my house dark. I pulled across the Curleys' driveway next door and surveyed the cars parked along the curbs. No gold Trans Am with an SHT license plate. I peered at the shadows surrounding my earthquake cottage. No strange shapes, and nothing moved except for a cat-sized form that was probably Ralph or Allie.

Suddenly a bittersweet longing swept over me. I wanted to be inside that house, curled up on the couch with a good book, a cat on either side of me and a glass of wine to hand. And at the same time I wanted to be exactly where I was—behind the wheel of the MG, primed for action. My life had been a series of such contradictions, the two sides of my personality pushing and pulling at each other. Finally I'd come to terms with the struggle, realized that the side that was drawn to excitement and danger would always win.

Next stop, Bernal Heights.

No Trans Am near the weedy little park that divided the street in front of All Souls. No Trans Am on any of the side streets, either. Again I idled across a driveway watching deceptively moving shadows. Saw nothing. And got moving again.

Quick check of Steuart Street. He hadn't returned to where he usually parked. Quick prowl through the South Beach area—trendy nightspots, condo and apartment complexes, bayside promenade, pierside diners. Miranda's was still open, and through its window I glimpsed Carmen holding court in a corner booth. Slowed, thinking one of the people might be Josh, but they were all strangers.

Where, dammit? *Where?*

And where was Suits?

I idled near the China Basin drawbridge, tapping my fingers on the steering wheel. The phone buzzed, and I started. The doorman, calling to say Josh had returned to Bay Vista? I snatched up the receiver. No reply to my hello, and then someone hung up. Wrong number? Or Josh trying to locate me?

Paranoid, McCone. As paranoid as Suits was when he—

Of course! How could I have forgotten? He'd started recording all his phone calls sometime last summer.

I drove to Bay Vista to get the evidence against Josh.

*　　*　　*

"He's not back yet," the doorman said.

I smiled, showed him the key that I'd neglected to return to Suits last August. "I'm picking up something for Mr. Gordon," I said. Then I slipped a ten-dollar bill into his hand. "Buzz me, will you, if Haddon shows up?"

The doorman nodded and ushered me into the lobby.

The elevator to the penthouse suites was high-speed, but it seemed to take forever. I crossed the vestibule and stood in front of Suits's door, listening. No sound inside. Quietly I inserted the key in the lock and let myself in.

I turned on the foyer light, went into the living room to shut the drapes. The stand with the phone and fax machine still stood near the wet bar, although the filing cabinets had been removed. The phone had a built-in answering machine; its green light shone steadily. I examined it; no extra wiring, no special equipment, but it might contain a bugging device that activated a concealed recorder.

Kitchen next. The extension that I'd used to call Nate Evans yesterday—with Josh no doubt listening in on the living room phone—was mounted on the wall next to the double oven. The room was immaculate; apparently Josh used it as seldom as Suits had. The cupboards were empty except for one next to the sink that held an assortment of mismatched glasses and dishes. One drawer contained a similar collection of flatware and utensils. On the counter were coffee, salt, pepper, and a box of Triscuits. The fridge would have made Mother Hubbard feel well provisioned.

So where was it?

I looked more closely at the wall phone. The paint was chipped around its edges and a small strip was several shades darker than the rest of the wall. Wires could have been run from it to . . . there.

It was one of those ornamental cupboards that they put over stoves to conceal the ducts for the exhaust fan. I stood on tiptoe, opened it. On either side of the duct were small spaces that had been covered with wood panels that didn't quite match that of the cabinetry. I reached up, pried one loose.

Got it!

When I had the recorder down from the cupboard, I set it on the counter and disconnected it from the wiring. It was a voice-activated type, and the tape cassette in it was more than three-quarters run, set at extended play. Quickly I replaced the panel, closed the cupboard. There were some paper bags stuffed between the fridge and the wall; I put the recorder into one, turned out the lights, and got out of there. I would listen to the tape in my car, where there was no risk of an unpleasant interruption.

*   *   *

I drove down the Embarcadero and turned onto Brannan Street. Pulled over to the curb in front of one of the many art galleries that dot the SoMa area. The gallery was closed, the nearby sidewalks dark and deserted; a streetlamp directly overhead gave me enough illumination so I could operate the recorder without having to use my flashlight or the dome light.

I reversed the tape partway, pressed the play button. Heard

my own voice repeating Nate Evans's directions to his house. Reversed again, this time winding it all the way back. Suits and Charles Loftus, his moneyman, were discussing returns on investment. I sped through several routine conversations between my client and his associates; listened with more interest to one in which he told Dottie Collier that he'd met with me and hoped I'd take his case. For a while after that there was nothing but a series of messages on the answering machine, some expressing condolences on Anna's death.

The only conversations Suits hadn't bothered to tape, it seemed, were the private ones between himself and his wife.

Next there was Josh: ordering a pizza, telling Noah Romanchek that the corporate aircraft were being maintained at Oakland's North Field. And finally something of real interest:

"Hey, Sid, I might have more work for you."

"Oh, yeah? What?"

"Better to talk it over in person. I can be out there in a couple of hours."

"Come on to the house."

"You know better than that. There's a new development being built on the east side—Orchard View."

"I've seen it."

"Meet me there, end of Apple Lane, at midnight. And don't tell anybody, even the wife, about this."

Nobody had ever claimed Sid Blessing was bright.

After that Josh didn't use the phone much. He canceled a dental appointment, ordered Chinese food. And then a woman's voice came onto the tape, shrill and urgent:

"Josh, you moved! I had to call the manager at your old building to find out where to reach you."

"What do you want, Brenda?"

"This investigator, Sharon McCone, is here in Lost Hope, claims she's working for your boss. She knows Anna was with him for a while. She came around to the store tonight asking about her stay here."

"What'd you tell her?"

"Nothing. I sent her to the sheriff's substation."

"Not smart. That'll make her all the more suspicious."

"Well, I didn't know what else to do. Why didn't you tell me he'd hired a private detective?"

"I had no idea she'd go to Nevada."

"What's this stuff about somebody harassing Gordon?"

"Just T.J.'s paranoia getting the best of him. Don't worry about it."

"Josh, what if she finds out—"

"How could she?"

"Well, there're a few people who know Leon's my half brother. What if she finds out and goes to see him? Leon . . . well, you know how he is. What if he tells her he saw us—"

"She's not going to find out about Leon. She's not going to go out there. And even if she did, what could she uncover?"

"Him . . . it. It's still there under that sculpture I had Leon make."

"For God's sake, Brenda, get a grip. If you're that worried, go out to Leon's and tell him not to say anything if she comes around."

"You can't *tell* Leon anything."

"Well, try. And keep an eye on him. Call me back if there're any problems."

Walker called him back:

"Well, I think I got through to Leon. I handed him a story in that crazy jargon he's always spouting, and he fell for it. I *think* it's going to be okay. But what if . . . ?"

"Just keep an eye on him. That's all you can do."

Another call from Walker, the next day:

"Josh, she was out there! I saw her, and she took a picture of the sculpture on the . . . place."

"How do you know that's what she was taking?"

"Because I stole the film from her camera and had it developed, that's how! And she was in the house with Leon for a while. God knows what he told her."

"You'd better get him away from there for a while. Take him on a camping trip or something. You know the desert; just go hide out. If McCone does find out about . . . it, if she does, you'll be safe till I can get to her and do some damage control."

"But the sheriff's deputy—"

"That deputy you've got there couldn't find his ass with both hands, and he sure won't be able to find you or anything else in the desert."

"Okay, that's what I'll do. I'll throw my gear in the truck and go get Leon right away. But what about this McCone woman?"

"I'll think of a way to take care of her."

The next call was from Romanchek, telling Josh I'd gone to Monora:

"I don't know if she's found out anything. She was very closemouthed about what she's doing there."

"You're pretty damn cool about this, Noah."

"What do you want me to do, work myself up into a frenzy? Besides, what's she going to do with the information? Implicate her own client in a drug frame? She's got to be sophisticated enough to know these things are done all the time."

"Maybe, maybe not. And I get the feeling she goes her own way, just like T.J."

"If she even tries, we'll slap a multimillion-dollar defamation suit on her, and that'll be the end of it."

"If you say so. . . . You really think we should fly up to Mendo tomorrow?"

"It wouldn't hurt. For some reason, McCone wants T.J. back here in the city. I want him back, too—it would make it easier to keep tabs on him."

"Then I'll see you at Oakland at nine-thirty."

There were no other calls until mine to Mick, Chuck Westerkamp, and Nate Evans on Sunday. If Josh had listened to all three, he'd known Bodine's body had been identified and that everything was falling apart. The pressure had made him desperate, sent him after me.

Sometime after I'd left, Brenda Walker called again:

"My God, where've you been, Josh? Why don't you at least leave your answering machine on?"

"Where are you?"

"Little town called Caliente; it's way to hell and gone over by Utah. I had to come in for supplies. Did you hear what happened?"

"What happened where?"

"Lost Hope, you fool! They dug up the drifter."

"I know. They've identified him, too."

"Oh, God! And they're looking for Leon and me; it was on the radio. We can't go back there, but we can't hold out in the desert much longer. It's getting cold, and anyway, Leon's driving me crazy."

"Okay, let me think a minute."

". . . Josh? Why can't we just give ourselves up and tell them?"

"Leon *must've* driven you crazy."

"No, I mean it. Leon didn't do anything. All I did was help you bury a body. You didn't do anything, not really. Anna's dead. And Gordon—"

"No."

"Why not?"

"It's complicated."

"Seems simple to me."

"You don't know the background on the guy they dug up. It's not a simple case of him assaulting Anna. But I think I'm getting an idea that'll get everybody but T.J. off the hook."

"You're forgetting about his detective."

"I can take care of her."

"That's what you said before. How?"

"Just leave it to me."

"You're not talking about—"

"Brenda, get your supplies and go back to wherever you're camped out. Call me in a couple of days. Once I take care of McCone, I'll go to the cops and make a painful confession about my employer."

"Josh, you can't—"

"Call me in a couple of days. Everything'll be under control by then."

I stopped the tape to think over what I'd heard so far. Josh had assumed he'd be on his way to having everything "under control" by now. Meaning I would be dead and he would be prepared to go to the authorities and confess that Suits had killed Ed Bodine and buried him in his desert grave.

Only things were not under control—not for Josh, not for Suits, and certainly not for me. Instead, they were veering out of control very badly, and there wasn't much left of this tape.

I pressed the play button again. My voice, asking for Gerry Butler's number in Garberville. Fast forward. Dottie Collier, letting Josh know about Romanchek's death.

And Suits's voice, saying hello.

"Hey boss, where you been?"

"Around and about. Josh, I need you to pick me up in the bird."

"Sure thing. But did you hear—"

"No time to talk now. Listen carefully. Is the bird ready to go?"

"It'll need some servicing, might take a while."

"Call the airport, get them started on it. I'll phone you there at eleven, give you exact instructions on where to meet me. Don't tell anybody you've heard from me, okay?"

"Boss, I think you better tell me where you are now."

"Can't. This is too important. Remember that, Josh. This

might be the most important flight of our lives. Are you with me?"

". . . Roger."

"I'll call you at eleven sharp."

One final segment on the tape—Josh calling the airport, asking that the JetRanger be serviced. Then nothing but a faint hiss as the cassette spun out. When it stopped, I removed it from the machine, held it tightly in my hand.

I had my evidence. And I could foresee the tragedy that was about to happen.

I turned on the dome light and looked at my watch. Ten-forty. In twenty minutes Suits would call Josh at Oakland's North Field. He'd give him a destination, probably in some rural area where he was camping out. And Josh would board the JetRanger—the bird, as Suits was fond of calling it.

I couldn't get to the airport in twenty minutes. No way.

Josh would contact Ground Control, request clearance to hover-taxi to the helipad for takeoff. If air traffic was light tonight, he'd be on his way in three to five minutes.

Dammit, I *couldn't* get there on time.

The JetRanger would cut through the airspace between Oakland and its destination. Josh would be thinking about a final confrontation with Suits. He'd plan how he'd help his boss aboard the copter . . . and then what? Kill him? Fake a suicide? It didn't matter.

Suits wouldn't board the helicopter. He wouldn't even let it land. Instead, as he'd told Howie Tso, he'd go bird hunting.

He'd take the AR-15 he'd bought and blow the copter out of the sky.

Twenty-four

I snatched up the car phone, called hangar 2C at Oakland Airport. Josh wasn't there, although the JetRanger was being serviced. I left a message: "Do not go to pick up Suits; call me immediately."

I doubted Josh would respond. He'd be afraid it was a trap.

There might be something else I could do, though. If I could locate Suits. If I could convince someone at the law-enforcement agency there that I wasn't playing a prank or suffering from a substance-induced hallucination. There just might be a way. . . .

*   *   *

Church Street was peaceful and dark. In my working-class neighborhood people go to bed early on weeknights. Even we baby boomers who are gradually gentrifying it don't go in for the wild life on Mondays.

At least not usually.

I shattered the silence by slamming the car door and running

317

up my front steps. Cursed as I fumbled with my keys. The
bulb in the hallway fixture had burned out over a week ago,
and both Mick and I had been too lazy to replace it. I groped
along to the sitting room, tripping over a pair of shoes that
I'd left there and cursing some more. Snapped on the lamp
next to the archway.

Mick's radio setup still sat on the card table by the window.
I squatted down in front of it, flipped it on. Turned the MHz
transceiver's tuning knob to 121.9, Oakland Ground Control.
Looked at my watch.

Eleven-oh-four.

At first there was nothing but buzzing and crackling. I
tuned more finely. Then the rhythms of the nighttime airwaves
became words, as clear as if I were in the cockpit of the Citabria.
I listened as Ground Control directed a corporate jet to runway
two-seven right, told a Piper Cub it was cleared for takeoff on
two-seven left.

"Ground Control, this is Cessna three-three-five-two-Delta.
I'm VFR northbound for Santa Rosa with Bravo . . ."

". . . Five-two-Delta, squawk is four-four-three-four, taxi
to runway thirty-four left . . ."

". . . Say again, Ground Control . . ."

I closed my eyes, clenched my fists, waiting for the familiar
voice and aircraft identification number. My fingernails dug
into my palms.

". . . Roger, one-six-Yankee . . ."

". . . Go ahead, three-four-niner . . ."

". . . Stand by, Oakland Ground . . ."

Nine minutes after eleven.

"Come on," I whispered, pounding my fists on my thighs.
"Come on!"

". . . One-six-Yankee, acknowledge . . ."

". . . Four-one-Romeo, proceed to executive terminal . . ."

". . . Ground Control, read back, please . . ."

Eleven-fourteen now.

How much longer?

"Come on, Josh, get into the copter and on the radio!"

". . . Correction, Ground Control . . ."

". . . VFR southbound to San Jose with Bravo . . ."

". . . Oakland Ground, this is JetRanger Echo-six-two-two-Tango . . ."

I leaned forward, intent on the radio's controls, as if they could bring Josh's face into focus.

". . . VFR westbound for Hunters Point with Bravo. Request permission to proceed to helipad B."

"Two-two-Tango, squawk is . . ."

Hunters Point!

All the time I'd been thinking rural encampment, and Suits was practically in my backyard. Down Church to Army Street, a straight shot east under the freeways, Third Street to—

Too far, too little time. And then there was the problem of getting past Security or over the fence.

The police. Call 911.

Sure, 911—you might as well send a letter through the Postal Service.

Take a chance, go yourself. You're the only person Suits might listen to.

I jumped up, ran downstairs to the garage. On the cluttered workbench—*somewhere* on the damned bench—was a pair of bolt cutters left over from the house renovations. I switched on the dim overhead, batted aside spiderwebs, pawed around until I found them. Rushed back upstairs.

". . . Oakland Ground, do you hear me . . ."

I adjusted the tuning to 118.3, Oakland Control Tower.

". . . this is one-six-Yankee . . ."

". . . One-six-Yankee, clear for takeoff . . ."

". . . this is two-two-Tango. What's the holdup?"

"Two-two-Tango, hold for incoming medevac helicopter. I say again, hold for incoming medevac. Acknowledge."

"Roger, Oakland Tower."

319

Somebody's medical emergency was buying me time. I wished the person well, flipped off the radio, and ran out to the car.

*　　*　　*

Church Street to Army. East on Army.

Signal out at Mission. Yield to a Muni bus, then shoot through the uncontrolled intersection.

Past Bernal Heights. Under the freeways. Right on Third, tires squealing.

Over Islais Creek Channel to Evans. Iron-barred storefronts, deep shadows where drug deals were likely going down.

Industrial park, security lights blazing. Quick jog down Innes. Something going on at the leased arts-and-crafts buildings: lights, voices, hammering—probably setting up for an exhibit. But beyond them, mostly darkness.

I drove along the potholed street, past the buildings. A new extra-high chain-link fence topped with coils of barbed wire blocked access to the dry docks and the acreage where Suits envisioned his container freight station. Trust his paranoia to prompt him to replace the old fence with a state-of-the-art model; it had probably gone up the instant he signed the final papers.

My headlights picked out the rusted Southern Pacific trunk line where it branched off to the west. A new guard shack sat outside a gate, light glowing in its windows. I cut my own lights, peered at the shack. No one inside.

No guard at night? Even if one was making rounds, another should man the shack.

Electrified fence? Didn't look like it.

Dogs? No, their presence would be posted. The same for any kind of alarm system.

So why . . . ?

Of course. Suits had sent the guards away. He wouldn't want witnesses who might interfere with his plan.

I pulled onto the shoulder and stopped the car. Looked at my watch. Thirteen minutes since I'd left my house.

I got out, stuck the bolt cutters in the back pocket of my jeans, reached into my purse for my .38. Locked the purse in the car and stood on the shoulder, listening.

Distant traffic sounds. Voices drifting from the arts-and-crafts buildings. Sirens, also distant.

No drone of a jet engine, no flap of a rotor. And no lights in the sky overhead.

I ran across the pavement to the fence. Touched it gingerly. Not electrified. The coils of barbed wire at the top made it nearly impossible to climb. I squatted down and attacked the chain links with the bolt cutters.

Snap-snap-snap.

How long before Josh gets here?

Snap-snap.

A quick trip across the Bay, even though the copter will be diverted up around the Bay Bridge to avoid the most sensitive part of the terminal control area.

Snap.

So he's still holding for the medevac copter. Or he's changed his mind about coming. Or . . .

Snap-snap-snap.

Suits—where? He's not totally crazy, is he? He doesn't want to kill himself, endanger other people, set the base on fire. Does he? No. He'll try to down the copter over vacant land or the water.

Snap.

So not over here. Not at the dry docks or India Basin. But over by South Basin . . . The contaminated area.

Snap.

Done!

I pushed the free section of fence inward. Stuffed the bolt cutters back in my pocket, wriggled through the hole, got to my feet.

Still nothing to hear. Just the same background noises and the wind whistling around the deserted buildings, gusting up the empty streets.

I began to run parallel to the fence, on unpaved ground that was illuminated only by dim security lights on the surrounding buildings. Ahead was a street that branched off toward the contaminated sector. I veered down it, heart pounding, muscles straining.

And then I heard the faint sound of a helicopter, far out over the Bay. When I glanced toward India Basin I could see its winking beacons as it approached; it was coming from the northeast, would fly along the dry docks.

Hurry, McCone!

I stuffed my .38 into the rear waistband of my jeans so I could pump more freely with both arms. Ran harder than I'd ever run in my life.

The street ended. A flat plain dotted with heaps of debris and half-collapsed buildings stretched between there and the slick black water. I could smell chemical odors mixed with the salt tang of the Bay.

Toxic waste. Untold horrors—

The copter flew lower now, angling along the ends of the northern dry docks. A flare went off by the shore of South Basin. Another, then a third and a fourth. Glowing red signals showing Josh where he should set down the JetRanger.

I sprinted toward the flares, dodging around the noxious trash heaps and ruined buildings. Off to my left a figure was slipping away into shadow. Suits, moving in his peculiar furtive gait.

The copter was passing the southern docks now, turning into the basin.

Suits had stopped, shielded from the copter by the tilted remains of a shed. He waited, then stepped out. Stood with legs apart. I saw the shape of the AR-15, braced against his shoulder and trained on the approaching copter.

Without slowing, I called out to him.

He slewed around. The rifle was now aimed at me. His black clothing blended into the darkness, but his pale face stood out. His face and his wild, wild eyes.

"Suits, don't! It's . . . Sherry-O!"

Hesitation, as if he couldn't quite place me. Then he lowered the rifle, glanced over his shoulder at the copter.

I made myself slow to a fast walk, closing on him.

He looked back at me, brought the rifle up again. "What the hell're you doing here?"

"Trying to help."

"I don't need your help, Sherry-O. Go away."

The copter was moving along the basin, within the AR-15's range. Descending slowly, carefully. This was a hazardous landing; Josh would concentrate on the flares, on what he could see of the ground. If Suits fired, he'd never know what happened. . . .

Suits still held the AR-15 on me. "Back off, Sherry-O."

"No."

The copter was just offshore now.

"Back off! Quit trying to save me from myself!" He jabbed the rifle's muzzle at my chest.

The gesture shattered the lid I'd been keeping on my anger. I warned myself not to do anything stupid.

The copter was directly over the flares now. As it began its clumsy descent, its landing light washed over us, momentarily blinding me. When my vision cleared, I saw that Suits had swung around, was aiming the AR-15 at the part of the fuselage where the fuel tanks were.

I rushed him, putting my hands out to deflect the rifle's barrel. They connected solidly, knocked it sideways. Suits staggered but maintained his grip. I grabbed him by the shoulders, spun him around, dragged him down.

He fell across my legs, still clinging to that damned rifle. I pushed him off, managed to yank the .38 free of my waistband. Suits was struggling to get up, his right hand clutching the rifle's stock. I brought the butt end of the .38 down on it, broke his hold, then shoved him onto his back and straddled him.

He was still fighting me, clawing for the rifle. I reversed my hold on the .38 and jammed its muzzle into his left ear. Hard.

"Don't move," I said.

His jumpy gaze focused on my gun hand, calculating.

I pulled back the hammer. Leaned forward until my face was close to his.

"Listen, asshole," I said, "I don't give a damn about saving you. I'm doing this for Anna."

He stopped struggling, stared into my eyes. The wildness was beginning to fade from his.

"Anna is the biggest and best part of you. If you kill Josh, you'll destroy that part, and then there'll be nothing left of her."

A shudder passed through his slight frame, and suddenly he went limp. Behind me the copter noise had altered, grown louder; when I looked back, I saw that it was ascending, fast. Josh had seen us, realized what had been about to happen.

I took my gun from Suits's ear and stuck it back into my waistband, at the same time reaching for the AR-15. I removed the cartridge from the rifle and tossed it away into darkness. Then I got up, hesitated, and extended a hand to Suits.

He pushed up to a sitting position, staring at my hand. But then he took it, and I pulled him upright. He stood panting, shoulders slumped, as if he'd run a long race and lost it.

The copter was swinging out over South Basin.

In a low voice Suits said, "He was responsible for it all."

"I know."

"And now he's going to get away."

Josh turned east toward the Bay.

"No, he's not," I said. "He's flying back to Oakland. We can have him picked up at North Field."

The JetRanger slowed, abruptly turned back. I watched its winking beacon as it glided over the middle of the basin.

"Even if he tries to escape, he won't get far," I added. "Given the range of that copter, where can he hide?"

My words echoed between us. I looked at Suits, saw my sudden thought mirrored in his expression.

He said, "Maybe he just realized that, too."

The copter had begun a steep ascent. Briefly it stopped, seemed to dance in the air. Then the engine cut out, the rotor slowed, and it plunged toward the water.

Seconds later a fireball blossomed and lit up the night sky.

Twenty-five

The narrow road climbed high into the Mendocino coast range, shadowed by giant redwoods, running in switchbacks. I drove at no more than thirty-five, slower on the curves; it had been nearly fifteen minutes since I'd encountered another vehicle, but that had been a logging truck traveling much too fast.

A week had passed since Josh Haddon destroyed himself and the JetRanger. Within twelve hours of the crash, Suits was back to his old self: downplaying the episode to the press, covering his ass with his moneymen, assembling a new organization from the remains of the old one. He acted like a man with a mission; perhaps he thought that purposeful activity would redeem him, make him worthy of the part of him where Anna still lived. To me he seemed somewhat frantic, hiding from the central issue—namely, that his life had to change.

As for me, I'd allowed him to cover up the events surrounding Josh's death. Had allowed him to weave a fabric of truths and half-truths. Josh, the official version went, had engineered the Bodine drug frame with the sole help of Noah Romanchek (half-truth); had shot Bodine when he followed Suits to Lost Hope and assaulted his wife (I had my opinion on that, but I kept it to myself); had begun a campaign of harassment against his boss that culminated in Anna's death (truth); and had taken his own life while on a routine run to pick up Suits at Hunters Point (again only half).

Once, I wouldn't have been party to such a sham, but as I'd told Mick, that was what life did to you. Old loyalties, as well as new ones, were at work there. And it was the new ones that today had prompted me to undertake a mission of my own— one that I'd almost decided would best be left undone.

Earlier this afternoon I'd visited Moonshine Cottage and confirmed a couple of details. Then I'd driven in to the town of Mendocino and checked the missing-persons reports filed with the sheriff's department. What I found was further confirmation.

Now I passed a logging road that cut far back into the timber. Climbed some more and crossed a one-lane bridge over a dry creek bed. The road switchbacked three more times, then straightened and came to a wide clearing.

Dwellings sprawled haphazardly on either side of the pavement: wooden shacks with iron or tar-paper roofs, old house trailers sitting on blocks, newer prefabs. A sign in front of a pair of rusted Quonset huts said Ridge Reservation School. Next to the huts was a dirt playing field with a pair of netless basketball hoops mounted on standards. The only person I saw was a heavy woman in a flowing orange dress sitting on a lounge chair under a tarp that stretched between two of the house trailers.

I pulled over to the side of the road and got out of the MG. A couple of brown mongrels bounded over, wagging tails giving the lie to their menacing barks. I scratched their ears, started across the road to the woman.

She got up and went inside her trailer, slamming its door.

I stopped, looked around for someone else. Saw a small girl of about seven peeping around a pile of old tires. I smiled at her, and she covered her mouth with her fingers. When I went that way, she drew back and ran toward the Quonset huts. I followed.

The little girl skirted the huts and took a zigzag path through a cluster of junked cars and trucks. A rubbish heap lay beyond them; she stopped beside it, glanced back, then veered toward the redwoods surrounding the clearing. I ran after her. The rough-barked tree trunks crowded closer together; the kid's footfalls were muted on the blanket of needles and moss. For a moment I lost her. Then I heard voices—hers and an adult woman's. I followed their sound and came to a smaller clearing.

It was the reservation's graveyard. Low metal fence, the kind you buy at the nursery to border your flower beds. Weathered tombstones and wooden markers, in some cases just piles of stones. Plastic flowers, mostly faded by the sun, blooming in profusion. At the far end on a broken-down redwood bench sat a woman.

Anna Gordon.

She had her arm around the little girl. When she saw me, she whispered to her, and the kid ran back toward the trees, giving me a hostile look as she passed.

Anna had changed markedly since I'd said good-bye to her at Moonshine House: the lines that bracketed her mouth were more pronounced; her hair was unkempt and dull; her jeans and T-shirt hung much too loose. But it was her eyes that told me she'd changed inside as well: self-containment had hardened into self-preservation. As she regarded me down the length of her ancestors' graveyard, their focus was cold and wary, a flicker of fear in their depths.

I said, "Nobody knows I'm here."

She watched me, waiting.

"And if you insist, I'll never tell anybody."

After a moment she nodded, motioned for me to join her on the bench. When I sat down beside her, the flimsy structure listed my way—she'd lost that much weight.

Neither of us spoke for a while. Finally Anna asked, "How'd you know?"

"The room where I stayed at Moonshine Cottage. When I was packing, you told me you were expecting Franny Silva that day, that changing the sheets would give you something to do after Suits and I left. I went up there in September—Suits holed up at the cottage after the explosion. The sheets were different—blue, rather than the ones I'd slept in. Recently I realized that Suits, bad off as he was, wouldn't have changed them, and I wondered if you'd been in the cottage rather than in the house when it exploded."

"That wasn't much to go on," she said. "Certainly not enough for you to drive all the way up here."

"No. At first I tried to convince myself I was mistaken, but it kept nagging at me, so today I went to the cottage and found the maroon striped sheets I'd slept in in the hamper. Then I checked with the sheriff's department in Mendocino. Franny Silva was reported missing a week after the explosion. She's never turned up. I suppose it was her fillings that your tribe's dentist identified as his work."

Anna winced and closed her eyes. "Franny. No one even told me she was missing; runaway teenagers are pretty commonplace up here. God, I never even knew a body was found at Moonshine House; my people don't bring back newspapers from the outside, and there's no TV up here."

The outside: she sounded as if she was speaking of a world she'd left for good. History had come full cycle for her, as it had for her parents. I wondered if I was too late to bring her back.

I asked, "What did you do after the explosion?"

"Ran. Away from the cottage, I don't remember where—it's pretty much a blur. Late that night I hitched a ride on the coast highway, had the driver drop me off at Ridge Road. And then . . . I came home."

"You walked all that way?"

She nodded. "For a long time after that I was pretty much out of it. I still am, in a way."

"Is that why you haven't gotten in touch with Suits?"

Her fingers tightened on the edge of the bench. She drew her knees up and hugged them to her breasts. Shivered, even though the warm autumn sun touched her shoulders. She looked toward the gravestones, and I followed her gaze to a wooden marker with plastic roses scattered at its base.

"That's where my mother's buried," she said. "My father used to beat her. Finally he went off with a woman from the Pomo reservation down on Stewart's Point Road. I never really expected much from a marriage."

"Anna, Suits had nothing to do with the explosion."

"I guess I know that now. The guy loves me. And I love him."

"So why didn't you come forward, ease his grief?"

"Fear. Sharon, he makes so many enemies. Don't you see that it doesn't matter who set that explosion? I was almost the victim of an enemy of his once before that; I can't live with the possibility always hanging over me."

"The enemy you're talking about was Ed Bodine, in Lost Hope?"

"If you know about that, you can understand why I can't leave here."

I hesitated, framing my reply carefully. "Anna, a lot of things have happened that you're unaware of. Josh Haddon, for instance."

"Josh?"

"Is the man who ordered the explosion. He didn't mean for you to die, but he was the one who was harassing Suits."

She stared at me, eyes filling with pain and dull horror. "And the person who actually set the charges?"

"Is dead now. Josh ran him down, probably to avenge your death."

"No . . ."

"Josh is dead, too."

" . . . How?"

"He died in a helicopter crash a week ago."

Anna covered her face with her hands, leaned her forehead against her raised knees. In the trees behind us a mockingbird began a monotonous trilling; a harsh chorus of jays joined in.

After a while Anna looked up. "You're not telling me everything."

"It's too complicated. I'll leave that to Suits."

"Suits . . ." The single syllable was full of longing. She stared bleakly at her mother's grave. "You know, what happened was all my fault."

"Your fault? Why, for God's sake?"

"I knew Josh was obsessed with me. I should've warned Suits."

"Josh hated him for other reasons besides you."

"I'm sure he did, but I was the big reason. After Monora . . . You know what happened there?"

I nodded.

"After that, Suits and I separated. For good, I thought. And Josh and I . . . became close again. He'd come to the house when Suits gave him time off. Once I let him make love to me."

"So when you and Suits reconciled . . . ?"

"Josh was upset, but he claimed he could accept my decision. What really tore it was Lost Hope. By then he was pretty sick of having to mop up after both Suits and me. Last summer when those things started to happen to Suits, I went to see Josh and asked if he was behind them. He lied, and I believed him, but I should've warned Suits anyway."

"Well, that's behind you now. And Suits needs you. He's

aware that he has to make some major changes, and you're the only person who can help him—and keep him honest."

She shook her head. "It's not all behind me. There's something about Lost Hope that you don't know."

I didn't know, but I suspected. And if I was right, this something would have to go unsaid between us. "I know that Josh shot Ed Bodine to protect you," I told her. "I know that he buried him in the wash with the help of your friend Brenda Walker. The deputy in charge of the case has my statement to that effect, and I'm sure Brenda will back it up."

"But that's wrong. I was down in the wash, going to see the bottle house, and I'd taken along my gun in case of rattlers—"

"But Bodine overpowered you. And Josh shot him."

"Sharon—"

"That is *exactly* the way it happened, Anna."

Our eyes locked. Finally she nodded and clasped my hand.

"I've got to talk to Franny Silva's parents, and say my good-byes," she said. "It'll take a little while. Wait for me."

I watched her disappear into the redwoods, then got up and moved restlessly among the graves of her people. They'd had little enough to begin with, and over time, harsh circumstance had forced them to accept the notion that life is often a series of givings-up. I suspected they'd understand the compromise I'd made here today. Sometimes the dead must bear the burden of a lie; sometimes the truth must be warped in favor of the living.

I didn't suppose Josh Haddon would have minded, anyway. After all, he would have done anything for Anna.

Touchstone

December 31

"I still don't understand why you wanted to spend New Year's here."

"Why not?" Hy rubbed his palms together, surveying with satisfaction the fire he'd built on the hearth at Moonshine Cottage. "It's cozier than the cabin in the Great Whites, which we can't even get to this time of year. It's got a killer view, and after this storm blows over we can walk on the beach and look for treasure."

I took a sip of champagne.

"McCone, don't tell me you're still spooked about the explosion and that girl dying?"

"Not really. Now that the debris is cleared away, it seems peaceful again. And it was nice of Anna and Suits to let us use the cottage. But we could just as easily have spent New Year's at my place."

"With your nephew? No thanks."

"He's almost always with his girlfriend these days, and he'll

335

be moving into her condo next week, after her roommate finally moves out."

"How'd his folks take the news?"

"Not very well at first. Then he took her home over Christmas, and now they're singing her praises. Charlene told me Maggie's a steadying influence—the implication being that I'm not."

"So you've got a permanent assistant."

"It's only temporary."

"It'll always be only temporary."

I was not to be diverted from the original topic of conversation. "Anyway, as I was saying, we really could've stayed in town."

"And then we'd've been obligated to go to All Souls's New Year's Eve party and meet Rae's computer-freak boyfriends. I'm not ready yet to see little Rae Kelleher in a ménage à trois."

"I'm not sure that's what it is."

"How do you define it, then?"

"It defies description. But I guess you're right; San Francisco would've been a bad idea. But why not your ranch, if you want privacy?"

Hy picked up his champagne glass and came to sit beside me on the floor in front of the fireplace. "Look, McCone, that wouldn't've been good, either. On holidays there're still ghosts of Julie stirring around. I like it when we're together at your place and at the ranch, but what we really need is a place of our own."

"Well, a borrowed cottage on the Mendocino coast isn't half bad."

"It's not exactly borrowed." He grinned lazily and handed me a sheaf of papers that had been sticking out of the pocket of his wool shirt. "Soon as you sign these, Moonshine Cottage is ours."

". . . Ours?"

"Uh-huh. Joint tenancy. I bought it from Anna. Someday maybe we'll build a bigger house; there's room for an airstrip, too. But for now this little beauty'll do just fine for us."

"Hy, I can't afford—"

"Won't cost you but fifty cents."

"Hy, I can't take—"

"I bought it for a dollar."

"What!"

"Anna wanted to offload it, and she wanted us to have it."

"Good Lord. Suits must've been furious."

"He wasn't too happy; the man's tight with a buck. But Anna gave him a look, and he backed off."

I knew that look and the effect it had on Suits.

"Oh, McCone," Hy said, "don't go getting sentimental on me."

"I'm not."

"You think I can't see that tear? Brush it away and sign the papers."

I signed where he indicated, handed them back to him.

"Where's my fifty cents?"

I found some change in my jeans pocket, counted it into his outstretched palm.

Hy folded the papers and tucked them away. Stoked the fire and poured more champagne. "Here's to us."

I returned the toast, still somewhat stunned at suddenly owning a piece of the California coastline.

Hy added, "We're going to have to change the name of this place. Moonshine Cottage—it's not us."

"No."

"So what'll we call it?"

A memory of last summer stirred. "How about Touchstone?"

"Touchstone." He nodded, and I saw he remembered, too. Then he raised his glass and motioned around the room. "I christen thee Touchstone. We'd break a bottle of champagne over you, but it's too expensive." To me he said, "So what do you have planned for the new year?"

"Well, I'm going to decide what to do about Mick."

"Uh-huh."

"No, really. And I'm going to get my pilot's license. Then maybe I'll have you teach me some of the fancy stuff."

He grinned.

"That the Citabria's capable of," I added.

He frowned.

"And . . ." I hesitated. "And," I went on, "I'm going to find out what you were up to all last fall if I have to mount a full-scale investigation."

"I was wondering when you'd ask."

"So?"

"Not much to it. I had a wild-hair, save-the-world kind of idea. Traveled around running it by people I know who're in that line of work and discovered I'd need more resources than either the Spaulding Foundation or I have got."

"What's the idea?"

"Has to do with human rights, helping people who need to get out of tight spots. It came to me after our little adventure last June."

"Mmm. So what did you decide to do?"

"Went to my old buddies Renshaw and Kessell."

"Six months ago they were gunning for you; now you're old buddies."

He shrugged. "It's always been an uneasy relationship. Anyway, they made me a gold-plated offer: ownership position; freedom to call my own shots and pursue my own projects."

"In exchange for . . . ?"

"My availability when a tricky situation like a hostage recovery comes up."

I was silent.

"Don't frown like that, McCone. The deal doesn't involve any major compromise on my part. What it all boils down to is that I was getting stale running a foundation; I need to get back to what Gage calls the old action—with a dash of idealism thrown in, of course."

I sipped champagne, looked into the fire. I could feel its heat, feel the heat of Hy's body pressing long and lanky next to mine. For a while I was silent, turning over a question in my mind. And decided that now was as good a time as any to ask it.

"So what about this old action? Are you going to keep me in the dark forever?"

"Thought you'd never ask that, either."

I stared at him.

"A while back I decided it was time to tell you about it."

"So why didn't you tell me then?"

"A man likes to be asked." He smiled complacently.

"All right—I'm asking!"

Hy got up and fetched some pillows. Fluffed them and tossed them to me. Stoked the fire, poured more champagne. Opened a bag of pretzels.

"It's a long story," he said. "We might as well be comfortable." He lay down alongside me, arranged a pillow under his head.

"I'm comfortable. Start talking."

"Well, it all began when I was a small boy in Fresno. I was a charming lad. . . ." To my outraged look he added, "Uh-uh, McCone. You want my life history, you're gonna get *all* of it."

I sighed. Reached for a pretzel. Settled back against the pillows. And waited for the good stuff.